PENGUIN TWENTIETH-C

COLLECTED SHORT STORIES
VOLUME 2

William Somerset Maugham was born in 1874 and lived in Paris until he was ten years old. He was educated at The King's School, Canterbury, and at Heidelberg University. He later walked the wards of St. Thomas's Hospital with a view to practicing medicine, but when he had qualified, the success of his first novel, *Liza of Lambeth* (1897), won him over to letters. Some of his hospital experience is reflected in the story, as well as in his later masterpiece, *Of Human Bondage* (1915). With *The Moon and Sixpence* (1919) and *Cakes and Ale* (1930), his reputation as a novelist was further enhanced.

A celebrity by the age of thirty-three, when he became one of the most successful playwrights on the London stage, Maugham's Edwardian comedy *Lady Frederick*, his first hit (1907), was followed by a string of successes just before and then after the First World War. At one point Maugham had four plays running at the same time in London's West End. His theatre career ended with *Sheppey* (1933).

His fame as a short-story writer began in 1921 with *The Trembling of a Leaf*, subtitled *Little Stories of the South Sea Islands*, which contained "Rain." After initial magazine publication of each story he wrote, there were ten more collections. Somerset Maugham's general nonfiction books also reflect his love of travel; they include *On a Chinese Screen* (1922) and *Don Fernando* (1935), essays, criticism, and the self-revealing *The Summing Up* (1938) and *A Writer's Notebook* (1949).

He traveled widely in the Far East and throughout Europe. His permanent home since before the Second World War was on the French Riviera, which he vacated temporarily in 1940. He became Companion of Honor in 1954 and he died in 1965.

W. Somerset Maugham

COLLECTED SHORT STORIES

VOLUME 2

PENGUIN BOOKS

in association with William Heinemann Ltd

PENGUIN BOOKS

Published by the Penguin Group
Penguin Books USA Inc., 375 Hudson Street, New York, New York 10014, U.S.A.
Penguin Books Ltd, 27 Wrights Lane, London W8 5TZ, England
Penguin Books Australia Ltd, Ringwood, Victoria, Australia
Penguin Books Canada Ltd, 10 Alcorn Avenue, Toronto, Ontario, Canada M4V 3B2
Penguin Books (NZ) Ltd, 182–190 Wairau Road, Auckland 10, New Zealand

Penguin Books Ltd, Registered Offices: Harmondsworth, Middlesex, England

20 19 18 17 16 15 14 13 12

Copyright © W. Somerset Maugham, 1951

ISBN 0 14 01.8590 9

Printed in the United States of America
Set in Monotype Times

CONTENTS

PREFACE

THERE is one point I want to make about these stories. The reader will notice that many of my stories are written in the first person singular. That is a literary convention which is as old as the hills. It was used by Petronius Arbiter in the *Satyricon* and by many of the story-tellers in *The Thousand and One Nights*. Its object is of course to achieve credibility, for when someone tells you what he states happened to himself you are more likely to believe that he is telling the truth than when he tells you what happened to somebody else. It has besides the merit from the story-teller's point of view that he need only tell you what he knows for a fact and can leave to your imagination what he doesn't or couldn't know. Some of the older novelists who wrote in the first person were in this respect very careless. They would narrate long conversations that they couldn't possibly have heard and incidents which in the nature of things they couldn't possibly have witnessed. Thus they lost the great advantage of verisimilitude which writing in the first person singular offers. But the *I* who writes is just as much a character in the story as the other persons with whom it is concerned. He may be the hero or he may be an onlooker or a confidant. But he is a character. The writer who uses this device is writing fiction and if he makes the *I* of his story a little quicker on the uptake, a little more level-headed, a little shrewder, a little braver, a little more ingenious, a little wittier, a little wiser than he, the writer, really is, the reader must show indulgence. He must remember that the author is not drawing a faithful portrait of himself, but creating a character for the particular purposes of his story.

THE VESSEL OF WRATH

THERE are few books in the world that contain more meat than the *Sailing Directions* published by the Hydrographic Department by order of the Lords Commissioners of the Admiralty. They are handsome volumes, bound (very flimsily) in cloth of different colours, and the most expensive of them is cheap. For four shillings you can buy the *Yangtse Kiang Pilot*, 'containing a description of, and sailing directions for, the Yangtse Kiang from the Wusung river to the highest navigable point, including the Han Kiang, the Kialing Kiang, and the Min Kiang'; and for three shillings you can get Part III of the *Eastern Archipelago Pilot*, 'comprising the N.E. end of Celebes, Molucca and Gilolo passages, Banda and Arafura Seas, and North, West, and South-West coasts of New Guinea'. But it is not very safe to do so if you are a creature of settled habits that you have no wish to disturb or if you have an occupation that holds you fast to one place. These business-like books take you upon enchanted journeys of the spirit; and their matter-of-fact style, the admirable order, the concision with which the material is set before you, the stern sense of the practical that informs every line, cannot dim the poetry that, like the spice-laden breeze that assails your senses with a more than material languor when you approach some of those magic islands of the Eastern seas, blows with so sweet a fragrance through the printed pages. They tell you the anchorages and the landing places, what supplies you can get at each spot, and where you can get water; they tell you the lights and buoys, tides, winds, and weather that you will find there. They give you brief information about the population and the trade. And it is strange when you think how sedately it is all set down, with no words wasted, that so much else is given you besides. What? Well, mystery and beauty, romance and the glamour of the unknown. It is no common book that offers you casually turning its pages such a paragraph as this: 'Supplies. A few jungle fowl are preserved, the island is also the resort of vast numbers of sea birds. Turtle are found in the lagoon, as well as quantities of various fish, including grey mullet, shark, and dog-fish; the seine cannot be used with any effect; but there is a fish which may be taken on a rod. A small store of tinned provisions and spirits is kept in a hut for the relief of shipwrecked persons. Good water may be obtained from a well near the landing-place.' Can the imagination want more material than this to go on a journey through time and space?

In the volume from which I have copied this passage, the compilers with the same restraint have described the Alas Islands. They are composed of a group or chain of islands, 'for the most part low and wooded, extending about 75 miles east and west, and 40 miles north and south'. The information about them, you are told, is very slight; there are channels between the different groups, and several vessels have passed through them, but the passages have not been thoroughly explored, and the positions of many of the dangers not yet determined; it is therefore advisable to avoid them. The population of the group is estimated at about 8,000, of whom 200 are Chinese and 400 Mohammedans. The rest are heathen. The principal island is called Baru, it is surrounded by a reef, and here lives a Dutch Contrôleur. His white house with its red roof on the top of a little hill is the most prominent object that the vessels of the Royal Netherlands Steam Packet Company see when every other month on their way up to Macassar and every four weeks on their way down to Merauke in Dutch New Guinea they touch at the island.

At a certain moment of the world's history the Contrôleur was Mynheer Evert Gruyter and he ruled the people who inhabited the Alas Islands with firmness tempered by a keen sense of the ridiculous. He had thought it a very good joke to be placed at the age of twenty-seven in a position of such consequence, and at thirty he was still amused by it. There was no cable communication between his islands and Batavia, and the mail arrived after so long a delay that even if he asked advice, by the time he received it, it was useless, and so he equably did what he thought best and trusted to his good fortune to keep out of trouble with the authorities. He was very short, not more than five feet four in height, and extremely fat; he was of a florid complexion. For coolness' sake he kept his head shaved and his face was hairless. It was round and red. His eyebrows were so fair that you hardly saw them; and he had little twinkling blue eyes. He knew that he had no dignity, but for the sake of his position made up for it by dressing very dapperly. He never went to his office, nor sat in court, nor walked abroad but in spotless white. His stengah-shifter, with its bright brass buttons, fitted him very tightly and displayed the shocking fact that, young though he was, he had a round and protruding belly. His good-humoured face shone with sweat and he constantly fanned himself with a palm-leaf fan.

But in his house Mr Gruyter preferred to wear nothing but a sarong and then with his white podgy little body he looked like a fat funny boy of sixteen. He was an early riser and his breakfast was always ready for him at six. It never varied. It consisted of a slice of papaia, three cold fried eggs, Edam cheese, sliced thin, and a cup of black coffee. When he had eaten it, he smoked a large Dutch cigar, read the papers if he had not read them through and through already, and then dressed to go down to his office.

One morning while he was thus occupied his head boy came into his bedroom and told him that Tuan Jones wanted to know if he could see him. Mr Gruyter was standing in front of a looking-glass. He had his trousers on and was admiring his smooth chest. He arched his back in order to throw it out and throw in his belly and with a good deal of satisfaction gave his breast three or four resounding slaps. It was a manly chest. When the boy brought the message he looked at his own eyes in the mirror and exchanged a slightly ironic smile with them. He asked himself what the devil his visitor could want. Evert Gruyter spoke English, Dutch, and Malay with equal facility, but he thought in Dutch. He liked to do this. It seemed to him a pleasantly ribald language.

'Ask the tuan to wait and say I shall come directly.' He put on his tunic, over his naked body, buttoned it up, and strutted into the sitting-room. The Rev. Owen Jones got up.

'Good morning, Mr Jones,' said the Contrôleur. 'Have you come in to have a peg with me before I start my day's work?'

Mr Jones did not smile.

'I've come to see you upon a very distressing matter, Mr Gruyter,' he answered.

The Contrôleur was not disconcerted by his visitor's gravity nor depressed by his words. His little blue eyes beamed amiably.

'Sit down, my dear fellow, and have a cigar.'

Mr Gruyter knew quite well that the Rev. Owen Jones neither drank nor smoked, but it tickled something prankish in his nature to offer him a drink and a smoke whenever they met. Mr Jones shook his head.

Mr Jones was in charge of the Baptist Mission on the Alas Islands. His headquarters were at Baru, the largest of them, with the greatest population, but he had meeting-houses under the care of native helpers in several other islands of the group. He was a tall, thin, melancholy man, with a long face, sallow and drawn, of about forty. His brown hair was already white on the temples and it receded from the forehead. This gave him a look of somewhat vacuous intellectuality. Mr Gruyter both disliked and respected him. He disliked him because he was narrow-minded and dogmatic. Himself a cheerful pagan who liked the good things of the flesh and was determined to get as many of them as his circumstances permitted, he had no patience with a man who disapproved of them all. He thought the customs of the country suited its inhabitants and had no patience with the missionary's energetic efforts to destroy a way of life that for centuries had worked very well. He respected him because he was honest, zealous, and good. Mr Jones, an Australian of Welsh descent, was the only qualified doctor in the group and it was a comfort to know that if you fell ill you need not rely only on a Chinese practitioner, and none knew better than the Contrôleur how useful to all Mr Jones's skill had been and with what charity he had given it. On the occasion of an epidemic of influenza the missionary had done the work of ten men and no storm short of a typhoon could prevent him from crossing to one island or another if his help was needed.

He lived with his sister in a little white house about half a mile from the village, and when the Contrôleur had arrived came on board to meet him and begged him to stay till he could get his own house in order. The Contrôleur had accepted and soon saw for himself with what simplicity the couple lived. It was more than he could stand. Tea at three sparse meals a day, and when he lit his cigar Mr Jones politely but firmly asked him to be good enough not to smoke, since both his sister and he strongly disapproved of it. In twenty-four hours Mr Gruyter moved into his own house. He fled, with panic in his heart, as though from a plague-stricken city. The Contrôleur was fond of a joke and he liked to laugh; to be with a man who took your nonsense in deadly earnest and never even smiled at your best story was more than flesh and blood could stand. The Rev. Owen Jones was a worthy man, but as a companion he was impossible. His sister was worse. Neither had a sense of humour, but whereas the missionary was of a melancholy turn, doing his duty so conscientiously, with the obvious conviction that everything in the world was hopeless, Miss Jones was resolutely cheerful. She grimly looked on the bright side of things. With the ferocity of an avenging angel she sought out the good in her fellow-men. Miss Jones taught in the mission school and helped her brother in his medical work. When he did operations she gave the anaesthetic and was matron, dresser, and nurse of the tiny hospital which on his own initiative Mr Jones had added to the mission. But the Contrôleur was an obstinate little fellow and he never lost his capacity of extracting amusement from the Rev. Owen's dour struggle with the infirmities of human nature, and Miss Jones's ruthless optimism. He had to get his fun where he could. The Dutch boats came in three times in two months for a few hours and then he could have a good old crack with the captain and chief engineer, and once in a blue moon a pearling lugger came in from Thursday Island or Port Darwin and for two or three days he had a grand time. They were rough fellows, the pearlers, for the most part, but they were full of guts, and they had plenty of liquor on board, and good stories to tell, and the Contrôleur had them up to his house and gave them a fine dinner, and the party was only counted a success if they were all too drunk to get back on the lugger again that night. But beside the missionary the only white man who lived on Baru was Ginger Ted, and he, of course, was a disgrace to civilization. There was not a single thing to be said in his favour. He cast discredit on the white race. All the same, but for Ginger Ted the Contrôleur sometimes thought he would find life on the island of Baru almost more than he could bear.

Oddly enough it was on account of this scamp that Mr Jones, when he should have been instructing the pagan young in the mysteries of the Baptist faith, was paying Mr Gruyter this early visit.

'Sit down, Mr Jones,' said the Contrôleur. 'What can I do for you?'

'Well, I've come to see you about the man they call Ginger Ted. What are you going to do now?'

'Why, what's happened?'

'Haven't you heard? I thought the sergeant would have told you.'

'I don't encourage the members of my staff to come to my private house unless the matter is urgent,' said the Contrôleur rather grandly. 'I am unlike you, Mr Jones, I only work in order to have leisure, and I like to enjoy my leisure without disturbance.'

But Mr Jones did not care much for small talk and he was not interested in general reflections.

'There was a disgraceful row in one of the Chinese shops last night. Ginger Ted wrecked the place and half killed a Chinaman.'

'Drunk again, I suppose,' said the Contrôleur placidly.

'Naturally. When is he anything else? They sent for the police and he assaulted the sergeant. They had to have six men to get him to the jail.'

'He's a hefty fellow,' said the Contrôleur.

'I suppose you'll send him to Macassar.'

Evert Gruyter returned the missionary's outraged look with a merry twinkle. He was no fool and he knew already what Mr Jones was up to. It gave him considerable amusement to tease him a little.

'Fortunately my powers are wide enough to enable me to deal with the situation myself,' he answered.

'You have power to deport anyone you like, Mr Gruyter, and I'm sure it would save a lot of trouble if you got rid of the man altogether.'

'I have the power of course, but I am sure you would be the last person to wish me to use it arbitrarily.'

'Mr Gruyter, the man's presence here is a public scandal. He's never sober from morning till night; it's notorious that he has relations with one native woman after another.'

'That is an interesting point, Mr Jones. I had always heard that alcoholic excess, though it stimulated sexual desire, prevented its gratification. What you tell me about Ginger Ted does not seem to bear out this theory.'

The missionary flushed a dull red.

'These are physiological matters which at the moment I have no wish to go into,' he said, frigidly. 'The behaviour of this man does incalculable damage to the prestige of the white race, and his example seriously hampers the efforts that are made in other quarters to induce the people of these islands to lead a less vicious life. He's an out-and-out bad lot.'

'Pardon my asking, but have you made any attempts to reform him?'

'When he first drifted here I did my best to get in touch with him. He repelled all my advances. When there was that first trouble I went to him and talked to him straight from the shoulder. He swore at me.'

'No one has a greater appreciation than I of the excellent work that you and other missionaries do on these islands, but are you sure that you always exercise your calling with all the tact possible?'

The Contrôleur was rather pleased with this phrase. It was extremely courteous and yet contained a reproof that he thought worth administering. The missionary looked at him gravely. His sad brown eyes were full of sincerity.

'Did Jesus exercise tact when he took a whip and drove the money-changers from the Temple? No, Mr Gruyter. Tact is the subterfuge the lax avail themselves of to avoid doing their duty.'

Mr Jones's remark made the Contrôleur feel suddenly that he wanted a bottle of beer. The missionary leaned forward earnestly.

'Mr Gruyter, you know this man's transgressions just as well as I do. It's unnecessary for me to remind you of them. There are no excuses for him. Now he really has overstepped the limit. You'll never have a better chance than this. I beg you to use the power you have and turn him out once for all.'

The Contrôleur's eyes twinkled more brightly than ever. He

was having a lot of fun. He reflected that human beings were much more amusing when you did not feel called upon in dealing with them to allot praise or blame.

'But, Mr Jones, do I understand you right? Are you asking me to give you an assurance to deport this man before I've heard the evidence against him and listened to his defence?'

'I don't know what his defence can be.'

The Contrôleur rose from his chair and really he managed to get quite a little dignity into his five feet four inches.

'I am here to administer justice according to the laws of the Dutch Government. Permit me to tell you that I am exceedingly surprised that you should attempt to influence me in my judicial functions.'

The missionary was a trifle flustered. It had never occurred to him that this little whipper-snapper of a boy, ten years younger than himself, would dream of adopting such an attitude. He opened his mouth to explain and apologize, but the Contrôleur raised a podgy little hand.

'It is time for me to go to my office, Mr Jones. I wish you good morning.'

The missionary, taken aback, bowed and without another word walked out of the room. He would have been surprised to see what the Contrôleur did when his back was turned. A broad grin broke on his lips and he put his thumb to his nose and cocked a snook at the Rev. Owen Jones.

A few minutes later he went down to his office. His head clerk, who was a Dutch half-caste, gave him his version of the previous night's row. It agreed pretty well with Mr Jones's. The court was sitting that day.

'Will you take Ginger Ted first, sir?' asked the clerk.

'I see no reason to do that. There are two or three cases held over from the last sitting. I will take him in his proper order.'

'I thought perhaps as he was a white man you would like to see him privately, sir.'

'The majesty of the law knows no difference between white and coloured, my friend,' said Mr Gruyter, somewhat pompously.

The court was a big square room with wooden benches on which, crowded together, sat natives of all kinds, Polynesians, Bugis, Chinese, Malays, and they all rose when a door was opened and a sergeant announced the arrival of the Contrôleur. He entered with his clerk and took his place on a little dais at a table of varnished pitch pine. Behind him was a large engraving of Queen Wilhelmina. He dispatched half a dozen cases and then Ginger Ted was brought in. He stood in the dock, handcuffed, with a warder on either side of him. The Contrôleur looked at him with a grave face, but he could not keep the amusement out of his eyes.

Ginger Ted was suffering from a hang-over. He swayed a little as he stood and his eyes were vacant. He was a man still young, thirty perhaps, of somewhat over the middle height, rather fat, with a bloated red face and a shock of curly red hair. He had not come out of the tussle unscathed. He had a black eye and his mouth was cut and swollen. He wore khaki shorts, very dirty and ragged, and his singlet had been almost torn off his back. A great rent showed the thick mat of red hair with which his chest was covered, but showed also the astonishing whiteness of his skin. The Contrôleur looked at the charge sheet. He called the evidence. When he had heard it, when he had seen the Chinaman whose head Ginger Ted had broken with a bottle, when he had heard the agitated story of the sergeant who had been knocked flat when he tried to arrest him, when he had listened to the tale of the havoc wrought by Ginger Ted who in his drunken fury had smashed everything he could lay hands on he turned and addressed the accused in English.

'Well, Ginger, what have you got to say for yourself?'

'I was blind. I don't remember a thing about it. If they say I half killed 'im I suppose I did. I'll pay the damage if they'll give me time.'

'You will, Ginger,' said the Contrôleur, 'but it's me who'll give you time.'

He looked at Ginger Ted for a minute in silence. He was an unappetizing object. A man who had gone completely to pieces. He was horrible. It made you shudder to look at him and if Mr Jones had not been so officious, at that moment the Contrôleur would certainly have ordered him to be deported.

'You've been a trouble ever since you came to the islands, Ginger. You're a disgrace. You're incorrigibly idle. You've been picked up in the street dead drunk time and time again. You've kicked up row after row. You're hopeless. I told you the last time you were brought here that if you were arrested again I should deal with you severely. You've gone the limit this time and you're for it. I sentence you to six months' hard labour.'

'Me?'

'You.'

'By God, I'll kill you when I come out.'

He burst into a string of oaths both filthy and blasphemous. Mr Gruyter listened scornfully. You can swear much better in Dutch than in English and there was nothing that Ginger Ted said that he could not have effectively capped.

'Be quiet,' he ordered. 'You make me tired.'

The Contrôleur repeated his sentence in Malay and the prisoner was led struggling away.

Mr Gruyter sat down to tiffin in high good-humour. It was astonishing how amusing life could be if you exercised a little ingenuity. There were people in Amsterdam, and even in Batavia and Surabaya, who looked upon his island home as a place of exile. They little knew how agreeable it was and what fun he could extract from unpromising material. They asked him whether he did not miss the club and the races and the cinema, the dances that were held once a week at the Casino and the society of Dutch ladies. Not at all. He liked comfort. The substantial furniture of the room in which he sat had a satisfying solidity. He liked reading French novels of a frivolous nature and he appreciated the sensation of reading one after the other without the uneasiness occasioned by the thought that he was wasting his time. It seemed to him a great luxury to waste time. When his young man's fancy turned to thoughts of love his head boy brought to the house a little dark-skinned bright-eyed creature in a sarong. He took care to form no connexion of a permanent nature. He thought that change kept the heart young. He enjoyed freedom and was not weighed down by a sense of responsibility. He did not mind the heat. It made a sluice over with cold water half a dozen times a day a pleasure that had almost an aesthetic quality. He played the piano. He wrote letters to his friends in Holland. He felt no need for the conversation of intellectual persons. He liked a good laugh, but he could get that out of a fool just as well as out of a professor of philosophy. He had a notion that he was a very wise little man.

Like all good Dutchmen in the Far East he began his lunch with a small glass of Hollands gin. It has a musty acrid flavour, and the taste for it must be acquired, but Mr Gruyter preferred it to any cocktail. When he drank it he felt besides that he was upholding the traditions of his race. Then he had *rijsttafel*. He had it every day. He heaped a soup-plate high with rice, and then, his three boys waiting on him, helped himself to the curry that one handed him, to the fried egg that another brought, and to the condiment presented by the third. Then each one brought another dish, of bacon, or bananas, or pickled fish, and presently his plate was piled high in a huge pyramid. He stirred it all together and began to eat. He ate slowly and with relish. He drank a bottle of beer.

He did not think while he was eating. His attention was applied to the mass in front of him and he consumed it with a happy concentration. It never palled on him. And when he had emptied the great plate it was a compensation to think that next day he would have *rijsttafel* again. He grew tired of it as little as the rest of us grow tired of bread. He finished his beer and lit his cigar. The boy brought him a cup of coffee. He leaned back in his chair then and allowed himself the luxury of reflection.

It tickled him to have sentenced Ginger Ted to the richly deserved punishment of six months' hard labour, and he smiled when he thought of him working on the roads with the other prisoners. It would have been silly to deport from the island the one man with whom he could occasionally have a heart-to-heart talk, and besides, the satisfaction it would have given the missionary would have been bad for that gentleman's character. Ginger Ted was a scamp and a scallywag, but the Contrôleur had a kindly feeling for him. They had drunk many a bottle of beer in one another's company, and when the pearl fishers from Port Darwin came in and they all made a night of it, they had got gloriously tight together. The Contrôleur liked the reckless way in which Ginger Ted squandered the priceless treasure of life.

Ginger Ted had wandered in one day on the ship that was going up from Merauke to Macassar. The captain did not know how he had found his way there, but he had travelled steerage with the natives, and he stopped off at the Alas Islands because he liked the look of them. Mr Gruyter had a suspicion that their attraction consisted perhaps in their being under the Dutch flag and so out of British jurisdiction. But his papers were in order, so there was no reason why he should not stay. He said that he was buying pearl-shell for an Australian firm, but it soon appeared that his commercial undertakings were not serious. Drink, indeed, took up so much of his time that he had little left over for other pursuits. He was in receipt of two pounds a week, paid monthly, which came regularly to him from England. The Contrôleur guessed that this sum was paid only so long as he kept well away from the persons who sent it. It was anyway too small to permit him any liberty of movement. Ginger Ted was reticent. The Contrôleur discovered that he was an Englishman, this he learnt from his passport, which described him as Edward Wilson, and that he had been in Australia. But why he had left England and what he had done in Australia he had no notion. Nor could he ever quite tell to what class Ginger Ted belonged. When you saw him in a filthy singlet and a pair of ragged trousers, a battered topee on his head, with the pearl-fishers and heard his conversation, coarse, obscene, and illiterate, you thought he must be a sailor before the mast who had deserted his ship, or a labourer, but when you saw his handwriting you were surprised to find that it was that of a man not without at least some education, and on occasion when you got him alone, if he had had a few drinks but was not yet drunk, he would talk of matters that neither a sailor nor a labourer would have been likely to know anything about. The Contrôleur had a certain sensitiveness and he realized that Ginger Ted did not speak to him as an inferior to a superior but as an equal. Most of his remittance was mortgaged before he received it, and the Chinamen to whom he owed money were standing at his elbow when the monthly letter was delivered to him, but with what was left he proceeded to get drunk. It was then that he made trouble, for when drunk he grew violent and was then likely to commit acts that brought him into the hands of the police. Hitherto Mr Gruyter had contented himself with keeping him in jail till he was sober and giving him a talking to. When he was out of money he cadged what drink he could from anyone who would give it him. Rum, brandy, arak, it was all the same to him. Two or three times Mr Gruyter had got him work on plantations run by Chinese in one or other of the islands, but he could not stick to it, and in a few weeks was back again at Baru on the beach. It was a miracle how he kept body and soul together. He had, of course, a way with him. He picked up the various dialects spoken on the islands, and knew how to make the natives laugh. They despised him, but they respected his physical strength, and they liked his company. He was as a result never at a loss for a meal or a mat to sleep on. The strange thing was, and it was this that chiefly outraged the Rev. Owen Jones, that he could do anything he liked with a woman. The Contrôleur could not imagine what it was they saw in him. He was casual with them and rather brutal. He took what they gave him, but seemed incapable of gratitude. He used them for his pleasure and then flung them indifferently away. Once or twice this had got him into trouble, and Mr Gruyter had had to sentence an angry father for sticking a knife in Ginger Ted's back one night, and a Chinese woman had sought to poison herself by swallowing opium because he had deserted her. Once Mr Jones came to the Contrôleur in a great state because the beachcomber had seduced one of his converts. The Contrôleur agreed that it was very deplorable, but could only advise Mr Jones to keep a sharp eye on these young persons. The Contrôleur liked it less when he discovered that a girl whom he fancied a good deal himself and had been seeing for several weeks had all the time been according her favours also to Ginger Ted. When he thought of this particular incident he smiled again at the thought of Ginger Ted doing six months' hard labour. It is seldom in this life that in the process of doing your bounden duty you can get back on a fellow who has played you a dirty trick.

A few days later Mr Gruyter was taking a walk, partly for exercise and partly to see that some job he wanted done was being duly proceeded with, when he passed a gang of prisoners working under the charge of a warder. Among them he saw Ginger Ted. He wore the prison sarong, a dingy tunic called in Malay a *baju*, and his own battered topee. They were repairing the road, and Ginger Ted was wielding a heavy pick. The way was narrow and the Contrôleur saw that he must pass within a foot of him. He remembered his threats. He knew that Ginger Ted was a man of violent passion, and the language he had used in the dock made it plain that he had not seen what a good joke it was of the Contrôleur's to sentence him to six months' hard labour. If Ginger Ted suddenly attacked him with the pick, nothing on God's earth could save him. It was true that the warder would immediately shoot him down, but meanwhile the Contrôleur's head would be bashed in. It was with a funny little feeling in the pit of his stomach that Mr Gruyter walked through the gang of prisoners. They were working in pairs a few feet from one another. He set his mind on neither hastening his pace nor slackening it. As he passed Ginger Ted, the man swung his pick into the ground and looked up at the Contrôleur and as he caught his eye winked. The Contrôleur checked the smile that rose to his lips and with official dignity strode on. But that wink, so lusciously full of sardonic humour, filled him with satisfaction. If he had been the Caliph of Bagdad instead of a junior official in the Dutch Civil Service, he would forthwith have released Ginger Ted, sent slaves to bath and perfume him, and having clothed him in a golden robe entertained him to a sumptuous repast.

Ginger Ted was an exemplary prisoner and in a month or two the Contrôleur, having occasion to send a gang to do some work on one of the outlying islands, included him in it. There was no jail there, so the ten fellows he sent, under the charge of a warder, were billeted on the natives and after their day's work lived like free men. The job was sufficient to take up the rest of Ginger Ted's sentence. The Contrôleur saw him before he left.

'Look here, Ginger,' he said to him, 'here's ten guilder for you so that you can buy yourself tobacco when you're gone.'

'Couldn't you make it a bit more? There's eight pounds a month coming in regularly.'

'I think that's enough. I'll keep the letters that come for you, and when you get back you'll have a tidy sum. You'll have enough to take you anywhere you want to go.'

'I'm very comfortable here,' said Ginger Ted.

'Well, the day you come back, clean yourself up and come over to my house. We'll have a bottle of beer together.'

'That'll be fine. I guess I'll be ready for a good crack then.'

Now chance steps in. The island to which Ginger Ted had been sent was called Maputiti, and like all the rest of them it was rocky, heavily wooded, and surrounded by a reef. There was a village among coconuts on the sea-shore opposite the opening of the reef and another village on a brackish lake in the middle of the island. Of this some of the inhabitants had been converted to Christianity. Communication with Baru was effected by a launch that touched at the various islands at irregular intervals. It carried passengers and produce. But the villagers were seafaring folk, and if they had to communicate urgently with Baru, manned a prahu and sailed the fifty miles or so that separated them from it. It happened that when Ginger Ted's sentence had but another fortnight to run the Christian headman of the village on the lake was taken suddenly ill. The native remedies availed him nothing and he writhed in agony. Messengers were sent to Baru imploring the missionary's help; but as ill luck would have it Mr Jones was suffering at the moment from an attack of malaria. He was in bed and unable to move. He talked the matter over with his sister.

'It sounds like acute appendicitis,' he told her.

'You can't go, Owen,' she said.

'I can't let the man die.'

Mr Jones had a temperature of a hundred and four. His head was aching like mad. He had been delirious all night. His eyes were shining strangely and his sister felt that he was holding on to his wits by a sheer effort of will.

'You couldn't operate in the state you're in.'

'No, I couldn't. Then Hassan must go.'

Hassan was the dispenser.

'You couldn't trust Hassan. He'd never dare to do an operation on his own responsibility. And they'd never let him. I'll go. Hassan can stay here and look after you.'

'You can't remove an appendix?'

'Why not? I've seen you do it. I've done lots of minor operations.'

Mr Jones felt he didn't quite understand what she was saying.

'Is the launch in?'

'No, it's gone to one of the islands. But I can go in the prahu the men came in.'

'You? I wasn't thinking of you. You can't go.'

'I'm going, Owen.'

'Going where?' he said.

She saw that his mind was wandering already. She put her hand soothingly on his dry forehead. She gave him a dose of medicine. He muttered something and she realized that he did not know where he was. Of course she was anxious about him, but she knew that his illness was not dangerous, and she could leave him safely to the mission boy who was helping her nurse him and to the native dispenser. She slipped out of the room. She put her toilet things, a night-dress, and a change of clothes into a bag. A little chest with surgical instruments, bandages, and antiseptic dressings was kept always ready. She gave them to the two natives who had come over from Maputiti, and telling the dispenser what she was going to do gave him instructions to inform her brother when he was able to listen. Above all he was not to be anxious about her. She put on her topee and sallied forth. The mission was about half a mile from the village. She walked quickly. At the end of the jetty the prahu was waiting. Six men manned it. She took her place in the stern and they set off with a rapid stroke. Within the reef the sea was calm, but when they crossed the bar they came upon a long swell. But this was not the first journey of the sort Miss Jones had taken and she was confident of the seaworthiness of the boat she was in. It was noon and the sun beat down from a sultry sky. The only thing that harassed her was that they could not arrive before dark, and if she found it necessary to operate at once she could count only on the light of hurricane lamps.

Miss Jones was a woman of hard on forty. Nothing in her appearance would have prepared you for such determination as she had just shown. She had an odd drooping gracefulness, which suggested that she might be swayed by every breeze; it was almost an affectation; and it made the strength of character which you soon discovered in her seem positively monstrous. She was flat-chested, tall, and extremely thin. She had a long sallow face and she was much afflicted with prickly heat. Her lank brown hair was drawn back straight from her forehead. She had rather small eyes, grey in colour, and because they were somewhat too close they gave her face a shrewish look. Her nose was long and thin and a trifle red. She suffered a good deal from indigestion. But this infirmity availed nothing against her ruthless determination to look upon the bright side of things. Firmly persuaded that the world was evil and men unspeakably vicious, she extracted any little piece of decency she could find in them with the modest pride with which a conjurer extracts a rabbit from a hat. She was quick, resourceful, and competent. When she arrived on the island she saw that there was not a moment to lose if she was to save the headman's life. Under the greatest difficulties, showing a native how to give the anaesthetic, she operated, and for the next three days nursed the patient with anxious assiduity. Everything went very well and she realized that her brother could not have made a better job of it. She waited long enough to take out the stitches and then prepared to go home. She could flatter herself that she had not wasted her time. She had given medical attention to such as needed it, she had strengthened the small Christian community in its faith, admonished such as were lax, and cast the good seed in places where it might be hoped under divine providence to take root.

The launch, coming from one of the other islands, put in somewhat late in the afternoon, but it was full moon and they expected to reach Baru before midnight. They brought her things down to the wharf and the people who were seeing her off stood about repeating their thanks. Quite a little crowd collected. The launch was loaded with sacks of copra, but Miss Jones was used to its strong smell and it did not incommode her. She made herself as comfortable a place to sit in as she could, and waiting for the launch to start, chatted with her grateful flock. She was the only passenger. Suddenly a group of natives emerged from the trees that embowered the little village on the lagoon and she saw that among them was a white man. He wore a prison sarong and a baju. He had long red hair. She at once recognized Ginger Ted. A policeman was with him. They shook hands and Ginger Ted shook hands with the villagers who accompanied him. They bore bundles of fruit and a jar which Miss Jones guessed contained native spirit, and these they put in the launch. She discovered to her surprise that Ginger Ted was coming with her. His term was up and instructions had arrived that he was to be returned to Baru in the launch. He gave her a glance, but did not nod – indeed Miss Jones turned away her head – and stepped in. The mechanic started his engine and in a moment they were jug-jugging through the channel in the lagoon. Ginger Ted clambered on to a pile of sacks and lit a cigarette.

Miss Jones ignored him. Of course she knew him very well. Her heart sank when she thought that he was going to be once more in Baru, creating a scandal and drinking, a peril to the women and a thorn in the flesh of all decent people. She knew the steps her brother had taken to have him deported and she had no patience with the Contrôleur, who would not see a duty that stared him so plainly in the face. When they had crossed the bar and were in the open sea Ginger Ted took the stopper out of the jar of arak and putting his mouth to it took a long pull. Then he handed the jar to the two mechanics who formed the crew. One was a middle-aged man and the other a youth.

'I do not wish you to drink anything while we are on the journey,' said Miss Jones sternly to the elder one.

He smiled at her and drank.

'A little arak can do no one any harm,' he answered. He passed the jar to his companion, who drank also.

'If you drink again I shall complain to the Contrôleur,' said Miss Jones.

The elder man said something she could not understand, but which she suspected was very rude, and passed the jar back to Ginger Ted. They went along for an hour or more. The sea was like glass and the sun set radiantly. It set behind one of the islands and for a few minutes changed it into a mystic city of the skies. Miss Jones turned round to watch it and her heart was filled with gratitude for the beauty of the world.

'And only man is vile,' she quoted to herself.

They went due east. In the distance was a little island which she knew they passed close by. It was uninhabited. A rocky islet thickly grown with virgin forest. The boatman lit his lamps. The night fell and immediately the sky was thick with stars. The moon had not yet risen. Suddenly there was a slight jar and the launch began to vibrate strangely. The engine rattled. The head mechanic, calling to his mate to take the helm, crept under the housing. They seemed to be going more slowly. The engine stopped. She asked the youth what was the matter, but he did not know. Ginger Ted got down from the top of the copra sacks and slipped under the housing. When he reappeared she would have liked to ask him what had happened, but her dignity prevented her. She sat still and occupied herself with her thoughts. There was a long swell and the launch rolled slightly. The mechanic emerged once more into view and started the engine. Though it rattled like mad they began to move. The launch vibrated from stem to stern. They went very slowly. Evidently something was amiss, but Miss Jones was exasperated rather than alarmed. The launch was supposed to do six knots, but now it was just crawling along; at that rate they would not get into Baru till long, long after midnight. The mechanic, still busy under the housing, shouted out something to the man at the helm. They spoke in Bugi, of which Miss Jones knew very little. But after a while she noticed that they had changed their course and seemed to be heading for the little uninhabited island a good deal to the lee of which they should have passed.

'Where are we going?' she asked the helmsman with sudden misgiving.

He pointed to the islet. She got up and went to the housing and called to the man to come out.

'You're not going there? Why? What's the matter?'

'I can't get to Baru,' he said.

'But you must. I insist. I order you to go to Baru.'

The man shrugged his shoulders. He turned his back on her and slipped once more under the housing. Then Ginger Ted addressed her.

'One of the blades of the propeller has broken off. He thinks he can get as far as that island. We shall have to stay the night there and he'll put on a new propeller in the morning when the tide's out.'

'I can't spend the night on an uninhabited island with three men,' she cried.

'A lot of women would jump at it.'

'I insist on going to Baru. Whatever happens we must get there tonight.'

'Don't get excited, old girl. We've got to beach the boat to put a new propeller on, and we shall be all right on the island.'

'How dare you speak to me like that! I think you're very insolent.'

'You'll be O.K. We've got plenty of grub and we'll have a snack when we land. You have a drop of arak and you'll feel like a house on fire.'

'You're an impertinent man. If you don t go to Baru I'll have you all put in prison.'

'We're not going to Baru. We can't. We're going to that island and if you don't like it you can get out and swim.'

'Oh, you'll pay for this.'

'Shut up, you old cow,' said Ginger Ted.

Miss Jones gave a gasp of anger. But she controlled herself. Even out there, in the middle of the ocean, she had too much dignity to bandy words with that vile wretch. The launch, the engine rattling horribly, crawled on. It was pitch dark now, and she could no longer see the island they were making for. Miss Jones, deeply incensed, sat with lips tight shut and a frown on her brow; she was not used to being crossed. Then the moon rose and she could see the bulk of Ginger Ted sprawling on the top of the piled sacks of copra. The glimmer of his cigarette was strangely sinister. Now the island was vaguely outlined against the sky. They reached it and the boatman ran the launch on to the beach. Suddenly Miss Jones gave a gasp. The truth had dawned on her and her anger changed to fear. Her heart beat violently. She shook in every limb. She felt dreadfully faint. She saw it all. Was the broken propeller a put-up job or was it an accident? She could not be certain; anyhow, she knew that Ginger Ted would seize the opportunity. Ginger Ted would rape her. She knew his character. He was mad about women. That was what he had done, practically, to the girl at the mission, such a good little thing she was and an excellent sempstress; they would have prosecuted him for that and he would have been sentenced to years of imprisonment only very unfortunately the innocent child had gone back to him several times and indeed had only complained of his ill usage when he left her for somebody else. They had gone to the Contrôleur about it, but he had refused to take any steps, saying in that coarse way of his that even if what the girl said was true, it didn't look very much as though it had been an altogether unpleasant experience. Ginger Ted was a scoundrel. And she was a white woman. What chance was there that he would spare her? None. She knew men. But she must pull herself together. She must keep her wits about her. She must have courage. She was determined to sell her virtue dearly, and if he killed her – well, she would rather die than yield. And if she died she would rest in the arms of Jesus. For a moment a great light blinded her eyes and she saw the mansions of her Heavenly Father. They were a grand and sumptuous mixture of a picture palace and a railway station. The mechanics and Ginger Ted jumped out of the launch and, waist-deep in water, gathered round the broken propeller. She took advantage of their preoccupation to get her case of surgical instruments out of the box. She took out the four scalpels it contained and secreted them in her clothing. If Ginger Ted touched her she would not hesitate to plunge a scalpel in his heart.

'Now then, miss, you'd better get out,' said Ginger Ted. 'You'll be better off on the beach than in the boat.'

She thought so too. At least here she would have freedom of action. Without a word she clambered over the copra sacks. He offered her his hand.

'I don't want your help,' she said coldly.

'You can go to hell,' he answered.

It was a little difficult to get out of the boat without showing her legs, but by the exercise of considerable ingenuity she managed it.

'Damned lucky we've got something to eat. We'll make a fire and then you'd better have a snack and a nip of arak.'

'I want nothing. I only want to be left alone.'

'It won't hurt me if you go hungry.'

She did not answer. She walked, with head erect, along the beach. She held the largest scalpel in her closed fist. The moon allowed her to see where she was going. She looked for a place to hide. The thick forest came down to the very edge of the beach; but, afraid of its darkness (after all, she was but a woman), she dared not plunge into its depth. She did not know what animals lurked there or what dangerous snakes. Besides, her instinct told her that it was better to keep those three bad men in sight; then if they came towards her she would be prepared. Presently she found a little hollow. She looked round. They seemed to be occupied with their own efforts and they could not see her. She slipped in. There was a rock between them and her so that she was hidden from them and yet could watch them. She saw them go to and from the boat carrying things. She saw them build a fire. It lit them luridly and she saw them sit around it and eat, and she saw the jar of arak passed from one to the other. They were all going to get drunk. What would happen to her then? It might be that she could cope with Ginger Ted, though his strength terrified her, but against three she would be powerless. A mad idea came to her to go to Ginger Ted and fall on her knees before him and beg him to spare her. He must have some spark of decent feeling in him and she had always been so convinced that there was good even in the worst of men. He must have had a mother. Perhaps he had a sister. Ah, but how could you appeal to a man blinded with lust and drunk with arak? She began to feel terribly weak. She was afraid she was going to cry. That would never do. She needed all her self-control. She bit her lip. She watched them, like a tiger watching his prey; no, not like that, like a lamb watching three hungry wolves. She saw them put more wood on the fire, and Ginger Ted, in his sarong, silhouetted by the flames. Perhaps after he had had his will of her he would pass her on to the others. How could she go back to her brother when such a thing had happened to her? Of course he would be sympathetic, but would he ever feel quite the same to her again? It would break his heart. And perhaps he would think that she ought to have resisted more. For his sake perhaps it would be better if she said nothing about it. Naturally the men would say nothing. It would mean twenty years in prison for them. But then supposing she had a baby. Miss Jones instinctively clenched her hands with horror and nearly cut herself with the scalpel. Of course it would only infuriate them if she resisted.

'What shall I do?' she cried. 'What have I done to deserve this?'

She flung herself down on her knees and prayed to God to save her. She prayed long and earnestly. She reminded God that she was a virgin and just mentioned, in case it had slipped the divine memory, how much St Paul had valued that excellent state. And then she peeped round the rock again. The three men appeared to be smoking and the fire was dying down. Now was the time that Ginger Ted's lewd thoughts might be expected to turn to the woman who was at his mercy. She smothered a cry, for suddenly he got up and walked in her direction. She felt all her muscles grow taut, and though her heart was beating furiously she clenched the scalpel firmly in her hand. But it was for another purpose that Ginger Ted had got up. Miss Jones blushed and looked away. He strolled slowly back to the others and sitting down again raised the jar of arak to his lips. Miss Jones, crouching behind the rock, watched with straining eyes. The conversation round the fire grew less and presently she divined, rather than saw, that the two natives wrapped themselves in blankets and composed themselves to slumber. She understood. This was the moment Ginger Ted had been waiting for. When they were fast asleep he would get up cautiously and without a sound, in order not to wake the others, creep stealthily towards her. Was it that he was unwilling to share her with them or did he know that his deed was so dastardly that he did not wish them to know of it? After all, he was a white man and she was a white woman. He could not have sunk so low as to allow her to suffer the violence of natives. But his plan, which was so obvious to her, had given her an idea; when she saw him coming she would scream, she would scream so loudly that it would wake the two mechanics. She remembered now that the elder, though he had only one eye, had a kind face. But Ginger Ted did not move. She was feeling terribly tired. She began to fear that she would not have the strength now to resist him. She had gone through too much. She closed her eyes for a minute.

When she opened them it was broad daylight. She must have fallen asleep and, so shattered was she by emotion, have slept till long after dawn. It gave her quite a turn. She sought to rise, but something caught in her legs. She looked and found that she was covered with two empty copra sacks. Someone had come in the night and put them over her. Ginger Ted! She gave a little scream. The horrible thought flashed through her mind that he had outraged her in her sleep. No. It was impossible. And yet he had had her at his mercy. Defenceless. And he had spared her. She blushed furiously. She raised herself to her feet, feeling a little stiff, and arranged her disordered dress. The scalpel had fallen from her hand and she picked it up. She took the two copra sacks and emerged from her hiding-place. She walked towards the boat. It was floating in the shallow water of the lagoon.

'Come on, Miss Jones,' said Ginger Ted. 'We've finished. I was just going to wake you up.'

She could not look at him, but she felt herself as red as a turkey cock.

'Have a banana?' he said.

Without a word she took it. She was very hungry, and ate it with relish.

'Step on this rock and you'll be able to get in without wetting your feet.'

Miss Jones felt as though she could sink into the ground with shame, but she did as he told her. He took hold of her arm – good heavens! his hand was like an iron vice, never, never could she have struggled with him – and helped her into the launch. The mechanic started the engine and they slid out of the lagoon. In three hours they were at Baru.

That evening, having been officially released, Ginger Ted went to the Contrôleur's house. He wore no longer the prison uniform, but the ragged singlet and the khaki shorts in which he had been arrested. He had had his hair cut and it fitted his head now like a little curly red cap. He was thinner. He had lost his bloated flabbiness and looked younger and better. Mr Gruyter, a friendly grin on his round face, shook hands with him and asked him to sit down. The boy brought two bottles of beer.

'I'm glad to see you hadn't forgotten my invitation, Ginger,' said the Contrôleur.

'Not likely. I've been looking forward to this for six months.'

'Here's luck, Ginger Ted.'

'Same to you, Contrôleur.'

They emptied their glasses and the Contrôleur clapped his hands. The boy brought two more bottles.

'Well, you don't bear me any malice for the sentence I gave you, I hope.'

'No bloody fear. I was mad for a minute, but I got over it. I didn't have half a bad time, you know. Nice lot of girls on that island, Contrôleur. You ought to give 'em a look over one of these days.'

'You're a bad lot, Ginger.'

'Terrible.'

'Good beer, isn't it?'

'Fine.'

'Let's have some more.'

Ginger Ted's remittance had been arriving every month and the

Contrôleur now had fifty pounds for him. When the damage he had done to the Chinaman's shop was paid for there would still be over thirty.

'That's quite a lot of money, Ginger. You ought to do something useful with it.'

'I mean to,' answered Ginger. 'Spend it.'

The Contrôleur sighed.

'Well, that's what money's for, I guess.'

The Contrôleur gave his guest the news. Not much had happened during the last six months. Time on the Alas Islands did not matter very much and the rest of the world did not matter at all.

'Any wars anywhere?' asked Ginger Ted.

'No. Not that I've noticed. Harry Jervis found a pretty big pearl. He says he's going to ask a thousand quid for it.'

'I hope he gets it.'

'And Charlie McCormack's married.'

'He always was a bit soft.'

Suddenly the boy appeared and said Mr Jones wished to know if he might come in. Before the Contrôleur could give an answer Mr Jones walked in.

'I won't detain you long,' he said. 'I've been trying to get hold of this good man all day and when I heard he was here I thought you wouldn't mind my coming.'

'How is Miss Jones?' asked the Contrôleur politely. 'None the worse for her night in the open, I trust.'

'She's naturally a bit shaken. She had a temperature and I've insisted on her going to bed, but I don't think it's serious.'

The two men had got up on the missionary's entrance, and now the missionary went up to Ginger Ted and held out his hand.

'I want to thank you. You did a great and noble thing. My sister is right, one should always look for the good in their fellowmen; I am afraid I misjudged you in the past: I beg your pardon.'

He spoke very solemnly. Ginger Ted looked at him with amazement. He had not been able to prevent the missionary taking his hand. He still held it.

'What the hell are you talking about?'

'You had my sister at your mercy and you spared her. I thought you were all evil and I am ashamed. She was defenceless. She was in your power. You had pity on her. I thank you from the bottom of my heart. Neither my sister nor I will ever forget. God bless and guard you always.'

Mr Jones's voice shook a little and he turned his head away. He released Ginger Ted's hand and strode quickly to the door. Ginger Ted watched him with a blank face.

'What the blazes does he mean?' he asked.

The Contrôleur laughed. He tried to control himself, but the more he did the more he laughed. He shook and you saw the folds of his fat belly ripple under the sarong. He leaned back in his long chair and rolled from side to side. He did not laugh only with his face, he laughed with his whole body, and even the muscles of his podgy legs shook with mirth. He held his aching ribs. Ginger Ted looked at him frowning, and because he did not understand what the joke was he grew angry. He seized one of the empty beer bottles by the neck.

'If you don't stop laughing, I'll break your bloody head open,' he said.

The Contrôleur mopped his face. He swallowed a mouthful of beer. He sighed and groaned because his sides were hurting him.

'He's thanking you for having respected the virtue of Miss Jones,' he spluttered at last.

'Me?' cried Ginger Ted.

The thought took quite a long time to travel through his head, but when at last he got it he flew into a violent rage. There flowed from his mouth such a stream of blasphemous obscenities as would have startled a marine.

'That old cow,' he finished. 'What does he take me for?'

'You have the reputation of being rather hot stuff with the girls, Ginger,' giggled the little Contrôleur.

'I wouldn't touch her with the fag-end of a barge-pole. It never entered my head. The nerve. I'll wring his blasted neck. Look here, give me my money, I'm going to get drunk.'

'I don't blame you,' said the Contrôleur.

'That old cow,' repeated Ginger Ted. 'That old cow.'

He was shocked and outraged. The suggestion really shattered his sense of decency.

The Contrôleur had the money at hand and having got Ginger Ted to sign the necessary papers gave it to him.

'Go and get drunk, Ginger Ted,' he said, 'but I warn you, if you get into mischief it'll be twelve months next time.'

'I shan't get into mischief,' said Ginger Ted sombrely. He was suffering from a sense of injury. 'It's an insult,' he shouted at the Contrôleur. 'That's what it is, it's a bloody insult.'

He lurched out of the house, and as he went he muttered to himself: 'Dirty swine, dirty swine.' Ginger Ted remained drunk for a week. Mr Jones went to see the Contrôleur again.

'I'm very sorry to hear that poor fellow has taken up his evil course again,' he said. 'My sister and I are dreadfully disappointed. I'm afraid it wasn't very wise to give him so much money at once.'

'It was his own money. I had no right to keep it back.'

'Not a legal right, perhaps, but surely a moral right.'

He told the Contrôleur the story of that fearful night on the island. With her feminine instinct, Miss Jones had realized that the man, inflamed with lust, was determined to take advantage of her, and, resolved to defend herself to the last, had armed herself with a scalpel. He told the Contrôleur how she had prayed and wept and how she had hidden herself. Her agony was indescribable, and she knew that she could never have survived the shame. She rocked to and fro and every moment she thought he was coming. And there was no help anywhere and at last she had fallen asleep; she was tired out, poor thing, she had undergone more than any human being could stand, and then when she awoke she found that he had covered her with copra sacks. He had found her asleep, and surely it was her innocence, her very helplessness that had moved him, he hadn't the heart to touch her; he covered her gently with two copra sacks and crept silently away.

'It shows you that deep down in him there is something sterling. My sister feels it's our duty to save him. We must do something for him.'

'Well, in your place I wouldn't try till he's got through all his money,' said the Contrôleur, 'and then if he's not in jail you can do what you like.'

But Ginger Ted didn't want to be saved. About a fortnight after his release from prison he was sitting on a stool outside a Chinaman's shop looking vacantly down the street when he saw Miss Jones coming along. He stared at her for a minute and once more amazement seized him. He muttered to himself and there can be little doubt that his mutterings were disrespectful. But then he noticed that Miss Jones had seen him and he quickly turned his head away; he was conscious, notwithstanding, that she was looking at him. She was walking briskly, but she sensibly diminished her pace as she approached him. He thought she was going to stop and speak to him. He got up quickly and went into the shop. He did not venture to come out for at least five minutes. Half an hour later Mr Jones himself came along and he went straight up to Ginger Ted with outstretched hand.

'How do you do, Mr Edward? My sister told me I should find you here.'

Ginger Ted gave him a surly look and did not take the proffered hand. He made no answer.

'We'd be so very glad if you'd come to dinner with us next Sunday. My sister's a capital cook and she'll make you a real Australian dinner.'

'Go to hell,' said Ginger Ted.

'That's not very gracious,' said the missionary, but with a little laugh to show that he was not affronted. 'You go and see the Contrôleur from time to time, why shouldn't you come and see us? It's pleasant to talk to white people now and then. Won't you let bygones be bygones? I can assure you of a very cordial welcome.'

'I haven't got clothes fit to go out in,' said Ginger Ted sulkily.

'Oh, never mind about that. Come as you are.'

'I won't.'

'Why not? You must have a reason.'

Ginger Ted was a blunt man. He had no hesitation in saying what we should all like to when we receive unwelcome invitations.

'I don't want to.'

'I'm sorry. My sister will be very disappointed.'

Mr Jones, determined to show that he was not in the least offended, gave him a breezy nod and walked on. Forty-eight hours later there mysteriously arrived at the house in which Ginger Ted lodged a parcel containing a suit of ducks, a tennis shirt, a pair of socks, and some shoes. He was unaccustomed to receiving presents and next time he saw the Contrôleur asked him if it was he who had sent the things.

'Not on your life,' replied the Contrôleur. 'I'm perfectly indifferent to the state of your wardrobe.'

'Well, then, who the hell can have?'

'Search me.'

It was necessary from time to time for Miss Jones to see Mr Gruyter on business and shortly after this she came to see him one morning in his office. She was a capable woman and though she generally wanted him to do something he had no mind to, she did not waste his time. He was a little surprised then to discover that she had come on a very trivial errand. When he told her that he could not take cognizance of the matter in question, she did not as was her habit try to convince him, but accepted his refusal as definite. She got up to go and then as though it were an afterthought said:

'Oh, Mr Gruyter, my brother is very anxious that we should have the man they call Ginger Ted to supper with us and I've written him a little note inviting him for the day after tomorrow. I think he's rather shy, and I wonder if you'd come with him.'

'That's very kind of you.'

'My brother feels that we ought to do something for the poor fellow.'

33

'A woman's influence and all that sort of thing,' said the Contrôleur demurely.

'Will you persuade him to come? I'm sure he will if you make a point of it, and when he knows the way he'll come again. It seems such a pity to let a young man like that go to pieces altogether.'

The Contrôleur looked up at her. She was several inches taller than he. He thought her very unattractive. She reminded him strangely of wet linen hung on a clothes-line to dry. His eyes twinkled, but he kept a straight face.

'I'll do my best,' he said.

'How old is he?' she asked.

'According to his passport he's thirty-one.'

'And what is his real name?'

'Wilson.'

'Edward Wilson,' she said softly.

'It's astonishing that after the life he's led he should be so strong,' murmured the Contrôleur. 'He has the strength of an ox.'

'Those red-headed men sometimes are very powerful,' said Miss Jones, but spoke as though she were choking.

'Quite so,' said the Contrôleur.

Then for no obvious reason Miss Jones blushed. She hurriedly said goodbye to the Contrôleur and left his office.

'*Godverdomme*!' said the Contrôleur.

He knew now who had sent Ginger Ted the new clothes.

He met him during the course of the day and asked him whether he had heard from Miss Jones. Ginger Ted took a crumpled ball of paper out of his pocket and gave it to him. It was the invitation. It ran as follows:

Dear Mr Wilson

My brother and I would be so very glad if you would come and have supper with us next Thursday at 7.30. The Contrôleur has kindly promised to come. We have some new records from Australia which I am sure you will like. I am afraid I was not very nice to you last time we met, but I did not know you so well then, and I am big enough to admit it when I have committed an error. I hope you will forgive me and let me be your friend,

Yours sincerely,
Martha Jones

The Contrôleur noticed that she addressed him as Mr Wilson and referred to his own promise to go, so that when she told him she had already invited Ginger Ted she had a little anticipated the truth.

'What are you going to do?'

'I'm not going, if that's what you mean. Damned nerve.'

34

'You must answer the letter.'

'Well, I won't.'

'Now look here, Ginger, you put on those new clothes and you come as a favour to me. I've got to go and, damn it all, you can't leave me in the lurch. It won't hurt you just once.'

Ginger Ted looked at the Contrôleur suspiciously, but his face was serious and his manner sincere: he could not guess that within him the Dutchman bubbled with laughter.

'What the devil do they want me for?'

'I don't know. The pleasure of your society, I suppose.'

'Will there be any booze?'

'No, but come up to my house at seven, and we'll have a tiddly before we go.'

'Oh, all right,' said Ginger Ted sulkily.

The Contrôleur rubbed his little fat hands with joy. He was expecting a great deal of amusement from the party. But when Thursday came and seven o'clock, Ginger Ted was dead drunk and Mr Gruyter had to go alone. He told the missionary and his sister the plain truth. Mr Jones shook his head.

'I'm afraid it's no good, Martha, the man's hopeless.'

For a moment Miss Jones was silent and the Contrôleur saw two tears trickle down her long thin nose. She bit her lip.

'No one is hopeless. Everyone has some good in him. I shall pray for him every night. It would be wicked to doubt the power of God.'

Perhaps Miss Jones was right in this, but the divine providence took a very funny way of effecting its ends. Ginger Ted began to drink more heavily than ever. He was so troublesome that even Mr Gruyter lost patience with him. He made up his mind that he could not have the fellow on the islands any more and resolved to deport him on the next boat that touched at Baru. Then a man died under mysterious circumstances after having been for a trip to one of the islands and the Contrôleur learnt that there had been several deaths on the same island. He sent the Chinese who was the official doctor of the group to look into the matter, and very soon received intelligence that the deaths were due to cholera. Two more took place at Baru and the certainty was forced upon him that there was an epidemic.

The Contrôleur cursed freely. He cursed in Dutch, he cursed in English, and he cursed in Malay. Then he drank a bottle of beer and smoked a cigar. After that he took thought. He knew the Chinese doctor would be useless. He was a nervous little man from Java and the natives would refuse to obey his orders. The Contrôleur was efficient and knew pretty well what must be done, but he could not do everything single-handed. He did not like Mr Jones, but just then he was thankful that he was at hand, and he sent for him at once. He was accompanied by his sister.

'You know what I want to see you about, Mr Jones,' he said abruptly.

'Yes. I've been expecting a message from you. That is why my sister has come with me. We are ready to put all our resources at your disposal. I need not tell you that my sister is as competent as a man.'

'I know. I shall be very glad of her assistance.'

They set to without further delay to discuss the steps that must be taken. Hospital huts would have to be erected and quarantine stations. The inhabitants of the various villages on the islands must be forced to take proper precautions. In a good many cases the infected villages drew their water from the same well as the uninfected, and in each case this difficulty would have to be dealt with according to circumstances. It was necessary to send round people to give orders and make sure that they were carried out. Negligence must be ruthlessly punished. The worst of it was that the natives would not obey other natives, and orders given by native policemen, themselves unconvinced of their efficacy, would certainly be disregarded. It was advisable for Mr Jones to stay at Baru, where the population was largest and his medical attention most wanted; and what with the official duties that forced him to keep in touch with his headquarters, it was impossible for Mr Gruyter to visit all the other islands himself. Miss Jones must go; but the natives of some of the outlying islands were wild and treacherous; the Contrôleur had had a good deal of trouble with them. He did not like the idea of exposing her to danger.

'I'm not afraid,' she said.

'I daresay. But if you have your throat cut I shall get into trouble, and besides, we're so short-handed I don't want to risk losing your help.'

'Then let Mr Wilson come with me. He knows the natives better than anyone and can speak all their dialects.'

'Ginger Ted?' The Contrôleur stared at her. 'He's just getting over an attack of D.T.s.'

'I know,' she answered.

'You know a great deal, Miss Jones.'

Even though the moment was so serious Mr Gruyter could not but smile. He gave her a sharp look, but she met it coolly.

'There's nothing like responsibility for bringing out what there is in a man, and I think something like this may be the making of him.'

'Do you think it would be wise to trust yourself for days at a time to a man of such infamous character?' said the missionary.

'I put my trust in God,' she answered gravely.

'Do you think he'd be any use?' asked the Contrôleur. 'You know what he is.'

'I'm convinced of it.' Then she blushed. 'After all, no one knows better than I that he's capable of self-control.'

The Contrôleur bit his lip.

'Let's send for him.'

He gave a message to the sergeant and in a few minutes Ginger Ted stood before them. He looked ill. He had evidently been much shaken by his recent attack and his nerves were all to pieces. He was in rags and he had not shaved for a week. No one could have looked more disreputable.

'Look here, Ginger,' said the Contrôleur, 'it's about this cholera business. We've got to force the natives to take precautions and we want you to help us.'

'Why the hell should I?'

'No reason at all. Except philanthropy.'

'Nothing doing, Contrôleur. I'm not a philanthropist.'

'That settles that. That was all. You can go.'

But as Ginger Ted turned to the door Miss Jones stopped him.

'It was my suggestion, Mr Wilson. You see, they want me to go to Labobo and Sakunchi, and the natives there are so funny I was afraid to go alone. I thought if you came I should be safer.'

He gave her a look of extreme distaste.

'What do you suppose I care if they cut your throat?'

Miss Jones looked at him and her eyes filled with tears. She began to cry. He stood and watched her stupidly.

'There's no reason why you should.' She pulled herself together and dried her eyes. 'I'm being silly. I shall be all right. I'll go alone.'

'It's damned foolishness for a woman to go to Labobo.'

She gave him a little smile.

'I daresay it is, but you see, it's my job and I can't help myself. I'm sorry if I offended you by asking you. You must forget about it. I daresay it wasn't quite fair to ask you to take such a risk.'

For quite a minute Ginger Ted stood and looked at her. He shifted from one foot to the other. His surly face seemed to grow black.

'Oh, hell, have it your own way,' he said at last. 'I'll come with you. When d'you want to start?'

They set out next day, with drugs and disinfectants, in the Government launch. Mr Gruyter as soon as he had put the

37

necessary work in order was to start off in a prahu in the other direction. For four months the epidemic raged. Though everything possible was done to localize it, one island after another was attacked. The Contrôleur was busy from morning to night. He had no sooner got back to Baru from one or other of the islands to do what was necessary there than he had to set off again. He distributed food and medicine. He cheered the terrified people. He supervised everything. He worked like a dog. He saw nothing of Ginger Ted, but he heard from Mr Jones that the experiment was working out beyond all hopes. The scamp was behaving himself. He had a way with the natives; and by cajolery, firmness, and on occasion the use of his fist, managed to make them take the steps necessary for their own safety. Miss Jones could congratulate herself on the success of the scheme. But the Contrôleur was too tired to be amused. When the epidemic had run its course he rejoiced because out of a population of eight thousand only six hundred had died.

Finally he was able to give the district a clean bill of health.

One evening he was sitting in his sarong on the veranda of his house and he read a French novel with the happy consciousness that once more he could take things easy. His head boy came in and told him that Ginger Ted wished to see him. He got up from his chair and shouted to him to come in. Company was just what he wanted. It had crossed the Contrôleur's mind that it would be pleasant to get drunk that night, but it is dull to get drunk alone, and he had regretfully put the thought aside. And heaven had sent Ginger Ted in the nick of time. By God, they would make a night of it. After four months they deserved a bit of fun. Ginger Ted entered. He was wearing a clean suit of white ducks. He was shaved. He looked another man.

'Why, Ginger, you look as if you'd been spending a month at a health resort instead of nursing a pack of natives dying of cholera. And look at your clothes. Have you just stepped out of a bandbox?'

Ginger Ted smiled rather sheepishly. The head boy brought two bottles of beer and poured them out.

'Help yourself, Ginger,' said the Contrôleur as he took his glass.

'I don't think I'll have any, thank you.'

The Contrôleur put down his glass and looked at Ginger Ted with amazement.

'Why, what's the matter? Aren't you thirsty?'

'I don't mind having a cup of tea.'

'A cup of what?'

'I'm on the wagon. Martha and I are going to be married.'

'Ginger!'

The Contrôleur's eyes popped out of his head. He scratched his shaven pate.

'You can't marry Miss Jones,' he said. 'No one could marry Miss Jones.'

'Well, I'm going to. That's what I've come to see you about. Owen's going to marry us in chapel, but we want to be married by Dutch law as well.'

'A joke's a joke, Ginger. What's the idea?'

'She wanted it. She fell for me that night we spent on the island when the propeller broke. She's not a bad old girl when you get to know her. It's her last chance, if you understand what I mean, and I'd like to do something to oblige her. And she wants someone to take care of her, there's no doubt about that.'

'Ginger, Ginger, before you can say knife she'll make you into a damned missionary.'

'I don't know that I'd mind that so much if we had a little mission of our own. She says I'm a bloody marvel with the natives. She says I can do more with a native in five minutes than Owen can do in a year. She says she's never known anyone with the magnetism I have. It seems a pity to waste a gift like that.'

The Contrôleur looked at him without speaking and slowly nodded his head three or four times. She'd nobbled him all right.

'I've converted seventeen already,' said Ginger Ted.

'You? I didn't know you believed in Christianity.'

'Well, I don't know that I did exactly, but when I talked to 'em and they just came into the fold like a lot of blasted sheep, well, it gave me quite a turn. Blimey, I said, I daresay there's something in it after all.'

'You should have raped her, Ginger. I wouldn't have been hard on you. I wouldn't have given you more than three years' and three years' is soon over.'

'Look here, Contrôleur, don't you ever let on that the thought never entered my head. Women are touchy, you know, and she'd be as sore as hell if she knew that.'

'I guessed she'd got her eye on you, but I never thought it would come to this.' The Contrôleur in an agitated manner walked up and down the veranda. 'Listen to me, old boy,' he said after an interval of reflection, 'we've had some grand times together and a friend's a friend. I'll tell you what I'll do, I'll lend you the launch and you can go and hide on one of the islands till the next ship comes along and then I'll get 'em to slow down and take you on board. You've only got one chance now and that's to cut and run.'

Ginger Ted shook his head.

'It's no good, Contrôleur, I know you mean well, but I'm going to marry the blasted woman, and that's that. You don't know the joy of bringing all them bleeding sinners to repentance, and Christ! that girl can make a treacle pudding. I haven't eaten a better one since I was a kid.'

The Contrôleur was very much disturbed. The drunken scamp was his only companion on the islands and he did not want to lose him. He discovered that he had even a certain affection for him. Next day he went to see the missionary.

'What's this I hear about your sister marrying Ginger Ted?' he asked him. 'It's the most extraordinary thing I've ever heard in my life.'

'It's true nevertheless.'

'You must do something about it. It's madness.'

'My sister is of full age and entitled to do as she pleases.'

'But you don't mean to tell me you approve of it. You know Ginger Ted. He's a bum and there are no two ways about it. Have you told her the risk she's running? I mean, bringing sinners to repentance and all that sort of thing's all right, but there are limits. And does the leopard ever change his spots?'

Then for the first time in his life the Contrôleur saw a twinkle in the missionary's eye.

'My sister is a very determined woman, Mr Gruyter,' he replied. 'From that night they spent on the island he never had a chance.'

The Contrôleur gasped. He was as surprised as the prophet when the Lord opened the mouth of the ass, and she said unto Balaam, What have I done unto thee, that thou hast smitten me these three times? Perhaps Mr Jones was human after all.

'*Allejezus!*' muttered the Contrôleur.

Before anything more could be said Miss Jones swept into the room. She was radiant. She looked ten years younger. Her cheeks were flushed and her nose was hardly red at all.

'Have you come to congratulate me, Mr Gruyter?' she cried, and her manner was sprightly and girlish. 'You see, I was right after all. Everyone has some good in them. You don't know how splendid Edward has been all through this terrible time. He's a hero. He's a saint. Even I was surprised.'

'I hope you'll be very happy, Miss Jones.'

'I know I shall. Oh, it would be wicked of me to doubt it. For it is the Lord who has brought us together.'

'Do you think so?'

'I know it. Don't you see? Except for the cholera Edward would never have found himself. Except for the cholera we should never have learnt to know one another. I have never seen the hand of God more plainly manifest.'

The Contrôleur could not but think that it was rather a clumsy device to bring those two together that necessitated the death of six hundred innocent persons, but not being well versed in the ways of omnipotence he made no remark.

'You'll never guess where we're going for our honeymoon,' said Miss Jones, perhaps a trifle archly.

'Java.'

'No, if you'll lend us the launch, we're going to that island where we were marooned. It has very tender recollections for both of us. It was there that I first guessed how fine and good Edward was. It's there I want him to have his reward.'

The Contrôleur caught his breath. He left quickly, for he thought that unless he had a bottle of beer at once he would have a fit. He was never so shocked in his life.

THE FORCE OF CIRCUMSTANCE

SHE was sitting on the veranda waiting for her husband to come in for luncheon. The Malay boy had drawn the blinds when the morning lost its freshness, but she had partly raised one of them so that she could look at the river. Under the breathless sun of midday it had the white pallor of death. A native was paddling along in a dug-out so small that it hardly showed above the surface of the water. The colours of the day were ashy and wan. They were but the various tones of the heat. (It was like an Eastern melody, in the minor key, which exacerbates the nerves by its ambiguous monotony; and the ear awaits impatiently a resolution, but waits in vain.) The cicadas sang their grating song with a frenzied energy; it was as continual and monotonous as the rustling of a brook over the stones; but on a sudden it was drowned by the loud singing of a bird, mellifluous and rich; and for an instant, with a catch at her heart, she thought of the English black-bird.

Then she heard her husband's step on the gravel path behind the bungalow, the path that led to the court-house in which he had been working, and she rose from her chair to greet him. He ran up the short flight of steps, for the bungalow was built on piles, and at the door the boy was waiting to take his topee. He came into the room which served them as a dining-room and parlour, and his eyes lit up with pleasure as he saw her.

'Hulloa, Doris. Hungry?'

'Ravenous.'

'It'll only take me a minute to have a bath and then I'm ready.'

'Be quick,' she smiled.

He disappeared into his dressing-room and she heard him whistling cheerily while, with the carelessness with which she was always remonstrating, he tore off his clothes and flung them on the floor. He was twenty-nine, but he was still a school-boy; he would never grow up. That was why she had fallen in love with him, perhaps, for no amount of affection could persuade her that he was good-looking. He was a little round man, with a red face like the full moon, and blue eyes. He was rather pimply. She had examined him carefully and had been forced to confess to him that he had not a single feature which she could praise. She had told him often that he wasn't her type at all.

'I never said I was a beauty,' he laughed.

'I can't think what it is I see in you.'

But of course she knew perfectly well. He was a gay, jolly little man, who took nothing very solemnly, and he was constantly laughing. He made her laugh too. He found life an amusing rather than a serious business, and he had a charming smile. When she was with him she felt happy and good-tempered. And the deep affection which she saw in those merry blue eyes of his touched her. It was very satisfactory to be loved like that. Once, sitting on his knees, during their honeymoon she had taken his face in her hands and said to him:

'You're an ugly, little fat man, Guy, but you've got charm. I can't help loving you.'

A wave of emotion swept over her and her eyes filled with tears. She saw his face contorted for a moment with the extremity of his feeling and his voice was a little shaky when he answered.

'It's a terrible thing for me to have married a woman who's mentally deficient,' he said.

She chuckled. It was the characteristic answer which she would have liked him to make.

It was hard to realize that nine months ago she had never even heard of him. She had met him at a small place by the seaside where she was spending a month's holiday with her mother. Doris was a secretary to a member of parliament. Guy was home on leave. They were staying at the same hotel, and he quickly told her all about himself. He was born in Sembulu, where his father had served for thirty years under the second Sultan, and on leaving school he had entered the same service. He was devoted to the country.

'After all, England's a foreign land to me,' he told her. 'My home's Sembulu.'

And now it was her home too. He asked her to marry him at the end of the month's holiday. She had known he was going to, and had decided to refuse him. She was her widowed mother's only child and she could not go so far away from her, but when the moment came she did not quite know what happened to her, she was carried off her feet by an unexpected emotion, and she accepted him. They had been settled now for four months in the little outstation of which he was in charge. She was very happy.

She told him once that she had quite made up her mind to refuse him.

'Are you sorry you didn't?' he asked, with a merry smile in his twinkling blue eyes.

'I should have been a perfect fool if I had. What a bit of luck that fate or chance or whatever it was stepped in and took the matter entirely out of my hands!'

Now she heard Guy clatter down the steps to the bath-house. He was a noisy fellow and even with bare feet he could not be quiet. But he uttered an exclamation. He said two or three words in the local dialect and she could not understand. Then she heard someone speaking to him, not aloud, but in a sibilant whisper. Really it was too bad of people to waylay him when he was going to have his bath. He spoke again and though his voice was low she could hear that he was vexed. The other voice was raised now; it was a woman's. Doris supposed it was someone who had a complaint to make. It was like a Malay woman to come in that surreptitious way. But she was evidently getting very little from Guy, for she heard him say: Get out. That at all events she understood, and then she heard him bolt the door. There was a sound of the water he was throwing over himself (the bathing arrangements still amused her, the bath-houses were under the bedrooms, on the ground; you had a large tub of water and you sluiced yourself with a little tin pail) and in a couple of minutes he was back again in the dining-room. His hair was still wet. They sat down to luncheon.

'It's lucky I'm not a suspicious or a jealous person,' she laughed. 'I don't know that I should altogether approve of your having animated conversations with ladies while you're having your bath.'

His face, usually so cheerful, had borne a sullen look when he came in, but now it brightened.

'I wasn't exactly pleased to see her.'

'So I judged by the tone of your voice. In fact, I thought you were rather short with the young person.'

'Damned cheek, waylaying me like that!'

'What did she want?'

'Oh, I don't know. It's a woman from the kampong. She's had a row with her husband or something.'

'I wonder if it's the same one who was hanging about this morning.'

He frowned a little.

'Was there someone hanging about?'

'Yes, I went into your dressing-room to see that everything was nice and tidy, and then I went down to the bath-house. I saw someone slink out of the door as I went down the steps and when I looked out I saw a woman standing there.'

'Did you speak to her?'

'I asked her what she wanted and she said something, but I couldn't understand.'

'I'm not going to have all sorts of stray people prowling about here,' he said. 'They've got no right to come.'

He smiled, but Doris, with the quick perception of a woman in love, noticed that he smiled only with his lips, not as usual with his eyes also, and wondered what it was that troubled him.

'What have you been doing this morning?' he asked.

'Oh, nothing much. I went for a little walk.'

'Through the kampong?'

'Yes. I saw a man send a chained monkey up a tree to pick coconuts, which rather thrilled me.'

'It's rather a lark, isn't it?'

'Oh, Guy, there were two little boys watching him who were much whiter than the others. I wondered if they were half-castes. I spoke to them, but they didn't know a word of English.'

'There are two or three half-caste children in the kampong,' he answered.

'Who do they belong to?'

'Their mother is one of the village girls.'

'Who is their father?'

'Oh, my dear, that's the sort of question we think it a little dangerous to ask out here.' He paused. 'A lot of fellows have native wives, and then when they go home or marry they pension them off and send them back to their village.'

Doris was silent. The indifference with which he spoke seemed a little callous to her. There was almost a frown on her frank, open, pretty English face when she replied.

'But what about the children?'

'I have no doubt they're properly provided for. Within his means, a man generally sees that there's enough money to have them decently educated. They get jobs as clerks in a government office, you know; they're all right.'

She gave him a slightly rueful smile.

'You can't expect me to think it's a very good system.'

'You mustn't be too hard,' he smiled back.

'I'm not hard. But I'm thankful you never had a Malay wife. I should have hated it. Just think if those two little brats were yours.'

The boy changed their plates. There was never much variety in their menu. They started luncheon with river fish, dull and insipid, so that a good deal of tomato ketchup was needed to make it palatable, and then went on to some kind of stew. Guy poured Worcester Sauce over it.

'The old Sultan didn't think it was a white woman's country,' he said presently. 'He rather encouraged people to – keep house with native girls. Of course things have changed now. The country's perfectly quiet and I suppose we know better how to cope with the climate.'

'But, Guy, the eldest of those boys wasn't more than seven or eight and the other was about five.'

'It's awfully lonely on an outstation. Why, often one doesn't see another white man for six months on end. A fellow comes out here when he's only a boy.' He gave her that charming smile of his which transfigured his round, plain face 'There are excuses, you know.'

She always found that smile irresistible. It was his best argument. Her eyes grew once more soft and tender.

'I'm sure there are.' She stretched her hand across the little table and put it on his. 'I'm very lucky to have caught you so young. Honestly, it would upset me dreadfully if I were told that you had lived like that.'

He took her hand and pressed it.

'Are you happy here, darling?'

'Desperately.'

She looked very cool and fresh in her linen frock. The heat did not distress her. She had no more than the prettiness of youth, though her brown eyes were fine; but she had a pleasing frankness of expression, and her dark, short hair was neat and glossy. She gave you the impression of a girl of spirit and you felt sure that the member of parliament for whom she worked had in her a very competent secretary.

'I loved the country at once,' she said. 'Although I'm alone so much I don't think I've ever once felt lonely.'

Of course she had read novels about the Malay Archipelago and she had formed an impression of a sombre land with great ominous rivers and a silent, impenetrable jungle. When the little coasting steamer set them down at the mouth of the river, where a large boat, manned by a dozen Dyaks, was waiting to take them to the station, her breath was taken away by the beauty, friendly rather than awe-inspiring, of the scene. It had a gaiety, like the joyful singing of birds in the trees, which she had never expected. On each bank of the river were mangroves and nipah palms, and behind them the dense green of the forest. In the distance stretched blue mountains, range upon range, as far as the eye could see. She had no sense of confinement nor of gloom, but rather of openness and wide spaces where the exultant fancy could wander with delight. The green glittered in the sunshine and the sky was blithe and cheerful. The gracious land seemed to offer her a smiling welcome.

They rowed on, hugging a bank, and high overhead flew a pair of doves. A flash of colour, like a living jewel, dashed across their path. It was a kingfisher. Two monkeys, with their dangling tails, sat side by side on a branch. On the horizon, over there on the other side of the broad and turbid river, beyond the jungle, was a row of little white clouds, the only clouds in the sky, and they looked like a row of ballet-girls, dressed in white, waiting at the back of the stage, alert and merry, for the curtain to go up. Her heart was filled with joy; and now, remembering it all, her eyes rested on her husband with a grateful, assured affection.

And what fun it had been to arrange their living-room! It was very big. On the floor, when she arrived, was torn and dirty matting; on the walls of unpainted wood hung (much too high up) photogravures of Academy pictures, Dyak shields, and parangs. The tables were covered with Dyak cloth in sombre colours, and on them stood pieces of Brunei brass-ware, much in need of cleaning, empty cigarette tins, and bits of Malay silver. There was a rough wooden shelf with cheap editions of novels and a number of old travel books in battered leather; and another shelf was crowded with empty bottles. It was a bachelor's room, untidy but stiff; and though it amused her she found it intolerably pathetic. It was a dreary, comfortless life that Guy had led there, and she threw her arms round his neck and kissed him.

'You poor darling,' she laughed.

She had deft hands and she soon made the room habitable. She arranged this and that, and what she could not do with she turned out. Her wedding-presents helped. Now the room was friendly and comfortable. In glass vases were lovely orchids and in great bowls huge masses of flowering shrubs. She felt an inordinate pride because it was her house (she had never in her life lived in anything but a poky flat) and she had made it charming for him.

'Are you pleased with me?' she asked when she had finished.

'Quite,' he smiled.

The deliberate understatement was much to her mind. How jolly it was that they should understand each other so well! They were both of them shy of displaying emotion, and it was only at rare moments that they used with one another anything but ironic banter.

They finished luncheon and he threw himself into a long chair to have a sleep. She went towards her room. She was a little surprised that he drew her to him as she passed and, making her bend down, kissed her lips. They were not in the habit of exchanging embraces at odd hours of the day.

'A full tummy is making you sentimental, my poor lamb,' she chaffed him.

'Get out and don't let me see you again for at least two hours.'

'Don't snore.'

She left him. They had risen at dawn and in five minutes were fast asleep.

Doris was awakened by the sound of her husband's splashing in the bath-house. The walls of the bungalow were like a sounding board and not a thing that one of them did escaped the other. She felt too lazy to move, but she heard the boy bring the tea things in, so she jumped up and ran down into her own bath-house. The water, not cold but cool, was deliciously refreshing. When she came into the sitting-room Guy was taking the rackets out of the press, for they played tennis in the short cool of the evening. The night fell at six.

The tennis-court was two or three hundred yards from the bungalow and after tea, anxious not to lose time, they strolled down to it.

'Oh, look,' said Doris, 'there's that girl that I saw this morning.'

Guy turned quickly. His eyes rested for a moment on a native woman, but he did not speak.

'What a pretty sarong she's got,' said Doris. 'I wonder where it comes from.'

They passed her. She was slight and small, with the large, dark, starry eyes of her race and a mass of raven hair. She did not stir as they went by, but stared at them strangely. Doris saw then that she was not quite so young as she had at first thought. Her features were a trifle heavy and her skin was dark, but she was very pretty. She held a small child in her arms. Doris smiled a little as she saw it, but no answering smile moved the woman's lips. Her face remained impassive. She did not look at Guy, she looked only at Doris, and he walked on as though he did not see her. Doris turned to him.

'Isn't that baby a duck?'

'I didn't notice.'

She was puzzled by the look of his face. It was deathly white, and the pimples which not a little distressed her were more than commonly red.

'Did you notice her hands and feet? She might be a duchess.'

'All natives have good hands and feet,' he answered, but not jovially as was his wont; it was as though he forced himself to speak.

But Doris was intrigued.

'Who is she, d'you know?'

'She's one of the girls in the kampong.'

They had reached the court now. When Guy went up to the net to see that it was taut he looked back. The girl was still standing where they had passed her. Their eyes met.

'Shall I serve?' said Doris.

'Yes, you've got the balls on your side.'

He played very badly. Generally he gave her fifteen and beat her, but today she won easily. And he played silently. Generally he was a noisy player, shouting all the time, cursing his foolishness when he missed a ball and chaffing her when he placed one out of her reach.

'You're off your game, young man,' she cried.

'Not a bit,' he said.

He began to slam the balls, trying to beat her, and sent one after the other into the net. She had never seen him with that set face. Was it possible that he was a little out of temper because he was not playing well? The light fell, and they ceased to play. The woman whom they had passed stood in exactly the same position as when they came and once more, with expressionless face, she watched them go.

The blinds on the veranda were raised now, and on the table between their two long chairs were bottles and soda-water. This was the hour at which they had the first drink of the day and Guy mixed a couple of gin slings. The river stretched widely before them, and on the further bank the jungle was wrapped in the mystery of the approaching night. A native was silently rowing up-stream, standing at the bow of the boat, with two oars.

'I played like a fool,' said Guy, breaking a silence. 'I'm feeling a bit under the weather.'

'I'm sorry. You're not going to have fever, are you?'

'Oh, no. I shall be all right tomorrow.'

Darkness closed in upon them. The frogs croaked loudly and now and then they heard a few short notes from some singing bird of the night. Fireflies flitted across the veranda and they made the trees that surrounded it look like Christmas trees lit with tiny candles. They sparkled softly. Doris thought she heard a little sigh. It vaguely disturbed her. Guy was always so full of gaiety.

'What is it, old man?' she said gently. 'Tell mother.'

'Nothing. Time for another drink,' he answered breezily.

Next day he was as cheerful as ever and the mail came. The coasting steamer passed the mouth of the river twice a month, once on its way to the coalfields and once on its way back. On the outward journey it brought mail, which Guy sent a boat down to fetch. Its arrival was the excitement of their uneventful lives. For the first day or two they skimmed rapidly all that had come, letters, English papers and papers from Singapore, magazines and books, leaving for the ensuing weeks a more exact perusal. They snatched the illustrated papers from one another. If Doris had not been so absorbed she might have noticed that there was a change in Guy. She would have found it hard to describe and harder still to explain. There was in his eyes a sort of watchfulness and in his mouth a slight droop of anxiety.

Then, perhaps a week later, one morning when she was sitting in the shaded room studying a Malay grammar (for she was industriously learning the language) she heard a commotion in the compound. She heard the house boy's voice, he was speaking angrily, the voice of another man, perhaps it was the water-carrier's, and then a woman's, shrill and vituperative. There was a scuffle. She went to the window and opened the shutters. The water-carrier had hold of a woman's arm and was dragging her along, while the house boy was pushing her from behind with both hands. Doris recognized her at once as the woman she had seen one morning loitering in the compound and later in the day outside the tennis-court. She was holding a baby against her breast. All three were shouting angrily.

'Stop,' cried Doris. 'What are you doing?'

At the sound of her voice the water-carrier let go suddenly and the woman, still pushed from behind, fell to the ground. There was a sudden silence and the house boy looked sullenly into space. The water-carrier hesitated a moment and then slunk away. The woman raised herself slowly to her feet, arranged the baby on her arm, and stood impassive, staring at Doris. The boy said something to her which Doris could not have heard even if she had understood; the woman by no change of face showed that his words meant anything to her; but she slowly strolled away. The boy followed her to the gate of the compound. Doris called to him as he walked back, but he pretended not to hear. She was growing angry now and she called more sharply.

'Come here at once,' she cried.

Suddenly, avoiding her wrathful glance, he came towards the bungalow. He came in and stood at the door. He looked at her sulkily.

'What were you doing with that woman?' she asked abruptly.

'Tuan say she no come here.'

'You mustn't treat a woman like that. I won't have it. I shall tell the tuan exactly what I saw.'

The boy did not answer. He looked away, but she felt that he was watching her through his long eyelashes. She dismissed him.

'That'll do.'

Without a word he turned and went back to the servants' quarters. She was exasperated and she found it impossible to give her attention once more to the Malay exercises. In a little while the boy came in to lay the cloth for luncheon. On a sudden he went to the door.

'What is it?' she asked.

'Tuan just coming.'

He went out to take Guy's hat from him. His quick ears had caught the footsteps before they were audible to her. Guy did not as usual come up the steps immediately; he paused, and Doris at once surmised that the boy had gone down to meet him in order to tell him of the morning's incident. She shrugged her shoulders. The boy evidently wanted to get his story in first. But she was astonished when Guy came in. His face was ashy.

'Guy, what on earth's the matter?'

He flushed a sudden hot red.

'Nothing. Why?'

She was so taken aback that she let him pass into his room without a word of what she had meant to speak of at once. It took him longer than usual to have his bath and change his clothes and luncheon was served when he came in.

'Guy,' she said, as they sat down, 'that woman we saw the other day was here again this morning.'

'So I've heard,' he answered.

'The boys were treating her brutally. I had to stop them. You must really speak to them about it.'

Though the Malay understood every word she said, he made no sign that he heard. He handed her the toast.

'She's been told not to come here. I gave instructions that if she showed herself again she was to be turned out.'

'Were they obliged to be so rough?'

'She refused to go. I don't think they were any rougher than they could help.'

'It was horrible to see a woman treated like that. She had a baby in her arms.'

'Hardly a baby. It's three years old.'

'How d'you know?'

'I know all about her. She hasn't the least right to come here pestering everybody.'

'What does she want?'

'She wants to do exactly what she did. She wants to make a disturbance.'

For a little while Doris did not speak. She was surprised at her husband's tone. He spoke tersely. He spoke as though all this were no concern of hers. She thought him a little unkind. He was nervous and irritable.

'I doubt if we shall be able to play tennis this afternoon,' he said. 'It looks to me as though we were going to have a storm.'

The rain was falling when she awoke and it was impossible to go out. During tea Guy was silent and abstracted. She got her sewing and began to work. Guy sat down to read such of the English papers as he had not yet gone through from cover to cover; but he was restless; he walked up and down the large room and then went out on the veranda. He looked at the steady rain. What was he thinking of? Doris was vaguely uneasy.

It was not till after dinner that he spoke. During the simple meal he had exerted himself to be his usual gay self, but the exertion was apparent. The rain had ceased and the night was starry. They sat on the veranda. In order not to attract insects they had put out the lamp in the sitting-room. At their feet, with a mighty, formidable sluggishness, silent, mysterious, and fatal, flowed the river. It had the terrible deliberation and the relentlessness of destiny.

'Doris, I've got something to say to you,' he said suddenly.

His voice was very strange. Was it her fancy that he had difficulty in keeping it quite steady? She felt a little pang in her heart because he was in distress, and she put her hand gently into his. He drew it away.

'It's rather a long story. I'm afraid it's not a very nice one and I find it rather difficult to tell. I'm going to ask you not to interrupt me, or to say anything, till I've finished.'

In the darkness she could not see his face, but she felt that it was haggard. She did not answer. He spoke in a voice so low that it hardly broke the silence of the night.

'I was only eighteen when I came out here. I came straight from school. I spent three months in Kuala Solor, and then I was sent to a station up the Sembulu river. Of course there was a Resident there and his wife. I lived in the court-house, but I used to have my meals with them and spend the evening with them. I had an awfully good time. Then the fellow who was here fell ill and had to go home. We were short of men on account of the war and I was put in charge of this place. Of course I was very young, but I spoke the language like a native, and they remembered my father. I was as pleased as punch to be on my own.'

He was silent while he knocked the ashes out of his pipe and refilled it. When he lit a match Doris, without looking at him, noticed that his hand was unsteady.

'I'd never been alone before. Of course at home there'd been father and mother and generally an assistant. And then at school naturally there were always fellows about. On the way out, on the boat, there were people all the time, and at K.S., and the same at my first post. The people there were almost like my own people. I seemed always to live in a crowd. I like people. I'm a noisy blighter. I like to have a good time. All sorts of things make me laugh and you must have somebody to laugh with. But it was different here. Of course it was all right in the day time; I had my work and I could talk to the Dyaks. Although they were head-hunters in those days and now and then I had a bit of trouble with them, they were an awfully decent lot of fellows. I got on very well with them. Of course I should have liked a white man to gas to, but they were better than nothing, and it was easier for me because they didn't look upon me quite as a stranger. I liked the work too. It was rather lonely in the evening to sit on the veranda and drink a gin and bitters by myself, but I could read. And the boys were about. My own boy was called Abdul. He'd known my father. When I got tired of reading I could give him a shout and have a bit of a jaw with him.

'It was the nights that did for me. After dinner the boys shut up and went away to sleep in the kampong. I was all alone. There wasn't a sound in the bungalow except now and then the croak of the chik-chak. It used to come out of the silence, suddenly, so that it made me jump. Over in the kampong I heard the sound of a gong or fire-crackers. They were having a good time, they weren't so far away, but I had to stay where I was. I was tired of reading. I couldn't have been more of a prisoner if I'd been in jail. Night after night it was the same. I tried drinking three or four whiskies, but it's poor fun drinking alone, and it didn't cheer me up; it only made me feel rather rotten next day. I tried going to bed immediately after dinner, but I couldn't sleep. I used to lie in bed, getting hotter and hotter, and more wide awake, till I didn't know what to do with myself. By George, those nights were long. D'you know, I got so low, I was so sorry for myself that sometimes – it makes me laugh now when I think of it, but I was only nineteen and a half – sometimes I used to cry.

'Then, one evening, after dinner, Abdul had cleared away and was just going off, when he gave a little cough. He said, wasn't I lonely in the house all night by myself? "Oh, no, that's all right," I said. I didn't want him to know what a damned fool I was, but

I expect he knew all right. He stood there without speaking, and I knew he wanted to say something to me. 'What is it?' I said. 'Spit it out.' Then he said that if I'd like to have a girl to come and live with me he knew one who was willing. She was a very good girl and he could recommend her. She'd be no trouble and it would be someone to have about the bungalow. She'd mend my things for me. . . . I felt awfully low. It had been raining all day and I hadn't been able to get any exercise. I knew I shouldn't sleep for hours. It wouldn't cost me very much money, he said, her people were poor and they'd be quite satisfied with a small present. Two hundred Straits dollars. "You look," he said. "If you don't like her you send her away." I asked him where she was. "She's here," he said. "I call her." He went to the door. She'd been waiting on the steps with her mother. They came in and sat down on the floor. I gave them some sweets. She was shy, of course, but cool enough, and when I said something to her she gave me a smile. She was very young, hardly more than a child, they said she was fifteen. She was awfully pretty, and she had her best clothes on. We began to talk. She didn't say much, but she laughed a lot when I chaffed her. Abdul said I'd find she had plenty to say for herself when she got to know me. He told her to come and sit by me. She giggled and refused, but her mother told her to come, and I made room for her on the chair. She blushed and laughed, but she came, and then she snuggled up to me. The boy laughed too. "You see, she's taken to you already," he said. "Do you want her to stay?" he asked. "Do you want to?" I said to her. She hid her face, laughing, on my shoulder. She was very soft and small. "Very well," I said, "let her stay."'

Guy leaned forward and helped himself to a whisky and soda.

'May I speak now?' asked Doris.

'Wait a minute, I haven't finished yet. I wasn't in love with her, not even at the beginning. I only took her so as to have somebody about the bungalow. I think I should have gone mad if I hadn't, or else taken to drink. I was at the end of my tether. I was too young to be quite alone. I was never in love with anyone but you.' He hesitated a moment. 'She lived here till I went home last year on leave. It's the woman you've seen hanging about.'

'Yes, I guessed that. She had a baby in her arms. Is that your child?'

'Yes. It's a little girl.'

'Is it the only one?'

'You saw the two small boys the other day in the kampong. You mentioned them.'

'She has three children then?'

'Yes.'

'It's quite a family you've got.'

She felt the sudden gesture which her remark forced from him, but he did not speak.

'Didn't she know that you were married till you suddenly turned up here with a wife?' asked Doris.

'She knew I was going to be married.'

'When?'

'I sent her back to the village before I left here. I told her it was all over. I gave her what I'd promised. She always knew it was only a temporary arrangement. I was fed up with it. I told her I was going to marry a white woman.'

'But you hadn't even seen me then.'

'No, I know. But I'd made up my mind to marry when I was home.' He chuckled in his old manner. 'I don't mind telling you that I was getting rather despondent about it when I met you. I fell in love with you at first sight and then I knew it was either you or nobody.'

'Why didn't you tell me? Don't you think it would have been only fair to give me a chance of judging for myself? It might have occurred to you that it would be rather a shock to a girl to find out that her husband had lived for ten years with another girl and had three children.'

'I couldn't expect you to understand. The circumstances out here are peculiar. It's the regular thing. Five men out of six do it. I thought perhaps it would shock you and I didn't want to lose you. You see, I was most awfully in love with you. I am now, darling. There was no reason that you should ever know. I didn't expect to come back here. One seldom goes back to the same station after home leave. When we came here I offered her money if she'd go to some other village. First she said she would and then she changed her mind.'

'Why have you told me now?'

'She's been making the most awful scenes. I don't know how she found out that you knew nothing about it. As soon as she did she began to blackmail me. I've had to give her an awful lot of money. I gave orders that she wasn't to be allowed in the compound. This morning she made that scene just to attract your attention. She wanted to frighten me. It couldn't go on like that. I thought the only thing was to make a clean breast of it.'

There was a long silence as he finished. At last he put his hand on hers.

'You do understand, Doris, don't you? I know I've been to blame.'

She did not move her hand. He felt it cold beneath his.

'Is she jealous?'

'I daresay there were all sorts of perks when she was living here, and I don't suppose she much likes not getting them any longer. But she was never in love with me any more than I was in love with her. Native women never do really care for white men, you know.'

'And the children?'

'Oh, the children are all right. I've provided for them. As soon as the boys are old enough I shall send them to school at Singapore.'

'Do they mean nothing to you at all?'

He hesitated.

'I want to be quite frank with you. I should be sorry if anything happened to them. When the first one was expected I thought I'd be much fonder of it than I ever had been of its mother. I suppose I should have been if it had been white. Of course, when it was a baby it was rather funny and touching, but I had no particular feeling that it was mine. I think that's what it is; you see, I have no sense of their belonging to me. I've reproached myself sometimes, because it seemed rather unnatural, but the honest truth is that they're no more to me than if they were somebody else's children. Of course a lot of slush is talked about children by people who haven't got any.'

Now she had heard everything. He waited for her to speak, but she said nothing. She sat motionless.

'Is there anything more you want to ask me, Doris?' he said at last.

'No, I've got rather a headache. I think I shall go to bed.' Her voice was as steady as ever. 'I don't quite know what to say. Of course it's been all very unexpected. You must give me a little time to think.'

'Are you very angry with me?'

'No. Not at all. Only – only I must be left to myself for a while. Don't move. I'm going to bed.'

She rose from her long chair and put her hand on his shoulder.

'It's so very hot tonight. I wish you'd sleep in your dressing-room. Good night.'

She was gone. He heard her lock the door of her bedroom.

She was pale next day and he could see that she had not slept. There was no bitterness in her manner, she talked as usual, but without ease; she spoke of this and that as though she were making conversation with a stranger. They had never had a quarrel, but it seemed to Guy that so would she talk if they had had a disagreement and the subsequent reconciliation had left her still wounded. The look in her eyes puzzled him; he seemed to read in them a strange fear. Immediately after dinner she said:

'I'm not feeling very well tonight. I think I shall go straight to bed.'

'Oh, my poor darling, I'm so sorry,' he cried.

'It's nothing. I shall be all right in a day or two.'

'I shall come in and say good night to you later.'

'No, don't do that. I shall try and get straight off to sleep.'

'Well, then, kiss me before you go.'

He saw that she flushed. For an instant she seemed to hesitate; then, with averted eyes, she leaned towards him. He took her in his arms and sought her lips, but she turned her face away and he kissed her cheek. She left him quickly and again he heard the key turn softly in the lock of her door. He flung himself heavily on the chair. He tried to read, but his ear was attentive to the smallest sound in his wife's room. She had said she was going to bed, but he did not hear her move. The silence in there made him unaccountably nervous. Shading the lamp with his hand he saw that there was a glimmer under her door; she had not put out her light. What on earth was she doing? He put down his book. It would not have surprised him if she had been angry and had made him a scene, or if she had cried; he could have coped with that; but her calmness frightened him. And then what was that fear which he had seen so plainly in her eyes? He thought once more over all he had said to her on the previous night. He didn't know how else he could have put it. After all, the chief point was that he'd done the same as everybody else, and it was all over long before he met her. Of course as things turned out he had been a fool, but anyone could be wise after the event. He put his hand to his heart. Funny how it hurt him there.

'I suppose that's the sort of thing people mean when they say they're heartbroken,' he said to himself. 'I wonder how long it's going on like this?'

Should he knock at the door and tell her he must speak to her? It was better to have it out. He *must* make her understand. But the silence scared him. Not a sound! Perhaps it was better to leave her alone. Of course it had been a shock. He must give her as long as she wanted. After all, she knew how devotedly he loved her. Patience, that was the only thing; perhaps she was fighting it out with herself; he must give her time; he must have patience. Next morning he asked her if she had slept better.

'Yes, much,' she said.

'Are you very angry with me?' he asked piteously.

She looked at him with candid, open eyes.

'Not a bit.'

'Oh, my dear, I'm so glad. I've been a brute and a beast. I know it's been hateful for you. But do forgive me. I've been so miserable.'

'I do forgive you. I don't even blame you.'

He gave her a little rueful smile, and there was in his eyes the look of a whipped dog.

'I haven't much liked sleeping by myself the last two nights.'

She glanced away. Her face grew a trifle paler.

'I've had the bed in my room taken away. It took up so much space. I've had a little camp bed put there instead.'

'My dear, what are you talking about?'

Now she looked at him steadily.

'I'm not going to live with you as your wife again.'

'Never?'

She shook her head. He looked at her in a puzzled way. He could hardly believe he had heard aright and his heart began to beat painfully.

'But that's awfully unfair to me, Doris.'

'Don't you think it was a little unfair to me to bring me out here in the circumstances?'

'But you just said you didn't blame me.'

'That's quite true. But the other's different. I can't do it.'

'But how are we going to live together like that?'

She stared at the floor. She seemed to ponder deeply.

'When you wanted to kiss me on the lips last night I – it almost made me sick.'

'Doris.'

She looked at him suddenly and her eyes were cold and hostile.

'That bed I slept on, is that the bed in which she had her children?' She saw him flush deeply. 'Oh, it's horrible. How could you?' She wrung her hands, and her twisting, tortured fingers looked like little writhing snakes. But she made a great effort and controlled herself. 'My mind is quite made up. I don't want to be unkind to you, but there are some things that you can't ask me to do. I've thought it all over. I've been thinking of nothing else since you told me, night and day, till I'm exhausted. My first instinct was to get up and go. At once. The steamer will be here in two or three days.'

'Doesn't it mean anything to you that I love you?'

'Oh, I know you love me. I'm not going to do that. I want to give us both a chance. I have loved you so, Guy.' Her voice broke, but she did not cry. 'I don't want to be unreasonable. Heaven knows, I don't want to be unkind. Guy, will you give me time?'

'I don't know quite what you mean.'

'I just want you to leave me alone. I'm frightened by the feelings that I have.'

He had been right then; she was afraid.

'What feelings?'

'Please don't ask me. I don't want to say anything to wound you. Perhaps I shall get over them. Heaven knows, I want to. I'll try, I promise you. I'll try. Give me six months. I'll do everything in the world for you, but just that one thing.' She made a little gesture of appeal. 'There's no reason why we shouldn't be happy enough together. If you really love me you'll – you'll have patience.'

He sighed deeply.

'Very well,' he said. 'Naturally I don't want to force you to do anything you don't like. It shall be as you say.'

He sat heavily for a little, as though, on a sudden grown old, it was an effort to move; then he got up.

'I'll be getting along to the office.'

He took his topee and went out.

A month passed. Women conceal their feelings better than men and a stranger visiting them would never have guessed that Doris was in any way troubled. But in Guy the strain was obvious; his round, good-natured face was drawn, and in his eyes was a hungry, harassed look. He watched Doris. She was gay and she chaffed him as she had been used to do; they played tennis together; they chatted about one thing and another. But it was evident that she was merely playing a part, and at last, unable to contain himself, he tried to speak again of his connexions with the Malay woman.

'Oh, Guy, there's no object in going back on all that,' she answered breezily. 'We've said all we had to say about it and I don't blame you for anything.'

'Why do you punish me then?'

'My poor boy, I don't want to punish you. It's not my fault if ...' she shrugged her shoulders. 'Human nature is very odd.'

'I don't understand.'

'Don't try.'

The words might have been harsh, but she softened them with a pleasant, friendly smile. Every night when she went to bed she leaned over Guy and lightly kissed his cheek. Her lips only touched it. It was as though a moth had just brushed his face in its flight.

A second month passed, then a third, and suddenly the six

months which had seemed so interminable were over. Guy asked himself whether she remembered. He gave a strained attention now to everything she said, to every look on her face and to every gesture of her hands. She remained impenetrable. She had asked him to give her six months; well, he had.

The coasting steamer passed the mouth of the river, dropped their mail, and went on its way. Guy busily wrote the letters which it would pick up on the return journey. Two or three days passed by. It was a Tuesday and the prahu was to start at dawn on Thursday to await the steamer. Except at meal time when Doris exerted herself to make conversation they had not of late talked very much together; and after dinner as usual they took their books and began to read; but when the boy had finished clearing away and was gone for the night Doris put down hers.

'Guy, I have something I want to say to you,' she murmured.

His heart gave a sudden thud against his ribs and he felt himself change colour.

'Oh, my dear, don't look like that, it's not so very terrible,' she laughed.

But he thought her voice trembled a little.

'Well?'

'I want you to do something for me.'

'My darling, I'll do anything in the world for you.'

He put out his hand to take hers, but she drew it away.

'I want you to let me go home.'

'You?' he cried, aghast. 'When? Why?'

'I've borne it as long as I can. I'm at the end of my tether.'

'How long do you want to go for? For always?'

'I don't know. I think so.' She gathered determination. 'Yes, for always.'

'Oh, my God!'

His voice broke and she thought he was going to cry.

'Oh, Guy, don't blame me. It really is not my fault. I can't help myself.'

'You asked me for six months. I accepted your terms. You can't say I've made a nuisance of myself.'

'No, no.'

'I've tried not to let you see what a rotten time I was having.'

'I know. I'm very grateful to you. You've been awfully kind to me. Listen, Guy, I want to tell you again that I don't blame you for a single thing you did. After all, you were only a boy, and you did no more than the others; I know what the loneliness is here. Oh, my dear, I'm so dreadfully sorry for you. I knew all that from the beginning. That's why I asked you for six months. My common sense tells me that I'm making a mountain out of a molehill. I'm unreasonable; I'm being unfair to you. But, you see, common sense has nothing to do with it; my whole soul is in revolt. When I see the woman and her children in the village I just feel my legs shaking. Everything in this house; when I think of that bed I slept in it gives me goose-flesh. . . . You don't know what I've endured.'

'I think I've persuaded her to go away. And I've applied for a transfer.'

'That wouldn't help. She'll be there always. You belong to them, you don't belong to me. I think perhaps I could have stood it if there'd only been one child, but three; and the boys are quite big boys. For ten years you lived with her.' And now she came out with what she had been working up to. She was desperate. 'It's a physical thing, I can't help it, it's stronger than I am. I think of those thin black arms of hers round you and it fills me with a physical nausea. I think of you holding those little black babies in your arms. Oh, it's loathsome. The touch of you is odious to me. Each night, when I've kissed you, I've had to brace myself up to it, I've had to clench my hands and force myself to touch your cheek.' Now she was clasping and unclasping her fingers in a nervous agony, and her voice was out of control. 'I know it's I who am to blame now. I'm a silly, hysterical woman. I thought I'd get over it. I can't, and now I never shall. I've brought it all on myself; I'm willing to take the consequences; if you say I must stay here, I'll stay, but if I stay I shall die. I beseech you to let me go.'

And now the tears which she had restrained so long overflowed and she wept broken-heartedly. He had never seen her cry before.

'Of course I don't want to keep you here against your will,' he said hoarsely.

Exhausted, she leaned back in her chair. Her features were all twisted and awry. It was horribly painful to see the abandonment of grief on that face which was habitually so placid.

'I'm so sorry, Guy. I've broken your life, but I've broken mine too. And we might have been so happy.'

'When do you want to go? On Thursday?'

'Yes.'

She looked at him piteously. He buried his face in his hands. At last he looked up.

'I'm tired out,' he muttered.

'May I go?'

'Yes.'

For two minutes perhaps they sat there without a word. She started when the chik-chak gave its piercing, hoarse, and strangely human cry. Guy rose and went out on to the veranda. He leaned against the rail and looked at the softly flowing water. He heard Doris go into her room.

Next morning, up earlier than usual, he went to her door and knocked.

'Yes?'

'I have to go up-river today. I shan't be back till late.'

'All right.'

She understood. He had arranged to be away all day in order not to be about while she was packing. It was heartbreaking work. When she had packed her clothes she looked round the sitting-room at the things that belonged to her. It seemed dreadful to take them. She left everything but the photograph of her mother. Guy did not come in till ten o'clock at night.

'I'm sorry I couldn't get back to dinner,' he said. 'The headman at the village I had to go to had a lot of things for me to attend to.'

She saw his eyes wander about the room and notice that her mother's photograph no longer stood in its place.

'Is everything quite ready?' he asked. 'I've ordered the boatman to be at the steps at dawn.'

'I told the boy to wake me at five.'

'I'd better give you some money.' He went to his desk and wrote out a cheque. He took some notes from a drawer. 'Here's some cash to take you as far as Singapore and at Singapore you'll be able to change the cheque.'

'Thank you.'

'Would you like me to come to the mouth of the river with you?'

'Oh, I think it would be better if we said good-bye here.'

'All right. I think I shall turn in. I've had a long day and I'm dead beat.'

He did not even touch her hand. He went into his room. In a few minutes she heard him throw himself on his bed. For a little while she sat looking for the last time round that room in which she had been so happy and so miserable. She sighed deeply. She got up and went into her own room. Everything was packed except the one or two things she needed for the night.

It was dark when the boy awakened them. They dressed hurriedly and when they were ready breakfast was waiting for them. Presently they heard the boat row up to the landing-stage below the bungalow, and then the servants carried down her luggage. It was a poor pretence they made of eating. The darkness thinned away and the river was ghostly. It was not yet day, but it was no longer night. In the silence the voices of the natives at the landing-stage were very clear. Guy glanced at his wife's untouched plate.

'If you've finished we might stroll down. I think you ought to be starting.'

She did not answer. She rose from the table. She went into her room to see that nothing had been forgotten and then side by side with him walked down the steps. A little winding path led them to the river. At the landing-stage the native guards in their smart uniform were lined up and they presented arms as Guy and Doris passed. The head boatman gave her his hand as she stepped into the boat. She turned and looked at Guy. She wanted desperately to say one last word of comfort, once more to ask for his forgiveness, but she seemed to be struck dumb.

He stretched out his hand.

'Well, good-bye, I hope you'll have a jolly journey.'

They shook hands.

Guy nodded to the head boatman and the boat pushed off. The dawn now was creeping along the river mistily, but the night lurked still in the dark trees of the jungle. He stood at the landing-stage till the boat was lost in the shadows of the morning. With a sigh he turned away. He nodded absent-mindedly when the guard once more presented arms. But when he reached the bungalow he called the boy. He went round the room picking out everything that had belonged to Doris.

'Pack all these things up,' he said. 'It's no good leaving them about.'

Then he sat down on the veranda and watched the day advance gradually like a bitter, an unmerited, and an overwhelming sorrow. At last he looked at his watch. It was time for him to go to the office.

In the afternoon he could not sleep, his head ached miserably, so he took his gun and went for a tramp in the jungle. He shot nothing, but he walked in order to tire himself out. Towards sunset he came back and had two or three drinks, and then it was time to dress for dinner. There wasn't much use in dressing now; he might just as well be comfortable; he put on a loose native jacket and a sarong. That was what he had been accustomed to wear before Doris came. He was barefoot. He ate his dinner listlessly and the boy cleared away and went. He sat down to read the *Tatler*. The bungalow was very silent. He could not read and let the paper fall on his knees. He was exhausted. He could not think and his mind was strangely vacant. The chik-chak was noisy that night and its hoarse and sudden cry seemed to mock him. You could hardly believe that this reverberating sound came from so small a throat. Presently he heard a discreet cough.

'Who's there?' he cried.

There was a pause. He looked at the door. The chik-chak laughed harshly. A small boy sidled in and stood on the threshold. It was a little half-caste boy in a tattered singlet and a sarong. It was the elder of his two sons.

'What do you want?' said Guy.

The boy came forward into the room and sat down, tucking his legs away under him.

'Who told you to come here?'

'My mother sent me. She says, do you want anything?'

Guy looked at the boy intently. The boy said nothing more. He sat and waited, his eyes cast down shyly. Then Guy in deep and bitter reflection buried his face in his hands. What was the use? It was finished. Finished! He surrendered. He sat back in his chair and sighed deeply.

'Tell your mother to pack up her things and yours. She can come back.'

'When?' asked the boy, impassively.

Hot tears trickled down Guy's funny, round spotty face.

'Tonight.'

FLOTSAM AND JETSAM

NORMAN GRANGE was a rubber-planter. He was up before day-break to take the roll-call of his labour and then walked over the estate to see that the tapping was properly done. This duty performed, he came home, bathed and changed, and now with his wife opposite him he was eating the substantial meal, half breakfast and half luncheon, which in Borneo is called brunch. He read as he ate. The dining-room was dingy. The worn electro-plate, the shabby cruet, the chipped dishes betokened poverty, but a poverty accepted with apathy. A few flowers would have brightened the table, but there was apparently no one to care how things looked. When Grange had finished he belched, filled his pipe and lit it, rose from the table and went out on to the veranda. He took no more notice of his wife than if she had not been there. He lay down in a long rattan chair and went on reading. Mrs Grange reached over for a tin of cigarettes and smoked while she sipped her tea. Suddenly she looked out, for the house boy came up the steps and accompanied by two men went up to her husband. One was a Dyak and the other Chinese. Strangers seldom came and she could not imagine what they wanted. She got up and went to the door to listen. Though she had lived in Borneo for so many years she knew no more Malay than was necessary to get along with the boys, and she only vaguely understood what was said. She gathered from her husband's tone that something had happened to annoy him. He seemed to be asking questions first of the Chink and then of the Dyak; it looked as though they were pressing him to do something he didn't want to do; at length, however, with a frown on his face he raised himself from his chair and followed by the men walked down the steps. Curious to see where he was going she slipped out on to the veranda. He had taken the path that led down to the river. She shrugged her thin shoulders and went to her room. Presently she gave a violent start, for she heard her husband call her.

'Vesta.'

She came out.

'Get a bed ready. There's a white man in a prahu at the landing-stage. He's damned ill.'

'Who is he?'

'How the hell should I know? They're just bringing him up.'

'We can't have anyone to stay here.'

'Shut up and do as I tell you.'

He left her on that and again went down to the river. Mrs Grange called the boy and told him to put sheets on the bed in the spare room. Then she stood at the top of the steps and waited. In a little while she saw her husband coming back and behind him a huddle of Dyaks carrying a man on a mattress. She stood aside to let them pass and caught a glimpse of a white face.

'What shall I do?' she asked her husband.

'Get out and keep quiet.'

'Polite, aren't you?'

The sick man was taken into the room, and in two or three minutes the Dyaks and Grange came out.

'I'm going to see about his kit. I'll have it brought up. His boy's looking after him and there's no cause for you to butt in!'

'What's the matter with him?'

'Malaria. His boatmen are afraid he's going to die and won't take him on. His name's Skelton.'

'He isn't going to die, is he?'

'If he does we'll bury him.'

But Skelton didn't die. He woke next morning to find himself in a room, in bed and under a mosquito-net. He couldn't think where he was. It was a cheap iron bed and the mattress was hard, but to lie on it was a relief after the discomfort of the prahu. He could see nothing of the room but a chest of drawers, roughly made by a native carpenter, and a wooden chair. Opposite was a doorway, with a blind down, and this he guessed led on to a veranda.

'Kong,' he called.

The blind was drawn aside and his boy came in. The Chinaman's face broke into a grin when he saw that his master was free from fever.

'You more better, Tuan. Velly glad.'

'Where the devil am I?'

Kong explained.

'Luggage all right?' asked Skelton.

'Yes, him all light.'

'What's the name of this fellow – the tuan whose house this is?'

'Mr Norman Grange.'

To confirm what he said he showed Skelton a little book in which the owner's name was written. It was Grange. Skelton noticed that the book was Bacon's *Essays*. It was curious to find it in a planter's house away up a river in Borneo.

'Tell him I'd be glad to see him.'

'Tuan out. Him come presently.'

'What about my having a wash? And by God, I want a shave.'

He tried to get out of bed, but his head swam and with a bewildered cry he sank back. But Kong shaved and washed him, and changed the shorts and singlet in which he had been lying ever since he fell ill for a sarong and a baju. After that he was glad to lie still. But presently Kong came in and said that the tuan of the house was back. There was a knock on the door and a large stoutish man stepped in.

'I hear you're better,' he said.

'Oh, much. It's terribly kind of you to have taken me in like this. It seems awful, planting myself on you.'

Grange answered a trifle harshly.

'That's all right. You were pretty bad, you know. No wonder those Dyaks wanted to get rid of you.'

'I don't want to impose myself on you longer than I need. If I could hire a launch here, or a prahu, I could get off this afternoon.'

'There's no launch to hire. You'd better stay a bit. You must be as weak as a rat.'

'I'm afraid I shall be a frightful bother.'

'I don't see why. You've got your own boy and he'll look after you.'

Grange had just come in from his round of the estate and wore dirty shorts, a khaki shirt open at the neck, and an old, battered terai hat. He looked as shabby as a beachcomber. He took off his hat to wipe his sweating brow; he had close-cropped grey hair; his face was red, a broad, fleshy face, with a large mouth under a stubble of grey moustache, a short, pugnacious nose and small, mean eyes.

'I wonder if you could let me have something to read,' said Skelton.

'What sort of thing?'

'I don't mind so long as it's lightish.'

'I'm not much of a novel reader myself, but I'll send you in two or three books. My wife can provide you with novels. They'll be trash, because that's all she reads. But it may suit you.'

With a nod he withdrew. Not a very likeable man. But he was obviously very poor, the room in which Skelton lay, something in Grange's appearance, indicated that; he was probably manager of an estate on a cut salary, and it was not unlikely that the expense of a guest and his servant was unwelcome. Living in that remote spot, and so seeing white men but seldom, it might be that he was ill at ease with strangers. Some people improve unbelievably on acquaintance. But his hard, shifty little eyes were disconcerting; they gave the lie to the red face and the massive frame which otherwise might have persuaded you that this was a jolly sort of fellow with whom you could quickly make friends.

After a while the house boy came in with a parcel of books. There were half a dozen novels by authors he had never heard of, and a glance told him they were slop; these must be Mrs Grange's; and then there was a Boswell's *Johnson*, Borrow's *Lavengro*, and Lamb's *Essays*. It was an odd choice. They were not the books you would have expected to find in a planter's house. In most planter's houses there is not more than a shelf or two of books and for the most part they're detective stories. Skelton had a disinterested curiosity in human creatures, and he amused himself now by trying to make out from the books Norman Grange had sent, from the look of him, and from the few words they had exchanged, what sort of a man he could be. Skelton was a little surprised that his host did not come to see him again that day; it looked as though he were going to content himself with giving his uninvited guest board and lodging, but were not sufficiently interested in him to seek his company. Next morning he felt well enough to get up, and with Kong's help settled himself in a long chair on the veranda. It badly needed a coat of paint. The bungalow stood on the brow of a hill, about fifty yards from the river; and on the opposite bank, looking very small across that great stretch of water, you could see native houses on piles nestling among the greenery. Skelton had not yet the activity of mind to read steadily, and after a page or two, his thoughts wandering, he found himself content to watch idly the sluggish flow of the turbid stream. Suddenly he heard a step. He saw a little elderly woman come towards him, and knowing that this must be Mrs Grange tried to get up.

'Don't move,' she said. 'I only came to see if you had everything you wanted.'

She wore a blue cotton dress, simple enough, but more suited to a young girl than to a woman of her age; her short hair was tousled, as though on getting out of bed she had scarcely troubled to pass a comb through it, and dyed a vivid yellow, but badly, and the roots showed white. Her skin was raddled and dry, and there was a great dab of rouge on each cheek-bone, put on however so clumsily that you could not for a moment take it for a natural colour, and a smear of lipstick on her mouth. But the strangest thing about her was a tic she had that made her jerk her head as though she were beckoning you to an inner room. It seemed to come at regular intervals, perhaps three times a minute, and her left hand was in almost constant movement; it was not quite a tremble, it was a rapid twirl as though she wanted to draw your attention to something behind her back. Skelton was startled by her appearance and embarrassed by her tic.

'I hope I'm not making myself too great a nuisance,' he said. 'I think I shall be well enough to make a move tomorrow or the day after.'

'It's not often we see anybody in a place like this, you know. It's a treat to have someone to talk to.'

'Won't you sit down? I'll tell my boy to bring you a chair.'

'Norman said I was to leave you alone.'

'I haven't spoken to a white person for two years. I've been longing for a good old talk.'

Her head twitched violently, more quickly than usual, and her hand gave that queer spasmodic gesture.

'He won't be back for another hour. I'll get a chair.'

Skelton told her who he was and what he had been doing, but he discovered that she had questioned his boy and already knew all about him.

'You must be crazy to get back to England?' she asked.

'I shan't be sorry.'

Suddenly Mrs Grange seemed to be attacked by what one could only describe as a nerve storm. Her head twitched so madly, her hand shook with such fury, that it was disconcerting. You could only look away.

'I haven't been to England for sixteen years,' she said.

'You don't mean that? Why, I thought all you planters went home every five years at the longest.'

'We can't afford it; we're broke to the wide. Norman put all the money he had into this plantation, and it hasn't really paid for years. It only just brings in enough to keep us from starvation. Of course it doesn't matter to Norman. He isn't English really.'

'He looks English enough.'

'He was born in Sarawak. His father was in the government service. If he's anything he's a native of Borneo.'

Then, without warning, she began to cry. It was horribly painful to see the tears running down the raddled, painted cheeks of that woman with the constant tic. Skelton knew neither what to say nor what to do. He did what was probably the best thing, he kept silent. She dried her eyes.

'You must think me a silly old fool. I sometimes wonder that after all these years I can still cry. I suppose it's in my nature. I always could cry very easy when I was on the stage.'

'Oh, were you on the stage?'

'Yes, before I married. That's how I met Norman. We were playing in Singapore and he was there on holiday. I don't suppose

I shall ever see England any more. I shall stay here till I die and every day of my life I shall look at that beastly river. I shall never get away now. Never.'

'How did you happen to find yourself in Singapore?'

'Well, it was soon after the war, I couldn't get anything to suit me in London, I'd been on the stage a good many years and I was fed up with playing small parts; the agents told me a fellow called Victor Palace was taking a company out East. His wife was playing lead, but I could play seconds. They'd got half a dozen plays, comedies, you know, and farces. The salary wasn't much, but they were going to Egypt and India, the Malay States and China and then down to Australia. It was a chance to see the world and I accepted. We didn't do badly in Cairo and I think we made money in India, but Burma wasn't much good, and Siam was worse; Penang was a disaster and so were the rest of the Malay States. Well, one day Victor called us together and said he was bust, he hadn't got the money for our fares on to Hong Kong, and the tour was a wash-out and he was very sorry but we'd have to get back home as best we could. Of course we told him he couldn't do that to us. You never heard such a row. Well, the long and short of it was that he said we could have the scenery and the props if we thought they was any good to us, but as to money it was no use asking for it because he damned well hadn't got it. And next day we found out that him and his wife, without saying a word to anybody, had got on a French boat and skipped. I was in a rare state, I can tell you. I had a few pounds I'd saved out of me salary, and that was all; somebody told me if we was absolutely stranded the government would have to send us home, but only steerage, and I didn't much fancy that. We got the Press to put our plight before the public and someone came along with the proposition that we should give a benefit performance. Well, we did, but it wasn't much without Victor or his wife, and by the time we'd paid the expenses we weren't any better off than we'd been before. I was at my wits' end, I don't mind telling you. It was then that Norman proposed to me. The funny thing is that I hardly knew him. He'd taken me for a drive round the island and we'd had tea two or three times at the Europe and danced. Men don't often do things for you without wanting something in return, and I thought he expected to get a little bit of fun, but I'd had a good deal of experience and I thought he'd be clever if he got round me. But when he asked me to marry him, well, I was so surprised, I couldn't hardly believe me own ears. He said he'd got his own estate in Borneo and it only wanted a little patience and he'd make a packet. And it was on the banks of a fine river and all round was the jungle. He made it sound very romantic. I was getting on, you know, I was thirty, it wasn't going to be any easier to get work as time went on, and it was tempting to have a house of me own and all that. Never to have to hang around agents' offices no more. Never to have to lay awake no more and wonder how you was going to pay next week's rent. He wasn't a bad-looking chap in those days, brown and big and virile. No one could say I was willing to marry anybody just to . . .' Suddenly she stopped. 'There he is. Don't say you've seen me.'

She picked up the chair she had been sitting in and quickly slipped away with it into the house. Skelton was bewildered. Her grotesque appearance, the painful tears, her story told with that incessant twitching; and then her obvious fear when she heard her husband's voice in the compound, and her hurried escape; he could make nothing of it.

In a few minutes Norman Grange stumped along the veranda.

'I hear you're better,' he said.

'Much, thanks.'

'If you care to join us at brunch I'll have a place laid for you.'

'I'd like it very much.'

'All right. I'm just going to have a bath and a change.'

He walked away. Presently a boy came along and told Skelton his tuan was waiting for him. Skelton followed him into a small sitting-room, with the jalousies drawn to keep out the heat, an uncomfortable, overcrowded room with a medley of furniture, English and Chinese, and occasional tables littered with worthless junk. It was neither cosy nor cool. Grange had changed into a sarong and baju and in the native dress looked coarse but powerful. He introduced Skelton to his wife. She shook hands with him as though she had never seen him before and uttered a few polite words of greeting. The boy announced that their meal was ready and they went into the dining-room.

'I hear that you've been in this bloody country for some time,' said Grange.

'Two years. I'm an anthropologist and I wanted to study the manners and customs of tribes that haven't had any contact with civilization.'

Skelton felt that he should tell his host how it had come about that he had been forced to accept a hospitality which he could not but feel was grudgingly offered. After leaving the village that had been his headquarters he had journeyed by land for ten days till he reached the river. There he had engaged a couple of prahus, one for himself and his luggage and the other for Kong, his Chinese servant, and the camp equipment, to take him to the coast. The long trek across country had been hard going and he found it very comfortable to lie on a mattress under an awning of rattan matting and take his ease. All the time he had been away Skelton had been in perfect health, and as he travelled down the river he could not but think that he was very lucky; but even as the thought passed through his mind, it occurred to him that if he happened just then to congratulate himself on his good fortune in this respect, it was because he did not feel quite so well as usual. It was true that he had been forced to drink a great deal of arak the night before at the long-house where he had put up, but he was used to it and that hardly accounted for his headache. He had a general sense of malaise. He was wearing nothing but shorts and a singlet, and he felt chilly; it was curious because the sun was shining fiercely and when he put his hand on the gunwale of the prahu the heat was hardly bearable. If he had had a coat handy he would have put it on. He grew colder and colder and presently his teeth began to chatter; he huddled up on his mattress, shivering all over in a desperate effort to get warm. He could not fail to guess what was the matter.

'Christ,' he groaned. 'Malaria.'

He called the headman, who was steering the prahu.

'Get Kong.'

The headman shouted to the second prahu and ordered his own paddlers to stop. In a moment the two boats were side by side and Kong stepped in.

'I've got fever, Kong,' gasped Skelton. 'Get me the medicine chest and, for God's sake, blankets. I'm freezing to death.'

Kong gave his master a big dose of quinine and piled on him what coverings they had. They started off again.

Skelton was too ill to be taken ashore when they tied up for the night and so passed it in the prahu. All next day and the day after he was very ill. Sometimes one or other of the crew came and looked at him, and often the headman stayed for quite a long while staring at him thoughtfully.

'How many days to the coast?' Skelton asked the boy.

'Four, five.' He paused for a minute. 'Headman, he no go coast. He say, he wantchee go home.'

'Tell him to go to hell.'

'Headman say, you velly sick, you die. If you die and he go coast he catchee trouble.'

'I'm not thinking of dying,' said Skelton. 'I shall be all right. It's just an ordinary go of malaria.'

Kong did not answer. The silence irritated Skelton. He knew that the Chinese had something in mind that he did not like to say.

'Spit it out, you fool,' he cried.

Skelton's heart sank when Kong told him the truth. When they reached their resting-place that night the headman was going to demand his money and slip away with the two prahus before dawn. He was too frightened to carry a dying man farther. Skelton had no strength to take the determined attitude that might have availed him; he could only hope by the offer of more money to persuade the headman to carry out his agreement. The day passed in long arguments between Kong and the headman, but when they tied up for the night the headman came to Skelton and told him sulkily that he would go no farther. There was a long-house near-by where he might get lodging till he grew better. He began to unload the baggage. Skelton refused to move. He got Kong to give him his revolver and swore to shoot anyone who came near him.

Kong, the crew, and the headman went up to the long-house and Skelton was left alone. Hour after hour he lay there, the fever burning his body and his mouth parched, while muddled thoughts hammered away in his brain. Then there were lights and the sound of men talking. The Chinese boy came with the headman and another man, whom Skelton had not yet seen, from the neighbouring long-house. He did his best to understand what Kong was telling him. It appeared that a few hours down-stream there lived a white man, and to his house, if that would satisfy Skelton, the headman was willing to take him.

'More better you say yes,' said Kong. 'Maybe white man has launch, then we go down to coast chop-chop.'

'Who is he?'

'Planter,' said Kong. 'This fellow say, him have rubber estate.'

Skelton was too tired to argue further. All he wanted just then was to sleep. He accepted the compromise.

'To tell you the truth,' he finished, 'I don't remember much more till I woke up yesterday morning to find myself an uninvited guest in your house.'

'I don't blame those Dyaks, you know,' said Grange. 'When I came down to the prahu and saw you, I thought you were for it.'

Mrs Grange sat silent while Skelton told his story, her head and her hand twitching regularly, as though by the action of some invisible clockwork, but when her husband addressed her, asking for the Worcester Sauce, and that was the only time he spoke to her, she was seized with such a paroxysm of involuntary movement that it was horrible to see. She passed him what he asked for without a word. Skelton got an uncomfortable impression that she was terrified of Grange. It was odd, because to all appearance he was not a bad sort. He was knowledgeable and far from stupid; and though you could not have said that his manner was cordial, it was plain that he was ready to be of what service he could.

They finished their meal and separated to rest through the heat of the day.

'See you again at six for a sun-downer,' said Grange.

When Skelton had had a good sleep, a bath, and a read, he went out on to the veranda. Mrs Grange came up to him. It looked as though she had been waiting.

'He's back from the office. Don't think it's funny if I don't speak to you. If he thought I liked having you here he'd turn you out tomorrow.'

She said these words in a whisper and slipped back into the house. Skelton was startled. It was a strange house he had come into in a strange manner. He went into the overcrowded sitting-room and there found his host. He had been worried by the evident poverty of the establishment and he felt that the Granges could ill afford even the small expense he must be putting them to. But he had already formed the impression that Grange was a quick-tempered, susceptible man and he did not know how he would take an offer to help. He made up his mind to risk it.

'Look here,' he said to him, 'it looks as though I might have to inflict myself on you for several days. I'd be so much more comfortable if you'd let me pay for my board and lodging.'

'Oh, that's all right, your lodging costs nothing, the house belongs to the mortgagees, and your board doesn't come to much.'

'Well, there are drinks anyway and I've had to come down on your stores of tobacco and cigarettes.'

'It's not more than once a year that anyone comes up here, and then it's only the D.O. or someone like that – besides, when one's as broke as I am nothing matters much.'

'Well, then, will you take my camp equipment? I shan't be wanting it any more, and if you'd like one of my guns, I'd be only too glad to leave it with you.'

Grange hesitated. There was a glimmer of cupidity in those small, cunning eyes of his.

'If you'd let me have one of your guns you'd pay for your board and lodging over and over again.'

'That's settled, then.'

They began to talk over the whisky and sparkler with which, following the Eastern habit, they celebrated the setting of the sun. Discovering that they both played chess they had a game. Mrs Grange did not join them till dinner. The meal was dull. An insi-

pid soup, a tasteless river fish, a tough piece of steak, and a
caramel pudding. Norman Grange and Skelton drank beer; Mrs
Grange water. She never of her own will uttered a word. Skelton
had again the uncomfortable impression that she was scared to
death of her husband. Once or twice, Skelton from common
politeness sought to bring her into the conversation, addressing
himself to her, telling her a story or asking her a question, but it
evidently distressed her so much, her head twitched so violently,
her hand was agitated by gestures so spasmodic that he thought
it kinder not to insist. When the meal was over she got up.

'I'll leave you gentlemen to your port,' she said.

Both the men got up as she left the room. It was rather absurd,
and somehow sinister, to see this social pretence in those poverty-
stricken surroundings on a Borneo river.

'I may add that there is no port. There might be a little
Benedictine left.'

'Oh, don't bother.'

They talked for a while and Grange began to yawn. He got up
every morning before sunrise and by nine o'clock at night could
hardly keep his eyes open.

'Well, I'm going to turn in,' he said.

He nodded to Skelton and without further ceremony left him.
Skelton went to bed, but he could not sleep. Though the heat was
oppressive, it was not the heat that kept him awake. There was
something horrible about that house and those two people who
lived in it. He didn't know what it was that affected him with this
peculiar uneasiness, but this he knew, that he would be heartily
thankful to be out of it and away from them. Grange had talked
a good deal about himself, but he knew no more of him than he
had learned at the first glance. To all appearances he was just the
commonplace planter who had fallen upon evil days. He had
bought his land immediately after the war and had planted trees;
but by the time they were bearing the slump had come and since
then it had been a constant struggle to keep going. The estate and
the house were heavily mortgaged, and now that rubber was once
more selling profitably all he made went to the mortgagees. That
was an old story in Malaya. What made Grange somewhat unusual was that he was a man without a country. Born in Borneo,
he had lived there with his parents till he was old enough to go to
school in England; at seventeen he had come back and had never
left it since except to go to Mesopotamia during the war. England
meant nothing to him. He had neither relations nor friends there.
Most planters, like civil servants, have come from England, go
back on leave now and then, and look forward to settling down

there when they retire. But what had England to offer Norman Grange?

'I was born here,' he said, 'and I shall die here. I'm a stranger in England. I don't like their ways over there and I don't understand the things they talk about. And yet I'm a stranger here too. To the Malays and the Chinese I'm a white man, though I speak Malay as well as they do, and a white man I shall always be.' Then he said a significant thing. 'Of course if I'd had any sense I'd have married a Malay girl and had half a dozen half-caste kids. That's the only solution really for us chaps who were born and bred here.'

Grange's bitterness was greater than could be explained by his financial embarrassment. He had little good to say of any of the white men in the colony. He seemed to think that they despised him because he was native-born. He was a sour, disappointed fellow, and a conceited one. He had shown Skelton his books. There were not many of them, but they were the best on the whole that English literature can show; he had read them over and over again; but it looked as though he had learnt from them neither charity nor loving-kindness, it looked as though their beauty had left him unmoved; and to know them so well had only made him self-complacent. His exterior, which was so hearty and English, seemed to have little relation to the man within; you could not resist the suspicion that it masked a very sinister being.

Early next morning, to enjoy the cool of the day, Skelton, with his pipe and a book, was sitting on the veranda outside his room. He was still very weak, but felt much better. In a little while Mrs Grange joined him. She held in her hand a large album.

'I thought I'd like to show you some of me old photos and me notices. You mustn't think I always looked like what I do now. He's off on his round and he won't be back for two or three hours yet.'

Mrs Grange, in the same blue dress she had worn the day before, her hair as untidy, appeared strangely excited.

'It's all I have to remind me of the past. Sometimes when I can't bear life any more I look at my album.'

She sat by Skelton's side as he turned the pages. The notices were from provincial papers, and the references to Mrs Grange, whose stage name had been apparently Vesta Blaise, were carefully underlined. From the photographs you could see that she had been pretty enough in an undistinguished way. She had acted in musical comedy and revue, in farce and comedy, and taking the photographs and the notices together it was easy to tell that here had been the common, dreary, rather vulgar career of the girl with no particular talent who has taken to the stage on the strength of a pretty face and a good figure. Her head twitching, her hand shaking, Mrs Grange looked at the photographs and read the notices with as much interest as if she had never seen them before.

'You've got to have influence on the stage, and I never had any,' she said. 'If I'd only had my chance I know I'd have made good. I had bad luck, there's no doubt about that.'

It was all sordid and somewhat pathetic.

'I daresay you're better off as you are,' said Skelton.

She snatched the book from him and shut it with a bang. She had a paroxysm so violent that it was really frightening to look at her.

'What d'you mean by that? What d'you know about the life I lead here? I'd have killed myself years ago only I know he wants me to die. That's the only way I can get back on him, by living, and I'm going to live; I'm going to live as long as he does. Oh, I hate him. I've often thought I'd poison him, but I was afraid. I didn't know how to do it really, and if he died the Chinks would foreclose and I'd be turned out. And where should I go then? I haven't a friend in the world.'

Skelton was aghast. It flashed through his mind that she was crazy. He hadn't a notion what to say. She gave him a keen look.

'I suppose it surprises you to hear me talk like that. I mean it, you know, every word of it. He'd like to kill me too, but he daren't either. And he knows how to do it all right. He knows how the Malays kill people. He was born here. There's nothing he doesn't know about the country.'

Skelton forced himself to speak.

'You know, Mrs Grange, I'm a total stranger. Don't you think it's rather unwise to tell me all sorts of things there's no need for me to know? After all, you live a very solitary life. I daresay you get on one another's nerves. Now that things are looking up perhaps you'll be able to take a trip to England.'

'I don't want to go to England. I'd be ashamed to let them see me like I am now. D'you know how old I am? Forty-six. I look sixty and I know it. That's why I showed you those photos, so as you might see I wasn't always like what I am now. Oh, my God, how I've wasted my life! They talk of the romance of the East. They can have it. I'd rather be a dresser in a provincial theatre, I'd rather be one of the sweepers that keep it clean, than what I am now. Until I came here I'd never been alone in me life, I'd always lived in a crowd; you don't know what it is to have nobody to talk to from year's end to year's end. To have to keep it all bottled up. How would you like to see no one, week in and week out, day after day for sixteen years, except the man you hate most in the world? How would you like to live for sixteen years with a man who hates you so he can't bear to look at you?'

'Oh, come, it can't be as bad as that.'

'I'm telling you the truth. Why should I tell you a lie? I shall never see you again; what do I care what you think of me? And if you tell them what I've said when you get down to the coast, what's the odds? They'll say: "God, you don't mean to say you stayed with those people? I pity you. He's an outsider and she's crazy; got a tic; they say it looks as if she was always trying to wipe the blood off her dress. They were mixed up in a damned funny business, but no one ever really knew the ins and outs of it; it all happened a long time ago and the country was pretty wild in those days." A damned funny business and no mistake. I'd tell you for two pins. That would be a bit of dirt for them at the club. You wouldn't have to pay for a drink for days. Damn them. Oh, Christ, how I hate this country. I hate that river. I hate this house. I hate that damned rubber. I loathe the filthy natives. And that's all I've got to look forward to till I die – till I die without a doctor to take care of me, without a friend to hold me hand.'

She began to cry hysterically. Mrs Grange had spoken with a dramatic intensity of which Skelton would never have thought her capable. Her coarse irony was as painful as her anguish. Skelton was young, he was not yet thirty, and he did not know how to deal with the difficult situation. But he could not keep silent.

'I'm terribly sorry, Mrs Grange. I wish I could do something to help you.'

'I'm not asking for your help. No one can help me.'

Skelton was distressed. From what she said he could not but suspect that she had been concerned in a mysterious and perhaps dreadful occurrence, and it might be that to tell him about it without fear of the consequences was just the relief she needed.

'I don't want to butt into what's no business of mine, but, Mrs Grange, if you think it would ease your mind to tell me – what you were referring to just now, I mean what you said was a damned funny business, I promise you on my word of honour that I'll never repeat it to a living soul.'

She stopped crying quite suddenly and gave him a long, intent look. She hesitated. He had an impression that the desire to speak was almost irresistible. But she shook her head and sighed.

'It wouldn't do any good. Nothing can do me any good.'

She got up and abruptly left him.

The two men sat down to brunch by themselves.

'My wife asks you to excuse her,' said Grange. 'She's got

one of her sick headaches and she's staying in bed today.'

'Oh, I'm sorry.'

Skelton had a notion that in the searching look that Grange gave him was mistrust and animosity. It flashed through his mind that somehow he had discovered that Mrs Grange had been talking to him and perhaps had said things that should have been left unsaid. Skelton made an effort at conversation, but his host was taciturn, and they ended the meal in a silence that was only broken by Grange when he got up.

'You seem pretty fit today and I don't suppose you want to stay in this God-forsaken place longer than you must. I've sent over the river to arrange for a couple of prahus to take you down to the coast. They'll be here at six tomorrow morning.'

Skelton felt sure then that he was right; Grange knew or guessed that his wife had spoken too freely, and he wanted to be rid as soon as possible of the dangerous visitor.

'That's terribly kind of you,' Skelton answered, smiling. 'I'm as fit as a fiddle.'

But in Grange's eyes was no answering smile. They were coldly hostile.

'We might have another game of chess later on,' said he.

'All right. When d'you get back from your office?'

'I haven't got much to do there today. I shall be about the house.'

Skelton wondered if it were only his fancy that there was something very like a threat in the tone in which Grange uttered these words. It looked as though he were going to make sure that his wife and Skelton should not again be left alone. Mrs Grange did not come to dinner. They drank their coffee and smoked their cheroots. Then Grange, pushing back his chair, said:

'You've got to make an early start tomorrow. I daresay you'd like to turn in. I shall have started out on my round by the time you go, so I'll say good-bye to you now.'

'Let me get my guns. I want you to take the one you like best.'

'I'll tell the boy to fetch them.'

The guns were brought and Grange made his choice. He gave no sign that he was pleased with the handsome gift.

'You quite understand that this gun's worth a damned sight more than what your food and drink and smoke have run me into?' he said.

'For all I know you saved my life. I don't think an old gun is an over-generous return for that.'

'Oh, well, if you like to look at it that way, I suppose it's your own business. Thank you very much all the same.'

They shook hands and parted.

Next morning, while the baggage was being stowed away in the prahus, Skelton asked the house boy whether, before starting, he could say good-bye to Mrs Grange. The house boy said he would go and see. He waited a little while. Mrs Grange came out of her room on to the veranda. She was wearing a pink dressing-gown, shabby, rumpled, and none too clean, of Japanese silk, heavily trimmed with cheap lace. The powder was thick on her face, her cheeks were rouged and her lips scarlet with lipstick. Her head seemed to twitch more violently than usual and her hand was agitated by that strange gesture. When first Skelton saw it he had thought that it suggested a wish to call attention to something behind her back, but now, after what she had told him yesterday, it did indeed look as though she were constantly trying to brush something off her dress. Blood, she had said.

'I didn't want to go without thanking you for all your kindness to me,' he said.

'Oh, that's all right.'

'Well, good-bye.'

'I'll walk down with you to the landing-stage.'

They hadn't far to go. The boatmen were still arranging the luggage. Skelton looked across the river where you could see some native houses.

'I suppose these men come from over there. It looks quite a village.'

'No, only those few houses. There used to be a rubber estate there, but the company went broke and it was abandoned.'

'D'you ever go over there?'

'Me?' cried Mrs Grange. Her voice rose shrill and her head, her hand, were on a sudden convulsed by a paroxysm of involuntary movement. 'No. Why should I?'

Skelton could not imagine why that simple question, asked merely for something to say, should so greatly upset her. But by now all was in order and he shook hands with her. He stepped into the boat and comfortably settled down. They pushed off. He waved to Mrs Grange. As the boat slid into the current she cried out with a harsh, strident scream:

'Give my regards to Leicester Square.'

Skelton heaved a great sigh of relief as with their powerful strokes the paddlers took him farther and farther away from that dreadful house and from those two unhappy and yet repellent people. He was glad now that Mrs Grange had not told him the story that was on the tip of her tongue to tell. He did not want some tragic tale of sin or folly to connect him with them in a recollection that he could not escape. He wanted to forget them as one forgets a bad dream.

But Mrs Grange watched the two prahus till a bend of the river took them out of sight. She walked slowly up to the house and went into her bedroom. The light was dim because the blinds were drawn to keep out the heat, but she sat down at her dressing-table and stared at herself in the glass. Norman had had the dressing-table made for her soon after they were married. It had been made by a native carpenter, of course, and they had had the mirror sent from Singapore, but it was made to her own design, of the exact size and shape she wanted, with plenty of room for all her toilet things and her make-up. It was the dressing-table she had hankered after for donkey's years and had never had. She remembered still how pleased she was when first she had it. She threw her arms round her husband's neck and kissed him.

'Oh, Norman, you are good to me,' she said. 'I'm a lucky little girl to have caught a chap like you, aren't I?'

But then everything delighted her. She was amused by the river life and the life of the jungle, the teeming growth of the forest, the birds with their gay plumage and the brilliant butterflies. She set about giving the house a woman's touch; she put out all her own photographs and she got vases to put flowers in; she routed around and got a lot of knick-knacks to place here and there. 'They make a room look homey,' she said. She wasn't in love with Norman, but she liked him all right; and it was lovely to be married; it was lovely to have nothing to do from morning till night, except play the gramophone, or patience, and read novels. It was lovely to think one hadn't got to bother about one's future. Of course it was a bit lonely sometimes, but Norman said she'd get used to that, and he'd promised that in a year, or two at the outside, he'd take her to England for three months. It would be a lark to show him off to her friends. She felt that what had caught him was the glamour of the stage and she'd made herself out a good deal more successful than she really had been. She wanted him to realize that she'd made a sacrifice when she'd thrown up her career to become a planter's wife. She'd claimed acquaintance with a good many stars that in point of fact she'd never even spoken to. That would need a bit of handling when they went home, but she'd manage it; after all, poor Norman knew no more about the stage than a babe unborn, if she couldn't cod a simple fellow like that, after twelve years on the stage, well, she'd wasted her time, that's all she could say. Things went all right the first year. At one moment she thought she was going to have a baby. They were both disappointed when it turned out not to be true.

Then she began to grow bored. It seemed to her that she'd done the same damned thing day after day for ever and it frightened her to think that she'd have to go on doing the same damned thing day after day for ever more. Norman said he couldn't leave the plantation that year. They had a bit of a scene. It was then that he'd said something that scared her.

'I hate England,' he said. 'If I had my way I'd never set foot in the damned country again.'

Living this lonely life Mrs Grange got into the habit of talking out loud to herself. Shut up in her room she could be heard chattering away hour after hour; and now, dipping the puff in her powder and plastering her face with it, she addressed her reflection in the mirror exactly as though she were talking to another person.

'That ought to have warned me. I should have insisted on going by myself, and who knows, I might have got a job when I got to London. With all the experience I had and everything. Then I'd have written to him and said I wasn't coming back.' Her thoughts turned to Skelton. 'Pity I didn't tell him,' she continued. 'I had half a mind to. P'raps he was right, p'raps it would have eased me mind. I wonder what he'd have said.' She imitated his Oxford accent. 'I'm so terribly sorry, Mrs Grange. I wish I could help you.' She gave a chuckle which was almost a sob. 'I'd have liked to tell him about Jack. Oh, Jack.'

It was when they had been married for two years that they got a neighbour. The price of rubber at that time was so high that new estates were being put under cultivation and one of the big companies had bought a great tract of land on the opposite bank of the river. It was a rich company and everything was done on a lavish scale. The manager they had put in had a launch at his disposal so that it was no trouble for him to pop over and have a drink whenever he felt inclined. Jack Carr his name was. He was quite a different sort of chap from Norman; for one thing he was a gentleman, he'd been to a public school and a university; he was about thirty-five, tall, not beefy like Norman, but slight, he had the sort of figure that looked lovely in evening dress; and he had crisply curling hair and a laughing look in his eyes. Just her type. She took to him at once. It was a treat, having someone you could talk about London to, and the theatre. He was gay and easy. He made the sort of jokes you could understand. In a week or two she felt more at home with him than she did with her husband after two years. There had always been something about Norman that she hadn't quite been able to get to the bottom of. He was crazy about her, of course, and he'd told her a lot about himself, but she had a funny feeling that there was something he kept from her, not because he wanted to, but – well, you couldn't hardly explain it, because it was so alien, you might say, that he couldn't put it into words. Later, when she knew Jack better, she mentioned it to him, and Jack said it was because he was country-born; even though he hadn't a drop of native blood in his veins, something of the country had gone to the making of him so that he wasn't white really; he had an Eastern streak in him. However hard he tried he could never be quite English.

She chattered away aloud, in that empty house, for the two boys, the cook and the house boy, were in their own quarters, and the sound of her voice, ringing along the wooden floors, piercing the wooden walls, was like the uncanny, unhuman gibber of new wine fermenting in a vat. She spoke just as though Skelton were there, but so incoherently that if he had been, he would have had difficulty in following the story she told. It did not take her long to discover that Jack Carr wanted her. She was excited. She'd never been promiscuous, but in all those years she'd been on the stage naturally there'd been episodes. You couldn't hardly have put up with being on tour month after month if you didn't have a bit of fun sometimes. Of course now she wasn't going to give in too easily, she didn't want to make herself cheap, but what with the life she led, she'd be a fool if she missed the chance; and as far as Norman was concerned, well, what the eye didn't see the heart didn't grieve over. They understood one another all right, Jack and her; they knew it was bound to happen sooner or later, it was only a matter of waiting for the opportunity; and the opportunity came. But then something happened that they hadn't bargained for: they fell madly in love with one another. If Mrs Grange really had been telling the story to Skelton it might have seemed as unlikely to him as it did to them. They were two very ordinary people, he a jolly, good-natured, commonplace planter, and she a small-part actress far from clever, not even very young, with nothing to recommend her but a neat figure and a prettyish face. What started as a casual affair turned without warning into a devastating passion, and neither of them was of a texture to sustain its exorbitant compulsion. They longed to be with one another; they were restless and miserable apart. She'd been finding Norman a bore for some time, but she'd put up with him because he was her husband; now he irritated her to frenzy because he stood between her and Jack. There was no question of their going off together, Jack Carr had nothing but his salary, and he couldn't throw up a job he'd been only too glad to get. It was difficult for them to meet. They had to run awful risks. Perhaps the chances they had to take, the obstacles they had to surmount, were fuel to their love; a year passed and it was as overwhelming as at the beginning; it was a year of agony and bliss, of fear and thrill. Then she discovered that she was pregnant. She had no doubt that Jack Carr was the father and she was wildly happy. It was true life was difficult, so difficult sometimes that she felt she just couldn't cope with it, but there'd be a baby, his baby, and that would make everything easy. She was going to Kuching for her confinement. It happened about then that Jack Carr had to go to Singapore on business and was to be away for several weeks; but he promised to get back before she left and he said he'd send word by a native the moment he arrived. When at last the message came she felt sick with the anguish of her joy. She had never wanted him so badly.

'I hear that Jack is back,' she told her husband at dinner. 'I shall go over tomorrow morning and get the things he promised to bring me.'

'I wouldn't do that. He's pretty sure to drop in towards sundown and he'll bring them himself.'

'I can't wait. I'm crazy to have them.'

'All right. Have it your own way.'

She couldn't help talking about him. For some time now they had seemed to have little to say to one another, Norman and she, but that night, in high spirits, she chattered away as she had done during the first months of their marriage. She always rose early, at six, and next morning she went down to the river and had a bathe. There was a little dent in the bank just there, with a tiny sandy beach, and it was delicious to splash about in the cool, transparent water. A kingfisher stood on the branch of a tree overhanging the pool and its reflection was brilliantly blue in the water. Lovely. She had a cup of tea and then stepped into a dug-out. A boy paddled her across the river. It took a good half-hour. As they got near she scanned the bank; Jack knew she would come at the earliest opportunity; he must be on the lookout. Ah, there he was. The delicious pain in her heart was almost unbearable. He came down to the landing-stage and helped her to get out of the boat. They walked hand in hand up the pathway and when they were out of sight of the boy who had paddled her over and of prying eyes from the house, they stopped. He put his arms round her and she yielded with ecstasy to his embrace. She clung to him. His mouth sought hers. In that kiss was all the agony of their separation and all the bliss of their reunion. The miracle of love transfused them so that they were unconscious of time and place. They were not human any more, but two spirits united by a divine fire. No thought passed through their minds. No words issued from their lips. Suddenly there was a brutal shock, like a blow, and immediately, almost simultaneously, a deafening noise. Horrified, not understanding, she clung to Jack more tightly and his grip on her was spasmodic, so that she gasped; then she felt that he was bearing her over.

'Jack.'

She tried to hold him up. His weight was too great for her and as he fell to the ground she fell with him. Then she gave a great cry, for she felt a gush of heat, and his blood sputtered over her. She began to scream. A rough hand seized her and dragged her to her feet. It was Norman. She was distraught. She could not understand.

'Norman, what have you done?'

'I've killed him.'

She stared at him stupidly. She pushed him aside.

'Jack. Jack.'

'Shut up. I'll go and get help. It was an accident.'

He walked quickly up the pathway. She fell to her knees and took Jack's head in her arms.

'Darling,' she moaned. 'Oh, my darling.'

Norman came back with some coolies and they carried him up to the house. That night she had a miscarriage and was so ill that for days it looked as if she would die. When she recovered she had the nervous tic that she'd had ever since. She expected that Norman would send her away; but he didn't, he had to keep her to allay suspicion. There was some talk among the natives, and after a while the District Officer came up and asked a lot of questions; but the natives were frightened of Norman, and the D.O. could get nothing out of them. The Dyak boy who paddled her over had vanished. Norman said something had gone wrong with his gun and Jack was looking at it to see what was the matter and it went off. They bury people quickly in that country and by the time they might have dug him up there wouldn't have been much left to show that Norman's story wasn't true. The D.O. hadn't been satisfied.

'It all looks damned fishy to me,' he said, 'but in the absence of any evidence, I suppose I must accept your version.'

She would have given anything to get away, but with that nervous affliction she had no ghost of a chance any longer of earning a living. She had to stay – or starve; and Norman had to keep her – or hang. Nothing had happened since then and now nothing ever would happen. The endless years one after another dragged out their weary length.

Mrs Grange on a sudden stopped talking. Her sharp ears had caught the sound of a footstep on the path and she knew that Norman was back from his round. Her head twitching furiously, her hand agitated by that sinister, uncontrollable gesture, she looked in the untidy mess of her dressing-table for her precious lipstick. She smeared it on her lips, and then, she didn't know why, on a freakish impulse daubed it all over her nose till she looked like a red-nose comedian in a music-hall. She looked at herself in the glass and burst out laughing.

'To hell with life!' she shouted.

THE ALIEN CORN

I HAD known the Blands a long time before I discovered that they had any connexion with Ferdy Rabenstein. Ferdy must have been nearly fifty when I first knew him and at the time of which I write he was well over seventy. He had altered little. His hair, coarse but abundant and curly, was white, but he had kept his figure and held himself as gallantly as ever. It was not hard to believe that in youth he had been as beautiful as people said. He had still his fine Semitic profile and the lustrous black eyes that had caused havoc in so many a Gentile breast. He was very tall, lean, with an oval face and a clear skin. He wore his clothes very well and in evening dress, even now, he was one of the handsomest men I had ever seen. He wore then large black pearls in his shirt-front and platinum and sapphire rings on his fingers. Perhaps he was rather flashy, but you felt it was so much in character that it would have ill become him to be anything else.

'After all, I am an Oriental,' he said. 'I can carry a certain barbaric magnificence.'

I have often thought that Ferdy Rabenstein would make an admirable subject for a biography. He was not a great man, but within the limits he set himself he made of his life a work of art. It was a masterpiece in little, like a Persian miniature, and derived its interest from its perfection. Unfortunately the materials are scanty. They would consist of letters that may very well have been destroyed and the recollections of people who are old now and will soon be dead. His memory is extraordinary, but he would never write his memoirs, for he looks upon his past as a source of purely private entertainment; and he is a man of the most perfect discretion. Nor do I know anyone who could do justice to the subject but Max Beerbohm. There is no one else in this hard world of today who can look upon the trivial with such tender sympathy and wring such a delicate pathos from futility. I wonder that Max, who must have known Ferdy much better than I, and long before, was never tempted to exercise his exquisite fancy on such a theme. He was born for Max to write about. And who should have illustrated the elegant book that I see in my mind's eye but Aubrey Beardsley? Thus would have been erected a monument of triple brass and the ephemera imprisoned to succeeding ages in the amber's translucency.

Ferdy's conquests were social and his venue was the great world. He was born in South Africa and did not come to England till he was twenty. For some time he was on the Stock Exchange, but on the death of his father he inherited a considerable fortune, and retiring from business devoted himself to the life of a man about town. At that period English society was still a closed body and it was not easy for a Jew to force its barriers, but to Ferdy they fell like the walls of Jericho. He was handsome, he was rich, he was a sportsman and he was good company. He had a house in Curzon Street, furnished with the most beautiful French furniture, and a French chef, and a brougham. It would be interesting to know the first steps in his wonderful career: they are lost in the dark abysm of time. When I first met him he had been long established as one of the smartest men in London: this was at a very grand house in Norfolk to which I had been asked as a promising young novelist by the hostess who took an interest in letters, but the company was very distinguished and I was overawed. We were sixteen, and I felt shy and alone among these Cabinet Ministers, great ladies, and peers of the realm who talked of people and things of which I knew nothing. They were civil to me, but indifferent, and I was conscious that I was somewhat of a burden to my hostess. Ferdy saved me. He sat with me, walked with me, and talked with me. He discovered that I was a writer and we discussed the drama and the novel; he learnt that I had lived much on the Continent and he talked to me pleasantly of France, Germany, and Spain. He seemed really to seek my society. He gave me the flattering impression that he and I stood apart from the other members of the company and by our conversation upon affairs of the spirit made that of the rest of them, the political situation, the scandal of somebody's divorce, and the growing disinclination of pheasants to be killed, seem a little ridiculous. But if Ferdy had at the bottom of his heart a feeling of ever so faint a contempt for the hearty British gentry that surrounded us I am sure that it was only to me that he allowed an inkling of it to appear, and looking back I cannot but wonder whether it was not after all a suave and very delicate compliment that he paid me. I think of course that he liked to exercise his charm and I dare say the obvious pleasure his conversation gave me gratified him, but he could have had no motive for taking so much trouble over an obscure novelist other than his real interest in art and letters. I felt that he and I at bottom were equally alien in that company, I because I was a writer and he because he was a Jew, but I envied the ease with which he bore himself. He was completely at home. Everyone called him Ferdy. He seemed to be always in good spirits. He was never at a loss for a quip, a jest, or a repartee. They liked him in that house because he made them laugh, but never made them uncomfortable by talking over their heads. He brought a faint savour of Oriental romance into their lives, but so cleverly that they only felt more English. You could never be dull when he was by and with him present you were safe from the fear of the devastating silences that sometimes overwhelm a British company. A pause looked inevitable and Ferdy Rabenstein had broken into a topic that interested everyone. An invaluable asset to any party. He had an inexhaustible fund of Jewish stories. He was a very good mimic and he assumed the Yiddish accent and reproduced the Jewish gestures to perfection; his head sank into his body, his face grew cunning, his voice oily, and he was a rabbi or an old clothes merchant or a smart commercial traveller or a fat procuress in Frankfort. It was as good as a play. Because he was himself a Jew and insisted on it you laughed without reserve, but for my own part not without an under-current of discomfort. I was not quite sure of a sense of humour that made such cruel fun of his own race. I discovered afterwards that Jewish stories were his speciality and I seldom met him anywhere without hearing him tell sooner or later the last he had heard.

But the best story he told me on this occasion was not a Jewish one. It struck me so that I have never forgotten it, but for one reason or another I have never had occasion to tell it again. I give it here because it is a curious little incident concerning persons whose names at least will live in the social history of the Victorian Era and I think it would be a pity if it were lost. He told me then that once when quite a young man he was staying in the country in a house where Mrs Langtry, at that time at the height of her beauty and astounding reputation, was also a guest. It happened to be within driving distance of that in which lived the Duchess of Somerset, who had been Queen of Beauty at the Eglinton Tournament, and knowing her slightly, it occurred to him that it would be interesting to bring the two women together. He suggested it to Mrs Langtry, who was willing, and forthwith wrote to the Duchess asking if he might bring the celebrated beauty to call on her. It was fitting, he said, that the loveliest woman of this generation (this was in the eighties) should pay her respects to the loveliest woman of the last. 'Bring her by all means,' answered the Duchess, 'but I warn you that it will be a shock to her.' They drove over in a carriage and pair, Mrs Langtry in a close-fitting blue bonnet with long satin strings, which showed the fine shape of her head and made her blue eyes even bluer, and were received by a little ugly old hag who looked with irony out of her beady eyes at the radiant beauty who had come to see her. They had tea, they talked, and they drove home again. Mrs Langtry was very silent and when Ferdy looked at her he saw that she was quietly weeping. When they got back to the house she went to her room and would not come down to dinner that night. For the first time she had realized that beauty dies.

Ferdy asked me for my address and a few days after I got back to London invited me to dinner. There were only six of us, an American woman married to an English peer, a Swedish painter, an actress, and a well-known critic. We ate very good food and drank excellent wine. The conversation was easy and intelligent. After dinner Ferdy was persuaded to play the piano. He only played Viennese waltzes, I discovered later that they were his speciality, and the light, tuneful, and sensual music seemed to accord well with his discreet flamboyance. He played without affectation, with a lilt, and he had a graceful touch. This was the first of a good many dinners I had with him, he would ask me two or three times a year, and as time passed I met him more and more frequently at other people's houses. I rose in the world and perhaps he came down a little. Of late years I had sometimes found him at parties where other Jews were and I fancied that I read in his shining liquid eyes, resting for a moment on these members of his race, a certain good-natured amusement at the thought of what the world was coming to. There were people who said he was a snob, but I do not think he was; it just happened that in his early days he had never met any but the great. He had a real passion for art and in his commerce with those that produced it was at his best. With them he had never that faint air of persiflage which when he was with very grand persons made you suspect that he was never quite the dupe of their grandeur. His taste was perfect and many of his friends were glad to avail themselves of his knowledge. He was one of the first to value old furniture and he rescued many a priceless piece from the attics of ancestral mansions and gave it an honourable place in the drawing-room. It amused him to saunter round the auction rooms and he was always willing to give his advice to great ladies who desired at once to acquire a beautiful thing and make a profitable investment. He was rich and good-natured. He liked to patronize the arts and would take a great deal of trouble to get commissions for some young painter whose talent he admired or an engagement to play at a rich man's house for a violinist who could in no other way get a hearing. But he never let his rich man down. His taste was too good to deceive and civil though he might be to the mediocre he would not lift a finger to help them. His own musical parties, very small and carefully chosen, were a treat.

He never married.

'I am a man of the world,' he said, 'and I flatter myself that I have no prejudices, *tous les goûts sont dans la nature*, but I do not think I could bring myself to marry a Gentile. There's no harm in going to the opera in a dinner jacket, but it just would never occur to me to do so.'

'Then why didn't you marry a Jewess?'

(I did not hear this conversation, but the lively and audacious creature who thus tackled him told me of it.)

'Oh, my dear, our women are so prolific. I could not bear the thought of peopling the world with a little Ikey and a little Jacob and a little Rebecca and a little Leah and a little Rachel.'

But he had had affairs of note and the glamour of past romance still clung to him. He was in his youth of an amorous complexion. I have met old ladies who told me that he was irresistible, and when in reminiscent mood they talked to me of this woman and that who had completely lost her head over him, I divined that, such was his beauty, they could not find it in their hearts to blame them. It was interesting to hear of great ladies that I had read of in the memoirs of the day or had met as respectable dowagers garrulous over their grandsons at Eton or making a mess of a hand at bridge and bethink myself that they had been consumed with sinful passion for the handsome Jew. Ferdy's most notorious amour was with the Duchess of Hereford, the loveliest, the most gallant and dashing of the beauties of the end of Queen Victoria's reign. It lasted for twenty years. He had doubtless flirtations meanwhile, but their relations were stable and recognized. It was proof of his marvellous tact that when at last they ended he exchanged an ageing mistress for a loyal friend. I remember meeting the pair not so very long ago at luncheon. She was an old woman, tall and of a commanding presence, but with a mask of paint on a ravaged face. We were lunching at the Carlton and Ferdy, our host, came a few minutes late. He offered us a cocktail and the Duchess told him we had already had one.

'Ah, I wondered why your eyes were so doubly bright,' he said. The old raddled woman flushed with pleasure.

My youth passed, I grew middle-aged, I wondered how soon I must begin to describe myself as elderly; I wrote books and plays, I travelled, I underwent experiences, I fell in love and out of it; and still I kept meeting Ferdy at parties. War broke out and was waged, millions of men were killed, and the face of the world was changed. Ferdy did not like the war. He was too old to take part in it, and his German name was awkward, but he was discreet and took care not to expose himself to humiliation. His old friends were faithful to him and he lived in a dignified but not too strict seclusion. But then peace came and with courage he set himself to making the best of changed conditions. Society was mixed now, parties were rowdy, but Ferdy fitted himself to the new life. He still told his funny Jewish stories, he still played charmingly the waltzes of Strauss, he still went round auction rooms and told the new rich what they ought to buy. I went to live abroad, but whenever I was in London I saw Ferdy and now there was something a little uncanny in him. He did not give in. He had never known a day's illness. He seemed never to grow tired. He still dressed beautifully. He was interested in everybody. His mind was alert and people asked him to dinner, not for old times' sake, but because he was worth his salt. He still gave charming little concerts at his house in Curzon Street.

It was when he invited me to one of these that I made the discovery that started the recollections of him I have here set down. We were dining at a house in Hill Street, a large party, and the women having gone upstairs Ferdy and I found ourselves side by side. He told me that Lea Makart was coming to play for him on the following Friday evening and he would be glad if I would come.

'I'm awfully sorry,' I said, 'but I'm going down to the Blands.'

'What Blands?'

'They live in Sussex at a place called Tilby.'

'I didn't know you knew them.'

He looked at me rather strangely. He smiled. I didn't know what amused him.

'Oh, yes, I've known them for years. It's a very nice house to stay at.'

'Adolf is my nephew.'

'Sir Adolphus?'

'It suggests one of the bucks of the Regency, doesn't it? But I will not conceal from you that he was named Adolf.'

'Everyone I know calls him Freddy.'

'I know, and I understand that Miriam, his wife, only answers to the name of Muriel.'

'How does he happen to be your nephew?'

'Because Hannah Rabenstein, my sister, married Alfons Bleikogel, who ended life as Sir Alfred Bland, first Baronet, and Adolf, their only son, in due course became Sir Adolphus Bland, second Baronet.'

'Then Freddy Bland's mother, the Lady Bland who lives in Portland Place, is your sister?'

'Yes, my sister Hannah. She was the eldest of the family. She's eighty, but in full possession of her faculties and a remarkable woman.'

'I've never met her.'

'I think your friends the Blands would just as soon you didn't. She has never lost her German accent.'

'Do you never see them?' I asked.

'I haven't spoken to them for twenty years. I am such a Jew and they are so English.' He smiled. 'I could never remember that their names were Freddy and Muriel. I used to come out with an Adolf or a Miriam at awkward moments. And they didn't like my stories. It was better that we should not meet. When the war broke out and I would not change my name it was the last straw. It was too late, I could never have accustomed my friends to think of me as anything but Ferdy Rabenstein; I was quite content. I was not ambitious to be a Smith, a Brown, or a Robinson.'

Though he spoke facetiously, there was in his tone the faintest possible derision and I felt, hardly felt even, the sensation was so shadowy, that, as it had often vaguely seemed to me before, there was in the depth of his impenetrable heart a cynical contempt for the Gentiles he had conquered.

'Then you don't know the two boys?' I said.

'No.'

'The eldest is called George, you know. I don't think he's so clever as Harry, the other one, but he's an engaging youth. I think you'd like him.'

'Where is he now?'

'Well, he's just been sent down from Oxford. I suppose he's at home. Harry's still at Eton.'

'Why don't you bring George to lunch with me?'

'I'll ask him. I should think he'd love to come.'

'It has reached my ears that he's been a little troublesome.'

'Oh, I don't know. He wouldn't go into the army, which is what they wanted. They rather fancied the Guards. And so he went to Oxford instead. He didn't work and he spent a great deal of money and he painted the town red. It was all quite normal.'

'What was he sent down for?'

'I don't know. Nothing of any consequence.'

At that moment our host rose and we went upstairs. When Ferdy bade me good night he asked me not to forget about his great-nephew.

'Ring me up,' he said. 'Wednesday would suit me. Or Friday.'

Next day I went down to Tilby. It was an Elizabethan mansion standing in a spacious park, in which roamed fallow deer, and from its windows you had wide views of rolling downs. It seemed to me that as far as the eye could reach the land belonged to the Blands. His tenants must have found Sir Adolphus a wonderful landlord, for I never saw farms kept in such order, the barns and cow-sheds were spick and span and the pigsties were a picture; the public-houses looked like Old English water-colours and the cottages he had built on the estate combined admirably picturesqueness and convenience. It must have cost him a pot of money to run the place on these lines. Fortunately he had it. The park with its grand old trees (and its nine-hole golf course) was tended like a garden, and the wide-stretching gardens were the pride of the neighbourhood. The magnificent house, with its steep roofs and mullioned windows, had been restored by the most celebrated architect in England and furnished by Lady Bland, with taste and knowledge, in a style that perfectly fitted it.

'Of course it's very simple,' she said. 'Just an English house in the country.'

The dining-room was adorned with old English sporting pictures and the Chippendale chairs were of incredible value. In the drawing-room were portraits by Reynolds and Gainsborough and landscapes by Old Crome and Richard Wilson. Even in my bedroom with its four-post bed were water-colours by Birket Foster. It was very beautiful and a treat to stay there, but though it would have distressed Muriel Bland beyond anything to know it, it entirely missed oddly enough the effect she had sought. It did not give you for a moment the impression of an English house. You had the feeling that every object had been bought with a careful eye to the general scheme. You missed the dull Academy portraits that hung in the dining-room beside a Carlo Dolci that an ancestor had brought back from the grand tour, and the water-colours painted by a great aunt that cluttered up the drawing-room so engagingly. There was no ugly Victorian sofa that had always been there and that it never occurred to anybody to take away and no needlework chairs that an unmarried daughter had so painstakingly worked at about the time of the Great Exhibition. There was beauty but no sentiment.

And yet how comfortable it was and how well looked after you were! And what a cordial greeting the Blands gave you! They seemed really to like people. They were generous and kindly. They were never happier than when they were entertaining the county, and though they had not owned the property for more than twenty years they had established themselves firmly in the favour of their neighbours. Except perhaps in their splendour and the competent way in which the estate was run there was nothing to suggest that they had not been settled there for centuries.

Freddy had been at Eton and Oxford. He was now in the early fifties. He was quiet in manner, courtly, very clever, I imagine, but a trifle reserved. He had great elegance, but it was not an English elegance; he had grey hair and a short pointed grey beard, fine dark eyes and an aquiline nose. He was just above middle height; I don't think you would have taken him for a Jew, but rather for a foreign diplomat of some distinction. He was a man of character, but gave you, strangely enough, notwithstanding the success he had had in life, an impression of faint melancholy. His successes had been financial and political; in the world of sport, for all his perseverance, he had never shone. For many years he had followed hounds, but he was a bad rider and I think it must have been a relief to him when he could persuade himself that middle age and pressure of business forced him to give up hunting. He had excellent shooting and gave grand parties for it, but he was a poor shot; and despite the course in his park he never succeeded in being more than an indifferent golfer. He knew only too well how much these things meant in England and his incapacity was a bitter disappointment to him. However George would make up for it.

George was scratch at golf, and though tennis was not his game he played much better than the average; the Blands had had him taught to shoot as soon as he was old enough to hold a gun and he was a fine shot; they had put him on a pony when he was two, and Freddy, watching him mount his horse, knew that out hunting when the boy came to a fence he felt exhilaration and not that sickening feeling in the pit of his stomach which, though he had chased the fox with such grim determination, had always made the sport a torture to him. George was so tall and slim, his curly hair, of a palish brown, was so fine, his eyes were so blue, he was the perfect type of the young Englishman. He had the engaging candour of the breed. His nose was straight, though perhaps a trifle fleshy, and his lips were perhaps a little full and sensual, but he had beautiful teeth, and his smooth skin was like ivory. George was the apple of his father's eye. He did not like Harry, his second son, so well. He was rather stocky, broad-shouldered and strong for his age, but his black eyes, shining with cleverness, his coarse dark hair, and his big nose revealed his race. Freddy was severe with him, and often impatient, but with George he was all indulgence. Harry would go into the business, he had brains and push, but George was the heir. George would be an English gentleman.

George had offered to motor me down in the roadster his father had given him as a birthday present. He drove very fast and we arrived before the rest of the guests. The Blands were sitting on the lawn and tea was laid out under a magnificent cedar.

'By the way,' I said presently, 'I saw Ferdy Rabenstein the other day and he wants me to bring George to lunch with him.'

I had not mentioned the invitation to George on the way because I thought that if there had been a family coldness I had better address his parents as well.

'Who in God's name is Ferdy Rabenstein?' said George.

How brief is human glory! A generation back such a question would have seemed grotesque.

'He's by way of being your great-uncle,' I replied.

A glance had passed from father to mother when I first spoke.

'He's a horrid old man,' said Muriel.

'I don't think it's in the least necessary for George to resume relationships that were definitely severed before he was born,' said Freddy with decision.

'Anyhow I've delivered the message,' said I, feeling somewhat snubbed.

'I don't want to see the old blighter,' said George.

The conversation was broken off by the arrival of other guests and in a little while George went off to play golf with one of his Oxford friends.

It was not till next day that the matter was referred to again. I had played an unsatisfactory round with Freddy Bland in the morning and several sets of what is known as country-house tennis in the afternoon and was sitting alone with Muriel on the terrace. In England we have so much bad weather that it is only fair that a beautiful day should be more beautiful than anywhere in the world and this June evening was perfect. The blue sky was cloudless and the air was balmy; before us stretched green rolling downs, and woods, and in the distance you saw the red roofs of a little village church. It was a day when to be alive was sufficient happiness. Detached lines of poetry hovered vaguely in my memory. Muriel and I had been chatting desultorily.

'I hope you didn't think it rather horrid of us to refuse to let George lunch with Ferdy,' she said suddenly. 'He's such a fearful snob, isn't he?'

'D'you think so? He's always been very nice to me.'

'We haven't been on speaking terms for twenty years. Freddy never forgave him for his behaviour during the war. So unpatriotic, I thought, and one really must draw the line somewhere. You know, he absolutely refused to drop his horrible German name. With Freddy in Parliament and running munitions and all that sort of thing it was quite impossible. I don't know why he should want to see George. He can't mean anything to him.'

'He's an old man. George and Harry are his great-nephews. He must leave his money to someone.'

'We'd rather not have his money,' said Muriel coldly.

Of course I didn't care a row of pins whether George went to lunch with Ferdy Rabenstein, and I was quite willing to let the matter drop, but evidently the Blands had talked it over and Muriel felt that some explanation was due to me.

'Of course you know that Freddy has Jewish blood in him,' she said.

She looked at me sharply. Muriel was rather a big blonde woman and she spent a great deal of time trying to keep down the corpulence to which she was predisposed. She had been very pretty when young, and even now was a comely person; but her round blue eyes, slightly prominent, her fleshy nose, the shape of her face and the back of her neck, her exuberant manner, betrayed her race. No Englishwoman, however fair-haired, ever looked like that. And yet her observation was designed to make me take it for granted that she was a Gentile. I answered discreetly:

'So many people have nowadays.'

'I know. But there's no reason to dwell on it, is there? After all, we're absolutely English; no one could be more English than George, in appearance and manner and everything; I mean, he's such a fine sportsman and all that sort of thing, I can't see any object in his knowing Jews just because they happen to be distant connexions of his.'

'It's very difficult in England now not to know Jews, isn't it?'

'Oh, I know, in London one does meet a good many, and I think some of them are very nice. They're so artistic. I don't go so far as to say that Freddy and I deliberately avoid them, of course I wouldn't do that, but it just happens that we don't really know any of them very well. And down here, there simply aren't any to know.'

I could not but admire the convincing manner in which she spoke. It would not have surprised me to be told that she really believed every word she said.

'You say that Ferdy might leave George his money. Well, I don't believe it's so very much anyway; it was quite a comfortable fortune before the war, but that's nothing nowadays. Besides we're hoping that George will go in for politics when he's a little older, and I don't think it would do him any good in the constituency to inherit money from a Mr Rabenstein.'

'Is George interested in politics?' I asked, to change the conversation.

'Oh, I do hope so. After all, there's the family constituency waiting for him. It's a safe Conservative seat and one can't expect Freddy to go on with the grind of the House of Commons indefinitely.'

Muriel was grand. She talked already of the constituency as though twenty generations of Blands had sat for it. Her remark, however, was my first intimation that Freddy's ambition was not satisfied.

'I suppose Freddy would go to the House of Lords when George was old enough to stand.'

'We've done a good deal for the party,' said Muriel.

Muriel was a Catholic and she often told you that she had been educated in a convent – 'Such sweet women, those nuns, I always said that if I had a daughter I should have sent her to a convent too' – but she liked her servants to be Church of England, and on Sunday evenings we had what was called supper because the fish was cold and there was ice-cream, so that they could go to church, and we were waited on by two footmen instead of four. It was still light when we finished and Freddy and I, smoking our cigars, walked up and down the terrace in the gloaming. I suppose Muriel had told him of her conversation with me, and it may be that his refusal to let George see his great-uncle still troubled him, but being subtler than she he attacked the question more indirectly. He told me that he had been very much worried about George. It had been a great disappointment that he had refused to go into the army.

'I should have thought he'd have loved the life,' he said.

'And he would certainly have looked marvellous in his Guards uniform.'

'He would, wouldn't he?' returned Freddy, ingenuously. 'I wonder he could resist that.'

He had been completely idle at Oxford; although his father had given him a very large allowance, he had got monstrously into debt; and now he had been sent down. But though he spoke so tartly I could see that he was not a little proud of his scapegrace son, he loved him with oh, such an unEnglish love, and in his heart it flattered him that George had cut such a dash.

'Why should you worry?' I said. 'You don't really care if George has a degree or not.'

Freddy chuckled.

'No, I don't suppose I do really. I always think the only important thing about Oxford is that people know you were there, and I dare say that George isn't any wilder than the other young men in his set. It's the future I'm thinking of. He's so damned idle. He doesn't seem to want to do anything but have a good time.'

'He's young, you know.'

'He's not interested in politics, and though he's so good at games he's not even very keen on sport. He seems to spend most of his time strumming the piano.'

'That's a harmless amusement.'

'Oh, yes, I don't mind that, but he can't go on loafing indefinitely. You see, all this will be his one day.' Freddy gave a sweeping gesture that seemed to embrace the whole county, but I knew that he did not own it all yet. 'I'm very anxious that he should be fit to assume his responsibilities. His mother is very ambitious for him, but I only want him to be an English gentleman.'

Freddy gave me a sidelong glance as though he wanted to say something but hesitated in case I thought it ridiculous; but there is one advantage in being a writer that, since people look upon you as of no account, they will often say things to you that they would not to their equals. He thought he would risk it.

'You know, I've got an idea that nowhere in the world now is the Greek ideal of life so perfectly cultivated as by the English country gentleman living on his estates. I think his life has the beauty of a work of art.'

I could not but smile when I reflected that it was impossible for the English country gentleman in these days to do anything of the sort without a packet of money safely invested in American Bonds, but I smiled with sympathy. I thought it rather touching that this Jewish financier should cherish so romantic a dream.

'I want him to be a good landlord. I want him to take his part in the affairs of the country. I want him to be a thorough sportsman.'

'Poor mutt,' I thought, but said: 'Well, what are your plans for George now?'

'I think he has a fancy for the diplomatic service. He's suggested going to Germany to learn the language.'

'A very good idea, I should have thought.'

'For some reason he's got it into his head that he wants to go to Munich.'

'A nice place.'

Next day I went back to London and shortly after my arrival rang up Ferdy.

'I'm sorry, but George isn't able to come to lunch on Wednesday.'

'What about Friday?'

'Friday's no good either.' I thought it useless to beat about the bush. 'The fact is, his people aren't keen on his lunching with you.'

There was a moment's silence. Then:

'I see. Well, will you come on Wednesday anyway?'

'Yes, I'd like to,' I answered.

So on Wednesday at half past one I strolled round to Curzon Street. Ferdy received me with the somewhat elaborate graciousness that he cultivated. He made no reference to the Blands. We sat in the drawing-room and I could not help reflecting what an eye for beautiful objects that family had. The room was more crowded than the fashion of today approves, and the gold snuffboxes in vitrines, the French china, appealed to a taste that was not mine; but they were no doubt choice pieces; and the Louis XV suite, with its beautiful *petit point*, must have been worth an enormous lot of money. The pictures on the walls by Lancret, Pater, and Watteau did not greatly interest me, but I recognized their intrinsic excellence. It was a proper setting for this aged man of the world. It fitted his period. Suddenly the door opened and George was announced. Ferdy saw my surprise and gave me a little smile of triumph.

'I'm very glad you were able to come after all,' he said as he shook George's hand.

I saw him in a glance take in his great-nephew whom he saw today for the first time. George was very well dressed. He wore a short black coat, striped trousers, and the grey double-breasted waistcoat which at that time was the mode. You could only wear it with elegance if you were tall and thin and your belly was slightly concave. I felt sure that Ferdy knew exactly who George's tailor was and what haberdasher he went to and approved of them. George, so smart and trim, wearing his clothes so beautifully, certainly looked very handsome. We went down to luncheon. Ferdy had the social graces at his fingers' ends and he put the boy at his ease, but I saw that he was carefully appraising him; then, I do not know why, he began to tell some of his Jewish stories. He told them with gusto and with his wonderful mimicry. I saw George flush, and though he laughed at them, I could see that it was with embarrassment. I wondered what on earth had induced Ferdy to be so tactless. But he was watching George and he told story after story. It looked as though he would never stop. I wondered if for some reason I could not grasp he was taking a malicious pleasure in the boy's obvious discomfiture. At last we went upstairs and to make things easier I asked Ferdy to play the piano. He played us three or four little waltzes. He had lost none of his exquisite lightness nor his sense of their lilting rhythm. Then he turned to George.

'Do you play?' he asked him.

'A little.'

'Won't you play something?'

'I'm afraid I only play classical music. I don't think it would interest you.'

Ferdy smiled slightly, but did not insist. I said it was time for me to go and George accompanied me.

'What a filthy old Jew,' he said as soon as we were in the street. 'I hated those stories of his.'

'They're his great stunt. He always tells them.'

'Would you if you were a Jew?'

I shrugged my shoulders.

'How is it you came to lunch after all?' I asked George.

He chuckled. He was a light-hearted creature, with a sense of humour, and he shook off the slight irritation his great-uncle had caused him.

'He went to see Granny. You don't know Granny, do you?'

'No.'

'She treats daddy like a kid in Etons. Granny said I was to go to lunch with great-uncle Ferdy and what Granny says goes.'

'I see.'

A week or two later George went to Munich to learn German. I happened then to go on a journey and it was not till the following spring that I was again in London. Soon after my arrival I found myself sitting next to Muriel Bland at dinner. I asked after George.

'He's still in Germany,' she said.

'I see in the papers that you're going to have a great beano at Tilby for his coming of age.'

'We're going to entertain the tenants and they're making George a presentation.'

She was less exuberant than usual, but I did not pay much attention to the fact. She led a strenuous life and it might be that she was tired. I knew she liked to talk of her son, so I continued.

'I suppose George has been having a grand time in Germany,' I said.

She did not answer for a moment and I gave her a glance. I was surprised to see that her eyes were filled with tears.

'I'm afraid George has gone mad,' she said.

'What *do* you mean?'

'We've been so frightfully worried. Freddy's so angry, he won't even discuss it. I don't know what we're going to do.'

Of course it immediately occurred to me that George, who, I supposed, like most young Englishmen sent to learn the language, had been put with a German family, had fallen in love with the daughter of the house and wanted to marry her. I had a pretty strong suspicion that the Blands were intent on his making a very grand marriage.

'Why, what's happened?' I asked.

'He wants to become a pianist.'

'A what?'

'A professional pianist.'

'What on earth put that idea in his head?'

'Heaven knows. We didn't know anything about it. We thought he was working for his exam. I went out to see him. I thought I'd like to know that he was getting on all right. Oh, my dear. He looks like nothing on earth. And he used to be so smart; I could have cried. He told me he wasn't going in for the exam. and had never had any intention of doing so; he'd only suggested the diplomatic service so that we'd let him go to Germany and he'd be able to study music.'

'But has he any talent?'

'Oh, that's neither here nor there. Even if he had the genius of Paderewski we couldn't have George traipsing around the country playing at concerts. No one can deny that I'm very artistic, and so is Freddy, we love music and we've always known a lot of artists, but George will have a very great position, it's out of the question. We've set our hearts on his going into Parliament. He'll be very rich one day. There's nothing he can't aspire to.'

'Did you point all that out to him?'

'Of course I did. He laughed at me. I told him he'd break his father's heart. He said his father could always fall back on Harry. Of course I'm devoted to Harry, and he's as clever as a monkey, but it was always understood that he was to go into the business; even though I am his mother I can see that he hasn't got the advantages that George has. Do you know what he said to me? He said that if his father would settle five pounds a week on him he would resign everything in Harry's favour and Harry could be his father's heir and succeed to the baronetcy and everything. It's too ridiculous. He said that if the Crown Prince of Roumania could abdicate a throne he didn't see why he couldn't abdicate a baronetcy. But you can't do that. Nothing can prevent him from being third baronet and if Freddy should be granted a peerage from succeeding to it at Freddy's death. Do you know, he even wants to drop the name of Bland and take some horrible German name.'

I could not help asking what.

'Bleikogel or something like that,' she answered.

That was a name I recognized. I remembered Ferdy telling me that Hannah Rabenstein had married Alfons Bleikogel who became eventually Sir Alfred Bland, first Baronet. It was all very strange. I wondered what had happened to the charming and so typically English boy whom I had seen only a few months before.

'Of course when I came home and told Freddy he was furious. I've never seen him so angry. He foamed at the mouth. He wired to George to come back immediately and George wired back to say he couldn't on account of his work.'

'Is he working?'

'From morning till night. That's the maddening part of it. He never did a stroke of work in his life. Freddy used to say he was born idle.'

'H'm.'

'Then Freddy wired to say that if he didn't come he'd stop his allowance and George wired back: "Stop it." That put the lid on. You don't know what Freddy can be when his back is up.'

I knew that Freddy had inherited a large fortune, but I knew also that he had immensely increased it, and I could well imagine that behind the courteous and amiable Squire of Tilby there was a ruthless man of affairs. He had been used to having his own way and I could believe that when crossed he would be hard and cruel.

'We'd been making George a very handsome allowance, but you know how frightfully extravagant he was. We didn't think he'd be able to hold out long and in point of fact within a month he wrote to Ferdy and asked him to lend him a hundred pounds. Ferdy went to my mother-in-law, she's his sister, you know, and asked her what it meant. Though they hadn't spoken for twenty years Freddy went to see him and begged him not to send George a penny, and he promised he wouldn't. I don't know how George has been making both ends meet. I'm sure Freddy's right, but I can't help being rather worried. If I hadn't given Freddy my word of honour that I wouldn't send him anything I think I'd have slipped a few notes in a letter in case of accident. I mean, it's awful to think that perhaps he hasn't got enough to eat.'

'It'll do him no harm to go short for a bit.'

'We were in an awful hole, you know. We'd made all sorts of preparations for his coming of age, and I'd issued hundreds of invitations. Suddenly George said he wouldn't come. I was simply frantic. I wrote and wired. I would have gone over to Germany only Freddy wouldn't let me. I practically went down on my bended knees to George. I begged him not to put us in such a humiliating position. I mean, it's the sort of thing it's so difficult to explain. Then my mother-in-law stepped in. You don't know her, do you? She's an extraordinary old woman. You'd never think she was Freddy's mother. She was German originally, but of very good family.'

'Oh?'

'To tell you the truth I'm rather frightened of her. She tackled Freddy and then she wrote to George herself. She said that if he'd come home for his twenty-first birthday she'd pay any debts he had in Munich and we'd all give a patient hearing to anything he had to say. He agreed to that and we're expecting him one day next week. But I'm not looking forward to it, I can tell you.'

She gave a deep sigh. When we were walking upstairs after dinner Freddy addressed me.

'I see Muriel has been telling you about George. The damned fool! I have no patience with him. Fancy wanting to be a pianist. It's so ungentlemanly.'

'He's very young, you know,' I said soothingly.

'He's had things too easy for him. I've been much too indulgent. There's never been a thing he wanted that I haven't given him. I'll learn him.'

The Blands had a discreet apprehension of the uses of advertisement and I gathered from the papers that the celebrations at Tilby of George's twenty-first birthday were conducted in accordance with the usage of English county families. There was a dinnerparty and a ball for the gentry and a collation and a dance in marquees on the lawn for the tenants. Expensive bands were brought down from London. In the illustrated papers were pictures of George surrounded by his family being presented with a solid silver tea-set by the tenantry. They had subscribed to have his portrait painted, but since his absence from the country had made it impossible for him to sit, the tea-service had been substituted. I read in the columns of the gossip writers that his father had given him a hunter, his mother a gramophone that changed its own records, his grandmother the dowager Lady Bland an *Encyclopaedia Britannica*, and his great-uncle Ferdinand Rabenstein a *Virgin and Child* by Pellegrino da Modena. I could not help observing that these gifts were bulky and not readily convertible into cash. From Ferdy's presence at the festivities I concluded that

George's unaccountable vagary had effected a reconciliation between uncle and nephew. I was right. Ferdy did not at all like the notion of his great-nephew becoming a professional pianist. At the first hint of danger to its prestige the family drew together and a united front was presented to oppose George's designs. Since I was not there I only know from hearsay what happened when the birthday celebrations were over. Ferdy told me something and so did Muriel, and later George gave me his version. The Blands had very much the impression that when George came home he found himself occupying the centre of the stage, when, surrounded by splendour, he saw for himself once more how much it meant to be the heir of a great estate, he would weaken. They surrounded him with love. They flattered him. They hung on his words. They counted on the goodness of his heart and thought that if they were very kind to him he would not have the courage to cause them pain. They seemed to take it for granted that he had no intention of going back to Germany and in conversation included him in all their plans. George did not say very much. He seemed to be enjoying himself. He did not open a piano. Things looked as though they were going very well. Peace descended on the troubled house. Then one day at luncheon when they were discussing a garden-party to which they had all been asked for one day of the following week, George said pleasantly:

'Don't count on me. I shan't be here.'

'Oh, George, why not?' asked his mother.

'I must get back to my work. I'm leaving for Munich on Monday.'

There was an awful pause. Everyone looked for something to say, but was afraid of saying the wrong thing, and at last it seemed impossible to break it. Luncheon was finished in silence. Then George went into the garden and the others, old Lady Bland and Ferdy, Muriel and Sir Adolphus, into the morning-room. There was a family council. Muriel wept. Freddy flew into a temper. Presently from the drawing-room they heard the sound of someone playing a nocturne of Chopin. It was George. It was as though now he had announced his decision he had gone for comfort, rest, and strength to the instrument he loved. Freddy sprang to his feet.

'Stop that noise,' he cried. 'I won't have him play the piano in my house.'

Muriel rang for a servant and gave him a message.

'Will you tell Mr Bland that her ladyship has a bad headache and would he mind not playing the piano.'

Ferdy, the man of the world, was deputed to have a talk with George. He was authorized to make him certain promises if he would give up the idea of becoming a pianist. If he did not wish to go into the diplomatic service his father would not insist, but if he would stand for Parliament he was prepared to pay his election expenses, give him a flat in London, and make him an allowance of five thousand a year. I must say it was a handsome offer. I do not know what Ferdy said to the boy. I suppose he painted to him the life that a young man could lead in London on such an income. I am sure he made it very alluring. It availed nothing. All George asked was five pounds a week to be able to continue his studies and to be left alone. He was indifferent to the position that he might some day enjoy. He didn't want to hunt. He didn't want to shoot. He didn't want to be a Member of Parliament. He didn't want to be a millionaire. He didn't want to be a baronet. He didn't want to be a peer. Ferdy left him defeated and in a state of considerable exasperation.

After dinner that evening there was a battle royal. Freddy was a quick-tempered man, unused to opposition, and he gave George the rough side of his tongue. I gather that it was very rough indeed. The women who sought to restrain his violence were sternly silenced. Perhaps for the first time in his life Freddy would not listen to his mother. George was obstinate and sullen. He had made up his mind and if his father didn't like it he could lump it. Freddy was peremptory. He forbade George to go back to Germany. George answered that he was twenty-one and his own master. He would go where he chose. Freddy swore he would not give him a penny.

'All right, I'll earn money.'

'You! You've never done a stroke of work in your life. What do you expect to do to earn money?'

'Sell old clothes,' grinned George.

There was a gasp from all of them. Muriel was so taken aback that she said a stupid thing.

'Like a Jew?'

'Well, aren't I a Jew? And aren't you a Jewess and isn't daddy a Jew? We're all Jews, the whole gang of us, and everyone knows it and what the hell's the good of pretending we're not?'

Then a very dreadful thing happened. Freddy burst suddenly into tears. I'm afraid he didn't behave very much like Sir Adolphus Bland. Bart, M.P., and the good old English gentleman he so much wanted to be, but like an emotional Adolf Bleikogel who loved his son and wept with mortification because the great hopes he had set on him were brought to nothing and the ambition of his life was frustrated. He cried noisily with great loud sobs and pulled his beard and beat his breast and rocked to and fro. Then they all began to cry, old Lady Bland and Muriel, and Ferdy, who sniffed and blew his nose and wiped the tears streaming down his face, and even George cried. Of course it was very painful, but to our rough Anglo-Saxon temperament I am afraid it must seem also a trifle ridiculous. No one tried to console anybody else. They just sobbed and sobbed. It broke up the party.

But it had no result on the situation. George remained obdurate. His father would not speak to him. There were more scenes. Muriel sought to excite his pity; he was deaf to her piteous entreaties, he did not seem to mind if he broke her heart, he did not care two hoots if he killed his father. Ferdy appealed to him as a sportsman and a man of the world. George was flippant and indeed personally offensive. Old Lady Bland with her guttural German accent and strong common sense argued with him, but he would not listen to reason. It was she, however, who at last found a way out. She made George acknowledge that it was no use to throw away all the beautiful things the world laid at his feet unless he had talent. Of course he thought he had, but he might be mistaken. It was not worth while to be a second-rate pianist. His only excuse, his only justification, was genius. If he had genius his family had no right to stand in his way.

'You can't expect me to show genius already,' said George. 'I shall have to work for years.'

'Are you sure you are prepared for that?'

'It's my only wish in the world. I'll work like a dog. I only want to be given my chance.'

This was the proposition she made. His father was determined to give him nothing and obviously they could not let the boy starve. He had mentioned five pounds a week. Well, she was willing to give him that herself. He could go back to Germany and study for two years. At the end of that time he must come back and they would get some competent and disinterested person to hear him play, and if then that person said he showed promise of becoming a first-rate pianist no further obstacles would be placed in his way. He would be given every advantage, help, and encouragement. If on the other hand that person decided that his natural gifts were not such as to ensure ultimate success he must promise faithfully to give up all thoughts of making music his profession and in every way accede to his father's wishes. George could hardly believe his ears.

'Do you mean that, Granny?'

'I do.'

'But will daddy agree?'

'I vill see dat he does,' she answered.

George seized her in his arms and impetuously kissed her on both cheeks.

'Darling,' he cried.

'Ah, but de promise?'

He gave her his solemn word of honour that he would faithfully abide by the terms of the arrangement. Two days later he went back to Germany. Though his father consented unwillingly to his going, and indeed could not help doing so, he would not be reconciled to him and when he left refused to say good-bye to him.

I imagine that in no manner could he have caused himself such pain. I permit myself a trite remark. It is strange that men, inhabitants for so short a while of an alien and inhuman world, should go out of their way to cause themselves so much unhappiness.

George had stipulated that during his two years of study his family should not visit him, so that when Muriel heard some months before he was due to come home that I was passing through Munich on my way to Vienna, whither business called me, it was not unnatural that she should ask me to look him up. She was anxious to have first-hand information about him. She gave me George's address and I wrote ahead, telling him I was spending a day in Munich, and asked him to lunch with me. His answer awaited me at the hotel. He said he worked all day and could not spare the time to lunch with me, but if I would come to his studio about six he would like to show me that and if I had nothing better to do would love to spend the evening with me. So soon after six I went to the address he gave me. He lived on the second floor of a large block of flats and when I came to his door I heard the sound of piano-playing. It stopped when I rang and George opened the door for me. I hardly recognized him. He had grown very fat. His hair was extremely long, it curled all over his head in picturesque confusion; and he had certainly not shaved for three days. He wore a grimy pair of Oxford bags, a tennis shirt, and slippers. He was not very clean and his finger-nails were rimmed with black. It was a startling change from the spruce, slim youth so elegantly dressed in such beautiful clothes that I had last seen. I could not but think it would be a shock to Ferdy to see him now. The studio was large and bare; on the walls were three or four unframed canvases of a highly cubist nature, there were several arm-chairs much the worse for wear, and a grand piano. Books were littered about and old newspapers and art magazines. It was dirty and untidy and there was a frowzy smell of stale beer and stale smoke.

'Do you live here alone?' I asked.

'Yes, I have a woman who comes in twice a week and cleans up. But I make my own breakfast and lunch.'

'Can you cook?'

'Oh, I only have bread and cheese and a bottle of beer for lunch. I dine at a *Bierstube*.'

It was pleasant to discover that he was very glad to see me. He seemed in great spirits and extremely happy. He asked after his relations and we talked of one thing and another. He had a lesson twice a week and for the rest of the time practised. He told me that he worked ten hours a day.

'That's a change,' I said.

He laughed.

'Daddy said I was born tired. I wasn't really lazy. I didn't see the use of working at things that bored me.'

I asked him how he was getting on with the piano. He seemed to be satisfied with his progress and I begged him to play to me.

'Oh, not now, I'm all in, I've been at it all day. Let's go out and dine and come back here later and then I'll play. I generally go to the same place, there are several students I know there, and it's rather fun.'

Presently we set out. He put on socks and shoes and a very old golf coat, and we walked together through the wide quiet streets. It was a brisk cold day. His step was buoyant. He looked round him with a sigh of delight.

'I love Munich,' he said. 'It's the only city in the world where there's art in the very air you breathe. After all, art is the only thing that matters, isn't it? I loathe the idea of going home.'

'All the same I'm afraid you'll have to.'

'I know. I'll go all right, but I'm not going to think about it till the time comes.'

'When you do, you might do worse than get a haircut. If you don't mind my saying so you look almost too artistic to be convincing.'

'You English, you're such Philistines,' he said.

He took me to a rather large restaurant in a side street, crowded even at that early hour with people dining, and furnished heavily in the German medieval style. A table covered with a red cloth, well away from the air, was reserved for George and his friends and when we went to it four or five youths were at it. There was a Pole studying Oriental languages, a student of philosophy, a painter (I suppose the author of George's cubist pictures), a Swede, and a young man who introduced himself to me, clicking his heels, as Hans Reiting, *Dichter*, namely Hans Reiting, poet. Not one of them was more than twenty-two and I felt a trifle out of it. They all addressed George as *du* and I noticed that his German was extremely fluent. I had not spoken it for some time and mine was rusty, so that I could not take much part in the lively conversation. But nevertheless I thoroughly enjoyed myself. They ate sparingly, but drank a good deal of beer. They talked of art and women. They were very revolutionary and though gay very much in earnest. They were contemptuous of everyone you had ever heard of, and the only point on which they all agreed was that in this topsy-turvy world only the vulgar could hope for success. They argued points of technique with animation, and contradicted one another, and shouted and were obscene. They had a grand time.

At about eleven George and I walked back to his studio. Munich is a city that frolics demurely and except about the Marienplatz the streets were still and empty. When we got in he took off his coat and said:

'Now I'll play to you.'

I sat in one of the dilapidated arm-chairs and a broken spring stuck into my behind, but I made myself as comfortable as I could. George played Chopin. I know very little of music and that is one of the reasons for which I have found this story difficult to write. When I go to a concert at the Queen's Hall and in the intervals read the programme it is all Greek to me. I know nothing of harmony and counterpoint. I shall never forget how humiliated I felt once when, having come to Munich for a Wagner Festival, I went to a wonderful performance of *Tristan und Isolde* and never heard a note of it. The first few bars sent me off and I began to think of what I was writing, my characters leapt into life and I heard their long conversations, I suffered their pains and was a party to their joy; the years swept by and all sorts of things happened to me, the spring brought me its rapture and in the winter I was cold and hungry; and I loved and I hated and I died. I suppose there were intervals in which I walked round and round the garden and probably ate *Schinken-Brödchen* and drank beer, but I have no recollection of them. The only thing I know is that when the curtain for the last time fell I woke with a start. I had had a wonderful time, but I could not help thinking it was very stupid of me to come such a long way and spend so much money if I couldn't pay attention to what I heard and saw.

I knew most of the things George played. They were the

familiar pieces of concert programmes. He played with a great deal of dash. Then he played Beethoven's *Appassionata*. I used to play it myself when I played the piano (very badly) in my far distant youth and I still knew every note of it. Of course it is a classic and a great work, it would be foolish to deny it, but I confess that at this time of day it leaves me cold. It is like *Paradise Lost*, splendid, but a trifle stolid. This too George played with vigour. He sweated profusely. At first I could not make out what was the matter with his playing, something did not seem to me quite right, and then it struck me that the two hands did not exactly synchronize, so that there was ever so slight an interval between the bass and the treble; but I repeat, I am ignorant of these things; what disconcerted me might have been merely the effect of his having drunk a good deal of beer that evening or indeed only my fancy. I said all I could think of to praise him.

'Of course I know I need a lot more work. I'm only a beginner, but I know I can do it. I feel it in my bones. It'll take me ten years, but then I shall be a pianist.'

He was tired and came away from the piano. It was after midnight and I suggested going, but he would not hear of it. He opened a couple of bottles of beer and lit his pipe. He wanted to talk.

'Are you happy here?' I asked him.

'Very,' he answered gravely. 'I'd like to stay for ever. I've never had such fun in my life. This evening, for instance. Wasn't it grand?'

'It was very jolly. But one can't go on leading the student's life. Your friends here will grow older and go away.'

'Others'll come. There are always students here and people like that.'

'Yes, but you'll grow older too. Is there anything more lamentable than the middle-aged man who tries to go on living the undergraduate's life? The old fellow who wants to be a boy among boys, and tries to persuade himself that they'll accept him as one of themselves – how ridiculous he is. It can't be done.'

'I feel so at home here. My poor father wants me to be an English gentleman. It gives me gooseflesh. I'm not a sportsman. I don't care a damn for hunting and shooting and playing cricket. I was only acting.'

'You gave a very natural performance.'

'It wasn't till I came here that I knew it wasn't real. I loved Eton, and Oxford was a riot, but all the same I knew I didn't belong. I played the part all right, because acting's in my blood, but there was always something in me that wasn't satisfied. The house in Grosvenor Square is a freehold and daddy paid a hundred and eighty thousand pounds for Tilby; I don't know if you understand what I mean, I felt they were just furnished houses we'd taken for the season and one of these days we'd pack up and the real owners would come back.'

I listened to him attentively, but I wondered how much he was describing what he had obscurely felt and how much he imagined now in his changed circumstances that he had felt.

'I used to hate hearing great-uncle Ferdy tell his Jewish stories. I thought it so damned mean. I understand now; it was a safety valve. My God, the strain of being a man about town. It's easier for daddy, he can play the old English squire at Tilby, but in the City he can be himself. He's all right. I've taken the make-up off and my stage clothes and at last I can be my real self too. What a relief! You know, I don't like English people. I never really know where I am with you. You're so dull and conventional. You never let yourselves go. There's no freedom in you, freedom of the soul, and you're such funks. There's nothing in the world you're so frightened of as doing the wrong thing.'

'Don't forget that you're English yourself, George,' I murmured.

He laughed.

'I? I'm not English. I haven't got a drop of English blood in me. I'm a Jew and you know it, and a German Jew into the bargain. I don't want to be English. I want to be a Jew. My friends are Jews. You don't know how much more easy I feel with them. I can be myself. We did everything we could to avoid Jews at home; Mummy, because she was blonde, thought she could get away with it and pretended she was a Gentile. What rot! D'you know, I have a lot of fun wandering about the Jewish parts of Munich and looking at the people. I went to Frankfort once, there are a lot of them there, and I walked about and looked at the frowzy old men with their hooked noses and the fat women with their false hair. I felt such a sympathy for them, I felt I belonged to them, I could have kissed them. When they looked at me I wondered if they knew that I was one of them. I wish to God I knew Yiddish. I'd like to become friends with them, and go into their houses and eat Kosher food and all that sort of thing. I wanted to go to a synagogue, but I was afraid I'd do the wrong thing and be kicked out. I like the smell of the Ghetto and the sense of life, and the mystery and the dust and the squalor and the romance. I shall never get the longing for it out of my head now. That's the real thing. All the rest is only pretence.'

'You'll break your father's heart,' I said.

'It's his or mine. Why can't he let me go? There's Harry. Harry would love to be squire of Tilby. He'd be an English gentleman all right. You know, mummy's set her heart on my marrying a Christian. Harry would love to. He'll found the good old English family all right. After all, I ask so little. I only want five pounds a week, and they can keep the title and the park and the Gainsboroughs and the whole bag of tricks.'

'Well, the fact remains that you gave your solemn word of honour to go back after two years.'

'I'll go back all right,' he said sullenly. 'Lea Makart has promised to come and hear me play.'

'What'll you do if she says you're no good?'

'Shoot myself,' he said gaily.

'What nonsense,' I answered in the same tone.

'Do *you* feel at home in England?'

'No,' I said, 'but then I don't feel at home anywhere else.'

But he was quite naturally not interested in me.

'I loathe the idea of going back. Now that I know what life has to offer I wouldn't be an English country gentleman for anything in the world. My God, the boredom of it!'

'Money's a very nice thing and I've always understood it's very pleasant to be an English peer.'

'Money means nothing to me. I want none of the things it can buy, and I don't happen to be a snob.'

It was growing very late and I had to get up early next day. It seemed unnecessary for me to pay too much attention to what George said. It was the sort of nonsense a young man might very well indulge in when thrown suddenly among painters and poets. Art is strong wine and needs a strong head to carry it. The divine fire burns most efficiently in those who temper its fury with horse sense. After all, George was not twenty-three yet. Time teaches. And when all was said and done his future was no concern of mine. I bade him good night and walked back to my hotel. The stars were shining in the indifferent sky. I left Munich in the morning.

I did not tell Muriel on my return to London what George had said to me, or what he looked like, but contented myself with assuring her that he was well and happy, working very hard, and seemed to be leading a virtuous and sober life. Six months later he came home. Muriel asked me to go down to Tilby for the week-end: Ferdy was bringing Lea Makart to hear George play and he particularly wished me to be there. I accepted. Muriel met me at the station.

'How did you find George?' I asked.

'He's very fat, but he seems in great spirits. I think he's pleased to be back again. He's been very sweet to his father.'

'I'm glad of that.'

'Oh, my dear, I do hope Lea Makart will say he's no good. It'll be such a relief to all of us.'

'I'm afraid it'll be a terrible disappointment to him.'

'Life is full of disappointments,' said Muriel crisply. 'But one learns to put up with them.'

I gave her a smile of amusement. We were sitting in a Rolls, and there was a footman as well as a chauffeur on the box. She wore a string of pearls that had probably cost forty thousand pounds. I recollected that in the birthday honours Sir Adolphus Bland had not been one of the three gentlemen on whom the King had been pleased to confer a peerage.

Lea Makart was able to make only a flying visit. She was playing that evening at Brighton and would motor over to Tilby on the Sunday morning for luncheon. She was returning to London the same day because she had a concert in Manchester on the Monday. George was to play in the course of the afternoon.

'He's practising very hard,' his mother told me. 'That's why he didn't come with me to meet you.'

We turned in at the park gates and drove up the imposing avenue of elms that led to the house. I found that there was no party.

I met the dowager Lady Bland for the first time. I had always been curious to see her. I had had in my mind's eye a somewhat sensational picture of an old, old Jewish woman who lived alone in her grand house in Portland Place, and, with a finger in every pie, ruled her family with a despotic hand. She did not disappoint me. She was of commanding presence, rather tall, and stout without being corpulent. Her countenance was markedly Hebraic. She wore a rather heavy moustache and a wig of a peculiarly metallic brown. Her dress was very grand, of black brocade, and she had a row of large diamond stars on her breast and round her neck a chain of diamonds. Diamond rings gleamed on her wrinkled hands. She spoke in a rather loud harsh voice and with a strong German accent. When I was introduced to her she fixed me with shining eyes. She summed me up with despatch and to my fancy at all events made no attempt to conceal from me that the judgement she formed was unfavourable.

'You have known my brother Ferdinand for many years, is it not so?' she said, rolling a guttural R. 'My brother Ferdinand has always moved in very good society. Where is Sir Adolphus,

Muriel? Does he know your guest is arrived? And will you not send for George? If he does not know his pieces by now he will not know them by tomorrow.'

Muriel explained that Freddy was finishing a round of golf with his secretary and that she had had George told I was there. Lady Bland looked as though she thought Muriel's replies highly unsatisfactory and turned again to me.

'My daughter-in-law tells me you have been in Italy?'

'Yes, I've only just come back.'

'It is a beautiful country. How is the King?'

I said I did not know.

'I used to know him when he was a little boy. He was not very strong then. His mother, Queen Margherita, was a great friend of mine. They thought he would never marry. The Duchess of Aosta was very angry when he fell in love with that Princess of Montenegro.'

She seemed to belong to some long-past period of history, but she was very alert and I imagine that little escaped her beady eyes. Freddy, very spruce in plus-fours, presently came in. It was amusing and yet a little touching to see this grey-bearded man, as a rule somewhat domineering, so obviously on his best behaviour with the old lady. He called her Mamma. Then George came in. He was as fat as ever, but he had taken my advice and had his hair cut; he was losing his boyish looks, but he was a powerful and well-set-up young man. It was good to see the pleasure he took in his tea. He ate quantities of sandwiches and great hunks of cake. He had still a boy's appetite. His father watched him with a tender smile and as I looked at him I could not be surprised at the attachment which they all so obviously felt for him. He had an ingenuousness, a charm, and an enthusiasm which were certainly very pleasant. There was about him a generosity of demeanour, a frankness, and a natural cordiality which could not but make people take to him. I do not know whether it was owing to a hint from his grandmother or merely of his own good nature, but it was plain that he was going out of his way to be nice to his father; and in his father's soft eyes, in the way he hung upon the boy's words, in his pleased, proud, and happy look, you felt how bitterly the estrangement of the last two years had weighed on him. He adored George.

We played golf in the morning, a three-ball match, since Muriel, having to go to Mass, could not join us, and at one Ferdy arrived in Lea Makart's car. We sat down to luncheon. Of course Lea Makart's reputation was well known to me. She was acknowledged to be the greatest woman pianist in Europe. She was a very old friend of Ferdy's, who with his interest and patronage had greatly helped her at the beginning of her career, and it was he who had arranged for her to come and give her opinion of George's chances. At one time I went as often as I could to hear her play. She had no affectations; she played as a bird sings, without any appearance of effort, very naturally, and the silvery notes dripped from her light fingers in a curiously spontaneous manner, so that it gave you the impression that she was improvising those complicated rhythms. They used to tell me that her technique was wonderful. I could never make up my mind how much the delight her playing gave me was due to her person. In those days she was the most ethereal thing you could imagine, and it was surprising that a creature so sylphlike should be capable of so much power. She was very slight, pale, with enormous eyes and magnificent black hair, and at the piano she had a child-like wistfulness that was most appealing. She was very beautiful in a hardly human way and when she played, a little smile on her closed lips, she seemed to be remembering things she had heard in another world. Now, however, a woman in the early forties, she was sylphlike no more; she was stout and her face had broadened; she had no longer that lovely remoteness, but the authority of her long succession of triumphs. She was brisk, business-like, and somewhat overwhelming. Her vitality lit her with a natural spotlight as his sanctity surrounds the saint with a halo. She was not interested in anything very much but her own affairs, but since she had humour and knew the world she was able to invest them with gaiety. She held the conversation, but did not absorb it. George talked little. Every now and then she gave him a glance, but did not try to draw him in. I was the only Gentile at the table. All but old Lady Bland spoke perfect English, yet I could not help feeling that they did not speak like English people; I think they rounded their vowels more than we do, they certainly spoke louder, and the words seemed not to fall, but to gush from their lips. I think if I had been in another room where I could hear the tone but not the words of their speech I should have thought it was in a foreign language that they were conversing. The effect was slightly disconcerting.

Lea Makart wished to set out for London at about six, so it was arranged that George should play at four. Whatever the result of the audition, I felt that I, a stranger in the circle which her departure must render exclusively domestic, would be in the way and so, pretending an early engagement in town next morning, I asked her if she would take me with her in her car.

At a little before four we all wandered into the drawing-room. Old Lady Bland sat on a sofa with Ferdy; Freddy, Muriel, and I made ourselves comfortable in arm-chairs; and Lea Makart sat by herself. She chose instinctively a high-backed Jacobean chair that had somewhat the air of a throne, and in a yellow dress, with her olive skin, she looked very handsome. She had magnificent eyes. She was very much made up and her mouth was scarlet.

George gave no sign of nervousness. He was already seated at the piano when I went in with his father and mother, and he watched us quietly settling ourselves down. He gave me the shadow of a smile. When he saw that we were all at our ease he began to play. He played Chopin. He played two waltzes that were familiar to me, a polonaise and an *étude*. He played with a great deal of brio. I wish I knew music well enough to give an exact description of his playing. It had strength, and a youthful exuberance, but I felt that he missed what to me is the peculiar charm of Chopin, the tenderness, the nervous melancholy, the wistful gaiety and the slightly faded romance that reminds me always of an Early Victorian keepsake. And again I had the vague sensation, so slight that it almost escaped me, that the two hands did not quite synchronize. I looked at Ferdy and saw him give his sister a look of faint surprise. Muriel's eyes were fixed on the pianist, but presently she dropped them and for the rest of the time stared at the floor. His father looked at him too, and his eyes were steadfast, but unless I was much mistaken he went pale and his face betrayed something like dismay. Music was in the blood of all of them, all their lives they had heard the greatest pianists in the world, and they judged with instinctive precision. The only person whose face betrayed no emotion was Lea Makart. She listened very attentively. She was as still as an image in a niche.

At last he stopped and turning round on his seat faced her. He did not speak.

'What is it you want me to tell you?' she asked.

They looked into one another's eyes.

'I want you to tell me whether I have any chance of becoming in time a pianist in the first rank.'

'Not in a thousand years.'

For a moment there was dead silence. Freddy's head sank and he looked down at the carpet at his feet. His wife put out her hand and took his. But George continued to look steadily at Lea Makart.

'Ferdy has told me the circumstances,' she said at last. 'Don't think I'm influenced by them. Nothing of this is very important.'

She made a great sweeping gesture that took in the magnificent room with the beautiful things it contained and all of us. 'If I thought you had in you the makings of an artist I shouldn't hesitate to beseech you to give up everything for art's sake. Art is the only thing that matters. In comparison with art, wealth and rank and power are not worth a straw.' She gave us a look so sincere that it was void of insolence. 'We are the only people who count. We give the world significance. You are only our raw material.'

I was not too pleased to be included with the rest under that heading, but that is neither here nor there.

'Of course I can see that you've worked very hard. Don't think it's been wasted. It will always be a pleasure to you to be able to play the piano and it will enable you to appreciate great playing as no ordinary person can hope to do. Look at your hands. They're not a pianist's hands.'

Involuntarily I glanced at George's hands. I had never noticed them before. I was astounded to see how podgy they were and how short and stumpy the fingers.

'Your ear is not quite perfect. I don't think you can ever hope to be more than a very competent amateur. In art the difference between the amateur and the professional is immeasurable.'

George did not reply. Except for his pallor no one would have known that he was listening to the blasting of all his hopes. The silence that fell was quite awful. Lea Makart's eyes suddenly filled with tears.

'But don't take my opinion alone,' she said. 'After all, I'm not infallible. Ask somebody else. You know how good and generous Paderewski is. I'll write to him about you and you can go down and play to him. I'm sure he'll hear you.'

George now gave a little smile. He had very good manners and whatever he was feeling did not want to make the situation too difficult for others.

'I don't think that's necessary, I am content to accept your verdict. To tell you the truth it's not so very different from my master's in Munich.'

He got up from the piano and lit a cigarette. It eased the strain. The others moved a little in their chairs. Lea Makart smiled at George.

'Shall I play to you?' she said.

'Yes, do.'

She got up and went to the piano. She took off the rings with which her fingers were laden. She played Bach. I do not know the names of the pieces, but I recognized the stiff ceremonial of the frenchified little German courts and the sober, thrifty comfort of the burghers, and the dancing on the village green, the green trees that looked like Christmas trees, and the sunlight on the wide German country, and a tender cosiness; and in my nostrils there was a warm scent of the soil and I was conscious of a sturdy strength that seemed to have its roots deep in mother earth, and of an elemental power that was timeless and had no home in space. She played beautifully, with a soft brilliance that made you think of the full moon shining at dusk in the summer sky. With another part of me I watched the others and I saw how intensely they were conscious of the experience. They were rapt. I wished with all my heart that I could get from music the wonderful exaltation that possessed them. She stopped, a smile hovered on her lips, and she put on her rings. George gave a little chuckle.

'That clinches it, I fancy,' he said.

The servants brought in tea and after tea Lea Makart and I bade the company farewell and got into the car. We drove up to London. She talked all the way, if not brilliantly at all events with immense gusto; she told me of her early years in Manchester and of the struggle of her beginnings. She was very interesting. She never even mentioned George; the episode was of no consequence, it was finished and she thought of it no more.

We little knew what was happening at Tilby. When we left George went out on the terrace and presently his father joined him. Freddy had won the day, but he was not happy. With his more than feminine sensitiveness he felt all that George was feeling, and George's anguish simply broke his heart. He had never loved his son more than then. When he appeared George greeted him with a little smile. Freddy's voice broke. In a sudden and overwhelming emotion he found it in him to surrender the fruits of his victory.

'Look here, old boy,' he said, 'I can't bear to think that you've had such a disappointment. Would you like to go back to Munich for another year and then see?'

George shook his head.

'No, it wouldn't be any good. I've had my chance. Let's call it a day.'

'Try not to take it too hard.'

'You see, the only thing in the world I want is to be a pianist. And there's nothing doing. It's a bit thick if you come to think of it.'

George, trying so hard to be brave, smiled wanly.

'Would you like to go round the world? You can get one of your Oxford pals to go with you and I'll pay all the expenses. You've been working very hard for a long time.'

'Thanks awfully, daddy, we'll talk about it. I'm just going for a stroll now.'

'Shall I come with you?'

'I'd rather go alone.'

Then George did a strange thing. He put his arm round his father's neck, and kissed him on the lips. He gave a funny little moved laugh and walked away. Freddy went back to the drawing-room. His mother, Ferdy, and Muriel were sitting there.

'Freddy, why don't you marry the boy?' said the old lady. 'He is twenty-three. It would take his mind off his troubles and when he is married and has a baby he will soon settle down like everybody else.'

'Whom is he to marry, mamma?' asked Sir Adolphus, smiling.

'That's not so difficult. Lady Frielinghausen came to see me the other day with her daughter Violet. She is a very nice maiden and she will have money of her own. Lady Frielinghausen gave me to understand that her Sir Jacob would come down very handsome if Violet made a good match.'

Muriel flushed.

'I hate Lady Frielinghausen. George is much too young to marry. He can afford to marry anyone he likes.'

Old Lady Bland gave her daughter a strange look.

'You are a very foolish girl, Miriam,' she said, using the name Muriel had long discarded. 'As long as I am here I shall not allow you to commit a foolishness.'

She knew as well as if Muriel had said it in so many words that she wanted George to marry a Gentile, but she knew also that so long as she was alive neither Freddy nor his wife would dare to suggest it.

But George did not go for a walk. Perhaps because the shooting season was about to open he took it into his head to go into the gun-room. He began to clean the gun that his mother had given him on his twentieth birthday. No one had used it since he went to Germany. Suddenly the servants were startled by a report. When they went into the gun-room they found George lying on the floor shot through the heart. Apparently the gun had been loaded and George while playing about with it had accidentally shot himself. One reads of such accidents in the paper often.

THE CREATIVE IMPULSE

I SUPPOSE that very few people know how Mrs Albert Forrester came to write *The Achilles Statue*; and since it has been acclaimed as one of the great novels of our time I cannot but think that a brief account of the circumstances that gave it birth must be of interest to all serious students of literature; and indeed, if, as the critics say, this is a book that will live, the following narrative, serving a better purpose than to divert an idle hour, may be regarded by the historian of the future as a curious footnote to the literary annals of our day.

Everyone of course remembers the success that attended the publication of *The Achilles Statue*. Month after month printers were kept busy printing, binders were kept busy binding, edition after edition; and the publishers, both in England and America, were hard put to it to fulfil the pressing orders of the booksellers. It was promptly translated into every European tongue and it has been recently announced that it will soon be possible to read it in Japanese and in Urdu. But it had previously appeared serially in magazines on both sides of the Atlantic and from the editors of these Mrs Albert Forrester's agent had wrung a sum that can only be described as thumping. A dramatization of the work was made, which ran for a season in New York, and there is little doubt that when the play is produced in London it will have an equal success. The film rights have been sold at a great price. Though the amount that Mrs Albert Forrester is reputed (in literary circles) to have made is probably exaggerated, there can be no doubt that she will have earned enough money from this one book to save her for the rest of her life from any financial anxiety.

It is not often that a book meets with equal favour from the public and the critics, and that she, of all persons, had (if I may so put it) squared the circle must have proved the more gratifying to Mrs Albert Forrester, since, though she had received the commendation of the critics in no grudging terms (and indeed had come to look upon it as her due), the public had always remained strangely insensible to her merit. Each work she published, a slender volume beautifully printed and bound in white buckram, was hailed as a masterpiece, always to the length of a column, and in the weekly reviews which you see only in the dusty library of a very long-established club even to the extent of a page; and all well-read persons read and praised it. But well-read persons apparently do not buy books, and she did not sell. It was indeed a scandal that so distinguished an author, with an imagination so delicate and a style so exquisite, should remain neglected of the vulgar. In America she was almost completely unknown; and though Mr Carl van Vechten had written an article berating the public for its obtuseness, the public remained callous. Her agent, a warm admirer of her genius, had blackmailed an American publisher into taking two of her books by refusing, unless he did so, to let him have others (trashy novels doubtless) that he badly wanted, and they had been duly published. The reception they received from the press was flattering and showed that in America the best minds were sensitive to her talent; but when it came to the third book the American publisher (in the coarse way publishers have) told the agent that any money he had to spare he preferred to spend on synthetic gin.

Since *The Achilles Statue* Mrs Albert Forrester's previous books have been republished (and Mr Carl van Vechten has written another article pointing out sadly, but firmly, that he had drawn the attention of the reading world to the merits of this exceptional writer fully fifteen years ago), and they have been so widely advertised that they can scarcely have escaped the cultured reader's attention. It is unnecessary, therefore, for me to give an account of them; and it would certainly be no more than cold potatoes after those two subtle articles by Mr Carl van Vechten. Mrs Albert Forrester began to write early. Her first work (a volume of elegies) appeared when she was a maiden of eighteen; and from then on she published, every two or three years, for she had too exalted a conception of her art to hurry her production, a volume either of verse or prose. When *The Achilles Statue* was written she had reached the respectable age of fifty-seven, so that it will be readily surmised that the number of her works was considerable. She had given the world half a dozen volumes of verse, published under Latin titles, such as *Felicitas*, *Pax Maris*, and *Aes Triplex*, all of the graver kind, for her muse, disinclined to skip on a light, fantastic toe, trod a somewhat solemn measure. She remained faithful to the Elegy, and the Sonnet claimed much of her attention; but her chief distinction was to revive the Ode, a form of poetry that the poets of the present day somewhat neglect; and it may be asserted with confidence that her *Ode to President Fallières* will find a place in every anthology of English verse. It is admirable not only for the noble sonority of its rhythms, but also for its felicitous description of the pleasant land of France. Mrs Albert Forrester wrote of the valley of the Loire with its memories of du Bellay, of Chartres and the jewelled windows of its cathedral, of the sun-swept cities of Provence, with a sympathy all the more remarkable since she had never penetrated further into France than Boulogne, which she visited shortly after her marriage on an excursion steamer from Margate. But the physical mortification of being extremely seasick and the intellectual humiliation of discovering that the inhabitants of that popular seaside resort could not understand her fluent and idiomatic French made her determine not to expose herself a second time to experiences that were at once undignified and unpleasant; and she never again embarked on the treacherous element which she, however, sang (*Pax Maris*) in numbers both grave and sweet.

There are some fine passages too in the *Ode to Woodrow Wilson*, and I regret that, owing to a change in her sentiments towards that no doubt excellent man, the author decided not to reprint it. But I think it must be admitted that Mrs Albert Forrester's most distinguished work was in prose. She wrote several volumes of brief, but perfectly constructed, essays on such subjects as Autumn in Sussex, Queen Victoria, Death, Spring in Norfolk, Georgian Architecture, Monsieur de Diaghileff, and Dante; she also wrote works, both erudite and whimsical, on the Jesuit Architecture of the Seventeenth Century and on the Literary Aspect of the Hundred Years' War. It was her prose that gained her that body of devoted admirers, fit though few, as with her rare gift of phrase she herself put it, that proclaimed her the greatest master of the English language that this century has seen. She admitted herself that it was her style, sonorous yet racy, polished yet eloquent, that was her strong point; and it was only in her prose that she had occasion to exhibit the delicious, but restrained, humour that her readers found so irresistible. It was not a humour of ideas, nor even a humour of words; it was much more subtle than that, it was a humour of punctuation: in a flash of inspiration she had discovered the comic possibilities of the semi-colon, and of this she had made abundant and exquisite use. She was able to place it in such a way that if you were a person of culture with a keen sense of humour, you did not exactly laugh a horse-collar, but you giggled delightedly, and the greater your culture the more delightedly you giggled. Her friends said that it made every other form of humour coarse and exaggerated. Several writers had tried to imitate her; but in vain: whatever else you might say about Mrs Albert Forrester you were bound to admit that she was able to get every ounce of humour out of the semi-colon and no one else could get within a mile of her.

Mrs Albert Forrester lived in a flat not far from the Marble Arch, which combined the advantage of a good address and a moderate rent. It had a handsome drawing-room on the street and a large bedroom for Mrs Albert Forrester, a darkish dining-room at the back, and a small poky bedroom, next door to the kitchen, for Mr Albert Forrester, who paid the rent. It was in the handsome drawing-room that Mrs Albert Forrester every Tuesday afternoon received her friends. It was a severe and chaste apartment. On the walls was a paper designed by William Morris himself, and on this, in plain black frames, mezzotints collected before mezzotints grew expensive; the furniture was of the Chippendale period, but for the roll-top desk, vaguely Louis XVI in character, at which Mrs Albert Forrester wrote her works. This was pointed out to visitors the first time they came to see her, and there were few who looked at it without emotion. The carpet was thick and the lights discreet. Mrs Albert Forrester sat in a straight-backed grandfather's chair covered with red damask. There was nothing ostentatious about it, but since it was the only comfortable chair in the room it set her apart as it were and above her guests. Tea was dispensed by a female of uncertain age, silent and colourless, who was never introduced to anyone but who was known to look upon it as a privilege to be allowed to save Mrs Albert Forrester from the irksome duty of pouring out tea. She was thus able to devote herself entirely to conversation, and it must be admitted that her conversation was excellent. It was not sprightly; and since it is difficult to indicate punctuation in speech it may have seemed to some slightly lacking in humour, but it was of wide range, solid, instructive, and interesting. Mrs Albert Forrester was well acquainted with social science, jurisprudence, and theology. She had read much and her memory was retentive. She had a pretty gift for quotation, which is a serviceable sub-stitute for wit, and having for thirty years known more or less intimately a great many distinguished people, she had a great many interesting anecdotes to tell, which she placed with tact and which she did not repeat more than was pardonable. Mrs Albert Forrester had the gift of attracting the most varied persons and you were liable at one and the same time to meet in her drawing-room an ex-Prime Minister, a newspaper proprietor, and the ambassador of a First Class Power. I always imagined that these great people came because they thought that here they rubbed shoulders with Bohemia, but with a Bohemia sufficiently neat and clean for them to be in no danger that the dirt would come off on them. Mrs Albert Forrester was deeply interested in politics and I myself heard a Cabinet Minister tell her frankly that she had a masculine intelligence. She had been opposed to Female Suffrage, but when it was at last granted to women she began to dally with the idea of going into Parliament. Her difficulty was that she did not know which party to choose.

'After all,' she said, with a playful shrug of her somewhat massive shoulders, 'I cannot form a party of one.'

Like many serious patriots, in her inability to know for certain which way the cat would jump she held her political opinions in suspense; but of late she had been definitely turning towards Labour as the best hope of the country, and if a safe seat were offered her it was felt fairly certain that she would not hesitate to come out into the open as a champion of the oppressed proletariat.

Her drawing-room was always open to foreigners, to Czecho-Slovaks, Italians, and Frenchmen, if they were distinguished, and to Americans even if they were obscure. But she was not a snob and you seldom met there a duke unless he was of a peculiarly serious turn and a peeress only if in addition to her rank she had the passport of some small social solecism such as having been divorced, written a novel, or forged a cheque, which might give her claim to Mrs Albert Forrester's catholic sympathies. She did not much care for painters, who were shy and silent; and musicians did not interest her: even if they consented to play, and if they were celebrated they were too often reluctant, their music was a hindrance to conversation: if people wanted music they could go to a concert; for her part she preferred the more subtle music of the soul. But her hospitality to writers, especially if they were promising and little known, was warm and constant. She had an eye for budding talent and there were few of the famous writers who from time to time drank a dish of tea with her whose first efforts she had not encouraged and whose early steps she had not guided. Her own position was too well assured for her to be capable of envy, and she had heard the word genius attached to her name too often to feel a trace of jealousy because the talents of others brought them a material success that was denied to her.

Mrs Albert Forrester, confident in the judgement of posterity, could afford to be disinterested. With these elements then it is no wonder that she had succeeded in creating something as near the French salon of the eighteenth century as our barbarous nation has ever reached. To be invited to 'eat a bun and drink a cup of tea on Tuesday' was a privilege that few failed to recognize; and when you sat on your Chippendale chair in the discreetly lit but austere room, you could not but feel that you were living literary history. The American Ambassador once said to Mrs Albert Forrester:

'A cup of tea with you, Mrs Forrester, is one of the richest intellectual treats which it has ever been my lot to enjoy.'

It was indeed on occasion a trifle overwhelming. Mrs Albert Forrester's taste was so perfect, she so inevitably admired the right thing and made the just observation about it, that sometimes you almost gasped for air. For my part I found it prudent to fortify myself with a cocktail or two before I exposed myself to the rarefied atmosphere of her society. Indeed, I very nearly found myself for ever excluded from it, for one afternoon, presenting myself at the door, instead of asking the maid who opened it: 'Is Mrs Forrester at home?' I asked: 'Is there Divine Service today?'

Of course it was said in pure inadvertence, but it was unfortunate that the maid sniggered, and one of Mrs Albert Forrester's most devoted admirers, Ellen Hannaway, happened to be at the moment in the hall taking off her goloshes. She told my hostess what I had said before I got into the drawing-room, and as I entered Mrs Albert Forrester fixed me with an eagle eye.

'Why did you ask if there was Divine Service today?' she inquired.

I explained that I was absent-minded, but Mrs Albert Forrester held me with a gaze that I can only describe as compelling.

'Do you mean to suggest that my parties are . . .' she searched for a word. 'Sacramental?'

I did not know what she meant, but did not like to show my ignorance before so many clever people, and I decided that the only thing was to seize my trowel and the butter.

'Your parties are like you, dear lady, perfectly beautiful and perfectly divine.'

A little tremor passed through Mrs Albert Forrester's substantial frame. She was like a man who enters suddenly a room filled with hyacinths; the perfume is so intoxicating that he almost staggers. But she relented.

'If you were trying to be facetious,' she said, 'I should prefer you to exercise your facetiousness on my guests rather than on my maids. . . . Miss Warren will give you some tea.'

Mrs Albert Forrester dismissed me with a wave of the hand, but she did not dismiss the subject, since for the next two or three years whenever she introduced me to someone she never failed to add:

'You must make the most of him, he only comes here as a penance. When he comes to the door he always asks: Is there Divine Service today? So amusing, isn't he?'

But Mrs Albert Forrester did not confine herself to weekly tea-parties: every Saturday she gave a luncheon of eight persons;

this according to her opinion being the perfect number for general conversation and her dining-room conveniently holding no more. If Mrs Albert Forrester flattered herself upon anything it was not that her knowledge of English prosody was unique, but that her luncheons were celebrated. She chose her guests with care, and an invitation to one of them was more than a compliment, it was a consecration. Over the luncheon-table it was possible to keep the conversation on a higher level than in the mixed company of a tea-party and few can have left her dining-room without taking away with them an enhanced belief in Mrs Albert Forrester's ability and a brighter faith in human nature. She only asked men, since, stout enthusiast for her sex as she was and glad to see women on other occasions, she could not but realize that they were inclined at table to talk exclusively to their next-door neighbours and thus hinder the general exchange of ideas that made her own parties an entertainment not only of the body but of the soul. For it must be said that Mrs Albert Forrester gave you uncommonly good food, excellent wine, and a first-rate cigar. Now to anyone who has partaken of literary hospitality this must appear very remarkable, since literary persons for the most part think highly and live plainly; their minds are occupied with the things of the spirit and they do not notice that the roast mutton is underdone and the potatoes cold: the beer is all right, but the wine has a sobering effect, and it is unwise to touch the coffee. Mrs Albert Forrester was pleased enough to receive compliments on the fare she provided.

'If people do me the honour to break bread with me,' she said, 'it is only fair that I should give them as good food as they can get at home.'

But if the flattery was excessive she deprecated it.

'You really embarrass me when you give me a meed of praise which is not my due. You must praise Mrs Bulfinch.'

'Who is Mrs Bulfinch?'

'My cook.'

'She's a treasure then, but you're not going to ask me to believe that she's responsible for the wine.'

'Is it good? I'm terribly ignorant of such things; I put myself entirely in the hands of my wine merchant.'

But if mention was made of the cigars Mrs Albert Forrester beamed.

'Ah, for them you must compliment Albert. It is Albert who chooses the cigars and I am given to understand that no one knows more about a cigar than Albert.'

She looked at her husband, who sat at the end of the table,

with the proud bright eyes of a pedigree hen (a Buff Orpington for choice) looking at her only chick. Then there was a quick flutter of conversation as the guests, anxious to be civil to their host and relieved at length to find an occasion, expressed their appreciation of his peculiar merit.

'You're very kind,' he said. 'I'm glad you like them.'

Then he would give a little discourse on cigars, explaining the excellencies he sought and regretting the deterioration in quality which had followed on the commercialization of the industry. Mrs Albert Forrester listened to him with a complacent smile, and it was plain that she enjoyed the little triumph of his. Of course you cannot go on talking of cigars indefinitely and as soon as she perceived that her guests were growing restive she broached a topic of more general, and it may be of more significant, interest. Albert subsided into silence. But he had had his moment.

It was Albert who made Mrs Forrester's luncheons to some less attractive than her tea-parties, for Albert was a bore; but though without doubt perfectly conscious of the fact, she made a point that he should come to them and in fact had fixed upon Saturdays (for the rest of the week he was busy) in order that he should be able to. Mrs Albert Forrester felt that her husband's presence on these festive occasions was an unavoidable debt that she paid to her own self-respect. She would never by a negligence admit to the world that she had married a man who was not spiritually her equal, and it may be that in the silent watches of the nights she asked herself where indeed such could have been found. Mrs Albert Forrester's friends were troubled by no such reticence and they said it was dreadful that such a woman should be burdened with such a man. They asked each other how she had ever come to marry him and (being mostly celibate) answered despairingly that no one ever knew why anybody married anybody else.

It was not that Albert was a verbose and aggressive bore; he did not buttonhole you with interminable stories or pester you with pointless jokes; he did not crucify you on a platitude or hamstring you with a commonplace; he was just dull. A cipher. Clifford Boyleston, for whom the French Romantics had no secrets and who was himself a writer of merit, had said that when you looked into a room into which Albert had just gone there was nobody there. This was thought very clever by Mrs Albert Forrester's friends, and Rose Waterford, the well-known novelist and the most fearless of women, had ventured to repeat it to Mrs Albert Forrester. Though she pretended to be annoyed, she had not been able to prevent the smile that rose to her lips. Her behaviour towards Albert could not but increase the respect in which her friends held her. She insisted that whatever in their secret hearts they thought of him, they should treat him with the decorum that was due to her husband. Her own demeanour was admirable. If he chanced to make an observation she listened to him with a pleasant expression and when he fetched her a book that she wanted or gave her his pencil to make a note of an idea that had occurred to her, she always thanked him. Nor would she allow her friends pointedly to neglect him, and though, being a woman of tact, she saw that it would be asking too much of the world if she took him about with her always, and she went out much alone, yet her friends knew that she expected them to ask him to dinner at least once a year. He always accompanied her to public banquets when she was going to make a speech, and if she delivered a lecture she took care that he should have a seat on the platform.

Albert was, I believe, of average height, but perhaps because you never thought of him except in connexion with his wife (of imposing dimensions) you only thought of him as a little man. He was spare and frail and looked older than his age. This was the same as his wife's. His hair, which he kept very short, was white and meagre, and he wore a stubby white moustache; his was a face, thin and lined, without a noticeable feature; and his blue eyes, which once might have been attractive, were now pale and tired. He was always very neatly dressed in pepper-and-salt trousers, which he chose always of the same pattern, a black coat, and a grey tie with a small pearl pin in it. He was perfectly unobtrusive, and when he stood in Mrs Albert Forrester's drawing-room to receive the guests whom she had asked to luncheon you noticed him as little as you noticed the quiet and gentlemanly furniture. He was well-mannered and it was with a pleasant, courteous smile that he shook hands with them.

'How do you do? I'm very glad to see you,' he said if they were friends of some standing. 'Keeping well, I hope?'

But if they were strangers of distinction coming for the first time to the house, he went to the door as they entered the drawing-room, and said:

'I am Mrs Albert Forrester's husband. I will introduce you to my wife.'

Then he led the visitor to where Mrs Albert Forrester stood with her back to the light, and she with a glad and eager gesture advanced to make the stranger welcome.

It was agreeable to see the demure pride he took in his wife's literary reputation and the self-effacement with which he furthered her interests. He was always there when he was wanted and never when he wasn't. His tact, if not deliberate, was instinctive. Mrs Albert Forrester was the first to acknowledge his merits.

'I really don't know what I should do without him,' she said. 'He's invaluable to me. I read him everything I write and his criticisms are often very useful.'

'Molière and his cook,' said Miss Waterford.

'Is that funny, dear Rose?' asked Mrs Forrester, somewhat acidly.

When Mrs Albert Forrester did not approve of a remark, she had a way that put many persons to confusion of asking you whether it was a joke which she was too dense to see. But it was impossible to embarrass Miss Waterford. She was a lady who in the course of a long life had had many affairs, but only one passion, and this was for printer's ink. Mrs Albert Forrester tolerated rather than approved her.

'Come, come, my dear,' she replied, 'you know very well that he wouldn't exist without you. He wouldn't know us. It must be wonderful to him to come in contact with all the best brains and the most distinguished people of our day.'

'It may be that the bee would perish without the hive which shelters it, but the bee nevertheless has a significance of its own.'

And since Mrs Albert Forrester's friends, though they knew all about art and literature, knew little about natural history, they had no reply to this observation. She went on.

'He doesn't interfere with me. He knows subconsciously when I don't want to be disturbed and, indeed, when I am following out a train of thought I find his presence in the room a comfort rather than a hindrance to me.'

'Like a Persian cat,' said Miss Waterford.

'But like a very well-trained, well-bred, and well-mannered Persian cat,' answered Mrs Forrester severely, thus putting Miss Waterford in her place.

But Mrs Albert Forrester had not finished with her husband.

'We who belong to the intelligentsia,' she said, 'are apt to live in a world too exclusively our own. We are interested in the abstract rather than in the concrete, and sometimes I think that we survey the bustling world of human affairs in too detached a manner and from too serene a height. Do you not think that we stand in danger of becoming a little inhuman? I shall always be grateful to Albert because he keeps me in contact with the man in the street.'

It was on account of this remark, to which none of her friends could deny the rare insight and subtlety that characterized so many of her utterances, that for some time Albert was known in her immediate circle as The Man in the Street. But this was only for a while, and it was forgotten. He then became known as The Philatelist. It was Clifford Boyleston, with his wicked wit, who invented the name. One day, his poor brain exhausted by the effort to sustain a conversation with Albert, he had asked in desperation:

'Do you collect stamps?'

'No,' answered Albert mildly. 'I'm afraid I don't.'

But Clifford Boyleston had no sooner asked the question than he saw its possibilities. He had written a book on Baudelaire's aunt by marriage, which had attracted the attention of all who were interested in French literature, and was well known in his exhaustive studies of the French spirit to have absorbed a goodly share of the Gallic quickness and the Gallic brilliancy. He paid no attention to Albert's disclaimer, but at the first opportunity informed Mrs Albert Forrester's friends that he had at last discovered Albert's secret. He collected stamps. He never met him afterwards without asking him:

'Well, Mr Forrester, how is the stamp collection?' Or: 'Have you been buying any stamps since I saw you last?'

It mattered little that Albert continued to deny that he collected stamps, the invention was too apt not to be made the most of; Mrs Albert Forrester's friends insisted that he did, and they seldom spoke to him without asking him how he was getting on. Even Mrs Albert Forrester, when she was in a specially gay humour, would sometimes speak of her husband as The Philatelist. The name really did seem to fit Albert like a glove. Sometimes they spoke of him thus to his face and they could not but appreciate the good nature with which he took it; he smiled unresentfully and presently did not even protest that they were mistaken.

Of course Mrs Albert Forrester had too keen a social sense to jeopardize the success of her luncheons by allowing her more distinguished guests to sit on either side of Albert. She took care that only her older and more intimate friends should do this, and when the appointed victims came in she would say to them:

'I know you won't mind sitting by Albert, will you?'

They could only say that they would be delighted, but if their faces too plainly expressed their dismay she would pat their hands playfully and add:

'Next time you shall sit by me. Albert is so shy with strangers and you know so well how to deal with him.'

They did: they simply ignored him. So far as they were

concerned the chair in which he sat might as well have been empty. There was no sign that it annoyed him to be taken no notice of by persons who after all were eating food he paid for, since the earnings of Mrs Forrester could certainly not have provided her guests with spring salmon and forced asparagus. He sat quiet and silent, and if he opened his mouth it was only to give a direction to one of the maids. If a guest were new to him he would let his eyes rest on him in a stare that would have been embarrassing if it had not been so childlike. He seemed to be asking himself what this strange creature was; but what answer his mild scrutiny gave him he never revealed. When the conversation grew animated he would look from one speaker to the other, but again you could not tell from his thin, lined face what he thought of the fantastic notions that were bandied across the table.

Clifford Boyleston said that all the wit and wisdom he heard passed over his head like water over a duck's back. He had given up trying to understand and now only made a semblance of listening. But Harry Oakland, the versatile critic, said that Albert was taking it all in; he found it all too, too marvellous, and with his poor, muddled brain he was trying desperately to make head or tail of the wonderful things he heard. Of course in the City he must boast of the distinguished persons he knew, perhaps there he was a light of learning and letters, an authority on the ideal; it would be perfectly divine to hear what he made of it all. Harry Oakland was one of Mrs Albert Forrester's staunchest admirers, and had written a brilliant and subtle essay on her style. With his refined and even beautiful features he looked like a San Sebastian who had had an accident with a hair-restorer; for he was uncommonly hirsute. He was a very young man, not thirty, but he had been in turn a dramatic critic, and a critic of fiction, a musical critic, and a critic of painting. But he was getting a little tired of art and threatened to devote his talents in future to the criticism of sport.

Albert, I should explain, was in the City and it was a misfortune that Mrs Forrester's friends thought she bore with meritorious fortitude that he was not even rich. There would have been something romantic in it if he had been a merchant prince who held the fate of nations in his hand or sent argosies, laden with rare spices, to those ports of the Levant the names of which have provided many a poet with so rich and rare a rhyme. But Albert was only a currant merchant and was supposed to make no more than just enabled Mrs Albert Forrester to conduct her life with distinction and even with liberality. Since his occupation kept him in his office till six o'clock he never managed to get to Mrs

Albert Forrester's Tuesdays till the most important visitors were gone. By the time he arrived, there were seldom more than three or four of her more intimate friends in the drawing-room, discussing with freedom and humour the guests who had departed, and when they heard Albert's key in the front door they realized with one accord that it was late. In a moment he opened the door in his hesitating way and looked mildly in. Mrs Albert Forrester greeted him with a bright smile.

'Come in, Albert, come in. I think you know everybody here.'
Albert entered and shook hands with his wife's friends.

'Have you just come from the City?' she asked eagerly, though she knew there was nowhere else he could have come from. 'Would you like a cup of tea?'

'No, thank you, my dear. I had tea in my office.'

Mrs Albert Forrester smiled still more brightly and the rest of the company thought she was perfectly wonderful with him.

'Ah, but I know you like a second cup. I will pour it out for you myself.'

She went to the tea-table and, forgetting that the tea had been stewing for an hour and a half and was stone cold, poured him out a cup and added milk and sugar. Albert took it with a word of thanks, and meekly stirred it, but when Mrs Forrester resumed the conversation which his appearance had interrupted, without tasting it put it quietly down. His arrival was the signal for the party finally to break up, and one by one the remaining guests took their departure. On one occasion, however, the conversation was so absorbing and the point at issue so important that Mrs Albert Forrester would not hear of their going.

'It must be settled once for all. And after all,' she remarked in a manner that for her was almost arch, 'this is a matter on which Albert may have something to say. Let us have the benefit of his opinion.'

It was when women were beginning to cut their hair and the subject of discussion was whether Mrs Albert Forrester should or should not shingle. Mrs Albert Forrester was a woman of authoritative presence. She was large-boned and her bones were well covered; had she not been so tall and strong it might have suggested itself to you that she was corpulent. But she carried her weight gallantly. Her features were a little larger than life-size and it was this that gave her face doubtless the look of virile intellectuality that it certainly possessed. Her skin was dark and you might have thought that she had in her veins some trace of Levantine blood: she admitted that she could not but think there was in her a gypsy strain and that would account, she felt, for the wild and lawless passion that sometimes characterized her poetry. Her eyes were large and black and bright, her nose like the great Duke of Wellington's, but more fleshy, and her chin square and determined. She had a big mouth, with full red lips, which owed nothing to cosmetics, for of these Mrs Albert Forrester had never deigned to make use; and her hair, thick, solid, and grey, was piled on the top of her head in such a manner as to increase her already commanding height. She was in appearance an imposing, not to say an alarming, female.

She was always very suitably dressed in rich materials of sombre hue and she looked every inch a women of letters; but in her discreet way (being after all human and susceptible to vanity) she followed the fashions and the cut of her gowns was modish. I think for some time she had hankered to shingle her hair, but she thought it more becoming to do it at the solicitation of her friends than on her own initiative.

'Oh, you must, you must,' said Harry Oakland, in his eager, boyish way. 'You'd look too, too wonderful.'

Clifford Boyleston, who was now writing a book on Madame de Maintenon, was doubtful. He thought it a dangerous experiment.

'I think,' he said, wiping his eye-glasses with a cambric handkerchief, 'I think when one has made a type one should stick to it. What would Louis XIV have been without his wig?'

'I'm hesitating,' said Mrs Forrester. 'After all, we must move with the times. I am of my day and I do not wish to lag behind. America, as Wilhelm Meister said, is here and now.' She turned brightly to Albert. 'What does my lord and master say about it? What is your opinion, Albert? To shingle or not to shingle, that is the question.'

'I'm afraid my opinion is not of great importance, my dear,' he answered mildly.

'To me it is of the greatest importance,' answered Mrs Albert Forrester, flatteringly.

She could not but see how beautifully her friends thought she treated The Philatelist.

'I insist,' she proceeded, 'I insist. No one knows me as you do, Albert. Will it suit me?'

'It might,' he answered. 'My only fear is that with your – statuesque appearance short hair would perhaps suggest – well, shall we say, the Isle of Greece where burning Sappho loved and sung.'

There was a moment's embarrassed pause. Rose Waterford smothered a giggle, but the others preserved a stony silence. Mrs

Forrester's smile froze on her lips. Albert had dropped a brick.

'I always thought Byron a very mediocre poet,' said Mrs Albert Forrester at last.

The company broke up. Mrs Albert Forrester did not shingle, nor indeed was the matter ever again referred to.

It was towards the end of another of Mrs Albert Forrester's Tuesdays that the event occurred that had so great an influence on her literary career.

It had been one of her most successful parties. The leader of the Labour Party had been there and Mrs Albert Forrester had gone as far as she could without definitely committing herself to intimate to him that she was prepared to throw in her lot with Labour. The time was ripe and if she was ever to adopt a political career she must come to a decision. A member of the French Academy had been brought by Clifford Boyleston and, though she knew he was wholly unacquainted with English, it had gratified her to receive his affable compliment on her ornate and yet pellucid style. The American Ambassador had been there and a young Russian prince whose authentic Romanoff blood alone prevented him from looking a gigolo. A duchess who had recently divorced her duke and married a jockey had been very gracious; and her strawberry leaves, albeit sere and yellow, undoubtedly added tone to the assembly. There had been quite a galaxy of literary lights. But now all, all were gone but Clifford Boyleston, Harry Oakland, Rose Waterford, Oscar Charles, and Simmons. Oscar Charles was a little, gnome-like creature, young but with the wizened face of a cunning monkey, with gold spectacles, who earned his living in a government office but spent his leisure in the pursuit of literature. He wrote little articles for the sixpenny weeklies and had a spirited contempt for the world in general. Mrs Albert Forrester liked him, thinking he had talent, but though he always expressed the keenest admiration for her style (it was indeed he who had named her the mistress of the semicolon), his acerbity was so general that she also somewhat feared him. Simmons was her agent; a round-faced man who wore glasses so strong that his eyes behind them looked strange and misshapen. They reminded you of the eyes of some uncouth crustacean that you had seen in an aquarium. He came regularly to Mrs Albert Forrester's parties, partly because he had the greatest admiration for her genius and partly because it was convenient for him to meet prospective clients in her drawing-room.

Mrs Albert Forrester, for whom he had long laboured with but a trifling recompense, was not sorry to put him in the way of earning an honest penny, and she took care to introduce him, with warm expressions of gratitude, to anyone who might be supposed to have literary wares to sell. It was not without pride that she remembered that the notorious and vastly lucrative memoirs of Lady St Swithin had been first mooted in her drawing-room.

They sat in a circle of which Mrs Albert Forrester was the centre and discussed brightly and, it must be confessed, some-what maliciously the various persons who had been that day present. Miss Warren, the pallid female who had stood for two hours at the tea-table, was walking silently round the room collecting cups that had been left here and there. She had some vague employment, but was always able to get off in order to pour out tea for Mrs Albert Forrester, and in the evening she typed Mrs Albert Forrester's manuscripts. Mrs Albert Forrester did not pay her for this, thinking quite rightly that as it was she did a great deal for the poor thing; but she gave her the seats for the cinema that were sent her for nothing and often presented her with articles of clothing for which she had no further use.

Mrs Albert Forrester in her rather deep, full voice was talking in a steady flow and the rest were listening to her with attention. She was in good form and the words that poured from her lips could have gone straight down on paper without alteration. Suddenly there was a noise in the passage as though something heavy had fallen and then the sound of an altercation.

Mrs Albert Forrester stopped and a slight frown darkened her really noble brow.

'I should have thought they knew by now that I will not have this devastating racket in the flat. Would you mind ringing the bell, Miss Warren, and asking what is the reason of this tumult?'

Miss Warren rang the bell and in a moment the maid appeared. Miss Warren at the door, in order not to interrupt Mrs Albert Forrester, spoke to her in undertones. But Mrs Albert Forrester somewhat irritably interrupted herself.

'Well, Carter, what is it? Is the house falling down or has the Red Revolution at last broken out?'

'If you please, ma'am, it's the new cook's box,' answered the maid. 'The porter dropped it as he was bringing it in and the cook got all upset about it.'

'What do you mean by "the new cook"?'

'Mrs Bulfinch went away this afternoon, ma'am,' said the maid.

Mrs Albert Forrester stared at her.

'This is the first I've heard of it. Had Mrs Bulfinch given

136

notice? The moment Mr Forrester comes in tell him that I wish to speak to him.'

'Very good, ma'am.'

The maid went out and Miss Warren slowly returned to the tea-table. Mechanically, though nobody wanted them, she poured out several cups of tea.

'What a catastrophe!' cried Miss Waterford.

'You must get her back,' said Clifford Boyleston. 'She's a treasure, that woman, a remarkable cook, and she gets better and better every day.'

But at that moment the maid came in again with a letter on a small plated salver and handed it to her mistress.

'What is this?' said Mrs Albert Forrester.

'Mr Forrester said I was to give you this letter when you asked for him, ma'am,' said the maid.

'Where is Mr Forrester then?'

'Mr Forrester's gone, ma'am,' answered the maid as though the question surprised her.

'Gone? That'll do. You can go.'

The maid left the room and Mrs Albert Forrester, with a look of perplexity on her large face, opened the letter. Rose Waterford has told me that her first thought was that Albert, fearful of his wife's displeasure at the departure of Mrs Bulfinch, had thrown himself in the Thames. Mrs Albert Forrester read the letter and a look of consternation crossed her face.

'Oh, monstrous,' she cried. 'Monstrous! Monstrous!'

'What is it, Mrs Forrester?'

Mrs Albert Forrester pawed the carpet with her foot like a restive, high-spirited horse pawing the ground, and crossing her arms with a gesture that is indescribable (but that you sometimes see in a fishwife who is going to make the very devil of a scene) bent her looks upon her curious and excessively startled friends.

'Albert has eloped with the cook.'

There was a gasp of dismay. Then something terrible happened. Miss Warren, who was standing behind the tea-table, suddenly choked. Miss Warren, who never opened her mouth and whom no one ever spoke to, Miss Warren, whom not one of them, though he had seen her every week for three years, would have recognized in the street, Miss Warren suddenly burst into uncontrollable laughter. With one accord, aghast, they turned and stared at her. They felt as Balaam must have felt when his ass broke into speech. She positively shrieked with laughter. There was a nameless horror about the sight, as though something had on a sudden gone wrong with a natural phenomenon, and you

were just as startled as though the chairs and tables without
warning began to skip about the floor in an antic dance. Miss
Warren tried to contain herself, but the more she tried the more
pitilessly the laughter shook her, and seizing a handkerchief she
stuffed it in her mouth and hurried from the room. The door
slammed behind her.

'Hysteria,' said Clifford Boyleston.

'Pure hysteria, of course,' said Harry Oakland.

But Mrs Albert Forrester said nothing.

The letter had dropped at her feet and Simmons, the agent,
picked it up and handed it to her. She would not take it.

'Read it,' she said. 'Read it aloud.'

Mr Simmons pushed his spectacles up on his forehead and
holding the letter very close to his eyes read as follows:

My Dear –

Mrs Bulfinch is in need of a change and has decided to leave, and as
I do not feel inclined to stay on here without her I am going too. I have
had all the literature I can stand and I am fed up with art.

Mrs Bulfinch does not care about marriage, but if you care to divorce
me she is willing to marry me. I hope you will find the new cook
satisfactory. She has excellent references. It may save you trouble if I
inform you that Mrs Bulfinch and I are living at 411 Kennington
Road, S.E.

Albert

No one spoke. Mr Simmons slipped his spectacles back on to
the bridge of his nose. The fact was that none of them, brilliant
as they were and accustomed to find topics of conversation to suit
every occasion, could think of an appropriate remark. Mrs Albert
Forrester was not the kind of woman to whom you could offer
condolences and each was too much afraid of the other's ridicule
to venture upon the obvious. At last Clifford Boyleston came
bravely to the rescue.

'One doesn't know what to say,' he observed.

There was another silence and then Rose Waterford spoke.

'What does Mrs Bulfinch look like?' she asked.

'How should I know?' answered Mrs Albert Forrester, somewhat peevishly. 'I never looked at her. Albert always engaged
the servants, she just came in for a moment so that I could see if
her aura was satisfactory.'

'But you must have seen her every morning when you did the
housekeeping.'

'Albert did the housekeeping. It was his own wish, so that I
might be free to devote myself to my work. In this life one has to
limit oneself.'

'Did Albert order your luncheons?' asked Clifford Boyleston.

'Naturally. It was his province.'

Clifford Boyleston slightly raised his eyebrows. What a fool he had been never to guess that it was Albert who was responsible for Mrs Forrester's beautiful food! And of course it was owing to him that the excellent Chablis was always just sufficiently chilled to run coolly over the tongue, but never so cold as to lose its bouquet and its savour.

'He certainly knew good food and good wine.'

'I always told you he had his points,' answered Mrs Albert Forrester, as though he were reproaching her. 'You all laughed at him. You would not believe me when I told you that I owed a great deal to him.'

There was no answer to this and once more silence, heavy and ominous, fell on the party. Suddenly Mr Simmons flung a bombshell.

'You must get him back.'

So great was her surprise that if Mrs Albert Forrester had not been standing against the chimney-piece she would undoubtedly have staggered two paces to the rear.

'What on earth do you mean?' she cried. 'I will never see him again as long as I live. Take him back? Never. Not even if he came and begged me on his bended knees.'

'I didn't say take him back; I said, get him back.'

But Mrs Albert Forrester paid no attention to the misplaced interruption.

'I have done everything for him. What would he be without me? I ask you. I have given him a position which never in his remotest dreams could he have aspired to.'

None could deny that there was something magnificent in the indignation of Mrs Albert Forrester, but it appeared to have little effect on Mr Simmons.

'What are you going to live on?'

Mrs Albert Forrester flung him a glance totally devoid of amiability.

'God will provide,' she answered in freezing tones.

'I think it very unlikely,' he returned.

Mrs Albert Forrester shrugged her shoulders. She wore an outraged expression. But Mr Simmons made himself as comfortable as he could on his chair and lit a cigarette.

'You know you have no warmer admirer of your art than me,' he said.

'Than I,' corrected Clifford Boyleston.

'Or than you,' went on Mr Simmons blandly. 'We all agree

that there is no one writing now whom you need fear comparison with. Both in prose and verse you are absolutely first class. And your style – well, everyone knows your style.'

'The opulence of Sir Thomas Browne with the limpidity of Cardinal Newman,' said Clifford Boyleston. 'The raciness of John Dryden with the precision of Jonathan Swift.'

The only sign that Mrs Albert Forrester heard was the smile that hesitated for a brief moment at the corners of her tragic mouth.

'And you have humour.'

'Is there anyone in the world,' cried Miss Waterford, 'who can put such a wealth of wit and satire and comic observation into a semi-colon?'

'But the fact remains that you don't sell,' pursued Mr Simmons imperturbably. 'I've handled your work for twenty years and I tell you frankly that I shouldn't have grown fat on my commission, but I've handled it because now and again I like to do what I can for good work. I've always believed in you and I've hoped that sooner or later we might get the public to swallow you. But if you think you can make your living by writing the sort of stuff you do I'm bound to tell you that you haven't a chance.'

'I have come into the world too late,' said Mrs Albert Forrester. 'I should have lived in the eighteenth century when the wealthy patron rewarded a dedication with a hundred guineas.'

'What do you suppose the currant business brings in?'

Mrs Albert Forrester gave a little sigh.

'A pittance. Albert always told me he made about twelve hundred a year.'

'He must be a very good manager. But you couldn't expect him on that income to allow you very much. Take my word for it, there's only one thing for you to do and that's to get him back.'

'I would rather live in a garret. Do you think I'm going to submit to the affront he has put upon me? Would you have me battle for his affections with my cook? Do not forget that there is one thing which is more valuable to a woman like me than her ease and that is her dignity.'

'I was just coming to that,' said Mr Simmons coldly.

He glanced at the others and those strange, lopsided eyes of his looked more than ever monstrous and fish-like.

'There is no doubt in my mind,' he went on, 'that you have a very distinguished and almost unique position in the world of letters. You stand for something quite apart. You never prostituted your genius for filthy lucre and you have held high the banner of pure art. You're thinking of going into Parliament. I don't think much of politics myself, but there's no denying that it would be a good advertisement and if you get in I daresay we could get you a lecture tour in America on the strength of it. You have ideals and this I can say, that even the people who've never read a word you've written respect you. But in your position there's one thing you can't afford to be and that's a joke.'

Mrs Albert Forrester gave a distinct start.

'What on earth do you mean by that?'

'I know nothing about Mrs Bulfinch and for all I know she's a very respectable woman, but the fact remains that a man doesn't run away with his cook without making his wife ridiculous. If it had been a dancer or a lady of title I daresay it wouldn't have done you any harm, but a cook would finish you. In a week you'd have all London laughing at you, and if there's one thing that kills an author or a politician it is ridicule. You must get your husband back and you must get him back pretty damned quick.'

A dark flush settled on Mrs Albert Forrester's face, but she did not immediately reply. In her ears there rang on a sudden the outrageous and unaccountable laughter that had sent Miss Warren flying from the room.

'We're all friends here and you can count on our discretion.'

Mrs Forrester looked at her friends and she thought that in Rose Waterford's eyes there was already a malicious gleam. On the wizened face of Oscar Charles was a whimsical look. She wished that in a moment of abandon she had not betrayed her secret. Mr Simmons, however, knew the literary world and allowed his eyes to rest on the company.

'After all you are the centre and head of their set. Your husband has not only run away from you but also from them. It's not too good for them either. The fact is that Albert Forrester has made you all look a lot of damned fools.'

'All,' said Clifford Boyleston. 'We're all in the same boat. He's quite right, Mrs Forrester, The Philatelist must come back.'

'*Et tu, Brute.*'

Mr Simmons did not understand Latin and if he had would probably not have been moved by Mrs Albert Forrester's exclamation. He cleared his throat.

'My suggestion is that Mrs Albert Forrester should go and see him tomorrow, fortunately we have his address, and beg him to reconsider his decision. I don't know what sort of things a woman says on these occasions, but Mrs Forrester has tact and imagination and she must say them. If Mr Forrester makes any conditions she must accept them. She must leave no stone unturned.'

'If you play your cards well there is no reason why you shouldn't bring him back here with you tomorrow evening,' said Rose Waterford lightly.

'Will you do it, Mrs Forrester?'

For two minutes, at least, turned away from them, she stared at the empty fireplace; then, drawing herself to her full height, she faced them.

'For my art's sake, not for mine. I will not allow the ribald laughter of the Philistine to besmirch all that I hold good and true and beautiful.'

'Capital,' said Mr Simmons, rising to his feet. 'I'll look in on my way home tomorrow and I hope to find you and Mr Forrester billing and cooing side by side like a pair of turtle-doves.'

He took his leave, and the others, anxious not to be left alone with Mrs Albert Forrester and her agitation, in a body followed his example.

It was latish in the afternoon next day when Mrs Albert Forrester, imposing in black silk and a velvet toque, set out from her flat in order to get a bus from the Marble Arch that would take her to Victoria Station. Mr Simmons had explained to her by telephone how to reach the Kennington Road with expedition and economy. She neither felt nor looked like Delilah. At Victoria she took the tram that runs down the Vauxhall Bridge Road. When she crossed the river she found herself in a part of London more noisy, sordid, and bustling than that to which she was accustomed, but she was too much occupied with her thoughts to notice the varied scene. She was relieved to find that the tram went along the Kennington Road and asked the conductor to put her down a few doors from the house she sought. When it did and rumbled on leaving her alone in the busy street, she felt strangely lost, like a traveller in an eastern tale set down by a djinn in an unknown city. She walked slowly, looking to right and left, and notwithstanding the emotions of indignation and embarrassment that fought for the possession of her somewhat opulent bosom, she could not but reflect that here was the material for a very pretty piece of prose. The little houses held about them the feeling of a bygone age when here it was still almost country, and Mrs Albert Forrester registered in her retentive memory a note that she must look into the literary associations of the Kennington Road. Number four hundred and eleven was one of a row of shabby houses that stood some way back from the street; in front of it was a narrow strip of shabby grass, and a paved way led up to a latticed wooden porch that badly needed a coat of paint. This and the straggling, stunted creeper that grew over the front of the house gave it a falsely rural air which was strange and even sinister in that road down which thundered a tumultuous traffic. There was something equivocal about the house that suggested that here lived women to whom a life of pleasure had brought an inadequate reward.

The door was opened by a scraggy girl of fifteen with long legs and a tousled head.

'Does Mrs Bulfinch live here, do you know?'

'You've rung the wrong bell. Second floor.' The girl pointed to the stairs and at the same time screamed shrilly: 'Mrs Bulfinch, a party to see you. Mrs Bulfinch.'

Mrs Albert Forrester walked up the dingy stairs. They were covered with torn carpet. She walked slowly, for she did not wish to get out of breath. A door opened as she reached the second floor and she recognized her cook.

'Good afternoon, Bulfinch,' said Mrs Albert Forrester, with dignity. 'I wish to see your master.'

Mrs Bulfinch hesitated for the shadow of a second, then held the door wide open.

'Come in, ma'am.' She turned her head. 'Albert, here's Mrs Forrester to see you.'

Mrs Forrester stepped by quickly and there was Albert sitting by the fire in a leather-covered, but rather shabby, arm-chair, with his feet in slippers, and in shirt-sleeves. He was reading the evening paper and smoking a cigar. He rose to his feet as Mrs Albert Forrester came in. Mrs Bulfinch followed her visitor into the room and closed the door.

'How are you, my dear?' said Albert cheerfully. 'Keeping well, I hope.'

'You'd better put on your coat, Albert,' said Mrs Bulfinch. 'What *will* Mrs Forrester think of you, finding you like that? I never.'

She took the coat, which was hanging on a peg, and helped him into it; and like a woman familiar with the peculiarities of masculine dress pulled down his waistcoat so that it should not ride over his collar.

'I received your letter, Albert,' said Mrs Forrester.

'I supposed you had, or you wouldn't have known my address, would you?'

'Won't you sit down, ma'am?' said Mrs Bulfinch, deftly dusting a chair, part of a suite covered in plum-coloured velvet, and pushing it forwards.

Mrs Albert Forrester with a slight bow seated herself.

'I should have preferred to see you alone, Albert,' she said. His eyes twinkled.

'Since anything you have to say concerns Mrs Bulfinch as much as it concerns me I think it much better that she should be present.'

'As you wish.'

Mrs Bulfinch drew up a chair and sat down. Mrs Albert Forrester had never seen her but with a large apron over a print dress. She was wearing now an open-work blouse of white silk, a black skirt, and high-heeled, patent-leather shoes with silver buckles. She was a woman of about five-and-forty, with reddish hair and a reddish face, not pretty, but with a good-natured look, and buxom. She reminded Mrs Albert Forrester of a serving-wench, somewhat overblown, in a jolly picture by an old Dutch master.

'Well, my dear, what have you to say to me?' asked Albert.

Mrs Albert Forrester gave him her brightest and most affable smile. Her great black eyes shone with tolerant good-humour.

'Of course you know that this is perfectly absurd, Albert. I think you must be out of your mind.'

'Do you, my dear? Fancy that.'

'I'm not angry with you, I'm only amused, but a joke's a joke and should not be carried too far. I've come to take you home.'

'Was my letter not quite clear?'

'Perfectly. I ask no questions and I will make no reproaches. We will look upon this as a momentary aberration and say no more about it.'

'Nothing will induce me ever to live with you again, my dear,' said Albert in, however, a perfectly friendly fashion.

'You're not serious?'

'Quite.'

'Do you love this woman?'

Mrs Albert Forrester still smiled with an eager and somewhat metallic brightness. She was determined to take the matter lightly. With her intimate sense of values she realized that the scene was comic. Albert looked at Mrs Bulfinch and a smile broke out on his withered face.

'We get on very well together, don't we, old girl?'

'Not so bad,' said Mrs Bulfinch.

Mrs Albert Forrester raised her eyebrows; her husband had never in all their married life called *her* 'old girl': nor indeed would she have wished it.

'If Bulfinch has any regard or respect for you she must know that the thing is impossible. After the life you've led and the society you've moved in she can hardly expect to make you permanently happy in miserable furnished lodgings.'

'They're not furnished lodgings, ma'am,' said Mrs Bulfinch. 'It's all me own furniture. You see, I'm very independent-like and I've always liked to have a home of me own. So I keep these rooms on whether I'm in a situation or whether I'm not, and so I always have some place to go back to.'

'And a very nice cosy little place it is,' said Albert.

Mrs Albert Forrester looked about her. There was a kitchen range in the fireplace on which a kettle was simmering and on the mantelshelf was a black marble clock flanked by black marble candelabra. There was a large table covered with a red cloth, a dresser, and a sewing-machine. On the walls were photographs and framed pictures from Christmas supplements. A door at the back, covered with a red plush portière, led into what, considering the size of the house, Mrs Albert Forrester (who in her leisure moments had made a somewhat extensive study of architecture) could not but conclude was the only bedroom. Mrs Bulfinch and Albert lived in a contiguity that allowed no doubt about their relations.

'Have you not been happy with me, Albert?' asked Mrs Forrester in a deeper tone.

'We've been married for thirty-five years, my dear. It's too long. It's a great deal too long. You're a good woman in your way, but you don't suit me. You're literary and I'm not. You're artistic and I'm not.'

'I've always taken care to make you share in all my interests. I've taken great pains that you shouldn't be overshadowed by my success. You can't say that I've ever left you out of things.'

'You're a wonderful writer, I don't deny it for a moment, but the truth is I don't like the books you write.'

'That, if I may be permitted to say so, merely shows that you have very bad taste. All the best critics admit their power and their charm.'

'And I don't like your friends. Let me tell you a secret, my dear. Often at your parties I've had an almost irresistible impulse to take off all my clothes just to see what would happen.'

'Nothing would have happened,' said Mrs Albert Forrester with a slight frown. 'I should merely have sent for the doctor.'

'Besides you haven't the figure for that, Albert,' said Mrs Bulfinch.

Mr Simmons had hinted to Mrs Albert Forrester that if the need arose she must not hesitate to use the allurements of her sex in order to bring back her erring husband to the conjugal roof, but she did not in the least know how to do this. It would have been easier, she could not but reflect, had she been in evening dress.

'Does the fidelity of five-and-thirty years count for nothing? I have never looked at another man, Albert. I'm used to you. I shall be lost without you.'

'I've left all my menus with the new cook, ma'am. You've only got to tell her how many to luncheon and she'll manage,' said Mrs Bulfinch. 'She's very reliable and she has as light a hand with pastry as anyone I ever knew.'

Mrs Albert Forrester began to be discouraged. Mrs Bulfinch's remark, well-meant no doubt, made it difficult to bring the conversation on to the plane on which emotion could be natural.

'I'm afraid you're only wasting your time, my dear,' said Albert. 'My decision is irrevocable. I'm not very young any more and I want someone to take care of me. I shall of course make you as good an allowance as I can. Corinne wants me to retire.'

'Who is Corinne?' asked Mrs Forrester with the utmost surprise.

'It's my name,' said Mrs Bulfinch. 'My mother was half French.'

'That explains a great deal,' replied Mrs Forrester, pursing her lips, for though she admired the literature of our neighbours she knew that their morals left much to be desired.

'What I say is, Albert's worked long enough, and it's about time he started enjoying himself. I've got a little bit of property at Clacton-on-Sea. It's a very healthy neighbourhood and the air is wonderful. We could live there very comfortable. And what with the beach and the pier there's always something to do. They're a very nice lot of people down there. If you don't interfere with nobody, nobody'll interfere with you.'

'I discussed the matter with my partners today and they're willing to buy me out. It means a certain sacrifice. When everything is settled I shall have an income of nine hundred pounds a year. There are three of us, so it gives us just three hundred a year apiece.'

'How am I to live on that?' cried Mrs Albert Forrester. 'I have my position to keep up.'

'You have a fluent, a fertile, and a distinguished pen, my dear.'

Mrs Albert Forrester impatiently shrugged her shoulders.

'You know very well that my books don't bring me in anything but reputation. The publishers always say that they lose by them and in fact they only publish them because it gives them prestige.'

It was then that Mrs Bulfinch had the idea that was to have consequences of such magnitude.

'Why don't you write a good thrilling detective story?' she asked.

'Me?' exclaimed Mrs Albert Forrester, for the first time in her life regardless of grammar.

'It's not a bad idea,' said Albert. 'It's not a bad idea at all.'

'I should have the critics down on me like a thousand bricks.'

'I'm not so sure of that. Give the highbrow the chance of being lowbrow without demeaning himself and he'll be so grateful to you, he won't know what to do.'

'For this relief much thanks,' murmured Mrs Albert Forrester reflectively.

'My dear, the critics'll eat it. And written in your beautiful English they won't be afraid to call it a masterpiece.'

'The idea is preposterous. It's absolutely foreign to my genius. I could never hope to please the masses.'

'Why not? The masses want to read good stuff, but they dislike being bored. They all know your name, but they don't read you, because you bore them. The fact is, my dear, you're dull.'

'I don't know how you can say that, Albert,' replied Mrs Albert Forrester, with as little resentment as the equator might feel if someone called it chilly. 'Everyone knows and acknowledges that I have an exquisite sense of humour and there is nobody who can extract so much good wholesome fun from a semi-colon as I can.'

'If you can give the masses a good thrilling story and let them think at the same time that they are improving their minds you'll make a fortune.'

'I've never read a detective story in my life,' said Mrs Albert Forrester. 'I once heard of a Mr Barnes of New York and I was told that he had written a book called *The Mystery of a Hansom Cab*. But I never read it.'

'Of course you have to have the knack,' said Mrs Bulfinch. 'The first thing to remember is that you don't want any love-making, it's out of place in a detective story, what you want is murder, and sleuth-hounds, and you don't want to be able to guess who done it till the last page.'

'But you must play fair with your reader, my dear,' said Albert. 'It always annoys me when suspicion has been thrown on the secretary or the lady of title and it turns out to be the second foot-man who's never done more than say, "The carriage is at the door." Puzzle your reader as much as you can, but don't make a fool of him.'

'I love a good detective story,' said Mrs Bulfinch. 'Give me a lady in evening dress, just streaming with diamonds, lying on the library floor with a dagger in her heart, and I know I'm going to have a treat.'

'There's no accounting for tastes,' said Albert. 'Personally, I prefer a respectable family solicitor, with side-whiskers, gold watch-chain, and a benign appearance, lying dead in Hyde Park.'

'With his throat cut?' asked Mrs Bulfinch eagerly.

'No, stabbed in the back. There's something peculiarly attractive to the reader in the murder of a middle-aged gentleman of spotless reputation. It is pleasant to think that the most apparently blameless of us have a mystery in our lives.'

'I see what you mean, Albert,' said Mrs Bulfinch. 'He was the repository of a fatal secret.'

'We can give you all the tips, my dear,' said Albert, smiling mildly at Mrs Albert Forrester. 'I've read hundreds of detective stories.'

'You!'

'That's what first brought Corinne and me together. I used to pass them on to her when I'd finished them.'

'Many's the time I've heard him switch off the electric light as the dawn was creeping through the window and I couldn't help smiling to myself as I said: "There, he's finished it at last, now he can have a good sleep."'

Mrs Albert Forrester rose to her feet. She drew herself up.

'Now I see what a gulf separates us,' she said, and her fine contralto shook a little. 'You have been surrounded for thirty years with all that was best in English literature and you read hundreds of detective novels.'

'Hundreds and hundreds,' interrupted Albert with a smile of satisfaction.

'I came here willing to make any reasonable concession so that you should come back to your home, but now I wish it no longer. You have shown me that we have nothing in common and never had. There is an abyss between us.'

'Very well, my dear,' said Albert gently, 'I will submit to your decision. But you think over the detective story.'

'I will arise and go now,' she murmured, 'and go to Innisfree.'

'I'll just show you downstairs,' said Mrs Bulfinch. 'One has to be careful of the carpet if one doesn't exactly know where the holes are.'

With dignity, but not without circumspection, Mrs Albert Forrester walked downstairs and when Mrs Bulfinch opened the door and asked her if she would like a taxi she shook her head.

'I shall take the tram.'

'You need not be afraid that I won't take good care of Mr Forrester, ma'am,' said Mrs Bulfinch pleasantly. 'He shall have every comfort. I nursed Mr Bulfinch for three years during his last illness and there's very little I don't know about invalids. Not that

Mr Forrester isn't very strong and active for his years. And of course he'll have a hobby. I always think a man should have a hobby. He's going to collect postage-stamps.'

Mrs Albert Forrester gave a little start of surprise. But just then a tram came in sight and, as a woman (even the greatest of them) will, she hurried at the risk of her life into the middle of the road and waved frantically. It stopped and she climbed in. She did not know how she was going to face Mr Simmons. He would be waiting for her when she got home. Clifford Boyleston would probably be there too. They would all be there and she would have to tell them that she had miserably failed. At that moment she had no warm feeling of friendship for her little group of devoted admirers. Wondering what the time was, she looked up at the man sitting opposite her to see whether he was the kind of person she could modestly ask, and suddenly started; for sitting there was a middle-aged gentleman of the most respectable appearance, with side-whiskers, a benign expression, and a gold watch-chain. It was the very man whom Albert had described lying dead in Hyde Park and she could not but jump to the conclusion that he was a family solicitor. The coincidence was extraordinary and really it looked as though the hand of fate were beckoning to her. He wore a silk hat, a black coat, and pepper-and-salt trousers, he was somewhat corpulent, of a powerful build, and by his side was a despatch-case. When the tram was half-way down the Vauxhall Bridge Road he asked the conductor to stop and she saw him go down a small, mean street. Why? Ah, why? When it reached Victoria, so deeply immersed in thought was she, until the conductor somewhat roughly told her where she was, she did not move. Edgar Allan Poe had written detective stories. She took a bus. She sat inside, buried in reflection, but when it arrived at Hyde Park Corner she suddenly made up her mind to get out. She couldn't sit still any longer. She felt she must walk. She entered the gates, walking slowly, and looked about her with an air that was at once intent and abstracted. Yes, there was Edgar Allan Poe; no one could deny that. After all he had invented the genre, and everyone knew how great his influence had been on the Parnassians. Or was it the Symbolists? Never mind. Baudelaire and all that. As she passed the Achilles Statue she stopped for a minute and looked at it with raised eyebrows.

At length she reached her flat and opening the door saw several hats in the hall. They were all there. She went into the drawing-room.

'Here she is at last,' cried Miss Waterford.

Mrs Albert Forrester advanced, smiling with animation, and

shook the proffered hands. Mr Simmons and Clifford Boyleston were there, Harry Oakland and Oscar Charles.

'Oh, you poor things, have you had no tea?' she cried brightly. 'I haven't an idea what the time is, but I know I'm fearfully late.'

'Well?' they said. 'Well?'

'My dears, I've got something quite wonderful to tell you. I've had an inspiration. Why should the devil have all the best tunes?'

'What *do* you mean?'

She paused in order to give full effect to the surprise she was going to spring upon them. Then she flung it at them without preamble.

'I'M GOING TO WRITE A DETECTIVE STORY.'

They stared at her with open mouths. She held up her hand to prevent them from interrupting her, but indeed no one had the smallest intention of doing so.

'I am going to raise the detective story to the dignity of Art. It came to me suddenly in Hyde Park. It's a murder story and I shall give the solution on the very last page. I shall write it in an impeccable English, and since it's occurred to me lately that perhaps I've exhausted the possibilities of the semi-colon, I am going to take up the colon. No one yet has explored its potentialities. Humour and mystery are what I aim at. I shall call it *The Achilles Statue*.'

'What a title!' cried Mr Simmons, recovering himself before any of the others. 'I can sell the serial rights on the title and your name alone.'

'But what about Albert?' asked Clifford Boyleston.

'Albert?' echoed Mrs Forrester. 'Albert?'

She looked at him as though for the life of her she could not think what he was talking about. Then she gave a little cry as if she had suddenly remembered.

'Albert! I knew I'd gone out on some errand and it absolutely slipped my memory. I was walking through Hyde Park and I had this inspiration. What a fool you'll all think me!'

'Then you haven't seen Albert?'

'My dear, I forgot all about him.' She gave an amused laugh. 'Let Albert keep his cook. I can't bother about Albert now. Albert belongs to the semi-colon period. I am going to write a detective story.'

'My dear, you're too, too wonderful,' said Harry Oakland.

VIRTUE

THERE are few things better than a good Havana. When I was young and very poor and smoked a cigar only when somebody gave me one, I determined that if ever I had money I would smoke a cigar every day after luncheon and after dinner. This is the only resolution of my youth that I have kept. It is the only ambition I have achieved that has never been embittered by disillusion. I like a cigar that is mild, but full-flavoured, neither so small that it is finished before you have become aware of it nor so large as to be irksome, rolled so that it draws without consciousness of effort on your part, with a leaf so firm that it doesn't become messy on your lips, and in such condition that it keeps its savour to the very end. But when you have taken the last pull and put down the shapeless stump and watched the final cloud of smoke dwindle blue in the surrounding air it is impossible, if you have a sensitive nature, not to feel a certain melancholy at the thought of all the labour, the care and pains that have gone, the thought, the trouble, the complicated organization that have been required to provide you with half an hour's delight. For this men have sweltered long years under tropical suns and ships have scoured the seven seas. These reflections become more poignant still when you are eating a dozen oysters (with half a bottle of dry white wine), and they become almost unbearable when it comes to a lamb cutlet. For these are animals and there is something that inspires awe in the thought that since the surface of the earth became capable of supporting life from generation to generation for millions upon millions of years creatures have come into existence to end at last upon a plate of crushed ice or on a silver grill. It may be that a sluggish fancy cannot grasp the dreadful solemnity of eating an oyster and evolution has taught us that the bivalve has through the ages kept itself to itself in a manner that inevitably alienates sympathy. There is an aloofness in it that is offensive to the aspiring spirit of man and a self-complacency that is obnoxious to his vanity. But I do not know how anyone can look upon a lamb cutlet without thoughts too deep for tears : here man himself has taken a hand and the history of the race is bound up with the tender morsel on your plate.

And sometimes even the fate of human beings is curious to consider. It is strange to look upon this man or that, the quiet ordinary persons of every day, the bank clerk, the dustman, the middle-aged girl in the second row of the chorus, and think of the interminable history behind them and of the long, long series of hazards by which from the primeval slime the course of events has brought them at this moment to such and such a place. When such tremendous vicissitudes have been needed to get them here at all one would have thought some huge significance must be attached to them; one would have thought that what befell them must matter a little to the Life Spirit or whatever else it is that has produced them. An accident befalls them. The thread is broken. The story that began with the world is finished abruptly and it looks as though it meant nothing at all. A tale told by an idiot. And is it not odd that this event, of an importance so dramatic, may be brought about by a cause so trivial?

An incident of no moment, that might easily not have happened, has consequences that are incalculable. It looks as though blind chance ruled all things. Our smallest actions may affect profoundly the whole lives of people who have nothing to do with us. The story I have to tell would never have happened if one day I had not walked across the street. Life is really very fantastic and one has to have a peculiar sense of humour to see the fun of it.

I was strolling down Bond Street one spring morning and having nothing much to do till lunch-time thought I would look in at Sotheby's, the auction rooms, to see whether there was anything on show that interested me. There was a block in the traffic and I threaded my way through the cars. When I reached the other side I ran into a man I had known in Borneo coming out of a hatter's.

'Hullo, Morton,' I said. 'When did you come home?'

'I've been back about a week.'

He was a District Officer. The Governor had given me a letter of introduction to him and I wrote and told him I meant to spend a week at the place he lived at and should like to put up at the government rest-house. He met me on the ship when I arrived and asked me to stay with him. I demurred. I did not see how I could spend a week with a total stranger, I did not want to put him to the expense of my board, and besides I thought I should have more freedom if I were on my own. He would not listen to me.

'I've got plenty of room,' he said, 'and the rest-house is beastly. I haven't spoken to a white man for six months and I'm fed to the teeth with my own company.'

But when Morton had got me and his launch had landed us at the bungalow and he had offered me a drink he did not in the least know what to do with me. He was seized on a sudden with shyness, and his conversation, which had been fluent and ready, ran dry. I did my best to make him feel at home (it was the least I could do, considering that it was his own house) and asked him if he had any new records. He turned on the gramophone and the sound of rag-time gave him confidence.

His bungalow overlooked the river and his living-room was a large veranda. It was furnished in the impersonal fashion that characterized the dwellings of government officials who were moved here and there at little notice according to the exigencies of the service. There were native hats as ornaments on the walls and the horns of animals, blow-pipes, and spears. In the book-shelf were detective novels and old magazines. There was a cottage piano with yellow keys. It was very untidy, but not uncomfortable.

Unfortunately I cannot very well remember what he looked like. He was young, twenty-eight, I learnt later, and he had a boyish and attractive smile. I spent an agreeable week with him. We went up and down the river and we climbed a mountain. We had tiffin one day with some planters who lived twenty miles away and every evening we went to the club. The only members were the managers of a kutch factory and his assistants, but they were not on speaking terms with one another and it was only on Morton's representations that they must not let him down when he had a visitor that we could get up a rubber of bridge. The atmosphere was strained. We came back to dinner, listened to the gramophone, and went to bed. Morton had little office work and one would have thought the time hung heavy on his hands, but he had energy and high spirits; it was his first post of the sort and he was happy to be independent. His only anxiety was lest he should be transferred before he had finished a road he was building. This was the joy of his heart. It was his own idea and he had wheedled the government into giving him the money to make it; he had surveyed the country himself and traced the path. He had solved unaided the technical problems that presented themselves. Every morning, before he went to his office, he drove out in a rickety old Ford to where the coolies were working and watched the progress that had been made since the day before. He thought of nothing else. He dreamt of it at night. He reckoned that it would be finished in a year and he did not want to take his leave till then. He could not have worked with more zest if he had been a painter or a sculptor creating a work of art. I think it was this eagerness that made me take a fancy to him. I liked his zeal. I liked his ingenuousness. And I was impressed by the passion for achievement that made him indifferent to the solitariness of his life, to promotion, and even to the thought of going home. I forget how long the road was, fifteen or twenty miles, I think, and I forget what purpose it was to serve. I don't believe Morton cared very much. His passion was the artist's and his triumph was the triumph of man over nature. He learnt as he went along. He had the jungle to contend against, torrential rains that destroyed the labour of weeks, accidents of topography; he had to collect his labour and hold it together; he had inadequate funds. His imagination sustained him. His labours gained a sort of epic quality and the vicissitudes of the work were a great saga that unrolled itself with an infinity of episodes.

His only complaint was that the day was too short. He had office duties, he was judge and tax collector, father and mother (at twenty-eight) of the people in his district; he had now and then to make tours that took him away from home. Unless he was on the spot nothing was done. He would have liked to be there twenty-four hours a day driving the reluctant coolies to further effort. It so happened that shortly before I arrived an incident had occurred that filled him with jubilation. He had offered a contract to a Chinese to make a certain section of the road and the Chinese had asked more than Morton could afford to pay. Notwithstanding interminable discussions they had been unable to arrive at an agreement and Morton with rage in his heart saw his work held up. He was at his wits' end. Then going down to his office one morning, he heard that there had been a row in one of the Chinese gambling houses the night before. A coolie had been badly wounded and his assailant was under arrest. This assailant was the contractor. He was brought into court, the evidence was clear, and Morton sentenced him to eighteen months' hard labour.

'Now he'll have to build the blasted road for nothing,' said Morton, his eyes glistening when he told me the story.

We saw the fellow at work one morning, in the prison sarong, unconcerned. He was taking his misfortune in good part.

'I've told him I'll remit the rest of his sentence when the road's finished,' said Morton, 'and he's as pleased as Punch. Bit of a snip for me, eh, what?'

When I left Morton I asked him to let me know when he came to England and he promised to write to me as soon as he landed. On the spur of the moment one gives these invitations and one is perfectly sincere about them. But when one is taken at one's word a slight dismay seizes one. People are so different at home from what they are abroad. There they are easy, cordial, and natural. They have interesting things to tell you. They are immensely kind. You are anxious when your turn comes to do something in return for the hospitality you have received. But it is not easy. The persons who were so entertaining in their own surroundings are very dull in yours. They are constrained and shy. You introduce them to your friends and your friends find them a crashing bore. They do their best to be civil, but sigh with relief when the strangers go and the conversation can once more run easily in its accustomed channels. I think the residents in far places early in their careers understand the situation pretty well, as the result maybe of bitter and humiliating experiences, for I have found that they seldom take advantage of the invitation which on some outstation on the edge of the jungle has been so cordially extended to them and by them as cordially accepted. But Morton was different. He was a young man and single. It is generally the wives that are the difficulty; other women look at their drab clothes, in a glance take in their provincial air, and freeze them with their indifference. But a man can play bridge and tennis, and dance. Morton had charm. I had had no doubt that in a day or two he would find his feet.

'Why didn't you let me know you were back?' I asked him.

'I thought you wouldn't want to be bothered with me,' he smiled.

'What nonsense!'

Of course now as we stood in Bond Street on the kerb and chatted for a minute he looked strange to me. I had never seen him in anything but khaki shorts and a tennis shirt, except when we got back from the club at night and he put on a pyjama jacket and a sarong for dinner. It is as comfortable a form of evening dress as has ever been devised. He looked a bit awkward in his blue serge suit. His face against a white collar was very brown.

'How about the road?' I asked him.

'Finished. I was afraid I'd have to postpone my leave, we struck one or two snags towards the end, but I made 'em hustle and the day before I left I drove the Ford to the end and back without stopping.'

I laughed. His pleasure was charming.

'What have you been doing with yourself in London?'

'Buying clothes.'

'Been having a good time?'

'Marvellous. A bit lonely, you know, but I don't mind that. I've been to a show every night. The Palmers, you know, I think you met them in Sarawak, were going to be in town and we were going to do the play together, but they had to go to Scotland because her mother's ill.'

His words, said so breezily, cut me to the quick. His was the common experience. It was heartbreaking. For months, for long months before it was due, these people planned their leave, and when they got off the ship they were in such spirits they could hardly contain themselves. London. Shops and clubs and theatres and restaurants. London. They were going to have the time of their lives. London. It swallowed them. A strange turbulent city, not hostile but indifferent, and they were lost in it. They had no friends. They had nothing in common with the acquaintances they made. They were more lonely than in the jungle. It was a relief when at a theatre they ran across someone they had known in the East (and perhaps been bored stiff by or disliked) and they could fix up an evening together and have a good laugh and tell one another what a grand time they were having and talk of common friends and at last confide to one another a little shyly that they would not be sorry when their leave was up and they were once again in harness. They went to see their families and of course they were glad to see them, but it wasn't the same as it had been, they did feel a bit out of it, and when you came down to brass tacks the life people led in England was deadly. It was grand fun to come home, but you couldn't live there any more, and sometimes you thought of your bungalow overlooking the river and your tours of the district and what a lark it was to run over once in a blue moon to Sandakan or Kuching or Singapore.

And because I remembered what Morton had looked forward to when, the road finished and off his chest, he went on leave, I could not but feel a pang when I thought of him dining by himself in a dismal club where he knew nobody or alone in a restaurant in Soho and then going off to see a play with no one by his side with whom he could enjoy it and no one to have a drink with during the interval. And at the same time I reflected that even if I had known he was in London I could have done nothing much for him, for during the last week I had not had a moment free. That very evening I was dining with friends and going to a play, and the next day I was going abroad.

'What are you doing tonight?' I asked him.

'I'm going to the Pavilion. It's packed jammed full, but there's a fellow over the road who's wonderful and he's got me a ticket that had been returned. You can often get one seat, you know, when you can't get two.'

'Why don't you come and have supper with me? I'm taking some people to the Haymarket and we're going on to Ciro's afterwards.'

'I'd love to.'

We arranged to meet at eleven and I left him to keep an engagement.

I was afraid the friends I had asked him to meet would not amuse Morton very much, for they were distinctly middle-aged, but I could not think of anyone young that at this season of the year I should be likely to get hold of at the last moment. None of the girls I knew would thank me for asking her to supper to dance with a shy young man from Malaya. I could trust the Bishops to do their best for him, and after all it must be jollier for him to have supper in a club with a good band where he could see pretty women dancing than to go home to bed at eleven because he had nowhere else in the world to go. I had known Charlie Bishop first when I was a medical student. He was then a thin little fellow with sandy hair and blunt features; he had fine eyes, dark and gleaming, but he wore spectacles. He had a round, merry, red face. He was very fond of the girls. I suppose he had a way with him, for, with no money and no looks, he managed to pick up a succession of young persons who gratified his roving desires. He was clever and bumptious, argumentative and quick-tempered. He had a caustic tongue. Looking back, I should say he was a rather disagreeable young man, but I do not think he was a bore. Now, half-way through the fifties, he was inclined to be stout and he was very bald, but his eyes behind the gold-rimmed spectacles were still bright and alert. He was dogmatic and somewhat conceited, argumentative still and caustic, but he was good-natured and amusing. After you have known a person so long his idiosyncrasies cease to trouble you. You accept them as you accept your own physical defects. He was by profession a pathologist and now and then he sent me a slim book he had just published. It was severe and extremely technical and grimly illustrated with photographs of bacteria. I did not read it. I gathered from what I sometimes heard that Charlie's views on the subjects with which he dealt were unsound. I do not believe that he was very popular with the other members of his profession, he made no secret of the fact that he looked upon them as a set of incompetent idiots; but he had his job, it brought him in six or eight hundred a year, I think, and he was completely indifferent to other people's opinion of him.

I liked Charlie Bishop because I had known him for thirty years, but I liked Margery, his wife, because she was very nice. I was extremely surprised when he told me he was going to be married. He was hard on forty at the time and so fickle in his affections that I had made up my mind he would remain single. He was very fond of women, but he was not in the least sentimental, and his aims were loose. His views on the female sex would in these idealistic days be thought crude. He knew what he wanted and he asked for it, and if he couldn't get it for love or money he shrugged his shoulders and went his way. To be brief, he did not look to women to gratify his ideal but to provide him with fornication. It was odd that though small and plain he found so many who were prepared to grant his wishes. For his spiritual needs he found satisfaction in unicellular organisms. He had always been a man who spoke to the point, and when he told me he was going to marry a young woman called Margery Hobson I did not hesitate to ask him why. He grinned.

'Three reasons. First, she won't let me go to bed with her without. Second, she makes me laugh like a hyena. And third, she's alone in the world, without a single relation, and she must have someone to take care of her.'

'The first reason is just swank and the second is eyewash. The third is the real one and it means that she's got you by the short hairs.'

His eyes gleamed softly behind his large spectacles.

'I shouldn't be surprised if you weren't dead right.'

'She's not only got you by the short hairs but you're as pleased as Punch that she has.'

'Come and lunch tomorrow and have a look at her. She's easy on the eye.'

Charlie was a member of a cock-and-hen club which at that time I used a good deal and we arranged to lunch there. I found Margery a very attractive young woman. She was then just under thirty. She was a lady. I noticed the fact with satisfaction, but with a certain astonishment, for it had not escaped my notice that Charlie was attracted as a rule by women whose breeding left something to be desired. She was not beautiful, but comely, with fine dark hair and fine eyes, a good colour and a look of health. She had a pleasant frankness and an air of candour that were very taking. She looked honest, simple, and dependable. I took an immediate liking to her. She was easy to talk to and though she did not say anything very brilliant she understood what other people were talking about; she was quick to see a joke and she was not shy. She gave you the impression of being competent and business-like. She had a happy placidity that suggested a good temper and an excellent digestion.

They seemed extremely pleased with one another. I had asked myself when I first saw her why Margery was marrying this irritable little man, baldish already and by no means young, but I discovered very soon that it was because she was in love with him. They chaffed one another a good deal and laughed a lot and every now and then their eyes met more significantly and they seemed to exchange a little private message. It was really rather touching.

A week later they were married at a registrar's office. It was a very successful marriage. Looking back now after sixteen years I could not but chuckle sympathetically at the thought of the lark they had made of their life together. I had never known a more devoted couple. They had never had very much money. They never seemed to want any. They had no ambitions. Their life was a picnic that never came to an end. They lived in the smallest flat I ever saw, in Panton Street, a small bedroom, a small sitting-room, and a bathroom that served also as a kitchen. But they had no sense of home, they ate their meals in restaurants, and only had breakfast in the flat. It was merely a place to sleep in. It was comfortable, though a third person coming in for a whisky and soda crowded it, and Margery with the help of a charwoman kept it as neat as Charlie's untidiness permitted, but there was not a single thing in it that had a personal note. They had a tiny car and whenever Charlie had a holiday they took it across the Channel and started off, with a bag each for all their luggage, to drive wherever the fancy took them. Breakdowns never disturbed them, bad weather was part of the fun, a puncture was no end of a joke, and if they lost their way and had to sleep out in the open they thought they were having the time of their lives.

Charlie continued to be irascible and contentious, but nothing he did ever disturbed Margery's lovely placidity. She could calm him with a word. She still made him laugh. She typed his monographs on obscure bacteria and corrected the proofs of his articles in the scientific magazines. Once I asked them if they ever quarrelled.

'No,' she said, 'we never seem to have anything to quarrel about. Charlie has the temper of an angel.'

'Nonsense,' I said, 'he's an overbearing, aggressive, and cantankerous fellow. He always has been.'

She looked at him and giggled and I saw that she thought I was being funny.

'Let him rave,' said Charlie. 'He's an ignorant fool and he uses words of whose meaning he hasn't the smallest idea.'

They were sweet together. They were very happy in one another's company and were never apart if they could help it. Even after the long time they had been married Charlie used to get into the car every day at luncheon-time to come west and meet Margery at a restaurant. People used to laugh at them, not unkindly, but perhaps with a little catch in the throat, because when they were asked to go and spend a week-end in the country Margery would write to the hostess and say they would like to come if they could be given a double bed. They had slept together for so many years that neither of them could sleep alone. It was often a trifle awkward. Husbands and wives as a rule not only demanded separate rooms, but were inclined to be peevish if asked to share the same bathroom. Modern houses were not arranged for domestic couples, but among their friends it became an understood thing that if you wanted the Bishops you must give them a room with a double bed. Some people of course thought it a little indecent, and it was never convenient, but they were a pleasant pair to have to stay and it was worth while to put up with their crankiness. Charlie was always full of spirits and in his caustic way extremely amusing, and Margery was peaceful and easy. They were no trouble to entertain. Nothing pleased them more than to be left to go out together for a long ramble in the country.

When a man marries, his wife sooner or later estranges him from his old friends, but Margery on the contrary increased Charlie's intimacy with them. By making him more tolerant she made him a more agreeable companion. They gave you the impression not of a married couple, but, rather amusingly, of two middle-aged bachelors living together; and when Margery, as was the rule, found herself the only woman among half a dozen men, ribald, argumentative, and gay, she was not a bar to good-fellowship but an asset. Whenever I was in England I saw them. They generally dined at the club of which I have spoken and if I happened to be alone I joined them.

When we met that evening for a snack before going to the play I told them I had asked Morton to come to supper.

'I'm afraid you'll find him rather dull,' I said. 'But he's a very decent sort of boy and he was awfully kind to me when I was in Borneo.'

'Why didn't you let me know sooner?' cried Margery. 'I'd have brought a girl along.'

'What do you want a girl for?' said Charlie. 'There'll be you.'

'I don't think it can be much fun for a young man to dance with a woman of my advanced years,' said Margery.

'Rot. What's your age got to do with it?' He turned to me. 'Have you ever danced with anyone who danced better?'

I had, but she certainly danced very well. She was light on her feet and she had a good sense of rhythm.

'Never,' I said heartily.

Morton was waiting for us when we reached Ciro's. He looked very sunburned in his evening clothes. Perhaps it was because I knew that they had been wrapped away in a tin box with moth-balls for four years that I felt he did not look quite at home in them. He was certainly more at ease in khaki shorts. Charlie Bishop was a good talker and liked to hear himself speak. Morton was shy. I gave him a cocktail and ordered some champagne. I had a feeling that he would be glad to dance, but was not quite sure whether it would occur to him to ask Margery. I was acutely conscious that we all belonged to another generation.

'I think I should tell you that Mrs Bishop is a beautiful dancer,' I said.

'Is she?' He flushed a little. 'Will you dance with me?'

She got up and they took the floor. She was looking peculiarly nice that evening, not at all smart, and I do not think her plain black dress had cost more than six guineas, but she looked a lady. She had the advantage of having extremely good legs and at that time skirts were still being worn very short. I suppose she had a little make-up on, but in contrast with the other women there she looked very natural. Shingled hair suited her; it was not even touched with white and it had an attractive sheen. She was not a pretty woman, but her kindliness, her wholesome air, her good health gave you, if not the illusion that she was, at least the feeling that it didn't at all matter. When she came back to the table her eyes were bright and she had a heightened colour.

'How does he dance?' asked her husband.

'Divinely.'

'You're very easy to dance with,' said Morton.

Charlie went on with his discourse. He had a sardonic humour and he was interesting because he was himself so interested in what he said. But he spoke of things that Morton knew nothing about and though he listened with a civil show of interest I could see that he was too much excited by the gaiety of the scene, the music, and the champagne to give his attention to conversation. When the music struck up again his eyes immediately sought Margery's. Charlie caught the look and smiled.

'Dance with him, Margery. Good for my figure to see you take exercise.'

They set off again and for a moment Charlie watched her with fond eyes.

'Margery's having the time of her life. She loves dancing and it makes me puff and blow. Not a bad youth.'

My little party was quite a success and when Morton and I, having taken leave of the Bishops, walked together towards Piccadilly Circus he thanked me warmly. He had really enjoyed himself. I said good-bye to him. Next morning I went abroad.

I was sorry not to have been able to do more for Morton and I knew that when I returned he would be on his way back to Borneo. I gave him a passing thought now and then, but by the autumn when I got home he had slipped my memory. After I had been in London a week or so I happened to drop in one night at the club to which Charlie Bishop also belonged. He was sitting with three or four men I knew and I went up. I had not seen any of them since my return. One of them, a man called Bill Marsh, whose wife, Janet, was a great friend of mine, asked me to have a drink.

'Where have you sprung from?' asked Charlie. 'Haven't seen you about lately.'

I noticed at once that he was drunk. I was astonished. Charlie had always liked his liquor, but he carried it well and never exceeded. In years gone by, when we were very young, he got tight occasionally, but probably more than anything to show what a great fellow he was, and it is unfair to bring up against a man the excesses of his youth. But I remembered that Charlie had never been very nice when he was drunk: his natural aggressiveness was exaggerated then and he talked too much and too loud; he was very apt to be quarrelsome. He was very dogmatic now, laying down the law and refusing to listen to any of the objections his rash statements called forth. The others knew he was drunk and were struggling between the irritation his cantankerousness aroused in them and the good-natured tolerance which they felt his condition demanded. He was not an agreeable object. A man of that age, bald and fattish, with spectacles, is disgusting drunk. He was generally rather dapper, but he was untidy now and there was tobacco ash all over him. Charlie called the waiter and ordered another whisky. The waiter had been at the club for thirty years.

'You've got one in front of you, sir.'

'Mind your own damned business,' said Charlie Bishop. 'Bring me a double whisky right away or I'll report you to the secretary for insolence.'

'Very good, sir,' said the waiter.

Charlie emptied his glass at a gulp, but his hand was unsteady and he spilled some of the whisky over himself.

'Well, Charlie, old boy, we'd better be toddling along,' said Bill Marsh. He turned to me. 'Charlie's staying with us for a bit.'

I was more surprised still. But I felt that something was wrong and thought it safer not to say anything.

'I'm ready,' said Charlie. 'I'll just have another drink before I go. I shall have a better night if I do.'

It did not look to me as though the party would break up for some time, so I got up and announced that I meant to stroll home.

'I say,' said Bill, as I was about to go, 'you wouldn't come and dine with us tomorrow night, would you, just me and Janet and Charlie?'

'Yes, I'll come with pleasure,' I said.

It was evident that something was up.

The Marshes lived in a terrace on the East side of Regent's Park. The maid who opened the door for me asked me to go in to Mr Marsh's study. He was waiting for me there.

'I thought I'd better have a word with you before you went upstairs,' he said as he shook hands with me. 'You know Margery's left Charlie?'

'No!'

'He's taken it very hard. Janet thought it was so awful for him alone in that beastly little flat that we asked him to stay here for a bit. We've done everything we could for him. He's been drinking like a fish. He hasn't slept a wink for a fortnight.'

'But she hasn't left him for good?'

I was astounded.

'Yes. She's crazy about a fellow called Morton.'

'Morton. Who's he?'

It never struck me it was my friend from Borneo.

'Damn it all, you introduced him and a pretty piece of work you did. Let's go upstairs. I thought I'd better put you wise.'

He opened the door and we went out. I was thoroughly confused.

'But look here,' I said.

'Ask Janet. She knows the whole thing. It beats me. I've got no patience with Margery, and he must be a mess.'

He preceded me into the drawing-room. Janet Marsh rose as I entered and came forward to greet me. Charlie was sitting at the window, reading the evening paper; he put it aside as I went up to him and shook his hand. He was quite sober and he spoke in his usual rather perky manner, but I noticed that he looked very ill. We had a glass of sherry and went down to dinner. Janet was a woman of spirit. She was tall and fair and good to look at. She kept the conversation going with alertness. When she left us to drink a glass of port it was with instructions not to stay more than ten minutes. Bill, as a rule somewhat taciturn, exerted himself now to talk. I tumbled to the game. I was hampered by my ignorance of what exactly had happened, but it was plain that the Marshes wanted to prevent Charlie from brooding, and I did my best to interest him. He seemed willing to play his part, he was always fond of holding forth, and he discussed, from the pathologist's standpoint, a murder that was just then absorbing the public. But he spoke without life. He was an empty shell, and one had the feeling that though for the sake of his host he forced himself to speak, his thoughts were elsewhere. It was a relief when a knocking on the floor above indicated to us that Janet was getting impatient. This was an occasion when a woman's presence eased the situation. We went upstairs and played family bridge. When it was time for me to go Charlie said he would walk with me as far as the Marylebone Road.

'Oh, Charlie, it's so late, you'd much better go to bed,' said Janet.

'I shall sleep better if I have a stroll before turning in,' he replied.

She gave him a worried look. You cannot forbid a middle-aged professor of pathology from going for a little walk if he wants to. She glanced brightly at her husband.

'I daresay it'll do Bill no harm.'

I think the remark was tactless. Women are often a little too managing. Charlie gave her a sullen look.

'There's absolutely no need to drag Bill out,' he said with some firmness.

'I haven't the smallest intention of coming,' said Bill, smiling. 'I'm tired out and I'm going to hit the hay.'

I fancy we left Bill Marsh and his wife to a little argument.

'They've been frightfully kind to me,' said Charlie, as we walked along by the railings. 'I don't know what I should have done without them. I haven't slept for a fortnight.'

I expressed regret but did not ask the reason, and we walked for a little in silence. I presumed that he had come with me in order to talk to me of what had happened, but I felt that he must take his own time. I was anxious to show my sympathy, but afraid of saying the wrong things; I did not want to seem eager to extract confidences from him. I did not know how to give him a lead. I was sure he did not want one. He was not a man given to beating about the bush. I imagined that he was choosing his words. We reached the corner.

'You'll be able to get a taxi at the church,' he said. 'I'll walk on a bit further. Good night.'

He nodded and slouched off. I was taken aback. There was nothing for me to do but to stroll on till I found a cab. I was having my bath next morning when a telephone call dragged me out of it, and with a towel round my wet body I took up the receiver. It was Janet.

'Well, what do you think of it all?' she said. 'You seem to have kept Charlie up pretty late last night. I heard him come home at three.'

'He left me at the Marylebone Road,' I answered. 'He said nothing to me at all.'

'Didn't he?'

There was something in Janet's voice that suggested that she was prepared to have a long talk with me. I suspected she had a telephone by the side of her bed.

'Look here,' I said quickly. 'I'm having my bath.'

'Oh, have you got a telephone in your bathroom?' she answered eagerly, and I think with envy.

'No, I haven't.' I was abrupt and firm. 'And I'm dripping all over the carpet.'

'Oh!' I felt disappointment in her tone and a trace of irritation. 'Well, when can I see you? Can you come here at twelve?'

It was inconvenient, but I was not prepared to start an argument.

'Yes, good-bye.'

I rang off before she could say anything more. In heaven when the blessed use the telephone they will say what they have to say and not a word beside.

I was devoted to Janet, but I knew that there was nothing that thrilled her more than the misfortunes of her friends. She was only too anxious to help them, but she wanted to be in the thick of their difficulties. She was the friend in adversity. Other people's business was meat and drink to her. You could not enter upon a love affair without finding her somehow your confidante nor be mixed up in a divorce case without discovering that she too had a finger in the pie. Withal she was a very nice woman. I could not help then chuckling in my heart when at noon I was shown in to Janet's drawing-room and observed the subdued eagerness with which she received me. She was very much upset by the catastrophe that had befallen the Bishops, but it was exciting, and she was tickled to death to have someone fresh to whom she could tell all about it. Janet had just that business-like expectancy that a mother has when she is discussing with the family doctor her married daughter's first confinement. Janet was conscious that the matter was very serious, and she would not for a moment have been thought to regard it flippantly, but she was determined to get every ounce of value out of it.

'I mean, no one could have been more horrified than I was when Margery told me she'd finally made up her mind to leave Charlie,' she said, speaking with the fluency of a person who has said the same thing in the same words a dozen times at least. 'They were the most devoted couple I'd ever known. It was a perfect marriage. They got on like a house on fire. Of course Bill and

I are devoted to one another, but we have awful rows now and then. I mean, I could kill him sometimes.'

'I don't care a hang about your relations with Bill,' I said. 'Tell me about the Bishops. That's what I've come here for.'

'I simply felt I must see you. After all you're the only person who can explain it.'

'Oh, God, don't go on like that. Until Bill told me last night I didn't know a thing about it.'

'That was my idea. It suddenly dawned on me that perhaps you didn't know and I thought you might put your foot in it too awfully.'

'Supposing you began at the beginning,' I said.

'Well, you're the beginning. After all you started the trouble. You introduced the young man. That's why I was so crazy to see you. You know all about him. I never saw him. All I know is what Margery has told me about him.'

'At what time are you lunching?' I asked.

'Half past one.'

'So am I. Get on with the story.'

But my remark had given Janet an idea.

'Look here, will you get out of your luncheon if I get out of mine? We could have a snack here. I'm sure there's some cold meat in the house, and then we needn't hurry. I don't have to be at the hairdresser's till three.'

'No, no, no,' I said. 'I hate the notion of that. I shall leave here at twenty minutes past one at the latest.'

'Then I shall just have to race through it. What do *you* think of Gerry?'

'Who's Gerry?'

'Gerry Morton. His name's Gerald.'

'How should I know that?'

'You stayed with him. Weren't there any letters lying about?'

'I daresay, but I didn't happen to read them,' I answered somewhat tartly.

'Oh, don't be so stupid. I meant the envelopes. What's he like?'

'All right. Rather the Kipling type, you know. Very keen on his work. Hearty. Empire-builder and all that sort of thing.'

'I don't mean that,' cried Janet, not without impatience. 'I mean, what does he look like?'

'More or less like everybody else, I think. Of course I should recognize him if I saw him again, but I can't picture him to myself very distinctly. He looks clean.'

'Oh, my God,' said Janet. 'Are you a novelist or are you not? What's the colour of his eyes?'

'I don't know.'

'You must know. You can't spend a week with anyone without knowing if their eyes are blue or brown. Is he fair or dark?'

'Neither.'

'Is he tall or short?'

'Average, I should say.'

'Are you trying to irritate me?'

'No. He's just ordinary. There's nothing in him to attract your attention. He's neither plain nor good-looking. He looks quite decent. He looks a gentleman.'

'Margery says he has a charming smile and a lovely figure.'

'I dare say.'

'He's absolutely crazy about her.'

'What makes you think that?' I asked dryly.

'I've seen his letters.'

'Do you mean to say she's shown them to you?'

'Why, of course.'

It is always difficult for a man to stomach the want of reticence that women betray in their private affairs. They have no shame. They will talk to one another without embarrassment of the most intimate matters. Modesty is a masculine virtue. But though a man may know this theoretically, each time he is confronted with women's lack of reserve he suffers a new shock. I wondered what Morton would think if he knew that not only were his letters read by Janet Marsh as well as by Margery, but that she had been kept posted from day to day with the progress of his infatuation. According to Janet he had fallen in love with Margery at first sight. The morning after they had met at my little supper party at Ciro's he had rung up and asked her to come and have tea with him at some place where they could dance. While I listened to Janet's story I was conscious of course that she was giving me Margery's view of the circumstances and I kept an open mind. I was interested to observe that Janet's sympathies were with Margery. It was true that when Margery left her husband it was her idea that Charlie should come to them for two or three weeks rather than stay on in miserable loneliness in the deserted flat and she had been extraordinarily kind to him. She lunched with him almost every day, because he had been accustomed to lunch every day with Margery; she took him for walks in Regent's Park and made Bill play golf with him on Sundays. She listened with wonderful patience to the story of his unhappiness and did what she could to console him. She was terribly sorry for him. But all the same she was definitely on Margery's side and when I expressed my disapproval of her she came down on me like a thousand of bricks. The affair thrilled her. She had been in it from the beginning when Margery, smiling, flattered, and a little doubtful, came and told her that she had a young man to the final scene when Margery, exasperated and distraught, announced that she could not stand the strain any more and had packed her things and moved out of the flat.

'Of course, at first I couldn't believe my ears,' she said. 'You know how Charlie and Margery were. They simply lived in one another's pockets. One couldn't help laughing at them, they were so devoted to one another. I never thought him a very nice little man and heaven knows he wasn't very attractive physically, but one couldn't help liking him because he was so awfully nice to Margery. I rather envied her sometimes. They had no money and they lived in a hugger-mugger sort of way, but they were frightfully happy. Of course I never thought anything would come of it. Margery was rather amused. "Naturally I don't take it very seriously," she told me, "but it is rather fun to have a young man at my time of life. I haven't had any flowers sent me for years. I had to tell him not to send any more because Charlie would think it so silly. He doesn't know a soul in London and he loves dancing and he says I dance like a dream. It's miserable for him going to the theatre by himself all the time and we've done two or three matinées together. It's pathetic to see how grateful he is when I say I'll go out with him." "I must say," I said, "he sounds rather a lamb." "He is," she said. "I knew you'd understand. You don't blame me, do you?" "Of course not, darling," I said, "surely you know me better than that. I'd do just the same in your place."'

Margery made no secret of her outings with Morton and her husband chaffed her good-naturedly about her beau. But he thought him a very civil, pleasant-spoken young man and was glad that Margery had someone to play with while he was busy. It never occurred to him to be jealous. The three of them dined together several times and went to a show. But presently Gerry Morton begged Margery to spend an evening with him alone; she said it was impossible, but he was persuasive, he gave her no peace; and at last she went to Janet and asked her to ring up Charlie one day and ask him to come to dinner and make a fourth at bridge. Charlie would never go anywhere without his wife, but the Marshes were old friends, and Janet made a point of it. She invented some cock-and-bull story that made it seem important that he should consent. Next day Margery and she met. The evening had been wonderful. They had dined at Maidenhead and danced there and then had driven home through the summer night.

'He says he's crazy about me,' Margery told her.

'Did he kiss you?' asked Janet.

'Of course,' Margery chuckled. 'Don't be silly, Janet. He is awfully sweet and, you know, he has such a nice nature. Of course I don't believe half the things he says to me.'

'My dear, you're not going to fall in love with him.'

'I have,' said Margery.

'Darling, isn't it going to be rather awkward?'

'Oh, it won't last. After all he's going back to Borneo in the autumn.'

'Well, one can't deny that it's made you look years younger.'

'I know, and I feel years younger.'

Soon they were meeting every day. They met in the morning and walked in the Park together or went to a picture gallery. They separated for Margery to lunch with her husband and after lunch met again and motored into the country or to some place on the river. Margery did not tell her husband. She very naturally thought he would not understand.

'How was it you never met Morton?' I asked Janet.

'Oh, she didn't want me to. You see, we belong to the same generation, Margery and I. I can quite understand that.'

'I see.'

'Of course I did everything I could. When she went out with Gerry she was always supposed to be with me.'

I am a person who likes to cross a 't' and dot an 'i'.

'Were they having an affair?' I asked.

'Oh, no. Margery isn't that sort of woman at all.'

'How do you know?'

'She would have told me.'

'I suppose she would.'

'Of course I asked her. But she denied it point-blank and I'm sure she was telling me the truth. There's never been anything of that sort between them at all.'

'It seems rather odd to me.'

'Well, you see, Margery is a very good woman.'

I shrugged my shoulders.

'She was absolutely loyal to Charlie. She wouldn't have deceived him for anything in the world. She couldn't bear the thought of having any secret from him. As soon as she knew she was in love with Gerry she wanted to tell Charlie. Of course I begged her not to. I told her it wouldn't do any good and it would only make Charlie miserable. And after all, the boy was going away in a couple of months, it didn't seem much good to make a lot of fuss about a thing that couldn't possibly last.'

But Gerry's imminent departure was the cause of the crash. The Bishops had arranged to go abroad as usual and proposed to motor through Belgium, Holland, and the North of Germany. Charlie was busy with maps and guides. He collected information from friends about hotels and roads. He looked forward to his holiday with the bubbling excitement of a schoolboy. Margery listened to him discussing it with a sinking heart. They were to be away four weeks and in September Gerry was sailing. She could not bear to lose so much of the short time that remained to them and the thought of the motor tour filled her with exasperation. As the interval grew shorter and shorter she grew more and more nervous. At last she decided that there was only one thing to do.

'Charlie, I don't want to come on this trip,' she interrupted him suddenly, one day when he was talking to her of some restaurant he had just heard of. 'I wish you'd get someone else to go with you.'

He looked at her blankly. She was startled at what she had said and her lips trembled a little.

'Why, what's the matter?'

'Nothing's the matter. I don't feel like it. I want to be by myself for a bit.'

'Are you ill?'

She saw the sudden fear in his eyes. His concern drove her beyond her endurance.

'No. I've never been better in my life. I'm in love.'

'You? Whom with?'

'Gerry.'

He looked at her in amazement. He could not believe his ears. She mistook his expression.

'It's no good blaming me. I can't help it. He's going away in a few weeks. I'm not going to waste the little time he has left.'

He burst out laughing.

'Margery, how can you make such a damned fool of yourself? You're old enough to be his mother.'

She flushed.

'He's just as much in love with me as I am with him.'

'Has he told you so?'

'A thousand times.'

'He's a bloody liar, that's all.'

He chuckled. His fat stomach rippled with mirth. He thought it a huge joke. I daresay Charlie did not treat his wife in the proper way. Janet seemed to think he should have been tender and compassionate. *He should have understood.* I saw the scene that was in her mind's eye, the stiff upper lip, the silent sorrow, and the final renunciation. Women are always sensitive to the beauty of the self-sacrifice of others. Janet would have sympathized also if he had flown into a violent passion, broken one or two pieces of furniture (which he would have had to replace), or given Margery a sock in the jaw. But to laugh at her was unpardonable. I did not point out that it is very difficult for a rather stout and not very tall professor of pathology, aged fifty-five, to act all of a sudden like a cave-man. Anyhow, the excursion to Holland was given up and the Bishops stayed in London through August. They were not very happy. They lunched and dined together every day because they had been in the habit of doing so for so many years and the rest of the time Margery spent with Gerry. The hours she passed with him made up for all she had to put up with and she had to put up with a good deal. Charlie had a ribald and sarcastic humour and he made himself very funny at her expense and at Gerry's. He persisted in refusing to take the matter seriously. He was vexed with Margery for being so silly, but apparently it never occurred to him that she might have been unfaithful to him. I commented upon this to Janet.

'He never suspected it even,' she said. 'He knew Margery much too well.'

The weeks passed and at last Gerry sailed. He went from Tilbury and Margery saw him off. When she came back she cried for forty-eight hours. Charlie watched her with increasing exasperation. His nerves were much frayed.

'Look here, Margery,' he said at last, 'I've been very patient with you, but now you must pull yourself together. This is getting past a joke.'

'Why can't you leave me alone?' she cried. 'I've lost everything that made life lovely to me.'

'Don't be such a fool,' he said.

I do not know what else he said. But he was unwise enough to tell her what he thought of Gerry and I gather that the picture he drew was virulent. It started the first violent scene they had ever had. She had borne Charlie's jibes when she knew that she would see Gerry in an hour or next day, but now that she had lost him for ever she could bear them no longer. She had held herself in for weeks: now she flung her self-control to the winds. Perhaps she never knew exactly what she said to Charlie. He had always been irascible and at last he hit her. They were both frightened when he had. He seized a hat and flung out of the flat. During all that miserable time they had shared the same bed, but when he came back, in the middle of the night, he found that she had made herself up a shake-down on the sofa in the sitting-room.

'You can't sleep there,' he said. 'Don't be so silly. Come to bed.'

'No, I won't, let me alone.'

For the rest of the night they wrangled, but she had her way and now made up her bed every night on the sofa. But in that tiny flat they could not get away from one another; they could not even get out of sight or out of hearing of one another. They had lived in such intimacy for so many years that it was an instinct for them to be together. He tried to reason with her. He thought her incredibly stupid and argued with her interminably in the effort to show her how wrong-headed she was. He could not leave her alone. He would not let her sleep, and he talked half through the night till they were both exhausted. He thought he could talk her out of love. For two or three days at a time they would not speak to one another. Then one day, coming home, he found her crying bitterly; the sight of her tears distracted him; he told her how much he loved her and sought to move her by the recollection of all the happy years they had spent together. He wanted to let bygones be bygones. He promised never to refer to Gerry again. Could they not forget the nightmare they had been through? But the thought of all that a reconciliation implied revolted her. She told him she had a racking headache and asked him to give her a sleeping draught. She pretended to be still asleep when he went out next morning, but the moment he was gone she packed up her things and left. She had a few trinkets that she had inherited and by selling them she got a little money. She took a room at a cheap boarding-house and kept her address a secret from Charlie.

It was when he found she had left him that he went all to pieces. The shock of her flight broke him. He told Janet that his loneliness was intolerable. He wrote to Margery imploring her to come back, and asked Janet to intercede for him; he was willing to promise anything; he abased himself. Margery was obdurate.

'Do you think she'll ever go back?' I asked Janet.

'She says not.'

I had to leave then, for it was nearly half past one and I was bound for the other end of London.

Two or three days later I got a telephone message from Margery asking if I could see her. She suggested coming to my rooms. I asked her to tea. I tried to be nice to her; her affairs were no business of mine, but in my heart I thought her a very silly woman and I dare say my manner was cold. She had never been handsome and the passing years had changed her little. She had still those fine dark eyes and her face was astonishingly unlined. She was very simply dressed and if she wore make-up it was so cunningly put on that I did not perceive it. She had still the charm she had always had of perfect naturalness and of a kindly humour.

'I want you to do something for me if you will,' she began without beating about the bush.

'What is it?'

'Charlie is leaving the Marshes today and going back to the flat. I'm afraid his first few days there will be rather difficult; it would be awfully nice of you if you'd ask him to dinner or something.'

'I'll have a look at my book.'

'I'm told he's been drinking heavily. It's such a pity. I wish you could give him a hint.'

'I understand he's had some domestic worries of late,' I said, perhaps acidly.

Margery flushed. She gave me a pained look. She winced as though I had struck her.

'Of course you've known him ever so much longer than you've known me. It's natural that you should take his part.'

'My dear, to tell you the truth I've known him all these years chiefly on your account. I have never very much liked him, but I thought you were awfully nice.'

She smiled at me and her smile was very sweet. She knew that I meant what I said.

'Do you think I was a good wife to him?'

'Perfect.'

'He used to put people's backs up. A lot of people didn't like him, but I never found him difficult.'

'He was awfully fond of you.'

'I know. We had a wonderful time together. For sixteen years we were perfectly happy.' She paused and looked down. 'I had to leave him. It became quite impossible. That cat-and-dog life we were leading was too awful.'

'I never see why two persons should go on living together if they don't want to.'

'You see, it was awful for us. We'd always lived in such close intimacy. We could never get away from one another. At the end I hated the sight of him.'

'I don't suppose the situation was easy for either of you.'

'It wasn't my fault that I fell in love. You see, it was quite a different love from the one I'd felt for Charlie. There was always something maternal in that and protective. I was so much more reasonable than he was. He was unmanageable, but I could always manage him. Gerry was different.' Her voice grew soft and her face was transfigured with glory. 'He gave me back my youth. I was a girl to him and I could depend on his strength and be safe in his care.'

'He seemed to me a very nice lad,' I said slowly. 'I imagine he'll do well. He was very young for the job he had when I ran across him. He's only twenty-nine now, isn't he?'

She smiled softly. She knew quite well what I meant.

'I never made any secret of my age to him. He says it doesn't matter.'

I knew this was true. She was not the woman to have lied about her age. She had found a sort of fierce delight in telling him the truth about herself.

'How old are you?'

'Forty-four.'

'What are you going to do now?'

'I've written to Gerry and told him I've left Charlie. As soon as I hear from him I'm going out to join him.'

I was staggered.

'You know, it's a very primitive little colony he's living in. I'm afraid you'll find your position rather awkward.'

'He made me promise that if I found my life impossible after he left I'd go to him.'

'Are you sure you're wise to attach so much importance to the things a young man says when he's in love?'

Again that really beautiful look of exaltation came into her face.

'Yes, when the young man happens to be Gerry.'

My heart sank. I was silent for a moment. Then I told her the story of the road Gerry Morton had built. I dramatized it, and I think I made it rather effective.

'What did you tell me that for?' she asked when I finished.

'I thought it rather a good story.'

She shook her head and smiled.

'No, you wanted to show me that he was very young and enthusiastic, and so keen on his work that he hadn't much time to waste on other interests. I wouldn't interfere with his work. You don't know him as I do. He's incredibly romantic. He looks upon himself as a pioneer. I've caught from him something of his excitement at the idea of taking part in the opening up of a new country. It *is* rather splendid, isn't it? It makes life here seem very humdrum and commonplace. But of course it's very lonely there. Even the companionship of a middle-aged woman may be worth having.'

'Are you proposing to marry him?' I asked.

'I leave myself in his hands. I want to do nothing that he does not wish.'

She spoke with so much simplicity, there was something so touching in her self-surrender, that when she left me I no longer felt angry with her. Of course I thought her very foolish, but if the folly of men made one angry one would pass one's life in a state of chronic ire. I thought all would come right. She said Gerry was romantic. He was, but the romantics in this workaday world only get away with their nonsense because they have at bottom a shrewd sense of reality: the mugs are the people who take their vapourings at their face value. The English are romantic; that is why other nations think them hypocritical; they are not: they set out in all sincerity for the Kingdom of God, but the journey is arduous and they have reason to pick up any gilt-edged investment that offers itself by the way. The British soul, like Wellington's armies, marches on its belly. I supposed that Gerry would go through a bad quarter of an hour when he received Margery's letter. My sympathies were not deeply engaged in the matter and I was only curious to see how he would extricate himself from the pass he was in. I thought Margery would suffer a bitter disappointment; well, that would do her no great harm, and then she would go back to her husband and I had no doubt the pair of them, chastened, would live in peace, quiet, and happiness for the rest of their lives.

The event was different. It happened that it was quite impossible for me to make any sort of engagement with Charlie Bishop for some days, but I wrote to him and asked him to dine with me one evening in the following week. I proposed, though with misgiving, that we should go to a play; I knew he was drinking like a fish, and when tight he was noisy. I hoped he would not make a nuisance of himself in the theatre. We arranged to meet at our club and dine at seven because the piece we were going to began at a quarter past eight. I arrived. I waited. He did not come. I rang up his flat, but could get no reply, so concluded that he was on his way. I hate missing the beginning of a play and I waited impatiently in the hall so that when he came we could go straight upstairs. To save time I had ordered dinner. The clock pointed to half past seven, then a quarter to eight; I did not see why I should wait for him any longer, so walked up to the dining-room and ate my dinner alone. He did not appear. I put a call through from the dining-room to the Marshes and presently was told by a waiter that Bill Marsh was at the end of the wire.

'I say, do you know anything about Charlie Bishop?' I said.

'We were dining together and going to a play and he hasn't turned up.'

'He died this afternoon.'

'What?'

My exclamation was so startled that two or three people within earshot looked up. The dining-room was full and the waiters were hurrying to and fro. The telephone was on the cashier's desk and a wine waiter came up with a bottle of hock and two long-stemmed glasses on a tray and gave the cashier a chit. The portly steward showing two men to a table jostled me.

'Where are you speaking from?' asked Bill.

I suppose he heard the clatter that surrounded me. When I told him he asked me if I could come round as soon as I had finished my dinner. Janet wanted to speak to me.

'I'll come at once,' I said.

I found Janet and Bill sitting in the drawing-room. He was reading the paper and she was playing patience. She came forward swiftly when the maid showed me in. She walked with a sort of spring, crouching a little, on silent feet, like a panther stalking his prey. I saw at once that she was in her element. She gave me her hand and turned her face away to hide her eyes brimming with tears. Her voice was low and tragic.

'I brought Margery here and put her to bed. The doctor has given her a sedative. She's all in. Isn't it awful?' She gave a sound that was something between a gasp and a sob. 'I don't know why these things always happen to me.'

The Bishops had never kept a servant but a charwoman went in every morning, cleaned the flat, and washed up the breakfast things. She had her own key. That morning she had gone in as usual and done the sitting-room. Since his wife had left him Charlie's hours had been irregular and she was not surprised to find him asleep. But the time passed and she knew he had his work to go to. She went to the bedroom door and knocked. There was no answer. She thought she heard him groaning. She opened the door softly. He was lying in bed, on his back, and was breathing stertorously. He did not wake. She called him. Something about him frightened her. She went to the flat on the same landing. It was occupied by a journalist. He was still in bed when she rang, and opened the door to her in pyjamas.

'Beg pardon, sir,' she said, 'but would you just come and 'ave a look at my gentleman. I don't think he's well.'

The journalist walked across the landing and into Charlie's flat. There was an empty bottle of veronal by the bed.

'I think you'd better fetch a policeman,' he said.

A policeman came and rang through to the police station for an ambulance. They took Charlie to Charing Cross Hospital. He never recovered consciousness. Margery was with him at the end.

'Of course there'll have to be an inquest,' said Janet. 'But it's quite obvious what happened. He'd been sleeping awfully badly for the last three or four weeks and I suppose he'd been taking veronal. He must have taken an overdose by accident.'

'Is that what Margery thinks?' I asked.

'She's too upset to think anything, but I told her I was positive he hadn't committed suicide. I mean, he wasn't that sort of a man. Am I right, Bill?'

'Yes, dear,' he answered.

'Did he leave any letter?'

'No, nothing. Oddly enough Margery got a letter from him this morning, well, hardly a letter, just a line. "I'm so lonely without you, darling." That's all. But of course that means nothing and she's promised to say nothing about it at the inquest. I mean, what is the use of putting ideas in people's heads? Every-one knows that you never can tell with veronal, I wouldn't take it myself for anything in the world, and it was quite obviously an accident. Am I right, Bill?'

'Yes, dear,' he answered.

I saw that Janet was quite determined to believe that Charlie Bishop had not committed suicide, but how far in her heart she believed what she wanted to believe I was not sufficiently expert in female psychology to know. And of course it might be that she was right. It is unreasonable to suppose that a middle-aged scientist should kill himself because his middle-aged wife leaves him and it is extremely plausible that, exasperated by sleeples-ness, and in all probability far from sober, he took a larger dose of the sleeping-draught than he realized. Anyhow that was the view the coroner took of the matter. It was indicated to him that of late Charles Bishop had given way to habits of intemperance which had caused his wife to leave him, and it was quite obvious that nothing was further from his thoughts than to put an end to himself. The coroner expressed his sympathy with the widow and commented very strongly on the dangers of sleeping-draughts.

I hate funerals, but Janet begged me to go to Charlie's. Several of his colleagues at the hospital had intimated their desire to come, but at Margery's wish they were dissuaded; and Janet and Bill, Margery and I were the only persons who attended it. We were to fetch the hearse from the mortuary and they offered to call for me on their way. I was on the look-out for the car and when I saw it drive up went downstairs, but Bill got out and met me just inside the door.

'Half a minute,' he said. 'I've got something to say to you. Janet wants you to come back afterwards and have tea. She says it's no good Margery moping and after tea we'll play a few rubbers of bridge. Can you come?'

'Like this?' I asked.

I had a tail coat on and a black tie and my evening dress trousers.

'Oh, that's all right. It'll take Margery's mind off.'

'Very well.'

But we did not play bridge after all. Janet, with her fair hair, was very smart in her deep mourning and she played the part of the sympathetic friend with amazing skill. She cried a little, wiping her eyes delicately so as not to disturb the black on her eyelashes, and when Margery sobbed broken-heartedly put her arm tenderly through hers. She was a very present help in trouble. We returned to the house. There was a telegram for Margery. She took it and went upstairs. I presumed it was a message of condolence from one of Charlie's friends who had just heard of his death. Bill went to change and Janet and I went up to the drawing-room and got the bridge table out. She took off her hat and put it on the piano.

'It's no good being hypocritical,' she said. 'Of course Margery has been frightfully upset, but she must pull herself together now. A rubber of bridge will help her to get back to her normal state. Naturally I'm dreadfully sorry about poor Charlie, but as far as he was concerned I don't believe he'd ever have got over Margery's leaving him and one can't deny that it has made things much easier for her. She wired to Gerry this morning.'

'What about?'

'To tell him about poor Charlie.'

At that moment the maid came to the room.

'Will you go up to Mrs Bishop, please, ma'am? She wants to see you.'

'Yes, of course.'

She went out of the room quickly and I was left alone. Bill joined me presently and we had a drink. At last Janet came back. She handed a telegram to me. It read as follows:

For God's sake await letter. Gerry

'What do you think it means?' she asked me.

'What it says,' I replied.

'Idiot! Of course I've told Margery that it doesn't mean anything, but she's rather worried. It must have crossed her cable telling him that Charles was dead. I don't think she feels very much like bridge after all. I mean, it would be rather bad form to play on the very day her husband has been buried.'

'Quite,' I said.

'Of course he may wire in answer to the cable. He's sure to do that, isn't he? The only thing we can do now is to sit tight and wait for his letter.'

I saw no object in continuing the conversation. I left. In a couple of days Janet rang me up to tell me that Margery had received a telegram of condolence from Morton. She repeated it to me:

Dreadfully distressed to hear sad news. Deeply sympathize with your great grief. Love. Gerry

'What do you think of it?' she asked me.

'I think it's very proper.'

'Of course he couldn't say he was as pleased as Punch, could he?'

'Not with any delicacy.'

'And he did put in *love*.'

I imagined how those women had examined the two telegrams from every point of view and scrutinized every word to press from it every possible shade of meaning. I almost heard their interminable conversations.

'I don't know what'll happen to Margery if he lets her down now,' Janet went on. 'Of course it remains to be seen if he's a gentleman.'

'Rot,' I said and rang off quickly.

In the course of the following days I dined with the Marshes a couple of times. Margery looked tired. I guessed that she awaited the letter that was on the way with sickening anxiety. Grief and fear had worn her to a shadow, she seemed very fragile now and she had acquired a spiritual look that I had never seen in her before. She was very gentle, very grateful for every kindness shown her, and in her smile, unsure and a little timid, was an infinite pathos. Her helplessness was very appealing. But Morton was several thousand miles away. Then one morning Janet rang me up.

'The letter has come. Margery says I can show it to you. Will you come round?'

Her tense voice told me everything. When I arrived Janet gave it to me. I read it. It was a very careful letter and I guessed that Morton had written it a good many times. It was very kind and he had evidently taken great pains to avoid saying anything that

could possibly wound Margery; but what transpired was his
terror. It was obvious that he was shaking in his shoes. He had
felt apparently that the best way to cope with the situation was to
be mildly facetious and he made very good fun of the white people
in the colony. What would they say if Margery suddenly turned
up? He would be given the order of the boot pretty damn quick.
People thought the East was free and easy; it wasn't, it was more
suburban than Clapham. He loved Margery far too much to bear
the thoughts of those horrible women out there turning up their
noses at her. And besides he had been sent to a station ten days
from anywhere; she couldn't live in his bungalow exactly and of
course there wasn't a hotel, and his work took him out into the
jungle for days at a time. It was no place for a woman anyhow.
He told her how much she meant to him, but she mustn't bother
about him and he couldn't help thinking it would be better if she
went back to her husband. He would never forgive himself if he
thought he had come between her and Charlie. Yes, I am quite
sure it had been a difficult letter to write.

'Of course he didn't know then that Charlie was dead. I've told
Margery that changes everything.'

'Does she agree with you?'

'I think she's being rather unreasonable. What do you make of
the letter?'

'Well, it's quite plain that he doesn't want her.'

'He wanted her badly enough two months ago.'

'It's astonishing what a change of air and a change of scene will
do for you. It must seem to him already like a year since he left
London. He's back among his old friends and his old interests.
My dear, it's no good Margery kidding herself; the life there has
taken him back and there's no place for her.'

'I've advised her to ignore the letter and go straight out to him.'

'I hope she's too sensible to expose herself to a very terrible
rebuff.'

'But then what's to happen to her? Oh, it's too cruel. She's the
best woman in the world. She has real goodness.'

'It's funny if you come to think of it, it's her goodness that has
caused all the trouble. Why on earth didn't she have an affair
with Morton? Charlie would have known nothing about it and
wouldn't have been a penny the worse. She and Morton could
have had a grand time and when he went away they could have
parted with the consciousness that a pleasant episode had come to
a graceful end. It would have been a jolly recollection, and she
could have gone back to Charlie satisfied and rested and continued to make him the excellent wife she had always been.'

Janet pursed her lips. She gave me a look of disdain.

'There is such a thing as virtue, you know.'

'Virtue be damned. A virtue that only causes havoc and un-happiness is worth nothing. You can call it virtue if you like. I call it cowardice.'

'The thought of being unfaithful to Charlie while she was living with him revolted her. There are women like that, you know.'

'Good gracious, she could have remained faithful to him in spirit while she was being unfaithful to him in the flesh. That is a feat of legerdemain that women find it easy to accomplish.'

'What an odious cynic you are.'

'If it's cynical to look truth in the face and exercise common sense in the affairs of life, then certainly I'm a cynic and odious if you like. Let's face it, Margery's a middle-aged woman, Charlie was fifty-five and they'd been married for sixteen years. It was natural enough that she should lose her head over a young man who made a fuss of her. But don't call it love. It was physiology. She was a fool to take anything he said seriously. It wasn't himself speaking, it was his starved sex, he'd suffered from sexual starvation, at least as far as white women are concerned, for four years; it's monstrous that she should seek to ruin his life by holding him to the wild promises he made then. It was an accident that Margery took his fancy; he wanted her, and because he couldn't get her wanted her more. I dare say he thought it love; believe me, it was only letch. If they'd gone to bed together Charlie would be alive today. It's her damned virtue that caused the whole trouble.

'How stupid you are. Don't you see that she couldn't help herself? She just doesn't happen to be a loose woman.'

'I prefer a loose woman to a selfish one and a wanton to a fool.'

'Oh, shut up. I didn't ask you to come here in order to make yourself absolutely beastly.'

'What did you ask me to come here for?'

'Gerry is your friend. You introduced him to Margery. If she's in the soup it's on his account. But *you* are the cause of the whole trouble. It's your duty to write to him and tell him he must do the right thing by her.'

'I'm damned if I will,' I said.

'Then you'd better go.'

I started to do so.

'Well, at all events it's a mercy that Charlie's life was insured,' said Janet.

Then I turned on her.

'And you have the nerve to call me a cynic.'

VIRTUE

I will not repeat the opprobrious word I flung at her as I slammed the door behind me. But Janet is all the same a very nice woman. I often think it would be great fun to be married to her.

THE MAN WITH THE SCAR

IT was on account of the scar that I first noticed him, for it ran, broad and red, in a great crescent from his temple to his chin. It must have been due to a formidable wound and I wondered whether this had been caused by a sabre or by a fragment of shell. It was unexpected on that round, fat, and good-humoured face. He had small and undistinguished features, and his expression was artless. His face went oddly with his corpulent body. He was a powerful man of more than common height. I never saw him in anything but a very shabby grey suit, a khaki shirt, and a battered sombrero. He was far from clean. He used to come into the Palace Hotel at Guatemala City every day at cocktail time and strolling leisurely round the bar offer lottery tickets for sale. If this was the way he made his living it must have been a poor one for I never saw anyone buy, but now and then I saw him offered a drink. He never refused it. He threaded his way among the tables with a sort of rolling walk as though he were accustomed to traverse long distances on foot, paused at each table, with a little smile mentioned the numbers he had for sale, and then, when no notice was taken of him, with the same smile passed on. I think he was for the most part a trifle the worse for liquor.

I was standing at the bar one evening, my foot on the rail, with an acquaintance – they make a very good dry Martini at the Palace Hotel in Guatemala City – when the man with the scar came up. I shook my head as for the twentieth time since my arrival he held out for my inspection his lottery tickets. But my companion nodded affably.

'*Qué tal, general?* How is life?'

'Not so bad. Business is none too good, but it might be worse.'

'What will you have, general?'

'A brandy.'

He tossed it down and put the glass back on the bar. He nodded to my acquaintance.

'*Gracias. Hasta luego.*'

Then he turned away and offered his tickets to the men who were standing next to us.

'Who is your friend?' I asked. 'That's a terrific scar on his face.'

'It doesn't add to his beauty, does it? He's an exile from Nicaragua. He's a ruffian of course and a bandit, but not a bad fellow. I give him a few *pesos* now and then. He was a revolution-

THE MAN WITH THE SCAR

ary general, and if his ammunition hadn't given out he'd have upset the government and be Minister of War now instead of selling lottery tickets in Guatemala. They captured him, along with his staff, such as it was, and tried him by court-martial. Such things are rather summary in these countries, you know, and he was sentenced to be shot at dawn. I guess he knew what was coming to him when he was caught. He spent the night in gaol and he and the others, there were five of them altogether, passed the time playing poker. They used matches for chips. He told me he'd never had such a run of bad luck in his life; they were playing with a short pack, Jacks to open, but he never held a card; he never improved more than half a dozen times in the whole sitting and no sooner did he buy a new stack than he lost it. When day broke and the soldiers came into the cell to fetch them for execution he had lost more matches than a reasonable man could use in a lifetime.

'They were led into the patio of the gaol and placed against a wall, the five of them side by side, with the firing party facing them. There was a pause and our friend asked the officer in charge of them what the devil they were keeping him waiting for. The officer said that the general commanding the government troops wished to attend the execution and they awaited his arrival.

'"Then I have time to smoke another cigarette," said our friend. "He was always unpunctual."

'But he had barely lit it when the general – it was San Ignacio, by the way: I don't know whether you ever met him – followed by his A.D.C. came into the patio. The usual formalities were performed and San Ignacio asked the condemned men whether there was anything they wished before the execution took place. Four of the five shook their heads, but our friend spoke.

'"Yes, I should like to say good-bye to my wife."

'"*Bueno*," said the general, "I have no objection to that. Where is she?"

'"She is waiting at the prison door."

'"Then it will not cause a delay of more than five minutes."

'"Hardly that, *Señor General*," said our friend.

'"Have him placed on one side."

'Two soldiers advanced and between them the condemned rebel walked to the spot indicated. The officer in command of the firing squad on a nod from the general gave an order, there was a ragged report, and the four men fell. They fell strangely, not together, but one after the other, with movements that were almost grotesque, as though they were puppets in a toy theatre. The officer went up to them and into one who was still alive emptied two barrels of his revolver. Our friend finished his cigarette and threw away the stub.

'There was a little stir at the gateway. A woman came into the patio, with quick steps, and then, her hand on her heart, stopped suddenly. She gave a cry and with outstretched arms ran forward.

'"*Caramba*," said the General.

'She was in black, with a veil over her hair, and her face was dead white. She was hardly more than a girl, a slim creature, with little regular features and enormous eyes. But they were distraught with anguish. Her loveliness was such that as she ran, her mouth slightly open and the agony of her face beautiful, a gasp of surprise was wrung from those indifferent soldiers who looked at her.

'The rebel advanced a step or two to meet her. She flung herself into his arms and with a hoarse cry of passion: *alma de mi corazón*, soul of my heart, he pressed his lips to hers. And at the same moment he drew a knife from his ragged shirt – I haven't a notion how he managed to retain possession of it – and stabbed her in the neck. The blood spurted from the cut vein and dyed his shirt. Then he flung his arms round her and once more pressed his lips to hers.

'It happened so quickly that many did not know what had occurred, but from the others burst a cry of horror; they sprang forward and seized him. They loosened his grasp and the girl would have fallen if the A.D.C. had not caught her. She was unconscious. They laid her on the ground and with dismay on their faces stood round watching her. The rebel knew where he was striking and it was impossible to staunch the blood. In a moment the A.D.C. who had been kneeling by her side rose.

'"She's dead," he whispered.

'The rebel crossed himself.

'"Why did you do it?" asked the general.

'"I loved her."

'A sort of sigh passed through those men crowded together and they looked with strange faces at the murderer. The general stared at him for a while in silence.

'"It was a noble gesture," he said at last. "I cannot execute this man. Take my car and have him led to the frontier. *Señor*, I offer you the homage which is due from one brave man to another."

'A murmur of approbation broke from those who listened. The A.D.C. tapped the rebel on the shoulder, and between the two soldiers without a word he marched to the waiting car.'

My friend stopped and for a little I was silent. I must explain that he was a Guatemalecan and spoke to me in Spanish. I have translated what he told me as well as I could, but I have made no attempt to tone down his rather high-flown language. To tell the truth I think it suits the story.

'But how then did he get the scar?' I asked at length.

'Oh, that was due to a bottle that burst when I was opening it. A bottle of ginger ale.'

'I never liked it,' said I.

THE CLOSED SHOP

NOTHING would induce me to tell the name of the happy country in which the incidents occurred that I am constrained to relate; but I see no harm in admitting that it is a free and independent state on the continent of America. This is vague enough in all conscience and can give rise to no diplomatic incident. Now the president of this free and independent state had an eye to a pretty woman and there came to his capital, a wide and sunny town with a *plaza*, a cathedral that was not without dignity, and a few old Spanish houses, a young person from Michigan of such a pleasing aspect that his heart went out to her. He lost no time in declaring his passion and was gratified to learn that it was returned, but he was mortified to discover that the young person regarded his possession of a wife and her possession of a husband as a bar to their union. She had a feminine weakness for marriage. Though it seemed unreasonable to the president, he was not the man to refuse a pretty woman the gratification of her whim and promised to make such arrangements as would enable him to offer her wedlock. He called his attorneys together and put the matter before them. He had long thought, he said, that for a progressive country their marriage laws were remarkably out of date and he proposed therefore radically to amend them. The attorneys retired and after a brief interval devised a divorce law that was satisfactory to the president. But the state of which I write was always careful to do things in a constitutional way, for it was a highly civilized, democratic, and reputable country. A president who respects himself and his oath of office cannot promulgate a law, even if it is to his own interest, without adhering to certain forms, and these things take time; the president had barely signed the decree that made the new divorce law valid when a revolution broke out and he was very unfortunately hanged on a lamp-post in the *plaza* in front of the cathedral that was not without dignity. The young person of pleasing aspect left town in a hurry, but the law remained. Its terms were simple. On the payment of one hundred dollars gold and after a residence of thirty days a man could divorce his wife or a wife her husband without even apprising the other party of the intended step. Your wife might tell you that she was going to spend a month with her aged mother and one morning at breakfast when you looked through your mail you might receive a letter from her informing you that she had divorced you and was already married to another.

Now it was not long before the happy news spread here and there that at a reasonable distance from New York was a country, the capital of which had an equable climate and tolerable accommodation, where a woman could release herself, expeditiously and with economy, from the irksome bonds of matrimony. The fact that the operation could be performed without the husband's knowledge saved her from those preliminary and acrimonious discussions that are so wearing to the nerves. Every woman knows that however much a man may argue about a proposition he will generally accept a fact with resignation. Tell him you want a Rolls-Royce and he will say he can't afford it, but buy it and he will sign his cheque like a lamb. So in a very short time beautiful women in considerable numbers began to come down to the pleasant, sunny town; tired business women and women of fashion, women of pleasure and women of leisure; they came from New York, Chicago, and San Francisco, they came from Georgia and they came from Dakota, they came from all the states in the Union. The passenger accommodation on the ships of the United Fruit Line was only just adequate to the demand, and if you wanted a stateroom to yourself you had to engage it six months in advance. Prosperity descended upon the capital of this enterprising state and in a very little while there was not a lawyer in it who did not own a Ford car. Don Agosto, the proprietor of the Grand Hotel, went to the expense of building several bathrooms, but he did not grudge it; he was making a fortune, and he never passed the lamp-post on which the outgoing president had been hanged without giving it a jaunty wave of his hand.

'He was a great man,' he said. 'One day they will erect a statue to him.'

I have spoken as though it were only women who availed themselves of this convenient and reasonable law, and this might indicate that in the United States it is they rather than men who desire release from the impediment of Holy Matrimony. I have no reason to believe that this is so. Though it was women in great majority who travelled to this country to get a divorce, I ascribe this to the fact that it is always easy for them to get away for six weeks (a week there, a week back, and thirty days to establish a domicile) but it is difficult for men to leave their affairs so long. It is true that they could go there during their summer holidays, but then the heat is somewhat oppressive; and besides, there are no golf links: it is reasonable enough to suppose that many a man will hesitate to divorce his wife when he can only do it at the cost of a month's golf. There were of course two or three males spending their thirty days at the Grand Hotel, but they were generally, for a reason that is obscure, commercial travellers. I can but imagine that by the nature of their avocations they were able at one and the same time to pursue freedom and profit.

Be this as it may, the fact remains that the inmates of the Grand Hotel were for the most part women, and very gay it was in the patio at luncheon and at dinner when they sat at little square tables under the arches discussing their matrimonial troubles and drinking champagne. Don Agosto did a roaring trade with the generals and colonels (there were more generals than colonels in the army of this state), the lawyers, bankers, merchants, and the young sparks of the town who came to look at these beautiful creatures. But the perfect is seldom realized in this world. There is always something that is not quite right and women engaged in getting rid of their husbands are very properly in an agitated condition. It makes them at times hard to please. Now it must be confessed that this delightful little city, notwithstanding its manifold advantages, somewhat lacked places of amusement. There was but one cinema and this showed films that had been wandering too long from their happy home in Hollywood. In the daytime you could have consultations with your lawyer, polish your nails, and do a little shopping, but the evenings were intolerable. There were many complaints that thirty days was a long time and more than one impatient young thing asked her lawyer why they didn't put a little pep into their law and do the whole job in eight and forty hours. Don Agosto, however, was a man of resource, and presently he had an inspiration: he engaged a troupe of wandering Guatemaltecans who played the marimba. There is no music in the world that sets the toes so irresistibly tingling and in a little while everyone in the patio began dancing. It is of course obvious that twenty-five beautiful women cannot dance with three commercial travellers, but there were all these generals and colonels and there were all the young sparks of the town. They danced divinely and they had great liquid black eyes. The hours flew, the days tripped one upon the heels of the other so quickly that the month passed before you realized it, and more than one of Don Agosto's guests when she bade him farewell confessed that she would willingly have stayed longer. Don Agosto was radiant. He liked to see people enjoy themselves. The marimba band was worth twice the money he paid for it, and it did his heart good to see his ladies dance with the gallant officers and the young men of the town. Since Don Agosto was thrifty he always turned off the electric light on the stairs and in the passages at ten o'clock at night and the gallant officers and the young men of the town improved their English wonderfully.

Everything went as merrily as a marriage bell, if I may use a phrase that, however hackneyed, in this connexion is irresistible, till one day Madame Coralie came to the conclusion that she had had enough of it. For one man's meat is another man's poison. She dressed herself and went to call on her friend Carmencita. After she had in a few voluble words stated the purpose of her visit, Carmencita called a maid and told her to run and fetch La Gorda. They had a matter of importance which they wished to discuss with her. La Gorda, a woman of ample proportions with a heavy moustache, soon joined them, and over a bottle of Malaga the three of them held a momentous conversation. The result of it was that they indited a letter to the president asking for an audience. The new president was a hefty young man in the early thirties who, a few years before, had been a stevedore in the employment of an American firm, and he had risen to his present exalted station by a natural eloquence and an effective use of his gun when he wanted to make a point or emphasize a statement. When one of his secretaries placed the letter before him he laughed.

'What do those three old faggots want with me?'

But he was a good-natured fellow and accessible. He did not forget that he had been elected by the people, as one of the people, to protect the people. He had also during his early youth been employed for some months by Madame Coralie to run errands. He told his secretary that he would see them at ten o'clock next morning. They went at the appointed hour to the palace and were led up a noble stairway to the audience chamber; the official who conducted them knocked softly on the door; a barred judas was opened and a suspicious eye appeared. The president had no intention of suffering the fate of his predecessor if he could help it and no matter who his visitors were did not receive them without precaution. The official gave the three ladies' names, the door was opened, but not too wide, and they slipped in. It was a handsome room and various secretaries at little tables, in their shirt-sleeves and with a revolver on each hip, were busy typing. One or two other young men, heavily armed, were lying on sofas reading the papers and smoking cigarettes. The president, also in his shirt-sleeves, with a revolver in his belt, was standing with his thumbs in the sleeve-holes of his waistcoat. He was tall and stout, of a handsome and even dignified presence.

'*Qué tal?*' he cried, jovially, with a flash of his white teeth. 'What brings you here, *señoras*?'

'How well you're looking, Don Manuel,' said La Gorda. 'You are a fine figure of a man.'

He shook hands with them, and his staff, ceasing their strenuous activity, leaned back and cordially waved their hands to the three ladies. They were old friends, and the greetings, if a trifle sardonic, were hearty. I must disclose the fact now (which I could without doubt do in a manner so discreet that I might be misunderstood; but if you have to say something you may just as well say it plainly as not) that these three ladies were the Madams of the three principal brothels in the capital of this free and independent state. La Gorda and Carmencita were of Spanish origin and were very decently dressed in black, with black silk shawls over their heads, but Madame Coralie was French and she wore a toque. They were all of mature age and of modest demeanour.

The president made them sit down, and offered them madeira and cigarettes, but they refused.

'No, thank you, Don Manuel,' said Madame Coralie. 'It is on business that we have come to see you.'

'Well, what can I do for you?'

La Gorda and Carmencita looked at Madame Coralie and Madame Coralie looked at La Gorda and Carmencita. They nodded and she saw that they expected her to be their spokeswoman.

'Well, Don Manuel, it is like this. We are three women who have worked hard for many years and not a breath of scandal has ever tarnished our good names. There are not in all the Americas three more distinguished houses than ours and they are a credit to this beautiful city. Why, only last year I spent five hundred dollars to supply my *sala principal* with plate-glass mirrors. We have always been respectable and we have paid our taxes with regularity. It is hard now that the fruits of our labours should be snatched away from us. I do not hesitate to say that after so many years of honest and conscientious attention to business it is unjust that we should have to submit to such treatment.'

The president was astounded.

'But, Coralie, my dear, I do not know what you mean. Has anyone dared to claim money from you that the law does not sanction or that I know nothing about?'

He gave his secretaries a suspicious glance. They tried to look innocent, but though they were, only succeeded in looking uneasy.

'It is the law we complain of. Ruin stares us in the face.'

'Ruin?'

'So long as this new divorce law is in existence we can do no business and we may just as well shut up our beautiful houses.'

Then Madame Coralie explained in a manner so frank that I

prefer to paraphrase her speech that owing to this invasion of the town by beautiful ladies from a foreign land the three elegant houses on which she and her two friends paid rates and taxes were utterly deserted. The young men of fashion preferred to spend their evenings at the Grand Hotel where they received for soft words entertainment which at the regular establishments they could only have got for hard cash.

'You cannot blame them,' said the president.

'I don't,' cried Madame Coralie. 'I blame the women. They have no right to come and take the bread out of our mouths. Don Manuel, you are one of the people, you are not one of these aristocrats; what will the country say if you allow us to be driven out of business by blacklegs? I ask you is it just, is it honest?'

'But what can I do?' said the president. 'I cannot lock them up in their rooms for thirty days. How am I to blame if these foreigners have no sense of decency?'

'It's different for a poor girl,' said La Gorda. 'She has her way to make. But that these women do that sort of thing when they're not obliged to, no, that I shall never understand.'

'It is a bad and wicked law,' said Carmencita.

The president sprang to his feet and threw his arms akimbo.

'You are not going to ask me to abrogate a law that has brought peace and plenty to this country. I am of the people and I was elected by the people, and the prosperity of my fatherland is very near my heart. Divorce is our staple industry and the law shall be repealed only over my dead body.'

'Oh, *Maria Santisima*, that it should come to this,' said Carmencita. 'And me with two daughters in a convent in New Orleans. Ah, in this business one often has unpleasantness, but I always consoled myself by thinking that my daughters would marry well, and when the time came for me to retire they would inherit my business. Do you think I can keep them in a convent in New Orleans for nothing?'

'And who is going to keep my son at Harvard if I have to close my house, Don Manuel?' asked La Gorda.

'As for myself,' said Madame Coralie, 'I do not care. I shall return to France. My dear mother is eighty-seven years of age and she cannot live very much longer. It will be a comfort to her if I spend her last remaining years by her side. But it is the injustice of it that hurts. You have spent many happy evenings in my house, Don Manuel, and I am wounded that you should let us be treated like this. Did you not tell me yourself that it was the proudest day of your life when you entered as an honoured guest the house in which you had once been employed as errand boy?'

'I do not deny it. I stood champagne all round.' Don Manuel walked up and down the large hall, shrugging his shoulders as he went, and now and then, deep in thought, he gesticulated. 'I am of the people, elected by the people,' he cried, 'and the fact is, these women are blacklegs.' He turned to his secretaries with a dramatic gesture. 'It is a stain on my administration. It is against all my principles to allow unskilled foreign labour to take the bread out of the mouths of honest and industrious people. These ladies are quite right to come to me and appeal for my protection. I will not allow the scandal to continue.'

It was of course a pointed and effective speech, but all who heard it knew that it left things exactly where they were. Madame Coralie powdered her nose and gave it, a commanding organ, a brief look in her pocket mirror.

'Of course I know what human nature is,' she said, 'and I can well understand that time hangs heavily on the hands of these creatures.'

'We could build a golf-course,' hazarded one of the secretaries. 'It is true that this would only occupy them by day.'

'If they want men why can't they bring them with them?' said La Gorda.

'*Caramba!*' cried the president, and with that stood on a sudden quite still. 'There is the solution.'

He had not reached his exalted station without being a man of insight and resource. He beamed.

'We will amend the law. Men shall come in as before without let or hindrance, but women only accompanied by their husbands or with their written consent.' He saw the look of consternation which his secretaries gave him, and he waved his hand. 'But the immigration authorities shall receive instructions to interpret the word husband with the widest latitude.'

'*María Santísima*!' cried Madame Coralie. 'If they come with a friend he will take care that no one else interferes with them and our customers will return to the houses where for so long they have been so hospitably entertained. Don Manuel, you are a great man and one of these days they will erect a statue to you.'

It is often the simplest expedients that settle the most formidable difficulties. The law was briefly amended according to the terms of Don Manuel's suggestion and, whereas prosperity continued to pour its blessings on the wide and sunny capital of this free and independent state, Madame Coralie was enabled profitably to pursue her useful avocations, Carmencita's two daughters completed their expensive education in the convent at New Orleans, and La Gorda's son successfully graduated at Harvard.

THE BUM

GOD knows how often I had lamented that I had not half the time I needed to do half the things I wanted. I could not remember when last I had had a moment to myself. I had often amused my fancy with the prospect of just one week's complete idleness. Most of us when not busy working are busy playing; we ride, play tennis or golf, swim or gamble; but I saw myself doing nothing at all. I would lounge through the morning, dawdle through the afternoon, and loaf through the evening. My mind would be a slate and each passing hour a sponge that wiped out the scribblings written on it by the world of sense. Time, because it is so fleeting, time, because it is beyond recall, is the most precious of human goods and to squander it is the most delicate form of dissipation in which man can indulge. Cleopatra dissolved in wine a priceless pearl, but she gave it to Antony to drink; when you waste the brief golden hours you take the beaker in which the gem is melted and dash its contents to the ground. The gesture is grand and like all grand gestures absurd. That of course is its excuse. In the week I promised myself I should naturally read, for to the habitual reader reading is a drug of which he is the slave; deprive him of printed matter and he grows nervous, moody, and restless; then, like the alcoholic bereft of brandy who will drink shellac or methylated spirit, he will make do with the advertisements of a paper five years old; he will make do with a telephone directory. But the professional writer is seldom a disinterested reader. I wished my reading to be but another form of idleness. I made up my mind that if ever the happy day arrived when I could enjoy untroubled leisure I would complete an enterprise that had always tempted me, but which hitherto, like an explorer making reconnaissances into an undiscovered country, I had done little more than enter upon: I would read the entire works of Nick Carter.

But I had always fancied myself choosing my moment with surroundings to my liking, not having it forced upon me; and when I was suddenly faced with nothing to do and had to make the best of it (like a steamship acquaintance whom in the wide waste of the Pacific Ocean you have invited to stay with you in London and who turns up without warning and with all his luggage) I was not a little taken aback. I had come to Vera Cruz from Mexico City to catch one of the Ward Company's white cool ships to Yucatan; and found to my dismay that, a dock strike having been declared over-night, my ship would not put in. I was stuck in Vera Cruz. I took a room in the Hotel Diligencias overlooking the *plaza*, and spent the morning looking at the sights of the town. I wandered down side streets and peeped into quaint courts. I sauntered through the parish church; it is picturesque with its gargoyles and flying buttresses, and the salt wind and the blazing sun have patined its harsh and massive walls with the mellowness of age; its cupola is covered with white and blue tiles. Then I found that I had seen all that was to be seen and I sat down in the coolness of the arcade that surrounded the square and ordered a drink. The sun beat down on the *plaza* with a merciless splendour. The coco-palms drooped dusty and bedraggled. Great black buzzards perched on them for a moment uneasily, swooped to the ground to gather some bit of offal, and then with lumbering wings flew up to the church tower. I watched the people crossing the square; negroes, Indians, Creoles, and Spanish, the motley people of the Spanish Main; and they varied in colour from ebony to ivory. As the morning wore on, the tables around me filled up, chiefly with men, who had come to have a drink before luncheon, for the most part in white ducks, but some notwithstanding the heat in the dark clothes of professional respectability. A small band, a guitarist, a blind fiddler, and a harpist, played rag-time and after every other tune the guitarist came round with a plate. I had already bought the local paper and I was adamant to the newsvendors who pertinaciously sought to sell me more copies of the same sheet. I refused, oh, twenty times at least, the solicitations of grimy urchins who wanted to shine my spotless shoes; and having come to the end of my small change I could only shake my head at the beggars who importuned me. They gave one no peace. Little Indian women, in shapeless rags, each one with a baby tied in the shawl on her back, held out skinny hands and in a whimper recited a dismal screed; blind men were led up to my table by small boys; the maimed, the halt, the deformed exhibited the sores and the monstrosities with which nature or accident had afflicted them; and half naked, underfed children whined endlessly their demand for coppers. But these kept their eyes open for the fat policeman who would suddenly dart out on them with a thong and give them a sharp cut on the back or over the head. Then they would scamper, only to return again when, exhausted by the exercise of so much energy, he relapsed into lethargy.

But suddenly my attention was attracted by a beggar who, unlike the rest of them and indeed the people sitting round me, swarthy and black-haired, had hair and beard of a red so vivid that it was startling. His beard was ragged and his long mop of hair looked as though it had not been brushed for months. He wore only a pair of trousers and a cotton singlet, but they were tatters, grimy and foul, that barely held together. I have never seen anyone so thin; his legs, his naked arms were but skin and bone, and through the rents of his singlet you saw every rib of his wasted body; you could count the bones of his dust-covered feet. Of that starveling band he was easily the most abject. He was not old, he could not well have been more than forty, and I could not but ask myself what had brought him to this pass. It was absurd to think that he would not have worked if work he had been able to get. He was the only one of the beggars who did not speak. The rest of them poured forth their litany of woe and if it did not bring the alms they asked continued until an impatient word from you chased them away. He said nothing. I suppose he felt that his look of destitution was all the appeal he needed. He did not even hold out his hand, he merely looked at you, but with such wretchedness in his eyes, such despair in his attitude, it was dreadful; he stood on and on, silent and immobile, gazing steadfastly, and then, if you took no notice of him, he moved slowly to the next table. If he was given nothing he showed neither disappointment nor anger. If someone offered him a coin he stepped forward a little, stretched out his claw-like hand, took it without a word of thanks, and impassively went his way. I had nothing to give him and when he came to me, so that he should not wait in vain, I shook my head.

'*Dispense Usted por Dios,*' I said, using the polite Castillian formula with which the Spaniards refuse a beggar.

But he paid no attention to what I said. He stood in front of me, for as long as he stood at the other tables, looking at me with tragic eyes. I have never seen such a wreck of humanity. There was something terrifying in his appearance. He did not look quite sane. At length he passed on.

It was one o'clock and I had lunch. When I awoke from my siesta it was still very hot, but towards evening a breath of air coming in through the windows which I had at last ventured to open tempted me into the *plaza*. I sat down under my arcade and ordered a long drink. Presently people in greater numbers filtered into the open space from the surrounding streets, the tables in the restaurants round it filled up, and in the kiosk in the middle the band began to play. The crowd grew thicker. On the free benches people sat huddled together like dark grapes clustered on a stalk. There was a lively hum of conversation. The big black buzzards flew screeching overhead, swooping down when they saw something to pick up, or scurrying away from under the feet of the

passers-by. As twilight descended they swarmed, it seemed from
all parts of the town, towards the church tower; they circled
heavily about it and hoarsely crying, squabbling, and jangling,
settled themselves uneasily to roost. And again bootblacks begged
me to have my shoes cleaned, newsboys pressed dank papers upon
me, beggars whined their plaintive demand for alms. I saw once
more that strange, red-bearded fellow and watched him stand
motionless, with the crushed and piteous air, before one table
after another. He did not stop before mine. I supposed he
remembered me from the morning and having failed to get anything from me then thought it useless to try again. You do not
often see a red-haired Mexican, and because it was only in Russia
that I had seen men of so destitute a mien I asked myself if he was
by chance a Russian. It accorded well enough with the Russian
fecklessness that he should have allowed himself to sink to such a
depth of degradation. Yet he had not a Russian face; his emaci-
ated features were clear-cut, and his blue eyes were not set in the
head in a Russian manner; I wondered if he could be a sailor,
English, Scandinavian, or American, who had deserted his ship
and by degrees sunk to this pitiful condition. He disappeared.
Since there was nothing else to do, I stayed on till I got hungry,
and when I had eaten came back. I sat on till the thinning crowd
suggested it was bed-time. I confess that the day had seemed long
and I wondered how many similar days I should be forced to
spend there.

But I woke after a little while and could not get to sleep again.
My room was stifling. I opened the shutters and looked out at the
church. There was no moon, but the bright stars faintly lit its
outline. The buzzards were closely packed on the cross above the
cupola and on the edges of the tower, and now and then they
moved a little. The effect was uncanny. And then, I have no
notion why, that red scarecrow recurred to my mind and I had
suddenly a strange feeling that I had seen him before. It was so
vivid that it drove away from me the possibility of sleep. I felt sure
that I had come across him, but when and where I could not tell.
I tried to picture the surroundings in which he might take his
place, but I could see no more than a dim figure against a background of fog. As the dawn approached it grew a little cooler and
I was able to sleep.

I spent my second day at Vera Cruz as I had spent the first.
But I watched for the coming of the red-haired beggar, and as he
stood at the tables near mine I examined him with attention. I felt
certain now that I had seen him somewhere. I even felt certain
that I had known him and talked to him, but I still could recall

none of the circumstances. Once more he passed my table without stopping and when his eyes met mine I looked in them for some gleam of recollection. Nothing. I wondered if I had made a mistake and thought I had seen him in the same way as sometimes, by some queer motion of the brain, in the act of doing something you are convinced that you are repeating an action that you have done at some past time. I could not get out of my head the impression that at some moment he had entered into my life. I racked my brains. I was sure now that he was either English or American. But I was shy of addressing him. I went over in my mind the possible occasions when I might have met him. Not to be able to place him exasperated me as it does when you try to remember a name that is on the tip of your tongue and yet eludes you. The day wore on.

Another day came, another morning, another evening. It was Sunday and the *plaza* was more crowded than ever. The tables under the arcade were packed. As usual the red-haired beggar came along, a terrifying figure in his silence, his threadbare rags, and his pitiful distress. He was standing in front of a table only two from mine, mutely beseeching, but without a gesture. Then I saw the policeman who at intervals tried to protect the public from the importunities of all these beggars sneak round a column and give him a resounding whack with his thong. His thin body winced, but he made no protest and showed no resentment; he seemed to accept the stinging blow as in the ordinary course of things, and with his slow movements slunk away into the gathering night of the plaza. But the cruel stripe had whipped my memory and suddenly I remembered.

Not his name, that escaped me still, but everything else. He must have recognized me, for I have not changed very much in twenty years, and that was why after that first morning he had never paused in front of my table. Yes, it was twenty years since I had known him. I was spending a winter in Rome and every evening I used to dine in a restaurant in the Via Sistina where you got excellent macaroni and a good bottle of wine. It was frequented by a little band of English and American art students, and one or two writers; and we used to stay late into the night engaged in interminable arguments upon art and literature. He used to come in with a young painter who was a friend of his. He was only a boy then, he could not have been more than twenty-two; and with his blue eyes, straight nose, and red hair he was pleasing to look at. I remembered that he spoke a great deal of Central America, he had had a job with the American Fruit Company, but had thrown it over because he wanted to be a writer. He was not popular among us because he was arrogant and we were none of us old enough to take the arrogance of youth with tolerance. He thought us poor fish and did not hesitate to tell us so. He would not show us his work, because our praise meant nothing to him and he despised our censure. His vanity was enormous. It irritated us; but some of us were uneasily aware that it might perhaps be justified. Was it possible that the intense consciousness of genius that he had, rested on no grounds? He had sacrificed everything to be a writer. He was so certain of himself that he infected some of his friends with his own assurance.

I recalled his high spirits, his vitality, his confidence in the future, and his disinterestedness. It was impossible that it was the same man, and yet I was sure of it. I stood up, paid for my drink, and went out into the plaza to find him. My thoughts were in a turmoil. I was aghast. I had thought of him now and then and idly wondered what had become of him. I could never have imagined that he was reduced to this frightful misery. There are hundreds, thousands of youths who enter upon the hard calling of the arts with extravagant hopes; but for the most part they come to terms with their mediocrity and find somewhere in life a niche where they can escape starvation. This was awful. I asked myself what had happened. What hopes deferred had broken his spirit, what disappointments shattered him, and what lost illusions ground him to the dust? I asked myself if nothing could be done. I walked round the plaza. He was not in the arcades. There was no hope of finding him in the crowd that circled round the bandstand. The light was waning and I was afraid I had lost him. Then I passed the church and saw him sitting on the steps. I cannot describe what a lamentable object he looked. Life had taken him, rent him on its racks, torn him limb from limb, and then flung him, a bleeding wreck, on the stone steps of that church. I went up to him.

'Do you remember Rome?' I said.

He did not move. He did not answer. He took no more notice of me than if I were not standing before him. He did not look at me. His vacant blue eyes rested on the buzzards that were screaming and tearing at some object at the bottom of the steps. I did not know what to do. I took a yellow-backed note out of my pocket and pressed it in his hand. He did not give it a glance. But his hand moved a little, the thin claw-like fingers closed on the note and scrunched it up; he made it into a little ball and then edging it on to his thumb flicked it into the air so that it fell among the jangling buzzards. I turned my head instinctively and saw one of them seize it in his beak and fly off followed by two others screaming behind it. When I looked back the man was gone.

I stayed three more days in Vera Cruz. I never saw him again.

THE DREAM

It chanced that in August 1917 the work upon which I was then engaged obliged me to go from New York to Petrograd, and I was instructed for safety's sake to travel by way of Vladivostok. I landed there in the morning and passed an idle day as best I could. The trans-Siberian train was due to start, so far as I remember, at about nine in the evening. I dined at the station restaurant by myself. It was crowded and I shared a small table with a man whose appearance entertained me. He was a Russian, a tall fellow, but amazingly stout, and he had so vast a paunch that he was obliged to sit well away from the table. His hands, small for his size, were buried in rolls of fat. His hair, long, dark, and thin, was brushed carefully across his crown in order to conceal his baldness, and his huge sallow face, with its enormous double chin, clean-shaven, gave you an impression of indecent nakedness. His nose was small, a funny little button upon that mass of flesh, and his black shining eyes were small too. But he had a large, red, and sensual mouth. He was dressed neatly enough in a black suit. It was not worn but shabby; it looked as if it had been neither pressed nor brushed since he had had it.

The service was bad and it was almost impossible to attract the attention of a waiter. We soon got into conversation. The Russian spoke good and fluent English. His accent was marked but not tiresome. He asked me many questions about myself and my plans, which – my occupation at the time making caution necessary – I answered with a show of frankness but with dissimulation. I told him I was a journalist. He asked me whether I wrote fiction and when I confessed that in my leisure moments I did, he began to talk of the later Russian novelists. He spoke intelligently. It was plain that he was a man of education.

By this time we had persuaded the waiter to bring us some cabbage soup, and my acquaintance pulled a small bottle of vodka from his pocket which he invited me to share. I do not know whether it was the vodka or the natural loquaciousness of his race that made him communicative, but presently he told me, unasked, a good deal about himself. He was of noble birth, it appeared, a lawyer by profession, and a radical. Some trouble with the authorities had made it necessary for him to be much abroad, but now he was on his way home. Business had detained him at Vladivostok, but he expected to start for Moscow in a week and if I went there he would be charmed to see me.

'Are you married?' he asked me.

I did not see what business it was of his, but I told him that I was. He sighed a little.

'I am a widower,' he said. 'My wife was a Swiss, a native of Geneva. She was a very cultivated woman. She spoke English, German, and Italian perfectly. French, of course, was her native tongue. Her Russian was much above the average for a foreigner. She had scarcely the trace of an accent.'

He called a waiter who was passing with a tray full of dishes and asked him, I suppose – for then I knew hardly any Russian – how much longer we were going to wait for the next course. The waiter, with a rapid but presumably reassuring exclamation, hurried on, and my friend sighed.

'Since the revolution the waiting in restaurants has become abominable.'

He lighted his twentieth cigarette and I, looking at my watch, wondered whether I should get a square meal before it was time for me to start.

'My wife was a very remarkable woman,' he continued. 'She taught languages at one of the best schools for the daughters of noblemen in Petrograd. For a good many years we lived together on perfectly friendly terms. She was, however, of a jealous temperament and unfortunately she loved me to distraction.'

It was difficult for me to keep a straight face. He was one of the ugliest men I had ever seen. There is sometimes a certain charm in the rubicund and jovial fat man, but this saturnine obesity was repulsive.

'I do not pretend that I was faithful to her. She was not young when I married her and we had been married for ten years. She was small and thin, and she had a bad complexion. She had a bitter tongue. She was a woman who suffered from a fury of possession, and she could not bear me to be attracted to anyone but her. She was jealous not only of the women I knew, but of my friends, my cat, and my books. On one occasion in my absence she gave away a coat of mine merely because I liked none of my coats so well. But I am of an equable temperament. I will not deny that she bored me, but I accepted her acrimonious disposition as an act of God and no more thought of rebelling against it than I would against bad weather or a cold in the head. I denied her accusations as long as it was possible to deny them, and when it was impossible I shrugged my shoulders and smoked a cigarette.

'The constant scenes she made me did not very much affect me. I led my own life. Sometimes, indeed, I wondered whether it was passionate love she felt for me or passionate hate. It seemed to me that love and hate were very near allied.

'So we might have continued to the end of the chapter if one night a very curious thing had not happened. I was awakened by a piercing scream from my wife. Startled, I asked her what was the matter. She told me that she had had a fearful nightmare; she had dreamt that I was trying to kill her. We lived at the top of a large house and the well round which the stairs climbed was broad. She had dreamt that just as we had arrived at our own floor I had caught hold of her and attempted to throw her over the balusters. It was six storeys to the stone floor at the bottom and it meant certain death.

'She was much shaken. I did my best to soothe her. But next morning, and for two or three days after, she referred to the subject again and, notwithstanding my laughter, I saw that it dwelt in her mind. I could not help thinking of it either, for this dream showed me something that I had never suspected. She thought I hated her, she thought I would gladly be rid of her; she knew of course that she was insufferable, and at some time or other the idea had evidently occurred to her that I was capable of murdering her. The thoughts of men are incalculable and ideas enter our minds that we should be ashamed to confess. Sometimes I had wished that she might run away with a lover, sometimes that a painless and sudden death might give me my freedom; but never, never had the idea come to me that I might deliberately rid myself of an intolerable burden.

'The dream made an extraordinary impression upon both of us. It frightened my wife, and she became for a little less bitter and more tolerant. But when I walked up the stairs to our apartment it was impossible for me not to look over the balusters and reflect how easy it would be to do what she had dreamt. The balusters were dangerously low. A quick gesture and the thing was done. It was hard to put the thought out of my mind. Then some months later my wife awakened me one night. I was very tired and I was exasperated. She was white and trembling. She had had the dream again. She burst into tears and asked me if I hated her. I swore by all the saints of the Russian calendar that I loved her. At last she went to sleep again. It was more than I could do. I lay awake. I seemed to see her falling down the well of the stairs, and I heard her shriek and the thud as she struck the stone floor. I could not help shivering.'

The Russian stopped and beads of sweat stood on his forehead. He had told the story well and fluently so that I had listened with attention. There was still some vodka in the bottle; he poured it out and swallowed it at a gulp.

'And how did your wife eventually die?' I asked after a pause.

He took out a dirty handkerchief and wiped his forehead.

'By an extraordinary coincidence she was found late one night at the bottom of the stairs with her neck broken.'

'Who found her?'

'She was found by one of the lodgers who came in shortly after the catastrophe.'

'And where were you?'

I cannot describe the look he gave me of malicious cunning. His little black eyes sparkled.

'I was spending the evening with a friend of mine. I did not come in till an hour later.'

At that moment the waiter brought us the dish of meat that we had ordered, and the Russian fell upon it with good appetite. He shovelled the food into his mouth in enormous mouthfuls.

I was taken aback. Had he really been telling me in this hardly veiled manner that he had murdered his wife? That obese and sluggish man did not look like a murderer; I could not believe that he would have had the courage. Or was he making a sardonic joke at my expense?

In a few minutes it was time for me to go and catch my train. I left him and I have not seen him since. But I have never been able to make up my mind whether he was serious or jesting.

THE TREASURE

RICHARD HARENGER was a happy man. Notwithstanding what the pessimists, from Ecclesiastes onwards, have said, this is not so rare a thing to find in this unhappy world, but Richard Harenger knew it, and that is a very rare thing indeed. The golden mean which the ancients so highly prized is out of fashion, and those who follow it must put up with polite derision from those who see no merit in self-restraint and no virtue in common sense. Richard Harenger shrugged a polite and amused shoulder. Let others live dangerously, let others burn with a hard gemlike flame, let others stake their fortunes on the turn of a card, walk the tightrope that leads to glory or the grave, or hazard their lives for a cause, a passion, or an adventure. He neither envied the fame their exploits brought them nor wasted his pity on them when their efforts ended in disaster.

But it must not be inferred from this that Richard Harenger was a selfish or a callous man. He was neither. He was considerate and of a generous disposition. He was always ready to oblige a friend and he was sufficiently well off to be able to indulge himself in the pleasure of helping others. He had some money of his own and he occupied in the Home Office a position that brought him an adequate stipend. The work suited him. It was regular, responsible, and pleasant. Every day when he left the office he went to his club to play bridge for a couple of hours, and on Saturdays and Sundays he played golf. He went abroad for his holidays, staying at good hotels, and visited churches, galleries, and museums. He was a regular first-nighter. He dined out a good deal. His friends liked him. He was easy to talk to. He was well-read, knowledgeable, and amusing. He was besides of a personable exterior, not remarkably handsome, but tall, slim, and erect of carriage, with a lean, intelligent face; his hair was growing thin, for he was now approaching the age of fifty, but his brown eyes retained their smile, and his teeth were all his own. He had from nature a good constitution and he had always taken care of himself. There was no reason in the world why he should not be a happy man, and if there had been in him a trace of self-complacency he might have claimed that he deserved to be.

He had the good fortune even to sail safely through those perilous, unquiet straits of marriage in which so many wise and good men have made shipwreck. Married for love in the early twenties, his wife and he, after some years of almost perfect felicity, had drifted gradually apart. Neither of them wished to marry anyone else, so there was no question of divorce (which indeed Richard Harenger's situation in the government service made undesirable), but for convenience' sake, with the help of the family lawyer, they arranged a separation which left them free to lead their lives as each one wished without interference from the other. They parted with mutual expressions of respect and good will.

Richard Harenger sold his house in St John's Wood and took a flat within convenient walking distance of Whitehall. It had a sitting-room which he lined with his books, a dining-room into which his Chippendale furniture just fitted, a nice-sized bedroom for himself, and beyond the kitchen a couple of maids' rooms. He brought his cook, whom he had had for many years, from St John's Wood, but needing no longer so large a staff dismissed the rest of the servants and applied at a registry office for a house-parlourmaid. He knew exactly what he wanted and he explained his needs to the superintendent of the agency with precision. He wanted a maid who was not too young, first because young women are flighty and secondly because, though he was of mature age and a man of principle, people would talk, the porter and the tradesmen if nobody else, and both for the sake of his own reputation and that of the young person he considered that the applicant should have reached years of discretion. Besides that he wanted a maid who could clean silver well. He had always had a fancy for old silver, and it was reasonable to demand that the forks and spoons that had been used by a woman of quality under the reign of Queen Anne should be treated with tenderness and respect. He was of a hospitable nature and liked to give at least once a week little dinners of not less than four people and not more than eight. He could trust his cook to send in a meal that his guests would take pleasure in eating and he desired his parlourmaid to wait with neatness and dispatch. Then he needed a perfect valet. He dressed well, in a manner that suited his age and condition, and he liked his clothes to be properly looked after. The parlourmaid he was looking for must be able to press trousers and iron a tie, and he was very particular that his shoes should be well shone. He had small feet and he took a good deal of trouble to have well-cut shoes. He had a large supply and he insisted that they should be treed up the moment he took them off. Finally the flat must be kept clean and tidy. It was of course understood that any applicant for the post must be of irreproachable character, sober, honest, reliable, and of a pleasing exterior. In return for this he was prepared to offer good wages, reasonable liberty, and ample holidays. The superintendent listened without batting an eyelash and, telling him that she was quite sure she could suit him, sent him a string of candidates which proved that she had not paid the smallest attention to a word he said. He saw them all personally. Some were obviously inefficient, some looked fast, some were too old, others too young, some lacked the presence he thought essential; there was not one to whom he was inclined even to give a trial. He was a kindly, polite man and he declined their services with a smile and a pleasant expression of regret. He did not lose patience. He was prepared to interview house-parlourmaids till he found one who was suitable.

Now it is a funny thing about life, if you refuse to accept anything but the best you very often get it: if you utterly decline to make do with what you can get, then somehow or other you are very likely to get what you want. It is as though fate said, this man's a perfect fool, he's asking for perfection, and then just out of her feminine wilfulness flung it in his lap. One day the porter of the flats said to Richard Harenger out of a blue sky:

'I hear you're lookin' for a house-parlourmaid, sir. There's someone I know lookin' for a situation as might do.'

'Can you recommend her personally?'

Richard Harenger had the sound opinion that one servant's recommendation of another was worth much more than that of an employer.

'I can vouch for her respectability. She's been in some very good situations.'

'I shall be coming in to dress about seven. If that's convenient to her I could see her then.'

'Very good, sir. I'll see that she's told.'

He had not been in more than five minutes when the cook, having answered a ring at the front door, came in and told him that the person the porter had spoken to him about had called.

'Show her in,' he said.

He turned on some more light so that he could see what the applicant looked like and, getting up, stood with his back to the fireplace. A woman came in and stood just inside the door in a respectful attitude.

'Good evening,' he said. 'What is your name?'

'Pritchard, sir.'

'How old are you?'

'Thirty-five, sir.'

'Well, that's a reasonable age.'

He gave his cigarette a puff and looked at her reflectively. She was on the tall side, nearly as tall as he, but he guessed that she wore high heels. Her black dress fitted her station. She held herself well. She had good features and a rather high colour.

'Will you take off your hat?' he asked.

She did so and he saw that she had pale brown hair. It was neatly and becomingly dressed. She looked strong and healthy. She was neither fat nor thin. In a proper uniform she would look very presentable. She was not inconveniently handsome, but she was certainly a comely, in another class of life you might almost have said a handsome, woman. He proceeded to ask her a number of questions. Her answers were satisfactory. She had left her last place for an adequate reason. She had been trained under a butler and appeared to be well acquainted with her duties. In her last place she had been head parlourmaid of three, but she did not mind undertaking the work of the flat single-handed. She had valeted a gentleman before who had sent her to a tailor's to learn how to press clothes. She was a little shy, but neither timid nor ill-at-ease. Richard asked her his questions in his amiable, leisurely way and she answered them with modest composure. He was considerably impressed. He asked her what references she could give. They seemed extremely satisfactory.

'Now look here,' he said, 'I'm very much inclined to engage you. But I hate changes, I've had my cook for twelve years: if you suit me and the place suits you I hope you'll stay. I mean, I don't want you to come to me in three or four months and say that you're leaving to get married.'

'There's not much fear of that, sir. I'm a widow. I don't believe marriage is much catch for anyone in my position, sir. My husband never did a stroke of work from the day I married him to the day he died, and I had to keep him. What I want now is a good home.'

'I'm inclined to agree with you,' he smiled. 'Marriage is a very good thing, but I think it's a mistake to make a habit of it.'

She very properly made no reply to this, but waited for him to announce his decision. She did not seem anxious about it. He reflected that if she was as competent as she appeared she must be well aware that she would have no difficulty in finding a place. He told her what wages he was offering and these seemed to be satisfactory to her. He gave her the necessary information about the place, but she gave him to understand that she was already apprised of this, and he received the impression, which amused rather than disconcerted him, that she had made certain inquiries about him before applying for the situation. It showed prudence on her part and good sense.

'When would you be able to come in if I engaged you? I haven't got anybody at the moment. The cook's managing as best she can with a char, but I should like to get settled as soon as possible.'

'Well, sir, I was going to give myself a week's holiday, but if it's a matter of obliging a gentleman I don't mind giving that up. I could come in tomorrow if it was convenient.'

Richard Harenger gave her his attractive smile.

'I shouldn't like you to do without a holiday that I dare say you've been looking forward to. I can very well go on like this for another week. Go and have your holiday and come to me when it's over.'

'Thank you very much, sir. Would it do if I came in tomorrow week?'

'Quite well.'

When she left, Richard Harenger felt he had done a good day's work. It looked as though he had found exactly what he was after. He rang for the cook and told her he had engaged a house-parlourmaid at last.

'I think you'll like her, sir,' she said. 'She came in and 'ad a talk with me this afternoon. I could see at once she knew her duties. And she's not one of them flighty ones.'

'We can but try, Mrs Jeddy. I hope you gave me a good character.'

'Well, I said you was particular, sir. I said you was a gentleman as liked things just so.'

'I admit that.'

'She said she didn't mind that. She said she liked a gentleman as knew what was what. She said there's no satisfaction in doing things proper if nobody notices. I expect you'll find she'll take a rare lot of pride in her work.'

'That's what I want her to do. I think we might go farther and fare worse.'

'Well, sir, there is that to it, of course. And the proof of the pudding's the eating. But if you ask my opinion I think she's going to be a real treasure.'

And that is precisely what Pritchard turned out. No man was ever better served. The way she shone shoes was marvellous, and he set out of a fine morning for his walk to the office with a more jaunty step because you could almost see yourself reflected in them. She looked after his clothes with such attention that his colleagues began to chaff him about being the best-dressed man in the Civil Service. One day, coming home unexpectedly, he found a line of socks and handkerchiefs hung up to dry in the bathroom. He called Pritchard.

'D'you wash my socks and handkerchiefs yourself, Pritchard?

I should have thought you had enough to do without that.'

'They do ruin them so at the laundry, sir. I prefer to do them at home if you have no objection.'

She knew exactly what he should wear on every occasion, and without asking him was aware whether she should put out a dinner jacket and a black tie in the evening or a dress coat and a white one. When he was going to a party where decorations were to be worn he found his neat little row of medals automatically affixed to the lapel of his coat. He soon ceased to choose every morning from his wardrobe the tie he wanted, for he found that she put out for him without fail the one he would have himself selected. Her taste was perfect. He supposed she read his letters, for she always knew what his movements were, and if he had forgotten at what hour he had an engagement he had no need to look in his book, for Pritchard could tell him. She knew exactly what tone to use with persons with whom she conversed on the telephone. Except with tradesmen, with whom she was apt to be peremptory, she was always polite, but there was a distinct difference in her manner if she was addressing one of Mr Harenger's literary friends or the wife of a Cabinet Minister. She knew by instinct with whom he wished to speak and with whom he didn't. From his sitting-room he sometimes heard her with placid sincerity assuring a caller that he was out, and then she would come in and tell him that So-and-So had rung up, but she thought he wouldn't wish to be disturbed.

'Quite right, Pritchard,' he smiled.

'I knew she only wanted to bother you about that concert,' said Pritchard.

His friends made appointments with him through her, and she would tell him what she had done on his return in the evening.

'Mrs Soames rang up, sir, and asked if you would lunch with her on Thursday, the eighth, but I said you were very sorry but you were lunching with Lady Versinder. Mr Oakley rang up and asked if you'd go to a cocktail party at the Savoy next Tuesday at six. I said you would if you possibly could, but you might have to go to the dentist's.'

'Quite right.'

'I thought you could see when the time came, sir.'

She kept the flat like a new pin. On one occasion soon after she entered his service, Richard coming back from a holiday took out a book from his shelves and at once noticed that it had been dusted. He rang the bell.

'I forgot to tell you when I went away under no circumstances ever to touch my books. When books are taken out to be dusted they're never put back in the right place. I don't mind my books being dirty, but I hate not being able to find them.'

'I'm very sorry, sir,' said Pritchard. 'I know some gentlemen are very particular and I took care to put back every book exactly where I took it from.'

Richard Harenger gave his books a glance. So far as he could see every one was in its accustomed place. He smiled.

'I apologize, Pritchard.'

'They were in a muck, sir. I mean, you couldn't open one without getting your hands black with dust.'

She certainly kept his silver as he had never had it kept before. He felt called upon to give her a special word of praise.

'Most of it's Queen Anne and George I, you know,' he explained.

'Yes, I know, sir. When you've got something good like that to look after it's a pleasure to keep it like it should be.'

'You certainly have a knack for it. I never knew a butler who kept his silver as well as you do.'

'Men haven't the patience women have,' she replied modestly.

As soon as he thought Pritchard had settled down in the place he resumed the little dinners he was fond of giving once a week. He had already discovered that she knew how to wait at table, but it was with a warm sense of complacency that he realized then how competently she could manage a party. She was quick, silent, and watchful. A guest had hardly felt the need of something before Pritchard was at his elbow offering him what he wanted. She soon learned the tastes of his more intimate friends and remembered that one liked water instead of soda with his whisky and that another particularly fancied the knuckle end of a leg of lamb. She knew exactly how cold a hock should be not to ruin its taste and how long claret should have stood in the room to bring out its bouquet. It was a pleasure to see her pour out a bottle of burgundy in such a fashion as not to disturb the grounds. On one occasion she did not serve the wine Richard had ordered. He somewhat sharply pointed this out to her.

'I opened the bottle sir, and it was slightly corked. So I got the Chambertin, as I thought it was safer.'

'Quite right, Pritchard.'

Presently he left this matter entirely in her hands, for he discovered that she knew perfectly what wines his guests would like. Without orders from him she would provide the best in his cellar and his oldest brandy if she thought they were the sort of people who knew what they were drinking. She had no belief in the palate of women, and when they were of the party was apt to serve the champagne which had to be drunk before it went off. She had the English servant's instinctive knowledge of social differences, and neither rank nor money blinded her to the fact that someone was not a gentleman, but she had favourites among his friends, and when someone she particularly liked was dining, with the air of a cat that has swallowed a canary she would pour out for him a bottle of a wine that Harenger kept for very special occasions. It amused him.

'You've got on the right side of Pritchard, old boy,' he exclaimed. 'There aren't many people she gives this wine to.'

Pritchard became an institution. She was known very soon to be the perfect parlourmaid. People envied Harenger the possession of her as they envied nothing else that he had. She was worth her weight in gold. Her price was above rubies. Richard Harenger beamed with self-complacency when they praised her.

'Good masters make good servants,' he said gaily.

One evening, when they were sitting over their port and she had left the room, they were talking about her.

'It'll be an awful blow when she leaves you.'

'Why should she leave me? One or two people have tried to get her away from me, but she turned them down. She knows where she's well off.'

'She'll get married one of these days.'

'I don't think she's that sort.'

'She's a good-looking woman.'

'Yes, she has quite a decent presence.'

'What are you talking about? She's a very handsome creature. In another class of life she'd be a well-known society beauty with her photograph in all the papers.'

At that moment Pritchard came in with the coffee. Richard Harenger looked at her. After seeing her every day, off and on, for four years it was now – my word, how time flies – he had really forgotten what she looked like. She did not seem to have changed much since he had first seen her. She was no stouter than then, she still had the high colour, and her regular features bore the same expression which was at once intent and vacuous. The black uniform suited her. She left the room.

'She's a paragon and there's no doubt about it.'

'I know she is,' answered Harenger. 'She's perfection. I should be lost without her. And the strange thing is that I don't very much like her.'

'Why not?'

'I think she bores me a little. You see, she has no conversation. I've often tried to talk to her. She answers when I speak to her, but that's all. In four years she's never volunteered a remark of her own. I know absolutely nothing about her. I don't know if she likes me or if she's completely indifferent to me. She's an automaton. I respect her, I appreciate her, I trust her. She has every quality in the world and I've often wondered why it is that with all that I'm so completely indifferent to her. I think it must be that she is entirely devoid of charm.'

They left it at that.

Two or three days after this, since it was Pritchard's night out and he had no engagement, Richard Harenger dined by himself at his club. A page-boy came to him and told him that they had just rung up from his flat to say that he had gone out without his keys and should they be brought along to him in a taxi? He put his hand to his pocket. It was a fact. By a singular chance he had forgotten to replace them when he had changed into a blue serge suit before coming out to dinner. His intention had been to play bridge, but it was an off-night at the club and there seemed little chance of a decent game; it occurred to him that it would be a good opportunity to see a picture that he had heard talked about, so he sent back the message by the page that he would call for the keys himself in half an hour.

He rang at the door of his flat and it was opened by Pritchard. She had the keys in her hand.

'What are you doing here, Pritchard?' he asked. 'It's your night out, isn't it?'

'Yes, sir. But I didn't care about going, so I told Mrs Jeddy she could go instead.'

'You ought to get out when you have the chance,' he said, with his usual thoughtfulness. 'It's not good for you to be cooped up here all the time.'

'I get out now and then on an errand, but I haven't been out in the evening for the last month.'

'Why on earth not?'

'Well, it's not very cheerful going out by yourself, and somehow I don't know anyone just now that I'm particularly keen on going out with.'

'You ought to have a bit of fun now and then. It's good for you.'

'I've got out of the habit of it somehow.'

'Look here, I'm just going to the cinema. Would you like to come along with me?'

He spoke in kindliness, on the spur of the moment, and the moment he had said the words half regretted them.

'Yes, sir, I'd like to,' said Pritchard.

'Run along then and put on a hat.'

'I shan't be a minute.'

She disappeared and he went into the sitting-room and lit a cigarette. He was a little amused at what he was doing, and pleased too; it was nice to be able to make someone happy with so little trouble to himself. It was characteristic of Pritchard that she had shown neither surprise nor hesitation. She kept him waiting about five minutes, and when she came back he noticed that she had changed her dress. She wore a blue frock in what he supposed was artificial silk, a small black hat with a blue brooch on it, and a silver fox round her neck. He was a trifle relieved to see that she looked neither shabby nor showy. It would never occur to anyone who happened to see them that this was a distinguished official in the Home Office taking his housemaid to the pictures.

'I'm sorry to have kept you waiting, sir.'

'It doesn't matter at all,' he said graciously.

He opened the front door for her and she went out before him. He remembered the familiar anecdote of Louis XIV and the courtier and appreciated the fact that she had not hesitated to precede him. The cinema for which they were bound was at no great distance from Mr Harenger's flat and they walked there. He talked about the weather and the state of the roads and Adolf Hitler. Pritchard made suitable replies. They arrived just as Mickey the Mouse was starting and this put them in a good humour. During the four years she had been in his service Richard Harenger had hardly ever seen Pritchard even smile, and now it diverted him vastly to hear her peal upon peal of joyous laughter. He enjoyed her pleasure. Then the principal attraction was thrown on the screen. It was a good picture and they both watched it with breathless excitement. Taking his cigarette-case out to help himself he automatically offered it to Pritchard.

'Thank you, sir,' she said, taking one.

He lit it for her. Her eyes were on the screen and she was almost unconscious of his action. When the picture was finished they streamed out with the crowd into the street. They walked back towards the flat. It was a fine starry night.

'Did you like it?' he said.

'Like anything, sir. It was a real treat.'

A thought occurred to him.

'By the way, did you have any supper tonight?'

'No, sir, I didn't have time.'

'Aren't you starving?'

'I'll have a bit of bread and cheese when I get in and I'll make meself a cup of cocoa.'

'That sounds rather grim.' There was a feeling of gaiety in the air, and the people who poured past them, one way and another, seemed filled with a pleasant elation. In for a penny, in for a pound, he said to himself. 'Look here, would you like to come and have a bit of supper with me somewhere?'

'If you'd like to, sir.'

'Come on.'

He hailed a cab. He was feeling very philanthropic and it was not a feeling that he disliked at all. He told the driver to go to a restaurant in Oxford Street which was gay, but at which he was confident there was no chance of meeting anyone he knew. There was an orchestra and people danced. It would amuse Pritchard to see them. When they sat down a waiter came up to them.

'They've got a set supper here,' he said, thinking that was what she would like. 'I suggest we have that. What would you like to drink? A little white wine?'

'What I really fancy is a glass of ginger beer,' she said.

Richard Harenger ordered himself a whisky and soda. She ate the supper with hearty appetite, and though Harenger was not hungry, to put her at her ease he ate too. The picture they had just seen gave them something to talk about. It was quite true what they had said the other night, Pritchard was not a bad-looking woman, and even if someone had seen them together he would not have minded. It would make rather a good story for his friends when he told them how he had taken the incomparable Pritchard to the cinema and then afterwards to supper. Pritchard was looking at the dancers with a faint smile on her lips.

'Do you like dancing?' he said.

'I used to be a rare one for it when I was a girl. I never danced much after I was married. My husband was a bit shorter than me and somehow I never think it looks well unless the gentleman's taller, if you know what I mean. I suppose I shall be getting too old for it soon.'

Richard was certainly taller than his parlourmaid. They would look all right. He was fond of dancing and he danced well. But he hesitated. He did not want to embarrass Pritchard by asking her to dance with him. It was better not to go too far perhaps. And yet what did it matter? It was a drab life she led. She was so sensible, if she thought it a mistake he was pretty sure she would find a decent excuse.

'Would you like to take a turn, Pritchard?' he said, as the band struck up again.

'I'm terribly out of practice, sir.'

'What does that matter?'

'If you don't mind, sir,' she answered coolly, rising from her seat.

She was not in the least shy. She was only afraid that she would not be able to follow his step. They moved on to the floor. He found she danced very well.

'Why, you dance perfectly, Pritchard,' he said.

'It's coming back to me.'

Although she was a big woman she was light on her feet and she had a natural sense of rhythm. She was very pleasant to dance with. He gave a glance at the mirrors that lined the walls and he could not help reflecting that they looked very well together. Their eyes met in the mirror; he wondered whether she was thinking that too. They had two more dances and then Richard Harenger suggested that they should go. He paid the bill and they walked out. He noticed that she threaded her way through the crowd without a trace of self-consciousness. They got into a taxi and in ten minutes were at home.

'I'll go up the back way, sir,' said Pritchard.

'There's no need to do that. Come up in the lift with me.'

He took her up, giving the night-porter an icy glance, so that he should not think it strange that he came back at that somewhat late hour with his parlourmaid, and with his latch-key let her into the flat.

'Well, good night, sir,' she said. 'Thank you very much. It's been a real treat for me.'

'Thank *you* Pritchard. I should have had a very dull evening by myself. I hope you've enjoyed your outing.'

'That I have, sir, more than I can say.'

It had been a success. Richard Harenger was satisfied with himself. It was a kindly thing for him to have done. It was a very agreeable sensation to give anyone so much real pleasure. His benevolence warmed him and for a moment he felt a great love in his heart for the whole human race.

'Good night, Pritchard,' he said, and because he felt happy and good he put his arm round her waist and kissed her on the lips.

Her lips were very soft. They lingered on his and she returned his kiss. It was the warm, hearty embrace of a healthy woman in the prime of life. He found it very pleasant and he held her to him a little more closely. She put her arms round his neck.

As a general rule he did not wake till Pritchard came in with his letters, but next morning he woke at half past seven. He had a curious sensation that he did not recognize. He was accustomed to sleep with two pillows under his head and he suddenly grew aware of the fact that he had only one. Then he remembered and with a start looked round. The other pillow was beside his own. Thank God, no sleeping head rested there, but it was plain that one had. His heart sank. He broke out into a cold sweat.

'My God, what a fool I've been!' he cried out loud.

How could he have done anything so stupid? What on earth had come over him? He was the last man to play about with servant girls. What a disgraceful thing to do! At his age and in his position. He had not heard Pritchard slip away. He must have been asleep. It wasn't even as if he'd liked her very much. She wasn't his type. And, as he had said the other night, she rather bored him. Even now he only knew her as Pritchard. He had no notion what her first name was. What madness! And what was to happen now? The position was impossible. It was obvious he couldn't keep her, and yet to send her away for what was his fault as much as hers seemed shockingly unfair. How idiotic to lose the best parlourmaid a man ever had just for an hour's folly!

'It's that damned kindness of heart of mine,' he groaned.

He would never find anyone else to look after his clothes so admirably or clean the silver so well. She knew all his friends' telephone numbers and she understood wine. But of course she must go. She must see for herself that after what had happened things could never be the same. He would make her a handsome present and give her an excellent reference. At any minute she would be coming in now. Would she be arch, would she be familiar? Or would she put on airs? Perhaps even she wouldn't trouble to come in with his letters. It would be awful if he had to ring the bell and Mrs Jeddy came in and said: Pritchard's not up yet, sir, she's having a lie in after last night.

'What a fool I've been! What a contemptible cad!'

There was a knock at the door. He was sick with anxiety.

'Come in.'

Richard Harenger was a very unhappy man.

Pritchard came in as the clock struck. She wore the print dress she was in the habit of wearing during the early part of the day.

'Good morning, sir,' she said.

'Good morning.'

She drew the curtains and handed him his letters and the papers. Her face was impassive. She looked exactly as she always looked. Her movements had the same competent deliberation that they always had. She neither avoided Richard's glance nor sought it.

'Will you wear your grey, sir? It came back from the tailor's yesterday.'

'Yes.'

He pretended to read his letters, but he watched her from under his eyelashes. Her back was turned to him. She took his vest and drawers and folded them over a chair. She took the studs out of the shirt he had worn the day before and studded a clean one. She put out some clean socks for him and placed them on the seat of a chair with the suspenders to match by the side. Then she put out his grey suit and attached the braces to the back buttons of the trousers. She opened his wardrobe and after a moment's reflection chose a tie to go with the suit. She collected on her arm the suit of the day before and picked up the shoes.

'Will you have breakfast now, sir, or will you have your bath first?'

'I'll have breakfast now,' he said.

'Very good, sir.'

With her slow quiet movements, unruffled, she left the room. Her face bore that rather serious, deferential, vacuous look it always bore. What had happened might have been a dream. Nothing in Pritchard's demeanour suggested that she had the smallest recollection of the night before. He gave a sigh of relief. It was going to be all right. She need not go, she need not go. Pritchard was the perfect parlourmaid. He knew that never by word nor gesture would she ever refer to the fact that for a moment their relations had been other than those of master and servant. Richard Harenger was a very happy man.

THE COLONEL'S LADY

ALL this happened two or three years before the outbreak of the war.

The Peregrines were having breakfast. Though they were alone and the table was long they sat at opposite ends of it. From the walls George Peregrine's ancestors, painted by the fashionable painters of the day, looked down upon them. The butler brought in the morning post. There were several letters for the colonel, business letters, *The Times*, and a small parcel for his wife Evie. He looked at his letters and then, opening *The Times*, began to read it. They finished breakfast and rose from the table. He noticed that his wife hadn't opened the parcel.

'What's that?' he asked.

'Only some books.'

'Shall I open it for you?'

'If you like.'

He hated to cut string and so with some difficulty untied the knots.

'But they're all the same,' he said when he had unwrapped the parcel. 'What on earth d'you want six copies of the same book for?' He opened one of them. 'Poetry.' Then he looked at the title page. *When Pyramids Decay*, he read, by E. K. Hamilton. Eva Katherine Hamilton: that was his wife's maiden name. He looked at her with smiling surprise. 'Have you written a book, Evie? You are a slyboots.'

'I didn't think it would interest you very much. Would you like a copy?'

'Well, you know poetry isn't much in my line, but – yes, I'd like a copy; I'll read it. I'll take it along to my study. I've got a lot to do this morning.'

He gathered up *The Times*, his letters, and the book, and went out. His study was a large and comfortable room, with a big desk, leather arm-chairs, and what he called 'trophies of the chase' on the walls. On the bookshelves were works of reference, books on farming, gardening, fishing, and shooting, and books on the last war, in which he had won an M.C. and a D.S.O. For before his marriage he had been in the Welsh Guards. At the end of the war he retired and settled down to the life of a country gentleman in the spacious house, some twenty miles from Sheffield, which one of his forebears had built in the reign of George III. George Peregrine had an estate of some fifteen hundred acres which he managed with ability; he was a Justice of the Peace and performed his duties conscientiously. During the season he rode to hounds two days a week. He was a good shot, a golfer, and though now a little over fifty could still play a hard game of tennis. He could describe himself with propriety as an all-round sportsman.

He had been putting on weight lately, but was still a fine figure of a man; tall, with grey curly hair, only just beginning to grow thin on the crown, frank blue eyes, good features, and a high colour. He was a public-spirited man, chairman of any number of local organizations and, as became his class and station, a loyal member of the Conservative Party. He looked upon it as his duty to see to the welfare of the people on his estate and it was a satisfaction to him to know that Evie could be trusted to tend the sick and succour the poor. He had built a cottage hospital on the outskirts of the village and paid the wages of a nurse out of his own pocket. All he asked of the recipients of his bounty was that at elections, county or general, they should vote for his candidate. He was a friendly man, affable to his inferiors, considerate with his tenants, and popular with the neighbouring gentry. He would have been pleased and at the same time slightly embarrassed if someone had told him he was a jolly good fellow. That was what he wanted to be. He desired no higher praise.

It was hard luck that he had no children. He would have been an excellent father, kindly but strict, and would have brought up his sons as gentlemen's sons should be brought up, sent them to Eton, you know, taught them to fish, shoot, and ride. As it was, his heir was a nephew, son of his brother killed in a motor accident, not a bad boy, but not a chip off the old block, no, sir, far from it; and would you believe it, his fool of a mother was sending him to a co-educational school. Evie had been a sad disappointment to him. Of course she was a lady, and she had a bit of money of her own; she managed the house uncommonly well and she was a good hostess. The village people adored her. She had been a pretty little thing when he married her, with a creamy skin, light brown hair, and a trim figure, healthy too, and not a bad tennis player; he couldn't understand why she'd had no children; of course she was faded now, she must be getting on for five and forty; her skin was drab, her hair had lost its sheen, and she was as thin as a rail. She was always neat and suitably dressed, but she didn't seem to bother how she looked, she wore no make-up and didn't even use lipstick; sometimes at night when she dolled herself up for a party you could tell that once she'd been quite attractive, but ordinarily she was – well, the sort of woman you simply didn't notice. A nice woman, of course, a good wife, and it wasn't her fault if she was barren, but it was tough on a fellow who wanted an heir of his own loins; she hadn't any vitality, that's what was the matter with her. He supposed he'd been in love with her when he asked her to marry him, at least sufficiently in love for a man who wanted to marry and settle down, but with time he discovered that they had nothing much in common. She didn't care about hunting, and fishing bored her. Naturally they'd drifted apart. He had to do her the justice to admit that she'd never bothered him. There'd been no scenes. They had no quarrels. She seemed to take it for granted that he should go his own way. When he went up to London now and then she never wanted to come with him. He had a girl there, well, she wasn't exactly a girl, she was thirty-five if she was a day, but she was blonde and luscious and he only had to wire ahead of time and they'd dine, do a show, and spend the night together. Well, a man, a healthy normal man had to have some fun in his life. The thought crossed his mind that if Evie hadn't been such a good woman she'd have been a better wife; but it was not the sort of thought that he welcomed and he put it away from him.

George Peregrine finished his *Times* and being a considerate fellow rang the bell and told the butler to take it to Evie. Then he looked at his watch. It was half past ten and at eleven he had an appointment with one of his tenants. He had half an hour to spare.

'I'd better have a look at Evie's book,' he said to himself.

He took it up with a smile. Evie had a lot of highbrow books in her sitting-room, not the sort of books that interested him, but if they amused her he had no objection to her reading them. He noticed that the volume he now held in his hand contained no more than ninety pages. That was all to the good. He shared Edgar Allan Poe's opinion that poems should be short. But as he turned the pages he noticed that several of Evie's had long lines of irregular length and didn't rhyme. He didn't like that. At his first school, when he was a little boy, he remembered learning a poem that began: *The boy stood on the burning deck*, and later, at Eton, one that started: *Ruin seize thee, ruthless king*; and then there was *Henry V*; they'd had to take that, one half. He stared at Evie's pages with consternation.

'That's not what I call poetry,' he said.

Fortunately it wasn't all like that. Interspersed with the pieces that looked so odd, lines of three or four words and then a line of ten or fifteen, there were little poems, quite short, that rhymed, thank God, with the lines all the same length. Several of the pages were just headed with the word *Sonnet*, and out of curiosity he counted the lines; there were fourteen of them. He read them. They seemed all right, but he didn't quite know what they were all about. He repeated to himself: *Ruin seize thee, ruthless king*.

'Poor Evie,' he sighed.

At that moment the farmer he was expecting was ushered into the study, and putting the book down he made him welcome. They embarked on their business.

'I read your book, Evie,' he said as they sat down to lunch. 'Jolly good. Did it cost you a packet to have it printed?'

'No, I was lucky. I sent it to a publisher and he took it.'

'Not much money in poetry, my dear,' he said in his good-natured, hearty way.

'No, I don't suppose there is. What did Bannock want to see you about this morning?'

Bannock was the tenant who had interrupted his reading of Evie's poems.

'He's asked me to advance the money for a pedigree bull he wants to buy. He's a good man and I've half a mind to do it.'

George Peregrine saw that Evie didn't want to talk about her book and he was not sorry to change the subject. He was glad she had used her maiden name on the title page; he didn't suppose anyone would ever hear about the book, but he was proud of his own unusual name and he wouldn't have liked it if some damned penny-a-liner had made fun of Evie's effort in one of the papers.

During the few weeks that followed he thought it tactful not to ask Evie any questions about her venture into verse, and she never referred to it. It might have been a discreditable incident that they had silently agreed not to mention. But then a strange thing happened. He had to go to London on business and he took Daphne out to dinner. That was the name of the girl with whom he was in the habit of passing a few agreeable hours whenever he went to town.

'Oh, George,' she said, 'is that your wife who's written a book they're all talking about?'

'What on earth d'you mean?'

'Well, there's a fellow I know who's a critic. He took me out to dinner the other night and he had a book with him. "Got anything for me to read?" I said. "What's that?" "Oh, I don't think that's your cup of tea," he said. "It's poetry. I've just been reviewing it." "No poetry for me," I said. "It's about the hottest stuff I ever read," he said. "Selling like hot cakes. And it's damned good."'

'Who's the book by?' asked George.

'A woman called Hamilton. My friend told me that wasn't her real name. He said her real name was Peregrine. "Funny," I said, "I know a fellow called Peregrine." "Colonel in the army," he said. "Lives near Sheffield."'

'I'd just as soon you didn't talk about me to your friends,' said George with a frown of vexation.

'Keep your shirt on, dearie. Who d'you take me for? I just said: "It's not the same one."' Daphne giggled. 'My friend said: "They say he's a regular Colonel Blimp."'

George had a keen sense of humour.

'You could tell them better than that,' he laughed. 'If my wife had written a book I'd be the first to know about it, wouldn't I?'

'I suppose you would.'

Anyhow the matter didn't interest her and when the colonel began to talk of other things she forgot about it. He put it out of his mind too. There was nothing to it, he decided, and that silly fool of a critic had just been pulling Daphne's leg. He was amused at the thought of her tackling that book because she had been told it was hot stuff and then finding it just a lot of bosh cut up into unequal lines.

He was a member of several clubs and next day he thought he'd lunch at one in St James's Street. He was catching a train back to Sheffield early in the afternoon. He was sitting in a comfortable arm-chair having a glass of sherry before going into the dining-room when an old friend came up to him.

'Well, old boy, how's life?' he said. 'How d'you like being the husband of a celebrity?'

George Peregrine looked at his friend. He thought he saw an amused twinkle in his eyes.

'I don't know what you're talking about,' he answered.

'Come off it, George. Everyone knows E. K. Hamilton is your wife. Not often a book of verse has a success like that. Look here, Henry Dashwood is lunching with me. He'd like to meet you.'

'Who the devil is Henry Dashwood and why should he want to meet me?'

'Oh, my dear fellow, what do you do with yourself all the time in the country? Henry's about the best critic we've got. He wrote a wonderful review of Evie's book. D'you mean to say she didn't show it you?'

Before George could answer his friend had called a man over. A tall, thin man, with a high forehead, a beard, a long nose, and a stoop, just the sort of man whom George was prepared to dislike at first sight. Introductions were effected. Henry Dashwood sat down.

'Is Mrs Peregrine in London by any chance? I should very much like to meet her,' he said.

'No, my wife doesn't like London. She prefers the country,' said George stiffly.

'She wrote me a very nice letter about my review. I was pleased. You know, we critics get more kicks than halfpence. I was simply bowled over by her book. It's so fresh and original, very modern without being obscure. She seems to be as much at her ease in free verse as in the classical metres.' Then because he was a critic he thought he should criticize. 'Sometimes her ear is a trifle at fault, but you can say the same of Emily Dickinson. There are several of those short lyrics of hers that might have been written by Landor.'

All this was gibberish to George Peregrine. The man was nothing but a disgusting highbrow. But the colonel had good manners and he answered with proper civility: Henry Dashwood went on as though he hadn't spoken.

'But what makes the book so outstanding is the passion that throbs in every line. So many of these young poets are so anaemic, cold, bloodless, dully intellectual, but here you have real naked, earthy passion; of course deep, sincere emotion like that is tragic – ah, my dear Colonel, how right Heine was when he said that the poet makes little songs out of his great sorrows. You know, now and then, as I read and re-read those heart-rending pages I thought of Sappho.'

This was too much for George Peregrine and he got up.

'Well, it's jolly nice of you to say such nice things about my wife's little book. I'm sure she'll be delighted. But I must bolt, I've got to catch a train and I want to get a bite of lunch.'

'Damned fool,' he said irritably to himself as he walked up-stairs to the dining-room.

He got home in time for dinner and after Evie had gone to bed he went into his study and looked for her book. He thought he'd just glance through it again to see for himself what they were making such a fuss about, but he couldn't find it. Evie must have taken it away.

'Silly,' he muttered.

He'd told her he thought it jolly good. What more could a fellow be expected to say? Well, it didn't matter. He lit his pipe and read the *Field* till he felt sleepy. But a week or so later it happened that he had to go into Sheffield for the day. He lunched there at his club. He had nearly finished when the Duke of

Haverel came in. This was the great local magnate and of course the colonel knew him, but only to say how d'you do to; and he was surprised when the Duke stopped at his table.

'We're so sorry your wife couldn't come to us for the week-end,' he said, with a sort of shy cordiality. 'We're expecting rather a nice lot of people.'

George was taken aback. He guessed that the Haverels had asked him and Evie over for the week-end and Evie, without saying a word to him about it, had refused. He had the presence of mind to say he was sorry too.

'Better luck next time,' said the Duke pleasantly and moved on.

Colonel Peregrine was very angry and when he got home he said to his wife:

'Look here, what's this about our being asked over to Haverel? Why on earth did you say we couldn't go? We've never been asked before and it's the best shooting in the county.'

'I didn't think of that. I thought it would only bore you.'

'Damn it all, you might at least have asked me if I wanted to go.'

'I'm sorry.'

He looked at her closely. There was something in her expression that he didn't quite understand. He frowned.

'I suppose *I* was asked?' he barked.

Evie flushed a little.

'Well, in point of fact you weren't.'

'I call it damned rude of them to ask you without asking me.'

'I suppose they thought it wasn't your sort of party. The Duchess is rather fond of writers and people like that, you know. She's having Henry Dashwood, the critic, and for some reason he wants to meet me.'

'It was damned nice of you to refuse, Evie.'

'It's the least I could do,' she smiled. She hesitated a moment. 'George, my publishers want to give a little dinner party for me one day towards the end of the month and of course they want you to come too.'

'Oh, I don't think that's quite my mark. I'll come up to London with you if you like. I'll find someone to dine with.'

Daphne.

'I expect it'll be very dull, but they're making rather a point of it. And the day after, the American publisher who's taken my book is giving a cocktail party at Claridge's. I'd like you to come to that if you wouldn't mind.'

'Sounds like a crashing bore, but if you really want me to come I'll come.'

'It would be sweet of you.'

George Peregrine was dazed by the cocktail party. There were a lot of people. Some of them didn't look so bad, a few of the women were decently turned out, but the men seemed to him pretty awful. He was introduced to everyone as Colonel Peregrine, E. K. Hamilton's husband, you know. The men didn't seem to have anything to say to him, but the women gushed.

'You *must* be proud of your wife. Isn't it *wonderful*? You know, I read it right through at a sitting, I simply couldn't put it down, and when I'd finished I started again at the beginning and read it right through a second time. I was simply *thrilled*.'

The English publisher said to him:

'We've not had a success like this with a book of verse for twenty years. I've never seen such reviews.'

The American publisher said to him:

'It's swell. It'll be a smash hit in America. You wait and see.'

The American publisher had sent Evie a great spray of orchids. Damned ridiculous, thought George. As they came in, people were taken up to Evie, and it was evident that they said flattering things to her, which she took with a pleasant smile and a word or two of thanks. She was a trifle flushed with the excitement, but seemed quite at her ease. Though he thought the whole thing a lot of stuff and nonsense George noted with approval that his wife was carrying it off in just the right way.

'Well, there's one thing,' he said to himself, 'you can see she's a lady and that's a damned sight more than you can say of anyone else here.'

He drank a good many cocktails. But there was one thing that bothered him. He had a notion that some of the people he was introduced to looked at him in rather a funny sort of way, he couldn't quite make out what it meant, and once when he strolled by two women who were sitting together on a sofa he had the impression that they were talking about him and after he passed he was almost certain they tittered. He was very glad when the party came to an end.

In the taxi on their way back to their hotel Evie said to him:

'You were wonderful, dear. You made quite a hit. The girls simply raved about you: they thought you so handsome.'

'Girls,' he said bitterly. 'Old hags.'

'Were you bored, dear?'

'Stiff.'

She pressed his hand in a gesture of sympathy.

'I hope you won't mind if we wait and go down by the afternoon train. I've got some things to do in the morning.'

'No, that's all right. Shopping?'

'I do want to buy one or two things, but I've got to go and be photographed. I hate the idea, but they think I ought to be. For America, you know.'

He said nothing. But he thought. He thought it would be a shock to the American public when they saw the portrait of the homely, desiccated little woman who was his wife. He'd always been under the impression that they liked glamour in America.

He went on thinking, and next morning when Evie had gone out he went to his club and up to the library. There he looked up recent numbers of *The Times Literary Supplement*, the *New Statesman*, and the *Spectator*. Presently he found reviews of Evie's book. He didn't read them very carefully, but enough to see that they were extremely favourable. Then he went to the bookseller's in Piccadilly where he occasionally bought books. He'd made up his mind that he had to read this damned thing of Evie's properly, but he didn't want to ask her what she'd done with the copy she'd given him. He'd buy one for himself. Before going in he looked in the window and the first thing he saw was a display of *When Pyramids Decay*. Damned silly title! He went in. A young man came forward and asked if he could help him.

'No, I'm just having a look round.' It embarrassed him to ask for Evie's book and he thought he'd find it for himself and then take it to the salesman. But he couldn't see it anywhere and at last, finding the young man near him, he said in a carefully casual tone: 'By the way, have you got a book called *When Pyramids Decay*?'

'The new edition came in this morning. I'll get a copy.'

In a moment the young man returned with it. He was a short, rather stout young man, with a shock of untidy carroty hair and spectacles. George Peregrine, tall, upstanding, very military, towered over him.

'Is this a new edition then?' he asked.

'Yes, sir. The fifth. It might be a novel the way it's selling.'

George Peregrine hesitated a moment.

'Why d'you suppose it's such a success? I've always been told no one reads poetry.'

'Well, it's good, you know. I've read it meself.' The young man, though obviously cultured, had a slight Cockney accent, and George quite instinctively adopted a patronizing attitude. 'It's the story they like. Sexy, you know, but tragic.'

George frowned a little. He was coming to the conclusion that the young man was rather impertinent. No one had told him anything about there being a story in the damned book and he had

228

not gathered that from reading the reviews. The young man went on:

'Of course it's only a flash in the pan, if you know what I mean. The way I look at it, she was sort of inspired like by a personal experience, like Housman was with *The Shropshire Lad*. She'll never write anything else.'

'How much is the book?' said George coldly to stop his chatter. 'You needn't wrap it up, I'll just slip it into my pocket.'

The November morning was raw and he was wearing a great-coat.

At the station he bought the evening papers and magazines and he and Evie settled themselves comfortably in opposite corners of a first-class carriage and read. At five o'clock they went along to the restaurant car to have tea and chatted a little. They arrived. They drove home in the car which was waiting for them. They bathed, dressed for dinner, and after dinner Evie, saying she was tired out, went to bed. She kissed him, as was her habit, on the forehead. Then he went into the hall, took Evie's book out of his greatcoat pocket and going into the study began to read it. He didn't read verse very easily and though he read with attention, every word of it, the impression he received was far from clear. Then he began at the beginning again and read it a second time. He read with increasing malaise, but he was not a stupid man and when he had finished he had a distinct understanding of what it was all about. Part of the book was in free verse, part in conventional metres, but the story it related was coherent and plain to the meanest intelligence. It was the story of a passionate love affair between an older woman, married, and a young man. George Peregrine made out the steps of it as easily as if he had been doing a sum in simple addition.

Written in the first person, it began with the tremulous surprise of the woman, past her youth, when it dawned upon her that the young man was in love with her. She hesitated to believe it. She thought she must be deceiving herself. And she was terrified when on a sudden she discovered that she was passionately in love with him. She told herself it was absurd; with the disparity of age between them nothing but unhappiness could come to her if she yielded to her emotion. She tried to prevent him from speaking but the day came when he told her that he loved her and forced her to tell him that she loved him too. He begged her to run away with him. She couldn't leave her husband, her home; and what life could they look forward to, she an ageing woman, he so young? How could she expect his love to last? She begged him to have mercy on her. But his love was impetuous. He wanted her, he wanted her with all his heart, and at last trembling, afraid, desirous, she yielded to him. Then there was a period of ecstatic happines. The world, the dull, humdrum world of every day, blazed with glory. Love songs flowed from her pen. The woman worshipped the young, virile body of her lover. George flushed darkly when she praised his broad chest and slim flanks, the beauty of his legs and the flatness of his belly.

Hot stuff, Daphne's friend had said. It was that all right. Disgusting.

There were sad little pieces in which she lamented the emptiness of her life when as must happen he left her, but they ended with a cry that all she had to suffer would be worth it for the bliss that for a while had been hers. She wrote of the long, tremulous nights they passed together and the languor that lulled them to sleep in one another's arms. She wrote of the rapture of brief stolen moments when, braving all danger, their passion overwhelmed them and they surrendered to its call.

She thought it would be an affair of a few weeks, but miraculously it lasted. One of the poems referred to three years having gone by without lessening the love that filled their hearts. It looked as though he continued to press her to go away with him, far away, to a hill town in Italy, a Greek island, a walled city in Tunisia, so that they could be together always, for in another of the poems she besought him to let things be as they were. Their happiness was precarious. Perhaps it was owing to the difficulties they had to encounter and the rarity of their meetings that their love had retained for so long its first enchanting ardour. Then on a sudden the young man died. How, when or where George could not discover. There followed a long, heartbroken cry of bitter grief, grief she could not indulge in, grief that had to be hidden. She had to be cheerful, give dinner-parties and go out to dinner, behave as she had always behaved, though the light had gone out of her life and she was bowed down with anguish. The last poem of all was a set of four short stanzas in which the writer, sadly resigned to her loss, thanked the dark powers that rule man's destiny that she had been privileged at least for a while to enjoy the greatest happiness that we poor human beings can ever hope to know.

It was three o'clock in the morning when George Peregrine finally put the book down. It had seemed to him that he heard Evie's voice in every line, over and over again he came upon turns of phrase he had heard her use, there were details that were as familiar to him as to her: there was no doubt about it; it was her own story she had told, and it was as plain as anything could be

that she had had a lover and her lover had died. It was not anger
so much that he felt, nor horror or dismay, though he was dis-
mayed and he was horrified, but amazement. It was as incon-
ceivable that Evie should have had a love affair, and a wildly
passionate one at that, as that the trout in a glass case over the
chimney piece in his study, the finest he had ever caught, should
suddenly wag its tail. He understood now the meaning of the
amused look he had seen in the eyes of that man he had spoken to
at the club, he understood why Daphne when she was talking
about the book had seemed to be enjoying a private joke, and why
those two women at the cocktail party had tittered when he
strolled past them.

He broke out into a sweat. Then on a sudden he was seized with
fury and he jumped up to go and awake Evie and ask her sternly
for an explanation. But he stopped at the door. After all, what
proof had he? A book. He remembered that he'd told Evie he
thought it jolly good. True, he hadn't read it, but he'd pretended
he had. He would look a perfect fool if he had to admit that.

'I must watch my step,' he muttered.

He made up his mind to wait for two or three days and think it
all over. Then he'd decide what to do. He went to bed, but he
couldn't sleep for a long time.

'Evie,' he kept on saying to himself. 'Evie, of all people.'

They met at breakfast next morning as usual. Evie was as she
always was, quiet, demure, and self-possessed, a middle-aged
woman who made no effort to look younger than she was, a
woman who had nothing of what he still called It. He looked at
her as he hadn't looked at her for years. She had her usual placid
serenity. Her pale blue eyes were untroubled. There was no sign of
guilt on her candid brow. She made the same little casual remarks
she always made.

'It's nice to get back to the country again after those two hectic
days in London. What are you going to do this morning?'

It was incomprehensible.

Three days later he went to see his solicitor. Henry Blane was
an old friend of George's as well as his lawyer. He had a place not
far from Peregrine's and for years they had shot over one another's
preserves. For two days a week he was a country gentleman and
for the other five a busy lawyer in Sheffield. He was a tall, robust
fellow, with a boisterous manner and a jovial laugh, which suggested that he liked to be looked upon essentially as a sportsman
and a good fellow and only incidentally as a lawyer. But he was
shrewd and wordly-wise.

'Well, George, what's brought you here today?' he boomed as

the colonel was shown into his office. 'Have a good time in London? I'm taking my missus up for a few days next week. How's Evie?'

'It's about Evie I've come to see you,' said Peregrine, giving him a suspicious look. 'Have you read her book?'

His sensitivity had been sharpened during those last days of troubled thought and he was conscious of a faint change in the lawyer's expression. It was as though he were suddenly on his guard.

'Yes, I've read it. Great success, isn't it? Fancy Evie breaking out into poetry. Wonders will never cease.'

George Peregrine was inclined to lose his temper.

'It's made me look a perfect damned fool.'

'Oh, what nonsense, George! There's no harm in Evie's writing a book. You ought to be jolly proud of her.'

'Don't talk such rot. It's her own story. You know it and everyone else knows it. I suppose I'm the only one who doesn't know who her lover was.'

'There is such a thing as imagination, old boy. There's no reason to suppose the whole thing isn't made up.'

'Look here, Henry, we've know one another all our lives. We've had all sorts of good times together. Be honest with me. Can you look me in the face and tell me you believe it's a made-up story?'

Harry Blane moved uneasily in his chair. He was disturbed by the distress in old George's voice.

'You've got no right to ask me a question like that. Ask Evie.'

'I daren't,' George answered after an anguished pause. 'I'm afraid she'd tell me the truth.'

There was an uncomfortable silence.

'Who was the chap?'

Harry Blane looked at him straight in the eye.

'I don't know, and if I did I wouldn't tell you.'

'You swine. Don't you see what a position I'm in? Do you think it's very pleasant to be made absolutely ridiculous?'

The lawyer lit a cigarette and for some moments silently puffed it.

'I don't see what I can do for you,' he said at last.

'You've got private detectives you employ, I suppose. I want you to put them on the job and let them find everything out.'

'It's not very pretty to put detectives on one's wife, old boy; and besides, taking for granted for a moment that Evie had an affair, it was a good many years ago and I don't suppose it would be possible to find out a thing. They seem to have covered their tracks pretty carefully.'

'I don't care. You put the detectives on. I want to know the truth.'

'I won't, George. If you're determined to do that you'd better consult someone else. And look here, even if you got evidence that Evie had been unfaithful to you what would you do with it? You'd look rather silly divorcing your wife because she'd committed adultery ten years ago.'

'At all events I could have it out with her.'

'You can do that now, but you know just as well as I do that if you do she'll leave you. D'you want her to do that?'

George gave him an unhappy look.

'I don't know. I always thought she'd been a damned good wife to me. She runs the house perfectly, we never have any servant trouble; she's done wonders with the garden and she's splendid with all the village people. But damn it, I have my self-respect to think of. How can I go on living with her when I know that she was grossly unfaithful to me?'

'Have you always been faithful to her?'

'More or less, you know. After all, we've been married for nearly twenty-four years and Evie was never much for bed.'

The solicitor slightly raised his eyebrows, but George was too intent on what he was saying to notice.

'I don't deny that I've had a bit of fun now and then. A man wants it. Women are different.'

'We only have men's word for that,' said Harry Blane, with a faint smile.

'Evie's absolutely the last woman I'd have suspected of kicking over the traces. I mean, she's a very fastidious, reticent woman. What on earth made her write the damned book?'

'I suppose it was a very poignant experience and perhaps it was a relief to her to get it off her chest like that.'

'Well, if she had to write it why the devil didn't she write it under an assumed name?'

'She used her maiden name. I suppose she thought that was enough, and it would have been if the book hadn't had this amazing boom.'

George Peregrine and the lawyer were sitting opposite one another with a desk between them. George, his elbow on the desk, his cheek on his hand, frowned at his thought.

'It's so rotten not to know what sort of a chap he was. One can't even tell if he was by way of being a gentleman. I mean, for all I know he may have been a farm-hand or a clerk in a lawyer's office.'

Harry Blane did not permit himself to smile and when he answered there was in his eyes a kindly, tolerant look.

'Knowing Evie so well I think the probabilities are that he was all right. Anyhow I'm sure he wasn't a clerk in my office.'

'It's been a shock to me,' the colonel sighed. 'I thought she was fond of me. She couldn't have written that book unless she hated me.'

'Oh, I don't believe that. I don't think she's capable of hatred.'

'You're not going to pretend that she loves me.'

'No.'

'Well, what does she feel for me?'

Harry Blane leaned back in his swivel chair and looked at George reflectively.

'Indifference, I should say.'

The colonel gave a little shudder and reddened.

'After all, you're not in love with her, are you?'

George Peregrine did not answer directly.

'It's been a great blow to me not to have any children, but I've never let her see that I think she's let me down. I've always been kind to her. Within reasonable limits I've tried to do my duty by her.'

The lawyer passed a large hand over his mouth to conceal the smile that trembled on his lips.

'It's been such an awful shock to me,' Peregrine went on. 'Damn it all, even ten years ago Evie was no chicken and God knows, she wasn't much to look at. It's so ugly.' He sighed deeply. 'What would *you* do in my place?'

'Nothing.'

George Peregrine drew himself bolt upright in his chair and he looked at Harry with the stern set face that he must have worn when he inspected his regiment.

'I can't overlook a thing like this. I've been made a laughing-stock. I can never hold up my head again.'

'Nonsense,' said the lawyer sharply, and then in a pleasant, kindly manner. 'Listen, old boy: the man's dead; it all happened a long while back. Forget it. Talk to people about Evie's book, rave about it, tell 'em how proud you are of her. Behave as though you had so much confidence in her, you *knew* she could never have been unfaithful to you. The world moves so quickly and people's memories are so short. They'll forget.'

'I shan't forget.'

'You're both middle-aged people. She probably does a great

deal more for you than you think and you'd be awfully lonely without her. I don't think it matters if you don't forget. It'll be all to the good if you can get it into that thick head of yours that there's a lot more in Evie than you ever had the gumption to see.'

'Damn it all, you talk as if I was to blame.'

'No, I don't think you were to blame, but I'm not so sure that Evie was either. I don't suppose she wanted to fall in love with this boy. D'you remember those verses right at the end? The impression they gave me was that though she was shattered by his death, in a strange sort of way she welcomed it. All through she'd been aware of the fragility of the tie that bound them. He died in the full flush of his first love and had never known that love so seldom endures; he'd only known its bliss and beauty. In her own bitter grief she found solace in the thought that he'd been spared all sorrow.'

'All that's a bit above my head, old boy. I see more or less what you mean.'

George Peregrine stared unhappily at the inkstand on the desk. He was silent and the lawyer looked at him with curious, yet sympathetic, eyes.

'Do you realize what courage she must have had never by a sign to show how dreadfully unhappy she was?' he said gently.

Colonel Peregrine sighed.

'I'm broken. I suppose you're right; it's no good crying over spilt milk and it would only make things worse if I made a fuss.'

'Well?'

George Peregrine gave a pitiful little smile.

'I'll take your advice. I'll do nothing. Let them think me a damned fool and to hell with them. The truth is, I don't know what I'd do without Evie. But I'll tell you what, there's one thing I shall never understand till my dying day: What in the name of heaven did the fellow ever see in her?'

LORD MOUNTDRAGO

DR AUDLIN looked at the clock on his desk. It was twenty minutes to six. He was surprised that his patient was late, for Lord Mountdrago prided himself on his punctuality; he had a sententious way of expressing himself which gave the air of an epigram to a commonplace remark, and he was in the habit of saying that punctuality is a compliment you pay to the intelligent and a rebuke you administer to the stupid. Lord Mountdrago's appointment was for five-thirty.

There was in Dr Audlin's appearance nothing to attract attention. He was tall and spare, with narrow shoulders and something of a stoop; his hair was grey and thin; his long, sallow face deeply lined. He was not more than fifty, but he looked older. His eyes, pale-blue and rather large, were weary. When you had been with him for a while you noticed that they moved very little; they remained fixed on your face, but so empty of expression were they that it was no discomfort. They seldom lit up. They gave no clue to his thoughts nor changed with the words he spoke. If you were of an observant turn it might have struck you that he blinked much less often than most of us. His hands were on the large side, with long, tapering fingers; they were soft, but firm, cool but not clammy. You could never have said what Dr Audlin wore unless you had made a point of looking. His clothes were dark. His tie was black. His dress made his sallow lined face paler, and his pale eyes more wan. He gave you the impression of a very sick man.

Dr Audlin was a psycho-analyst. He had adopted the profession by accident and practised it with misgiving. When the war broke out he had not been long qualified and was getting experience at various hospitals; he offered his services to the authorities, and after a time was sent out to France. It was then that he discovered his singular gift. He could allay certain pains by the touch of his cool, firm hands, and by talking to them often induce sleep in men who were suffering from sleeplessness. He spoke slowly. His voice had no particular colour, and its tone did not alter with the words he uttered, but it was musical, soft, and lulling. He told the men that they must rest, that they mustn't worry, that they must sleep; and rest stole into their jaded bones, tranquillity pushed their anxieties away, like a man finding a place for himself on a crowded bench, and slumber fell on their tired eyelids like the light rain of spring upon the fresh-turned earth. Dr Audlin found that by speaking to men with that low, monotonous voice of his, by looking at them with his pale, quiet eyes, by stroking their weary foreheads with his long firm hands, he could soothe their perturbations, resolve the conflicts that distracted them, and banish the phobias that made their lives a torment. Sometimes he effected cures that seemed miraculous. He restored speech to a man who, after being buried under the earth by a bursting shell, had been struck dumb, and he gave back the use of his limbs to another who had been paralysed after a crash in a plane. He could not understand his powers; he was of a sceptical turn, and though they say that in circumstances of this kind the first thing is to believe in yourself, he never quite succeeded in doing that; and it was only the outcome of his activities, patent to the most incredulous observer, that obliged him to admit that he had some faculty, coming from he knew not where, obscure and uncertain, that enabled him to do things for which he could offer no explanation. When the war was over he went to Vienna and studied there, and afterwards to Zürich; and then settled down in London to practise the art he had so strangely acquired. He had been practising now for fifteen years, and had attained, in the speciality he followed, a distinguished reputation. People told one another of the amazing things he had done, and though his fees were high, he had as many patients as he had time to see. Dr Audlin knew that he had achieved some very extraordinary results; he had saved men from suicide, others from the lunatic asylum, he had assuaged griefs that embittered useful lives, he had turned unhappy marriages into happy ones, he had eradicated abnormal instincts and thus delivered not a few from a hateful bondage, he had given health to the sick in spirit; he had done all this, and yet at the back of his mind remained the suspicion that he was little more than a quack.

It went against his grain to exercise a power that he could not understand, and it offended his honesty to trade on the faith of the people he treated when he had no faith in himself. He was rich enough now to live without working, and the work exhausted him; a dozen times he had been on the point of giving up practice. He knew all that Freud and Jung and the rest of them had written. He was not satisfied; he had an intimate conviction that all their theory was hocus-pocus, and yet there the results were, incomprehensible, but manifest. And what had he not seen of human nature during the fifteen years that patients had been coming to his dingy back room in Wimpole Street? The revelations that had been poured into his ears, sometimes only too willingly, sometimes with shame, with reservations, with anger, had long ceased to surprise him. Nothing could shock him any longer. He knew by now that men were liars, he knew how extravagant was their

vanity; he knew far worse than that about them; but he knew
that it was not for him to judge or to condemn. But year by year
as these terrible confidences were imparted to him his face grew
a little greyer, its lines a little more marked, and his pale eyes
more weary. He seldom laughed, but now and again when for
relaxation he read a novel he smiled. Did their authors really
think the men and women they wrote of were like that? If they
only knew how much more complicated they were, how much
more unexpected, what irreconcilable elements coexisted within
their souls and what dark and sinister contentions afflicted them!

It was a quarter to six. Of all the strange cases he had been
called upon to deal with Dr Audlin could remember none stranger
than that of Lord Mountdrago. For one thing the personality of
his patient made it singular. Lord Mountdrago was an able and a
distinguished man. Appointed Secretary for Foreign Affairs when
still under forty, now after three years in office he had seen his
policy prevail. It was generally acknowledged that he was the
ablest politician in the Conservative Party and only the fact that
his father was a peer, on whose death he would no longer be able
to sit in the House of Commons, made it impossible for him to
aim at the premiership. But if in these democratic times it is out
of the question for a Prime Minister of England to be in the
House of Lords, there was nothing to prevent Lord Mountdrago
from continuing to be Secretary for Foreign Affairs in successive
Conservative administrations and so for long directing the
foreign policy of his country.

Lord Mountdrago had many good qualities. He had intelligence and industry. He was widely travelled, and spoke several
languages fluently. From early youth he had specialized in foreign
affairs, and had conscientiously made himself acquainted with the
political and economic circumstances of other countries. He had
courage, insight, and determination. He was a good speaker, both
on the platform and in the House, clear, precise, and often witty.
He was a brilliant debater and his gift of repartee was celebrated.
He had a fine presence: he was a tall, handsome man, rather bald
and somewhat too stout, but this gave him solidity and an air of
maturity that were of service to him. As a young man he had been
something of an athlete and had rowed in the Oxford boat, and
he was known to be one of the best shots in England. At twenty-
four he had married a girl of eighteen whose father was a duke
and her mother a great American heiress, so that she had both
position and wealth, and by her he had had two sons. For several
years they had lived privately apart, but in public united, so that
appearances were saved, and no other attachment on either side

had given the gossips occasion to whisper. Lord Mountdrago indeed was too ambitious, too hard-working, and it must be added too patriotic, to be tempted by any pleasures that might interfere with his career. He had, in short, a great deal to make him a popular and successful figure. He had unfortunately great defects.

He was a fearful snob. You would not have been surprised at this if his father had been the first holder of the title. That the son of an ennobled lawyer, a manufacturer, or a distiller should attach an inordinate importance to his rank is understandable. The earldom held by Lord Mountdrago's father was created by Charles II, and the barony held by the first Earl dated from the Wars of the Roses. For three hundred years the successive holders of the title had allied themselves with the noblest families of England. But Lord Mountdrago was as conscious of his birth as a *nouveau riche* is conscious of his money. He never missed an opportunity of impressing it upon others. He had beautiful manners when he chose to display them, but this he did only with people whom he regarded as his equals. He was coldly insolent to those whom he looked upon as his social inferiors. He was rude to his servants and insulting to his secretaries. The subordinate officials in the government offices to which he had been success- ively attached feared and hated him. His arrogance was horrible. He knew that he was a great deal cleverer than most of the persons he had to do with, and never hesitated to apprise them of the fact. He had no patience with the infirmities of human nature. He felt himself born to command and was irritated with people who expected him to listen to their arguments or wished to hear the reasons for his decisions. He was immeasurably selfish. He looked upon any service that was rendered him as a right due to his rank and intelligence and therefore deserving of no gratitude. It never entered his head that he was called upon to do anything for others. He had many enemies: he despised them. He knew no one who merited his assistance, his sympathy, or his compassion. He had no friends. He was distrusted by his chiefs, because they doubted his loyalty; he was unpopular with his party, because he was over-bearing and discourteous; and yet his merit was so great, his patriotism so evident, his intelligence so solid, and his management of affairs so brilliant that they had to put up with him. And what made it possible to do this was that on occasion he could be enchanting: when he was with persons whom he considered his equals, or whom he wished to captivate, in the company of foreign dignitaries or women of distinction, he could be gay, witty, and debonair; his manners then reminded you that in his veins ran the same blood as had run in the veins of Lord Chesterfield; he could tell a story with point, he could be natural, sensible, and even profound. You were surprised at the extent of his knowledge and the sensitiveness of his taste. You thought him the best company in the world; you forgot that he had insulted you the day before and was quite capable of cutting you dead the next.

Lord Mountdrago almost failed to become Dr Audlin's patient. A secretary rang up the doctor and told him that his lordship, wishing to consult him, would be glad if he would come to his house at ten o'clock on the following morning. Dr Audlin answered that he was unable to go to Lord Mountdrago's house, but would be pleased to give him an appointment at his consulting-room at five o'clock on the next day but one. The secretary took the message and presently rang back to say that Lord Mountdrago insisted on seeing Dr Audlin in his own house and the doctor could fix his own fee. Dr Audlin replied that he only saw patients in his consulting-room and expressed his regret that unless Lord Mountdrago was prepared to come to him he could not give him his attention. In a quarter of an hour a brief message was delivered to him that his lordship would come not next day but one, but next day, at five.

When Lord Mountdrago was then shown in he did not come forward, but stood at the door and insolently looked the doctor up and down. Dr Audlin perceived that he was in a rage; he gazed at him, silently, with still eyes. He saw a big heavy man, with greying hair, receding on the forehead so that it gave nobility to his brow, a puffy face with bold regular features and an expression of haughtiness. He had somewhat the look of one of the Bourbon sovereigns of the eighteenth century.

'It seems that it is as difficult to see you as a Prime Minister, Dr Audlin. I'm an extremely busy man.'

'Won't you sit down?' said the doctor.

His face showed no sign that Lord Mountdrago's speech in any way affected him. Dr Audlin sat in his chair at the desk. Lord Mountdrago still stood and his frown darkened.

'I think I should tell you that I am His Majesty's Secretary for Foreign Affairs,' he said acidly.

'Won't you sit down?' the doctor repeated.

Lord Mountdrago made a gesture, which might have suggested that he was about to turn on his heel and stalk out of the room; but if that was his intention he apparently thought better of it. He seated himself. Dr Audlin opened a large book and took up his pen. He wrote without looking at his patient.

'How old are you?'

'Forty-two.'

'Are you married?'

'Yes.'

'How long have you been married?'

'Eighteen years.'

'Have you any children?'

'I have two sons.'

Dr Audlin noted down the facts as Lord Mountdrago abruptly answered his questions. Then he leaned back in his chair and looked at him. He did not speak; he just looked, gravely, with pale eyes that did not move.

'Why have you come to see me?' he asked at length.

'I've heard about you. Lady Canute is a patient of yours, I understand. She tells me you've done her a certain amount of good.'

Dr Audlin did not reply. His eyes remained fixed on the other's face, but they were so empty of expression that you might have thought he did not even see him.

'I can't do miracles,' he said at length. Not a smile, but the shadow of a smile flickered in his eyes. 'The Royal College of Physicians would not approve of it if I did.'

Lord Mountdrago gave a brief chuckle. It seemed to lessen his hostility. He spoke more amiably.

'You have a very remarkable reputation. People seem to believe in you.'

'Why have you come to me?' repeated Dr Audlin.

Now it was Lord Mountdrago's turn to be silent. It looked as though he found it hard to answer. Dr Audlin waited. At last Lord Mountdrago seemed to make an effort. He spoke.

'I'm in perfect health. Just as a matter of routine I had myself examined by my own doctor the other day, Sir Augustus Fitzherbert, I daresay you've heard of him, and he tells me I have the physique of a man of thirty. I work hard, but I'm never tired, and I enjoy my work. I smoke very little and I'm an extremely moderate drinker. I take a sufficiency of exercise and I lead a regular life. I am a perfectly sound, normal, healthy man. I quite expect you to think it very silly and childish of me to consult you.'

Dr Audlin saw that he must help him.

'I don't know if I can do anything to help you. I'll try. You're distressed?'

Lord Mountdrago frowned.

'The work that I'm engaged in is important. The decisions I am called upon to make can easily affect the welfare of the country and even the peace of the world. It is essential that my judgement should be balanced and my brain clear. I look upon it as my duty to eliminate any cause of worry that may interfere with my usefulness.'

Dr Audlin had never taken his eyes off him. He saw a great deal. He saw behind his patient's pompous manner and arrogant pride an anxiety that he could not dispel.

'I asked you to be good enough to come here because I know by experience that it's easier for someone to speak openly in the dingy surroundings of a doctor's consulting-room than in his accustomed environment.'

'They're certainly dingy,' said Lord Mountdrago acidly. He paused. It was evident that this man who had so much self-assurance, so quick and decided a mind that he was never at a loss, at this moment was embarrassed. He smiled in order to show the doctor that he was at his ease, but his eyes betrayed his disquiet. When he spoke again it was with unnatural heartiness.

'The whole thing's so trivial that I can hardly bring myself to bother you with it. I'm afraid you'll just tell me not to be a fool and waste your valuable time.'

'Even things that seem very trivial may have their importance. They can be a symptom of a deep-seated derangement. And my time is entirely at your disposal.'

Dr Audlin's voice was low and grave. The monotone in which he spoke was strangely soothing. Lord Mountdrago at length made up his mind to be frank.

'The fact is I've been having some very tiresome dreams lately. I know it's silly to pay any attention to them, but – well, the honest truth is that I'm afraid they've got on my nerves.'

'Can you describe any of them to me?'

Lord Mountdrago smiled, but the smile that tried to be careless was only rueful.

'They're so idiotic, I can hardly bring myself to narrate them.'

'Never mind.'

'Well, the first I had was about a month ago. I dreamt that I was at a party at Connemara House. It was an official party. The King and Queen were to be there and of course decorations were worn. I was wearing my ribbon and my star. I went into a sort of cloakroom they have to take off my coat. There was a little man there called Owen Griffiths, who's a Welsh Member of Parliament, and to tell you the truth, I was surprised to see him. He's very common, and I said to myself: "Really, Lydia Connemara is going too far, whom will she ask next?" I thought he looked at me rather curiously, but I didn't take any notice of him; in fact I cut the little bounder and walked upstairs. I suppose you've never been there?'

'Never.'

'No, it's not the sort of house you'd ever be likely to go to. It's a rather vulgar house, but it's got a very fine marble staircase, and the Connemaras were at the top receiving their guests. Lady Connemara gave me a look of surprise when I shook hands with her, and began to giggle; I didn't pay much attention, she's a very silly, ill-bred woman and her manners are no better than those of her ancestor whom King Charles II made a duchess. I must say the reception rooms at Connemara House are stately. I walked through, nodding to a number of people and shaking hands; then I saw the German Ambassador talking with one of the Austrian Archdukes. I particularly wanted to have a word with him, so I went up and held out my hand. The moment the Archduke saw me he burst into a roar of laughter. I was deeply affronted. I looked him up and down sternly, but he only laughed the more. I was about to speak to him rather sharply, when there was a sudden hush and I realized that the King and Queen had come. Turning my back on the Archduke, I stepped forward, and then, quite suddenly, I noticed that I hadn't got any trousers on. I was in short silk drawers, and I wore scarlet sock-suspenders. No wonder Lady Connemara had giggled; no wonder the Archduke had laughed! I can't tell you what that moment was. An agony of shame. I awoke in a cold sweat. Oh, you don't know the relief I felt to find it was only a dream.'

'It's the kind of dream that's not so very uncommon,' said Dr Audlin.

'I dare say not. But an odd thing happened next day. I was in the lobby of the House of Commons, when that fellow Griffiths walked slowly past me. He deliberately looked down at my legs and then he looked me full in the face and I was almost certain he winked. A ridiculous thought came to me. He'd been there the night before and seen me make that ghastly exhibition of myself and was enjoying the joke. But of course I knew that was impossible because it was only a dream. I gave him an icy glare and he walked on. But he was grinning his head off.'

Lord Mountdrago took his handkerchief out of his pocket and wiped the palms of his hands. He was making no attempt now to conceal his perturbation. Dr Audlin never took his eyes off him.

'Tell me another dream.'

'It was the night after, and it was even more absurd than the first one. I dreamt that I was in the House. There was a debate on foreign affairs which not only the country, but the world, had been looking forward to with the gravest concern. The government had decided on a change in their policy which vitally affected the future of the Empire. The occasion was historic. Of course the House was crowded. All the ambassadors were there. The galleries were packed. It fell to me to make the important speech of the evening. I had prepared it carefully. A man like me has enemies, there are a lot of people who resent my having achieved the position I have at an age when even the cleverest men are content with situations of relative obscurity, and I was determined that my speech should not only be worthy of the occasion, but should silence my detractors. It excited me to think that the whole world was hanging on my lips. I rose to my feet. If you've ever been in the House you'll know how members chat to one another during a debate, rustle papers and turn over reports. The silence was the silence of the grave when I began to speak. Suddenly I caught sight of that odious little bounder on one of the benches opposite, Griffiths the Welsh member; he put out his tongue at me. I don't know if you've ever heard a vulgar music-hall song called *A Bicycle Made for Two*. It was very popular a great many years ago. To show Griffiths how completely I despised him I began to sing it. I sang the first verse right through. There was a moment's surprise, and when I finished they cried "Hear, hear," on the opposite benches. I put up my hand to silence them and sang the second verse. The House listened to me in stony silence and I felt the song wasn't going down very well. I was vexed, for I have a good baritone voice, and I was determined that they should do me justice. When I started the third verse the members began to laugh; in an instant the laughter spread; the ambassadors, the strangers in the Distinguished Strangers' Gallery, the ladies in the Ladies' Gallery, the reporters, they shook, they bellowed, they held their sides, they rolled in their seats; everyone was overcome with laughter except the ministers on the Front Bench immediately behind me. In that incredible, in that unprecedented uproar, they sat petrified. I gave them a glance, and suddenly the enormity of what I had done fell upon me. I had made myself the laughing-stock of the whole world. With misery I realized that I should have to resign. I woke and knew it was only a dream.'

Lord Mountdrago's grand manner had deserted him as he narrated this, and now having finished he was pale and trembling. But with an effort he pulled himself together. He forced a laugh to his shaking lips.

'The whole thing was so fantastic that I couldn't help being amused. I didn't give it another thought, and when I went into the House on the following afternoon I was feeling in very good form.

The debate was dull, but I had to be there, and I read some documents that required my attention. For some reason I chanced to look up and I saw that Griffiths was speaking. He has an unpleasant Welsh accent and an unprepossessing appearance. I couldn't imagine that he had anything to say that it was worth my while to listen to, and I was about to return to my papers when he quoted two lines from *A Bicycle Made for Two*. I couldn't help glancing at him and I saw that his eyes were fixed on me with a grin of bitter mockery. I faintly shrugged my shoulders. It was comic that a scrubby little Welsh member should look at me like that. It was an odd coincidence that he should quote two lines from that disastrous song that I'd sung all through in my dream. I began to read my papers again, but I don't mind telling you that I found it difficult to concentrate on them. I was a little puzzled. Owen Griffiths had been in my first dream, the one at Connemara House, and I'd received a very definite impression afterwards that he knew the sorry figure I'd cut. Was it a mere coincidence that he had just quoted those two lines? I asked myself if it was possible that he was dreaming the same dreams as I was. But of course the idea was preposterous and I determined not to give it a second thought.'

There was a silence. Dr Audlin looked at Lord Mountdrago and Lord Mountdrago looked at Dr Audlin.

'Other people's dreams are very boring. My wife used to dream occasionally and insist on telling me her dreams next day with circumstantial detail. I found it maddening.'

Dr Audlin faintly smiled.

'You're not boring me.'

'I'll tell you one more dream I had a few days later. I dreamt that I went into a public-house at Limehouse. I've never been to Limehouse in my life and I don't think I've ever been in a public-house since I was at Oxford, and yet I saw the street and the place I went into as exactly as if I were at home there. I went into a room, I don't know whether they call it the saloon bar or the private bar; there was a fireplace and a large leather arm-chair on one side of it, and on the other a small sofa; a bar ran the whole length of the room and over it you could see into the public bar. Near the door was a round marble-topped table and two arm-chairs beside it. It was a Saturday night and the place was packed. It was brightly lit, but the smoke was so thick that it made my eyes smart. I was dressed like a rough, with a cap on my head and a handkerchief round my neck. It seemed to me that most of the people there were drunk. I thought it rather amusing. There was a gramophone going, or the radio, I don't know which, and in front of the fireplace two women were doing a grotesque dance. There was a little crowd round them, laughing, cheering, and singing. I went up to have a look and some man said to me: "'Ave a drink, Bill?" There were glasses on the table full of a dark liquid which I understand is called brown ale. He gave me a glass and not wishing to be conspicuous I drank it. One of the women who were dancing broke away from the other and took hold of the glass. "'Ere, what's the idea?" she said. "That's my beer you're putting away." "Oh, I'm so sorry," I said, "this gentleman offered it me and I very naturally thought it was his to offer." "All right, mate," she said, "I don't mind. You come an' 'ave a dance with me." Before I could protest she'd caught hold of me and we were dancing together. And then I found myself sitting in the arm-chair with the woman on my lap and we were sharing a glass of beer. I should tell you that sex has never played any great part in my life. I married young because in my position it was desirable that I should marry, but also in order to settle once for all the question of sex. I had the two sons I had made up my mind to have, and then I put the whole matter on one side. I've always been too busy to give much thought to that kind of thing, and living so much in the public eye as I do it would have been madness to do anything that might give rise to scandal. The greatest asset a politician can have is a blameless record as far as women are concerned. I have no patience with the men who smash up their careers for women. I only despise them. The woman I had on my knees was drunk; she wasn't pretty and she wasn't young: in fact, she was just a blowsy old prostitute. She filled me with disgust, and yet when she put her mouth to mine and kissed me, though her breath stank of beer and her teeth were decayed, though I loathed myself, I wanted her – I wanted her with all my soul. Suddenly I heard a voice. "That's right, old boy, have a good time." I looked up and there was Owen Griffiths. I tried to spring out of the chair, but that horrible woman wouldn't let me. "Don't you pay no attention to 'im," she said, "'e's only one of them nosy-parkers." "You go to it," he said. "I know Moll. She'll give you your money's worth all right." You know, I wasn't so much annoyed at his seeing me in that absurd situation as angry that he should address me as "old boy". I pushed the woman aside and stood up and faced him. "I don't know you and I don't want to know you," I said. "I know you all right," he said. "And my advice to you, Molly, is, see that you get your money, he'll bilk you if he can." There was a bottle of beer on the table close by. Without a word I seized it by the neck and hit him over the head with it as hard as I could. I made such a violent gesture that it woke me up.'

A dream of that sort is not incomprehensible,' said Dr Audlin. 'It is the revenge nature takes on persons of unimpeachable character.'

'The story's idiotic. I haven't told it you for its own sake. I've told it you for what happened next day. I wanted to look up something in a hurry and I went into the library of the House. I got the book and began reading. I hadn't noticed when I sat down that Griffiths was sitting in a chair close by me. Another of the Labour Members came in and went up to him. "Hullo, Owen," he said to him, "you're looking pretty dicky today." "I've got an awful headache," he answered. "I feel as if I'd been cracked over the head with a bottle."'

Now Lord Mountdrago's face was grey with anguish.

'I knew then that the idea I'd had and dismissed as preposterous was true. I knew that Griffiths was dreaming my dreams and that he remembered them as well as I did.'

'It may also have been a coincidence.'

'When he spoke he didn't speak to his friend, he deliberately spoke to me. He looked at me with sullen resentment.'

'Can you offer any suggestion why this same man should come into your dreams?'

'None.'

Dr Audlin's eyes had not left his patient's face and he saw that he lied. He had a pencil in his hand and he drew a straggling line or two on his blotting-paper. It often took a long time to get people to tell the truth, and yet they knew that unless they told it he could do nothing for them.

'The dream you've just described to me took place just over three weeks ago. Have you had any since?'

'Every night.'

'And does this man Griffiths come into them all?'

'Yes.'

The doctor drew more lines on his blotting-paper. He wanted the silence, the drabness, the dull light of that little room to have its effect on Lord Mountdrago's sensibility. Lord Mountdrago threw himself back in his chair and turned his head away so that he should not see the other's grave eyes.

'Dr Audlin, you must do something for me. I'm at the end of my tether. I shall go mad if this goes on. I'm afraid to go to sleep. Two or three nights I haven't. I've sat up reading and when I felt drowsy put on my coat and walked till I was exhausted. But I must have sleep. With all the work I have to do I must be at concert pitch; I must be in complete control of all my faculties. I need rest; sleep brings me none. I no sooner fall asleep than my dreams begin, and he's always there, that vulgar little cad, grinning at me, mocking me, despising me. It's a monstrous persecution. I tell you, doctor, I'm not the man of my dreams; it's not fair to judge me by them. Ask anyone you like. I'm an honest, upright, decent man. No one can say anything against my moral character either private or public. My whole ambition is to serve my country and maintain its greatness. I have money, I have rank, I'm not exposed to many of the temptations of lesser men, so that it's no credit to me to be incorruptible; but this I can claim, that no honour, no personal advantage, no thought of self would induce me to swerve by a hair's breadth from my duty. I've sacrificed everything to become the man I am. Greatness is my aim. Greatness is within my reach and I'm losing my nerve. I'm not that mean, despicable, cowardly, lewd creature that horrible little man sees. I've told you three of my dreams; they're nothing; that man has seen me do things that are so beastly, so horrible, so shameful, that even if my life depended on it I wouldn't tell them. And he remembers them. I can hardly meet the derision and disgust I see in his eyes and I even hesitate to speak because I know my words can seem to him nothing but utter humbug. He's seen me do things that no man with any self-respect would do, things for which men are driven out of the society of their fellows and sentenced to long terms of imprisonment; he's heard the foulness of my speech; he's seen me not only ridiculous, but revolting. He despises me and he no longer pretends to conceal it. I tell you that if you can't do something to help me I shall either kill myself or kill him.'

'I wouldn't kill him if I were you,' said Dr Audlin, coolly, in that soothing voice of his. 'In this country the consequences of killing a fellow-creature are awkward.'

'I shouldn't be hanged for it, if that's what you mean. Who would know that I'd killed him? That dream of mine has shown me how. I told you, the day after I'd hit him over the head with a beer-bottle he had such a headache that he couldn't see straight. He said so himself. That shows that he can feel with his waking body what happens to his body asleep. It's not with a bottle I shall hit him next time. One night, when I'm dreaming, I shall find myself with a knife in my hand or a revolver in my pocket, I must because I want to so intensely, and then I shall seize my opportunity. I'll stick him like a pig; I'll shoot him like a dog. In the heart. And then I shall be free of this fiendish persecution.'

Some people might have thought that Lord Mountdrago was mad; after all the years during which Dr Audlin had been treating the diseased souls of men he knew how thin a line divides those whom we call sane from those whom we call insane. He knew how often in men who to all appearance were healthy and normal, who were seemingly devoid of imagination, and who fulfilled the duties of common life with credit to themselves and with benefit to their fellows, when you gained their confidence, when you tore away the mask they wore to the world, you found not only hideous abnormality, but kinks so strange, mental extravagances so fantastic, that in that respect you could call them lunatic. If you put them in an asylum not all the asylums in the world would be large enough. Anyhow, a man was not certifiable because he had strange dreams and they had shattered his nerve. The case was singular, but it was only an exaggeration of others that had come under Dr Audlin's observation; he was doubtful, however, whether the methods of treatment that he had so often found efficacious would here avail.

'Have you consulted any other member of my profession?' he asked.

'Only Sir Augustus. I merely told him that I suffered from nightmares. He said I was overworked and recommended me to go for a cruise. That's absurd. I can't leave the Foreign Office just now when the international situation needs constant attention. I'm indispensable, and I know it. On my conduct at the present juncture my whole future depends. He gave me sedatives. They had no effect. He gave me tonics. They were worse than useless. He's an old fool.'

'Can you give any reason why it should be this particular man who persists in coming into your dreams?'

'You asked me that question before. I answered it.'

That was true. But Dr Audlin had not been satisfied with the answer.

'Just now you talked of persecution. Why should Owen Griffiths want to persecute you?'

'I don't know.'

Lord Mountdrago's eyes shifted a little. Dr Audlin was sure that he was not speaking the truth.

'Have you ever done him an injury?'

'Never.'

Lord Mountdrago made no movement, but Dr Audlin had a queer feeling that he shrank into his skin. He saw before him a large, proud man who gave the impression that the questions put to him were an insolence, and yet for all that, behind that façade, was something shifting and startled that made you think of a frightened animal in a trap. Dr Audlin leaned forward and by the power of his eyes forced Lord Mountdrago to meet them.

'Are you quite sure?'

'Quite sure. You don't seem to understand that our ways lead along different paths. I don't wish to harp on it, but I must remind you that I am a Minister of the Crown and Griffiths is an obscure member of the Labour Party. Naturally there's no social connexion between us; he's a man of very humble origin, he's not the sort of person I should be likely to meet at any of the houses I go to; and politically our respective stations are so far separated that we could not possibly have anything in common.'

'I can do nothing for you unless you tell me the complete truth.'

Lord Mountdrago raised his eyebrows. His voice was rasping.

'I'm not accustomed to having my word doubted, Dr Audlin. If you're going to do that I think to take up any more of your time can only be a waste of mine. If you will kindly let my secretary know what your fee is he will see that a cheque is sent to you.'

For all the expression that was to be seen on Dr Audlin's face you might have thought that he simply had not heard what Lord Mountdrago said. He continued to look steadily into his eyes and his voice was grave and low.

'Have you done anything to this man that *he* might look upon as an injury?'

Lord Mountdrago hesitated. He looked away, and then, as though there were in Dr Audlin's eyes a compelling force that he could not resist, looked back. He answered sulkily:

'Only if he was a dirty, second-rate little cad.'

'But that is exactly what you've described him to be.'

Lord Mountdrago sighed. He was beaten. Dr Audlin knew that the sigh meant he was going at last to say what he had till then held back. Now he had no longer to insist. He dropped his eyes and began again drawing vague geometrical figures on his blotting-paper. The silence lasted two or three minutes.

'I'm anxious to tell you everything that can be of any use to you. If I didn't mention this before, it's only because it was so unimportant that I didn't see how it could possibly have anything to do with the case. Griffiths won a seat at the last election and he began to make a nuisance of himself almost at once. His father's a miner, and he worked in a mine himself when he was a boy; he's been a schoolmaster in the board schools and a journalist. He's that half-baked, conceited intellectual, with inadequate knowledge, ill-considered ideas, and impracticable plans, that compulsory education has brought forth from the working-classes. He's a scrawny, grey-faced man, who looks half-starved, and he's always very slovenly in appearance; heaven knows members nowadays don't bother much about their dress, but his clothes are an outrage to the dignity of the House. They're ostentatiously shabby, his collar's never clean and his tie's never tied properly; he looks as if he hadn't had a bath for a month and his hands are filthy. The Labour Party have two or three fellows on the Front Bench who've got a certain ability, but the rest of them don't amount to much. In the kingdom of the blind the one-eyed man is king: because Griffiths is glib and has a lot of superficial information on a number of subjects, the Whips on his side began to put him up to speak whenever there was a chance. It appeared that he fancied himself on foreign affairs, and he was continually asking me silly, tiresome questions. I don't mind telling you that I made a point of snubbing him as soundly as I thought he deserved. From the beginning I hated the way he talked, his whining voice and his vulgar accent; he had nervous mannerisms that intensely irritated me. He talked rather shyly, hesitatingly, as though it were torture to him to speak and yet he was forced on by some inner passion, and often he used to say some very disconcerting things. I'll admit that now and again he had a sort of tub-thumping eloquence. It had a certain influence over the ill-regulated minds of the members of his party. They were impressed by his earnestness and they weren't, as I was, nauseated by his sentimentality. A certain sentimentality is the common coin of political debate. Nations are governed by self-interest, but they prefer to believe that their aims are altruistic, and the politician is justified if with fair words and fine phrases he can persuade the electorate that the hard bargain he is driving for his country's advantage tends to the good of humanity. The mistake people like Griffiths make is to take these fair words and fine phrases at their face value. He's a crank, and a noxious crank. He calls himself an idealist. He has at his tongue's end all the tedious blather that the intelligentsia have been boring us with for years. Non-resistance. The brotherhood of man. You know the hopeless rubbish. The worst of it was that it impressed not only his own party, it even shook some of the sillier, more sloppy-minded members of ours. I heard rumours that Griffiths was likely to get office when a Labour Government came in; I even heard it suggested that he might get the Foreign Office. The notion was grotesque but not impossible. One day I had occasion to wind up a debate on foreign affairs which Griffiths had opened. He'd spoken for an hour. I thought it a very good opportunity to cook his goose, and by God, sir, I cooked it. I tore his speech to pieces. I pointed out the faultiness of his reasoning and emphasized the deficiency of his knowledge. In the House of Commons the most devastating weapon is ridicule: I mocked him; I bantered him; I was in good form that day and the House rocked with laughter. Their laughter excited me and I excelled myself. The Opposition sat glum and silent, but even some of them couldn't help laughing once or twice; it's not intolerable, you know, to see a colleague, perhaps a rival, made a fool of. And if ever a man was made a fool of I made a fool of Griffiths. He shrank down in a seat, I saw his face go white, and presently he buried it in his hands. When I sat down I'd killed him. I'd destroyed his prestige for ever; he had no more chance of getting office when a Labour Government came in than the policeman at the door. I heard afterwards that his father, the old miner, and his mother had come up from Wales, with various supporters of his in the constituency, to watch the triumph they expected him to have. They had seen only his utter humiliation. He'd won the constituency by the narrowest margin. An incident like that might very easily lose him his seat. But that was no business of mine.'

'Should I be putting it too strongly if I said you had ruined his career?' asked Dr Audlin.

'I don't suppose you would.'

'That is a very serious injury you've done him.'

'He brought it on himself.'

'Have you never felt any qualms about it?'

'I think perhaps if I'd known that his father and mother were there I might have let him down a little more gently.'

There was nothing further for Dr Audlin to say, and he set about treating his patient in such a manner as he thought might avail. He sought by suggestion to make him forget his dreams when he awoke; he sought to make him sleep so deeply that he would not dream. He found Lord Mountdrago's resistance impossible to break down. At the end of an hour he dismissed him. Since then he had seen Lord Mountdrago half a dozen times. He had done him no good. The frightful dreams continued every night to harass the unfortunate man, and it was clear that his general condition was growing rapidly worse. He was worn out. His irritability was uncontrollable. Lord Mountdrago was angry because he received no benefit from his treatment, and yet continued it, not only because it seemed his only hope, but because it was a relief to him to have someone with whom he could talk openly. Dr Audlin came to the conclusion at last that there was only one way in which Lord Mountdrago could achieve deliverance, but he knew him well enough to be assured that of his own free will he would never, never take it. If Lord Mountdrago was to be saved from the breakdown that was threatening he must be induced to take a step that must be abhorrent to his pride of birth and his self-complacency. Dr Audlin was convinced that to delay was impossible. He was treating his patient by suggestion, and after several visits found him more susceptible to it. At length he managed to get him into a condition of somnolence. With his low, soft, monotonous voice he soothed his tortured nerves. He repeated the same words over and over again. Lord Mountdrago lay quite still, his eyes closed; his breathing was regular, and his limbs were relaxed. Then Dr Audlin in the same quiet tone spoke the words he had prepared.

'You will go to Owen Griffiths and say that you are sorry that you caused him that great injury. You will say that you will do whatever lies in your power to undo the harm that you have done him.'

The words acted on Lord Mountdrago like the blow of a whip across his face. He shook himself out of his hypnotic state and sprang to his feet. His eyes blazed with passion and he poured forth upon Dr Audlin a stream of angry vituperation such as even he had never heard. He swore at him. He cursed him. He used language of such obscenity that Dr Audlin, who had heard every sort of foul word, sometimes from the lips of chaste and distinguished women, was surprised that he knew it.

'Apologize to that filthy little Welshman? I'd rather kill myself.'

'I believe it to be the only way in which you can regain your balance.'

Dr Audlin had not often seen a man presumably sane in such a condition of uncontrollable fury. He grew red in the face and his eyes bulged out of his head. He did really foam at the mouth. Dr Audlin watched him coolly, waiting for the storm to wear itself out, and presently he saw that Lord Mountdrago, weakened by the strain to which he had been subjected for so many weeks, was exhausted.

'Sit down,' he said then, sharply.

Lord Mountdrago crumpled up into a chair.

'Christ, I feel all in. I must rest a minute and then I'll go.'

For five minutes perhaps they sat in complete silence. Lord Mountdrago was a gross, blustering bully, but he was also a gentleman. When he broke the silence he had recovered his self-control.

'I'm afraid I've been very rude to you. I'm ashamed of the things I've said to you and I can only say you'd be justified if you refused to have anything more to do with me. I hope you won't do that. I feel that my visits to you do help me. I think you're my only chance.'

'You mustn't give another thought to what you said. It was of no consequence.'

'But there's one thing you mustn't ask me to do, and that is to make excuses to Griffiths.'

'I've thought a great deal about your case. I don't pretend to understand it, but I believe that your only chance of release is to do what I proposed. I have a notion that we're none of us one self, but many, and one of the selves in you has risen up against the injury you did Griffiths and has taken on the form of Griffiths in your mind and is punishing you for what you cruelly did. If I were a priest I should tell you that it is your conscience that has adopted the shape and lineaments of this man to scourge you to repentance and persuade you to reparation.'

'My conscience is clear. It's not my fault if I smashed the man's career. I crushed him like a slug in my garden. I regret nothing.'

It was on these words that Lord Mountdrago had left him. Reading through his notes, while he waited, Dr Audlin considered how best he could bring his patient to the state of mind that, now that his usual methods of treatment had failed, he thought alone could help him. He glanced at his clock. It was six. It was strange that Lord Mountdrago did not come. He knew he had intended to because a secretary had rung up that morning to say that he would be with him at the usual hour. He must have been detained by pressing work. This notion gave Dr Audlin something else to think of: Lord Mountdrago was quite unfit for work and in no condition to deal with important matters of state. Dr Audlin wondered whether it behoved him to get in touch with someone in authority, the Prime Minister or the Permanent Under-Secretary for Foreign Affairs, and impart to him his conviction that Lord Mountdrago's mind was so unbalanced that it was dangerous to leave affairs of moment in his hands. It was a ticklish thing to do. He might cause needless trouble and get roundly snubbed for his pains. He shrugged his shoulders.

'After all,' he reflected, 'the politicians have made such a mess of the world during the last five-and-twenty years, I don't suppose it makes much odds if they're mad or sane.'

He rang the bell.

'If Lord Mountdrago comes now will you tell him that I have another appointment at six-fifteen and so I'm afraid I can't see him.'

'Very good, sir.'

'Has the evening paper come yet?'

'I'll go and see.'

In a moment the servant brought it in. A huge headline ran across the front page: Tragic Death of Foreign Minister.

'My God!' cried Dr Audlin.

For once he was wrenched out of his wonted calm. He was shocked, horribly shocked, and yet he was not altogether surprised. The possibility that Lord Mountdrago might commit suicide had occurred to him several times, for that it was suicide he could not doubt. The paper said that Lord Mountdrago had been waiting in a Tube station, standing on the edge of the platform, and as the train came in was seen to fall on the rail. It was supposed that he had had a sudden attack of faintness. The paper went on to say that Lord Mountdrago had been suffering for some weeks from the effects of overwork, but had felt it impossible to absent himself while the foreign situation demanded his unremitting attention. Lord Mountdrago was another victim of the strain that modern politics placed upon those who played the more important parts in it. There was a neat little piece about the talents and industry, the patriotism and vision, of the deceased statesman, followed by various surmises upon the Prime Minister's choice of his successor. Dr Audlin read all this. He had not liked Lord Mountdrago. The chief emotion that his death caused in him was dissatisfaction with himself because he had been able to do nothing for him.

Perhaps he had done wrong in not getting into touch with Lord Mountdrago's doctor. He was discouraged, as always when failure frustrated his conscientious efforts, and repulsion seized him for the theory and practice of this empiric doctrine by which he earned his living. He was dealing with dark and mysterious forces that it was perhaps beyond the powers of the human mind to understand. He was like a man blindfold trying to feel his way to he knew not whither. Listlessly he turned the pages of the paper. Suddenly he gave a great start, and an exclamation once more was forced from his lips. His eyes had fallen on a small paragraph near the bottom of a column. Sudden Death of an M.P., he read. Mr Owen Griffiths, member for so-and-so, had been taken ill in Fleet Street that afternoon and when he was brought to Charing Cross Hospital life was found to be extinct. It was supposed that death was due to natural causes, but an inquest would be held. Dr Audlin could hardly believe his eyes. Was it possible that the night before Lord Mountdrago had at last in his dream found himself possessed of the weapon, knife or gun, that he had wanted, and had killed his tormentor, and had that ghostly murder, in the same way as the blow with the bottle had given him a racking headache on the following day, taken effect a certain number of hours later on the waking man? Or was it, more mysterious and more frightful, that when Lord Mountdrago sought relief in death, the enemy he had so cruelly wronged, unappeased, escaping from his own mortality, had pursued him to some other sphere there to torment him still? It was strange. The sensible thing was to look upon it merely as an odd coincidence. Dr Audlin rang the bell.

'Tell Mrs Milton that I'm sorry I can't see her this evening. I'm not well.'

It was true; he shivered as though of an ague. With some kind of spiritual sense he seemed to envisage a bleak, a horrible void. The dark night of the soul engulfed him, and he felt a strange, primeval terror of he knew not what.

THE SOCIAL SENSE

I DO not like long-standing engagements. How can you tell whether on a certain day three or four weeks ahead you will wish to dine with a certain person? The chances are that in the interval something will turn up that you would much sooner do and so long a notice presages a large and formal party. But what help is there? The date has been fixed thus far away so that the guests bidden may be certainly disengaged and it needs a very adequate excuse to prevent your refusal from seeming churlish. You accept, and for a month the engagement hangs over you with gloomy menace. It interferes with your cherished plans. It disorganizes your life. There is really only one way to cope with the situation and that is to put yourself off at the last moment. But it is one that I have never had the courage or the want of scruple to adopt.

It was with a faint sense of resentment then that one June evening towards half past eight I left my lodging in Half Moon Street to walk round the corner to dine with the Macdonalds. I liked them. Many years ago I made up my mind not to eat the food of persons I disliked or despised, and though I have on this account enjoyed the hospitality of far fewer people than I otherwise should have done I still think the rule a good one. The Macdonalds were nice, but their parties were a toss-up. They suffered from the delusion that if they asked six persons to dine with them who had nothing in the world to say to one another the party would be a failure, but if they multiplied it by three and asked eighteen it must be a success. I arrived a little late, which is almost inevitable when you live so near the house you are going to that it is not worth while to take a taxi, and the room into which I was shown was filled with people. I knew few of them and my heart sank as I saw myself laboriously making conversation through a long dinner with two total strangers. It was a relief to me when I saw Thomas and Mary Warton come in and an unexpected pleasure when I found on going in to dinner that I had been placed next to Mary.

Thomas Warton was a portrait-painter who at one time had had considerable success, but he had never fulfilled the promise of his youth and had long ceased to be taken seriously by the critics. He made an adequate income, but at the Private View of the Royal Academy no one gave more than a passing glance at the dull but conscientious portraits of fox-hunting squires and prosperous merchants which with unfailing regularity he sent to the annual exhibition. One would have liked to admire his work because he

257

was an amiable and kindly man. If you happened to be a writer he was so genuinely enthusiastic over anything you had done, so charmed with any success you might have had, that you wished your conscience would allow you to speak with decent warmth of his own productions. It was impossible and you were driven to the last refuge of the portrait painter's friend.

'It looks as if it were a marvellous likeness,' you said.

Mary Warton had been in her day a well-known concert singer and she had still the remains of a lovely voice. She must in her youth have been very handsome. Now, at fifty-three, she had a haggard look. Her features were rather mannish and her skin was weather-beaten; but her short grey hair was thick and curly and her fine eyes were bright with intelligence. She dressed picturesquely rather than fashionably and she had a weakness for strings of beads and fantastic ear-rings. She had a blunt manner, a quick sense of human folly, and a sharp tongue, so that many people did not like her. But no one could deny that she was clever. She was not only an accomplished musician, but she was a great reader and she was passionately interested in painting. She had a very rare feeling for art. She liked the modern, not from pose but from natural inclination, and she had bought for next to nothing the pictures of unknown painters who later became famous. You heard at her house the most recent and difficult music and no poet or novelist in Europe could offer the world something new and strange without her being ready to fight on his behalf the good fight against the philistines. You might say she was a highbrow; she was; but her taste was almost faultless, her judgement sound, and her enthusiasm honest.

No one admired her more than Thomas Warton. He had fallen in love with her when she was still a singer and had pestered her to marry him. She had refused him half a dozen times and I had a notion that she had married him in the end with hesitation. She thought that he would become a great painter and when he turned out to be no more than a decent craftsman, without originality or imagination, she felt that she had been cheated. She was mortified by the contempt with which the connoisseurs regarded him. Thomas Warton loved his wife. He had the greatest respect for her judgement and would sooner have had a word of praise from her than columns of eulogy in all the papers in London. She was too honest to say what she did not think. It wounded him bitterly that she held his work in such poor esteem, and though he pretended to make a joke of it you could see that at heart he resented her outspoken comments. Sometimes his long, horse-like face grew red with the anger he tried to control and his eyes dark with hatred.

It was notorious among their friends that the couple did not get on. They had the distressing habit of fripping in public. Warton never spoke to others of Mary but with admiration, but she was less discreet and her confidants knew how exasperating she found him. She admitted his goodness, his generosity, his unselfishness; she admitted them ungrudgingly; but his defects were of the sort that make a man hard to live with, for he was narrow, argumentative, and conceited. He was not an artist and Mary Warton cared more for art than for anything in the world. It was a matter on which she could not compromise. It blinded her to the fact that the faults in Warton that maddened her were due in large part to his hurt feelings. She wounded him continually and he was dogmatic and intolerant in self-protection. There cannot be anything much worse than to be despised by the one person whose approval is all in all to you; and though Thomas Warton was intolerable it was impossible not to feel sorry for him. But if I have given the impression that Mary was a discontented, rather tiresome, pretentious woman I have been unjust to her. She was a loyal friend and a delightful companion. You could talk to her of any subject under the sun. Her conversation was humorous and witty. Her vitality was immense.

She was sitting now on the left hand of her host and the talk around her was general. I was occupied with my next-door neighbour, but I guessed by the laughter with which Mary's sallies were greeted that she was at her brilliant best. When she was in the vein no one could approach her.

'You're in great form tonight,' I remarked, when at last she turned to me.

'Does it surprise you?'

'No, it's what I expect of you. No wonder people tumble over one another to get you to their houses. You have the inestimable gift of making a party go.'

'I do my little best to earn my dinner.'

'By the way, how's Manson? Someone told me the other day that he was going into a nursing-home for an operation. I hope it's nothing serious.'

Mary paused for a moment before answering, but she still smiled brightly.

'Haven't you seen the paper tonight?'

'No, I've been playing golf. I only got home in time to jump into a bath and change.'

'He died at two o'clock this afternoon.' I was about to make an exclamation of horrified surprise, but she stopped me. 'Take care. Tom is watching me like a lynx. They're all watching me. They all know I adored him, but they none of them know for certain if he was my lover, even Tom doesn't know; they want to see how I'm taking it. Try to look as if you were talking of the Russian Ballet.'

At that moment someone addressed her from the other side of the table, and throwing back her head a little with a gesture that was habitual with her, a smile on her large mouth, she flung at the speaker so quick and apt an answer that everyone round her burst out laughing. The talk once more became general and I was left to my consternation.

I knew, everyone knew, that for five and twenty years there had existed between Gerrard Manson and Mary Warton a passionate attachment. It had lasted so long that even the more strait-laced of their friends, if ever they had been shocked by it, had long since learnt to accept it with tolerance. They were middle-aged people, Manson was sixty and Mary not much younger, and it was absurd that at their age they should not do what they liked. You met them sometimes sitting in a retired corner of an obscure restaurant or walking together in the Zoo and you wondered why they still took care to conceal an affair that was nobody's business but their own. But of course there was Thomas. He was insanely jealous of Mary. He made many violent scenes and indeed, at the end of one tempestuous period, not so very long ago, he forced her to promise never to see Manson again. Of course she broke the promise, and though she knew that Thomas suspected this, she took precautions to prevent him from discovering it for a fact.

It was hard on Thomas. I think he and Mary would have jogged on well enough together and she would have resigned herself to the fact that he was a second-rate painter if her intercourse with Manson had not embittered her judgement. The contrast between her husband's mediocrity and her lover's brilliance was too galling.

'With Tom I feel as if I were stifling in a closed room full of dusty knick-knacks,' she told me. 'With Gerrard I breathe the pure air of the mountain tops.'

'Is it possible for a woman to fall in love with a man's mind?' I asked in a pure spirit of inquiry.

'What else is there in Gerrard?'

That, I admit, was a poser. For my part I thought, nothing; but the sex is extraordinary and I was quite ready to believe that Mary saw in Gerrard Manson a charm and a physical attractiveness to which most people were blind. He was a shrivelled little man, with a pale intellectual face, faded blue eyes behind his spectacles, and a high dome of shiny bald head. He had none of the appearance of a romantic lover. On the other hand he was certainly a very subtle critic and a felicitous essayist. I resented somewhat his contemptuous attitude towards English writers unless they were safely dead and buried; but this was only to his credit with the intelligentsia, who are ever ready to believe that there can be no good in what is produced in their own country, and with them his influence was great. On one occasion I told him that one had only to put a commonplace in French for him to mistake it for an epigram and he had thought well enough of the joke to use it as his own in one of his essays. He reserved such praise as he was willing to accord his contemporaries to those who wrote in a foreign tongue. The exasperating thing was that no one could deny that he was himself a brilliant writer. His style was exquisite. His knowledge was vast. He could be profound without pomposity, amusing without frivolity, and polished without affectation. His slightest article was readable. His essays were little masterpieces. For my part I did not find him a very agreeable companion. Perhaps I did not get the best out of him. Though I knew him a great many years I never heard him say an amusing thing. He was not talkative and when he made a remark it was oracular. The prospect of spending an evening alone with him would have filled me with dismay. It never ceased to puzzle me that this dull and mannered little man should be able to write with so much grace, wit, and gaiety.

It puzzled me even more that a gallant and vivacious creature like Mary Warton should have cherished for him so consuming a passion. These things are inexplicable and there was evidently something in that odd, crabbed, irascible creature that appealed to women. His wife adored him. She was a fat, frowsy, boring person. She had led Gerrard a dog's life, but had always refused to give him his freedom. She swore to kill herself if he left her and since she was unbalanced and hysterical he was never quite certain that she would not carry out her threat. One day, when I was having tea with Mary, I saw that she was distraught and nervous and when I asked her what was the matter she burst into tears. She had been lunching with Manson and had found him shattered after a terrific scene with his wife.

'We can't go on like this,' Mary cried. 'It's ruining his life. It's ruining all our lives.'

'Why don't you take the plunge?'

'What do you mean?'

'You've been lovers so long, you know the best and the worst of one another by now; you're getting old and you can't count on many more years of life; it seems a pity to waste a love that has endured so long. What good are you doing to Mrs Manson or to Tom? Are they happy because you two are making yourselves miserable?'

'No.'

'Then why don't you chuck everything and just go off together and let come what may?'

Mary shook her head.

'We've talked that over endlessly. We've talked it over for a quarter of a century. It's impossible. For years Gerrard couldn't on account of his daughters. Mrs Manson may have been a very fond mother, but she was a very bad one, and there was no one to see the girls were properly brought up but Gerrard. And now that they're married off he's set in his habits. What should we do? Go to France or Italy? I couldn't tear Gerrard away from his surroundings. He'd be wretched. He's too old to make a fresh start. And besides, though Thomas nags me and makes scenes and we frip and get on one another's nerves, he loves me. When it came to the point I simply shouldn't have the heart to leave him. He'd be lost without me.'

'It's a situation without an issue. I'm dreadfully sorry for you.'

On a sudden Mary's haggard, weather-beaten face was lit by a smile that broke on her large red mouth; and upon my word at that moment she was beautiful.

'You need not be. I was rather low a little while ago, but now I've had a good cry I feel better. Notwithstanding all the pain, all the unhappiness this affair has caused me, I wouldn't have missed it for all the world. For those few moments of ecstasy my love has brought me I would be willing to live all my life over again. And I think he'd tell you the same thing. Oh, it's been so infinitely worth while.'

I could not help but be moved.

'There's no doubt about it,' I said. 'That's love all right.'

'Yes, it's love, and we've just got to go through with it. There's no way out.'

And now with this tragic suddenness the way out had come. I turned a little to look at Mary and she, feeling my eyes upon her, turned too. There was a smile on her lips.

'Why did you come here tonight? It must be awful for you.'

She shrugged her shoulders.

'What could I do? I read the news in the evening paper while I was dressing. He'd asked me not to ring up the nursing-home on account of his wife. It's death to me. Death. I had to come. We'd been engaged for a month. What excuse could I give Tom? I'm not supposed to have seen Gerrard for two years. Do you know that for twenty years we've written to one another every day?' Her lower lip trembled a little, but she bit it and for a moment her face was twisted to a strange grimace; then with a smile she pulled herself together. 'He was everything I had in the world, but I couldn't let the party down, could I? He always said I had a social sense.'

'Happily we shall break up early and you can go home.'

'I don't want to go home. I don't want to be alone. I daren't cry because my eyes will get red and swollen, and we've got a lot of people lunching with us tomorrow. Will you come, by the way? I want an extra man. I must be in good form; Tom expects to get a commission for a portrait out of it.'

'By George, you've got courage.'

'D'you think so? I'm heartbroken, you know. I suppose that's what makes it easier for me. Gerrard would have liked me to put a good face on it. He would have appreciated the irony of the situation. It's the sort of thing he always thought the French novelists described so well.'

THE VERGER

THERE had been a christening that afternoon at St Peter's, Neville Square, and Albert Edward Foreman still wore his verger's gown. He kept his new one, its folds as full and stiff as though it were made not of alpaca but of perennial bronze, for funerals and weddings (St Peter's, Neville Square, was a church much favoured by the fashionable for these ceremonies) and now he wore only his second-best. He wore it with complacence, for it was the dignified symbol of his office, and without it (when he took it off to go home) he had the disconcerting sensation of being somewhat insufficiently clad. He took pains with it; he pressed it and ironed it himself. During the sixteen years he had been verger of this church he had had a succession of such gowns, but he had never been able to throw them away when they were worn out and the complete series, neatly wrapped up in brown paper, lay in the bottom drawers of the wardrobe in his bedroom.

The verger busied himself quietly, replacing the painted wooden cover on the marble font, taking away a chair that had been brought for an infirm old lady, and waited for the vicar to have finished in the vestry so that he could tidy up in there and go home. Presently he saw him walk across the chancel, genuflect in front of the high altar, and come down the aisle; but he still wore his cassock.

'What's he 'anging about for?' the verger said to himself. 'Don't 'e know I want my tea?'

The vicar had been but recently appointed, a red-faced energetic man in the early forties, and Albert Edward still regretted his predecessor, a clergyman of the old school who preached leisurely sermons in a silvery voice and dined out a great deal with his more aristocratic parishioners. He liked things in church to be just so, but he never fussed; he was not like this new man who wanted to have his finger in every pie. But Albert Edward was tolerant. St Peter's was in a very good neighbourhood and the parishioners were a very nice class of people. The new vicar had come from the East End and he couldn't be expected to fall in all at once with the discreet ways of his fashionable congregation.

'All this 'ustle,' said Albert Edward. 'But give 'im time, he'll learn.'

When the vicar had walked down the aisle so far that he could address the verger without raising his voice more than was becoming in a place of worship he stopped.

'Foreman, will you come into the vestry for a minute. I have something to say to you.'

'Very good, sir.'

The vicar waited for him to come up and they walked up the church together.

'A very nice christening, I thought, sir. Funny 'ow the baby stopped cryin' the moment you took him.'

'I've noticed they very often do,' said the vicar, with a little smile. 'After all I've had a good deal of practice with them.'

It was a source of subdued pride to him that he could nearly always quiet a whimpering infant by the manner in which he held it and he was not unconscious of the amused admiration with which mothers and nurses watched him settle the baby in the crook of his surpliced arm. The verger knew that it pleased him to be complimented on his talent.

The vicar preceded Albert Edward into the vestry. Albert Edward was a trifle surprised to find the two churchwardens there. He had not seen them come in. They gave him pleasant nods.

'Good afternoon, my lord. Good afternoon, sir,' he said to one after the other.

They were elderly men, both of them, and they had been churchwardens almost as long as Albert Edward had been verger. They were sitting now at a handsome refectory table that the old vicar had brought many years before from Italy and the vicar sat down in the vacant chair between them. Albert Edward faced them, the table between him and them, and wondered with slight uneasiness what was the matter. He remembered still the occasion on which the organist had got into trouble and the bother they had all had to hush things up. In a church like St Peter's, Neville Square, they couldn't afford a scandal. On the vicar's red face was a look of resolute benignity, but the others bore an expression that was slightly troubled.

'He's been naggin' them, he 'as,' said the verger to himself. 'He's jockeyed them into doin' something, but they don't 'alf like it. That's what it is, you mark my words.'

But his thoughts did not appear on Albert Edward's clean-cut and distinguished features. He stood in a respectful but not obsequious attitude. He had been in service before he was appointed to his ecclesiastical office, but only in very good houses, and his deportment was irreproachable. Starting as a page-boy in the household of a merchant-prince, he had risen by due degrees from the position of fourth to first footman, for a year he had been single-handed butler to a widowed peeress, and, till the vacancy occurred at St Peter's, butler with two men under him in the house of a retired ambassador. He was tall, spare, grave, and dignified. He looked, if not like a duke, at least like an actor of the old school who specialized in dukes' parts. He had tact, firmness, and self-assurance. His character was unimpeachable.

The vicar began briskly.

'Foreman, we've got something rather unpleasant to say to you. You've been here a great many years and I think his lordship and the general agree with me that you've fulfilled the duties of your office to the satisfaction of everybody concerned.'

The two churchwardens nodded.

'But a most extraordinary circumstance came to my knowledge the other day and I felt it my duty to impart it to the churchwardens. I discovered to my astonishment that you could neither read nor write.'

The verger's face betrayed no sign of embarrassment.

'The last vicar knew that, sir,' he replied. 'He said it didn't make no difference. He always said there was a great deal too much education in the world for 'is taste.'

'It's the most amazing thing I ever heard,' cried the general. 'Do you mean to say that you've been verger of this church for sixteen years and never learned to read or write?'

'I went into service when I was twelve, sir. The cook in the first place tried to teach me once, but I didn't seem to 'ave the knack for it, and then what with one thing and another I never seemed to 'ave the time. I've never really found the want of it. I think a lot of these young fellows waste a rare lot of time readin' when they might be doin' something useful.'

'But don't you want to know the news?' said the other churchwarden. 'Don't you ever want to write a letter?'

'No, me lord, I seem to manage very well without. And of late years now they've all these pictures in the papers I get to know what's goin' on pretty well. Me wife's quite a scholar and if I want to write a letter she writes it for me. It's not as if I was a bettin' man.'

The two churchwardens gave the vicar a troubled glance and then looked down at the table.

'Well, Foreman, I've talked the matter over with these gentlemen and they quite agree with me that the situation is impossible. At a church like St Peter's, Neville Square, we cannot have a verger who can neither read nor write.'

Albert Edward's thin, sallow face reddened and he moved uneasily on his feet, but he made no reply.

'Understand me, Foreman, I have no complaint to make against you. You do your work quite satisfactorily; I have the highest opinion both of your character and of your capacity; but we haven't the right to take the risk of some accident that might happen owing to your lamentable ignorance. It's a matter of prudence as well as of principle.'

'But couldn't you learn, Foreman?' asked the general.

'No, sir, I'm afraid I couldn't, not now. You see, I'm not as young as I was and if I couldn't seem able to get the letters in me 'ead when I was a nipper I don't think there's much chance of it now.'

'We don't want to be harsh with you, Foreman,' said the vicar. 'But the churchwardens and I have quite made up our minds. We'll give you three months and if at the end of that time you cannot read and write I'm afraid you'll have to go.'

Albert Edward had never liked the new vicar. He'd said from the beginning that they'd made a mistake when they gave him St Peter's. He wasn't the type of man they wanted with a classy congregation like that. And now he straightened himself a little. He knew his value and he wasn't going to allow himself to be put upon.

'I'm very sorry, sir, I'm afraid it's no good. I'm too old a dog to learn new tricks. I've lived a good many years without knowin' 'ow to read and write, and without wishin' to praise myself, self-praise is no recommendation, I don't mind sayin' I've done my duty in that state of life in which it 'as pleased a merciful providence to place me, and if I *could* learn now I don't know as I'd want to.'

'In that case, Foreman, I'm afraid you must go.'

'Yes, sir, I quite understand. I shall be 'appy to 'and in my resignation as soon as you've found somebody to take my place.'

But when Albert Edward with his usual politeness had closed the church door behind the vicar and the two churchwardens he could not sustain the air of unruffled dignity with which he had borne the blow inflicted upon him and his lips quivered. He walked slowly back to the vestry and hung up on its proper peg his verger's gown. He sighed as he thought of all the grand funerals and smart weddings it had seen. He tidied everything up, put on his coat, and hat in hand walked down the aisle. He locked the church door behind him. He strolled across the square, but deep in his sad thoughts he did not take the street that led him home, where a nice strong cup of tea awaited him; he took the wrong turning. He walked slowly along. His heart was heavy. He did not know what he should do with himself. He did not fancy the notion of going back to domestic service; after being his own master for so many years, for the vicar and churchwardens could say what they liked, it was he that had run St

Peter's, Neville Square, he could scarcely demean himself by accepting a situation. He had saved a tidy sum, but not enough to live on without doing something, and life seemed to cost more every year. He had never thought to be troubled with such questions. The vergers of St Peter's, like the popes of Rome, were there for life. He had often thought of the pleasant reference the vicar would make in his sermon at evensong the first Sunday after his death to the long and faithful service, and the exemplary character of their late verger, Albert Edward Foreman. He sighed deeply. Albert Edward was a non-smoker and a total abstainer, but with a certain latitude; that is to say he liked a glass of beer with his dinner and when he was tired he enjoyed a cigarette. It occurred to him now that one would comfort him and since he did not carry them he looked about him for a shop where he could buy a packet of Gold Flakes. He did not at once see one and walked on a little. It was a long street, with all sorts of shops in it, but there was not a single one where you could buy cigarettes.

'That's strange,' said Albert Edward.

To make sure he walked right up the street again. No, there was no doubt about it. He stopped and looked reflectively up and down.

'I can't be the only man as walks along this street and wants a fag,' he said. 'I shouldn't wonder but what a fellow might do very well with a little shop here. Tobacco and sweets, you know.'

He gave a sudden start.

'That's an idea,' he said. 'Strange 'ow things come to you when you least expect it.'

He turned, walked home, and had his tea.

'You're very silent this afternoon, Albert,' his wife remarked.

'I'm thinkin',' he said.

He considered the matter from every point of view and next day he went along the street and by good luck found a little shop to let that looked as though it would exactly suit him. Twenty-four hours later he had taken it, and when a month after that he left St Peter's, Neville Square, for ever, Albert Edward Foreman set up in business as a tobacconist and newsagent. His wife said it was a dreadful come-down after being verger of St Peter's, but he answered that you had to move with the times, the church wasn't what it was, and 'enceforward he was going to render unto Caesar what was Caesar's. Albert Edward did very well. He did so well that in a year or so it struck him that he might take a second shop and put a manager in. He looked for another long street that hadn't got a tobacconist in it and when he found it, and a shop to let, took it and stocked it. This was a success too. Then it occurred to him that if he could run two he could run half a dozen, so he began walking about London, and whenever he found a long street that had no tobacconist and a shop to let he took it. In the course of ten years he had acquired no less than ten shops and he was making money hand over fist. He went round to all of them himself every Monday, collected the week's takings, and took them to the bank.

One morning when he was there paying in a bundle of notes and a heavy bag of silver the cashier told him that the manager would like to see him. He was shown into an office and the manager shook hands with him.

'Mr Foreman, I wanted to have a talk to you about the money you've got on deposit with us. D'you know exactly how much it is?'

'Not within a pound or two, sir; but I've got a pretty rough idea.'

'Apart from what you paid in this morning it's a little over thirty thousand pounds. That's a very large sum to have on deposit and I should have thought you'd do better to invest it.'

'I wouldn't want to take no risk, sir. I know it's safe in the bank.'

'You needn't have the least anxiety. We'll make you out a list of absolutely gilt-edged securities. They'll bring you in a better rate of interest than we can possibly afford to give you.'

A troubled look settled on Mr Foreman's distinguished face. 'I've never 'ad anything to do with stocks and shares and I'd 'ave to leave it all in your 'ands,' he said.

The manager smiled. 'We'll do everything. All you'll have to do next time you come in is just to sign the transfers.'

'I could do that all right,' said Albert uncertainly. 'But 'ow should I know what I was signin'?'

'I suppose you can read,' said the manager a trifle sharply.

Mr Foreman gave him a disarming smile.

'Well, sir, that's just it. I can't. I know it sounds funny-like, but there it is, I can't read or write, only me name, an' I only learnt to do that when I went into business.'

The manager was so surprised that he jumped up from his chair. 'That's the most extraordinary thing I ever heard.'

'You see, it's like this, sir, I never 'ad the opportunity until it was too late and then some'ow I wouldn't. I got obstinate-like.'

The manager stared at him as though he were a prehistoric monster.

'And do you mean to say that you've built up this important business and amassed a fortune of thirty thousand pounds without being able to read or write? Good God, man, what would you be now if you had been able to?'

'I can tell you that, sir,' said Mr Foreman, a little smile on his still aristocratic features. 'I'd be verger of St Peter's, Neville Square.'

IN A STRANGE LAND

I AM of a roving disposition; but I travel not to see imposing monuments, which indeed somewhat bore me, nor beautiful scenery, of which I soon tire; I travel to see men. I avoid the great. I would not cross the road to meet a president or a king; I am content to know the writer in the pages of his book and the painter in his picture; but I have journeyed a hundred leagues to see a missionary of whom I had heard a strange story and I have spent a fortnight in a vile hotel in order to improve my acquaintance with a billiard-marker. I should be inclined to say that I am not surprised to meet any sort of person were it not that there is one sort that I am constantly running against and that never fails to give me a little shock of amused astonishment. This is the elderly Englishwoman, generally of adequate means, who is to be found living alone, up and down the world, in unexpected places. You do not wonder when you hear of her living in a villa on a hill outside a small Italian town, the only Englishwoman in the neighbourhood, and you are almost prepared for it when a lonely *hacienda* is pointed out to you in Andalusia and you are told that there has dwelt for many years an English lady. But it is more surprising when you hear that the only white person in a Chinese city is an Englishwoman, not a missionary, who lives there none knows why; and there is another who inhabits an island in the South Seas, and a third who has a bungalow on the outskirts of a large village in the centre of Java. They live solitary lives, these women, without friends, and they do not welcome the stranger. Though they may not have seen one of their own race for months they will pass you on the road as though they did not see you, and if, presuming on your nationality, you should call, as likely as not they will decline to see you; but if they do, they will give you a cup of tea from a silver teapot and on a plate of Old Worcester you will find Scotch scones. They will talk to you politely, as though they were entertaining you in a Kentish vicarage, but when you take your leave will show no particular desire to continue the acquaintance. One wonders in vain what strange instinct it is that has driven them to separate themselves from their kith and kin and thus to live apart from all their natural interests in an alien land. Is it romance they have sought, or freedom?

But of all these Englishwomen whom I have met or perhaps only heard of (for as I have said they are difficult of access) the one who remains most vividly in my memory is an elderly person who lived in Asia Minor. I had arrived after a tedious journey at a little town from which I proposed to make the ascent of a celebrated mountain and I was taken to a rambling hotel that stood at its foot. I arrived late at night and signed my name in the book. I went up to my room. It was cold and I shivered as I undressed, but in a moment there was a knock at the door and the dragoman came in.

'Signora Niccolini's compliments,' he said.

To my astonishment he handed me a hot-water bottle. I took it with grateful hands.

'Who is Signora Niccolini?' I asked.

'She is the proprietor of this hotel,' he answered.

I sent her my thanks and he withdrew. The last thing I expected in a scrubby hotel in Asia Minor kept by an old Italian woman was a beautiful hot-water bottle. There is nothing I like more (if we were not all sick to death of the war I would tell you the story of how six men risked their lives to fetch a hot-water bottle from a chateau in Flanders that was being bombarded); and next morning, so that I might thank her in person, I asked if I might see the Signora Niccolini. While I waited for her I racked my brains to think what hot-water bottle could possibly be in Italian. In a moment she came in. She was a little stout woman, not without dignity, and she wore a black apron trimmed with lace and a small black lace cap. She stood with her hands crossed. I was astonished at her appearance for she looked exactly like a house-keeper in a great English house.

'Did you wish to speak to me, sir?'

She was an Englishwoman and in those few words I surely recognized the trace of a cockney accent.

'I wanted to thank you for the hot-water bottle,' I replied in some confusion.

'I saw by the visitors' book that you were English, sir, and I always send up a 'ot-water bottle to English gentlemen.'

'Believe me, it was very welcome.'

'I was for many years in the service of the late Lord Ormskirk, sir. He always used to travel with a 'ot-water bottle. Is there anything else, sir?'

'Not at the moment, thank you.'

She gave me a polite little nod and withdrew. I wondered how on earth it came about that a funny old Englishwoman like that should be the landlady of a hotel in Asia Minor. It was not easy to make her acquaintance, for she knew her place, as she would herself have put it, and she kept me at a distance. It was not for nothing that she had been in service in a noble English family.

But I was persistent and I induced her at last to ask me to have a cup of tea in her own little parlour. I learnt that she had been lady's-maid to a certain Lady Ormskirk, and Signor Niccolini (for she never alluded to her deceased husband in any other way) had been his lordship's chef. Signor Niccolini was a very handsome man and for some years there had been an 'understanding' between them. When they had both saved a certain amount of money they were married, retired from service, and looked about for a hotel. They had bought this one on an advertisement because Signor Niccolini thought he would like to see something of the world. That was nearly thirty years ago and Signor Niccolini had been dead for fifteen. His widow had not once been back to England. I asked her if she was never homesick.

'I don't say as I wouldn't like to go back on a visit, though I expect I'd find many changes. But my family didn't like the idea of me marrying a foreigner and I 'aven't spoken to them since. Of course there are many things here that are not the same as what they 'ave at 'ome, but it's surprising what you get used to. I see a lot of life. I don't know as I should care to live the 'umdrum life they do in a place like London.'

I smiled. For what she said was strangely incongruous with her manner. She was a pattern of decorum. It was extraordinary that she could have lived for thirty years in this wild and almost barbaric country without its having touched her. Though I knew no Turkish and she spoke it with ease I was convinced that she spoke it most incorrectly and with a cockney accent. I suppose she had remained the precise, prim English lady's-maid, knowing her place, through all these vicissitudes because she had no faculty of surprise. She took everything that came as a matter of course. She looked upon everyone who wasn't English as a foreigner and therefore as someone, almost imbecile, for whom allowances must be made. She ruled her staff despotically – for did she not know how an upper servant in a great house should exercise his authority over the under servants? – and everything about the hotel was clean and neat.

'I do my best,' she said, when I congratulated her on this, standing, as always when she spoke to me, with her hands respectfully crossed. 'Of course one can't expect foreigners to 'ave the same ideas what we 'ave, but as his lordship used to say to me, what we've got to do, Parker, he said to me, what we've got to do in this life is to make the best of our raw material.'

But she kept her greatest surprise for the eve of my departure.

'I'm glad you're not going before you've seen my two sons, sir.'

'I didn't know you had any.'

'They've been away on business, but they've just come back. You'll be surprised when you've seen them. I've trained them with me own 'ands so to speak, and when I'm gone they'll carry on the 'otel between them.'

In a moment two tall, swarthy, strapping young fellows entered the hall. Her eyes lit up with pleasure. They went up to her and took her in their arms and gave her resounding kisses.

'They don't speak English, sir, but they understand a little, and of course they speak Turkish like natives, and Greek and Italian.'

I shook hands with the pair and then Signora Niccolini said something to them and they went away.

'They're handsome fellows, Signora,' I said. 'You must be very proud of them.'

'I am, sir, and they're good boys, both of them. They've never give me a moment's trouble from the day they was born and they're the very image of Signor Niccolini.'

'I must say no one would think they had an English mother.'

'I'm not exactly their mother, sir. I've just sent them along to say 'ow do you do to 'er.'

I dare say I looked a little confused.

'They're the sons that Signor Niccolini 'ad by a Greek girl that used to work in the 'otel, and 'aving no children of me own I adopted them.'

I sought for some remark to make.

'I 'ope you don't think that there's any blame attaches to Signor Niccolini,' she said, drawing herself up a little. 'I shouldn't like you to think that, sir.' She folded her hands again and with a mixture of pride, primness, and satisfaction added the final word: 'Signor Niccolini was a very full-blooded man.'

THE TAIPAN

No one knew better than he that he was an important person. He was number one in not the least important branch of the most important English firm in China. He had worked his way up through solid ability and he looked back with a faint smile at the callow clerk who had come out to China thirty years before. When he remembered the modest home he had come from, a little red house in a long row of little red houses, in Barnes, a suburb which, aiming desperately at the genteel, achieves only a sordid melancholy, and compared it with the magnificent stone mansion, with its wide verandas and spacious rooms, which was at once the office of the company and his own residence, he chuckled with satisfaction. He had come a long way since then. He thought of the high tea to which he sat down when he came home from school (he was at St Paul's), with his father and mother and his two sisters, a slice of cold meat, a great deal of bread and butter and plenty of milk in his tea, everybody helping himself, and then he thought of the state in which now he ate his evening meal. He always dressed and whether he was alone or not he expected the three boys to wait at table. His number one boy knew exactly what he liked and he never had to bother himself with the details of housekeeping; but he always had a set dinner with soup and fish, entrée, roast, sweet, and savoury, so that if he wanted to ask anyone in at the last moment he could. He liked his food and he did not see why when he was alone he should have less good a dinner than when he had a guest.

He had indeed gone far. That was why he did not care to go home now, he had not been to England for ten years, and he took his leave in Japan or Vancouver, where he was sure of meeting old friends from the China coast. He knew no one at home. His sisters had married in their own station, their husbands were clerks and their sons were clerks; there was nothing between him and them; they bored him. He satisfied the claims of relationship by sending them every Christmas a piece of fine silk, some elaborate embroidery, or a case of tea. He was not a mean man and as long as his mother lived he had made her an allowance. But when the time came for him to retire he had no intention of going back to England, he had seen too many men do that and he knew how often it was a failure; he meant to take a house near the racecourse in Shanghai: what with bridge and his ponies and golf he expected to get through the rest of his life very comfortably. But he had a

good many years before he need think of retiring. In another five
or six Higgins would be going home and then he would take charge
of the head office in Shanghai. Meanwhile he was very happy
where he was, he could save money, which you couldn't do in
Shanghai, and have a good time into the bargain. This place had
another advantage over Shanghai: he was the most prominent
man in the community and what he said went. Even the consul
took care to keep on the right side of him. Once a consul and he
had been at loggerheads and it was not he who had gone to the
wall. The taipan thrust out his jaw pugnaciously as he thought of
the incident.

But he smiled, for he felt in an excellent humour. He was walking back to his office from a capital luncheon at the Hong-Kong
and Shanghai Bank. They did you very well there. The food was
first-rate and there was plenty of liquor. He had started with a
couple of cocktails, then he had some excellent sauterne, and he
had finished up with two glasses of port and some fine old brandy.
He felt good. And when he left he did a thing that was rare with
him; he walked. His bearers with his chair kept a few paces behind
him in case he felt inclined to slip into it, but he enjoyed stretching
his legs. He did not get enough exercise these days. Now that he
was too heavy to ride it was difficult to get exercise. But if he was
too heavy to ride he could still keep ponies, and as he strolled
along in the balmy air he thought of the spring meeting. He had a
couple of griffins that he had hopes of and one of the lads in his
office had turned out a fine jockey (he must see they didn't sneak
him away, old Higgins in Shanghai would give a pot of money to
get him over there) and he ought to pull off two or three races. He
flattered himself that he had the finest stable in the city. He pouted
his broad chest like a pigeon. It was a beautiful day, and it was
good to be alive.

He paused as he came to the cemetery. It stood there, neat and
orderly, as an evident sign of the community's opulence. He never
passed the cemetery without a little glow of pride. He was pleased
to be an Englishman. For the cemetery stood in a place, valueless
when it was chosen, which with the increase of the city's affluence
was now worth a great deal of money. It had been suggested that
the graves should be moved to another spot and the land sold for
building, but the feeling of the community was against it. It gave
the taipan a sense of satisfaction to think that their dead rested on
the most valuable site on the island. It showed that there were things
they cared for more than money. Money be blowed! When it came
to 'the things that mattered' (this was a favourite phrase with the
taipan), well, one remembered that money wasn't everything.

And now he thought he would take a stroll through. He looked at the graves. They were neatly kept and the pathways were free from weeds. There was a look of prosperity. And as he sauntered along he read the names on the tombstones. Here were three side by side: the captain, the first mate, and the second mate of the barque *Mary Baxter*, who had all perished together in the typhoon of 1908. He remembered it well. There was a little group of two missionaries, their wives and children, who had been massacred during the Boxer troubles. Shocking thing that had been! Not that he took much stock in missionaries; but, hang it all, one couldn't have these damned Chinese massacring them. Then he came to a cross with a name on it he knew. Good chap, Edward Mulock, but he couldn't stand his liquor, drank himself to death, poor devil, at twenty-five; the taipan had known a lot of them do that; there were several more neat crosses with a man's name on them and the age, twenty-five, twenty-six, or twenty-seven; it was always the same story: they had come out to China; they had never seen so much money before, they were good fellows and they wanted to drink with the rest: they couldn't stand it, and there they were in the cemetery. You had to have a strong head and a fine constitution to drink drink for drink on the China coast. Of course it was very sad, but the taipan could hardly help a smile when he thought how many of those young fellows he had drunk underground. And there was a death that had been useful, a fellow in his own firm, senior to him and a clever chap too: if that fellow had lived he might not have been taipan now. Truly the ways of fate were inscrutable. Ah, and here was little Mrs Turner, Violet Turner, she had been a pretty little thing, he had had quite an affair with her; he had been devilish cut up when she died. He looked at her age on the tombstone. She'd be no chicken if she were alive now. And as he thought of all those dead people a sense of satisfaction spread through him. He had beaten them all. They were dead and he was alive, and by George he'd scored them off. His eyes collected in one picture all those crowded graves and he smiled scornfully. He very nearly rubbed his hands.

'No one ever thought I was a fool,' he muttered.

He had a feeling of good-natured contempt for the gibbering dead. Then, as he strolled along, he came suddenly upon two coolies digging a grave. He was astonished, for he had not heard that anyone in the community was dead.

'Who the devil's that for?' he said aloud.

The coolies did not even look at him, they went on with their work, standing in the grave, deep down, and they shovelled up heavy clods of earth. Though he had been so long in China he knew no Chinese, in his day it was not thought necessary to learn the damned language, and he asked the coolies in English whose grave they were digging. They did not understand. They answered him in Chinese and he cursed them for ignorant fools. He knew that Mrs Broome's child was ailing and it might have died, but he would certainly have heard of it, and besides, that wasn't a child's grave, it was a man's and a big man's too. It was uncanny. He wished he hadn't gone into that cemetery; he hurried out and stepped into his chair. His good-humour had all gone and there was an uneasy frown on his face. The moment he got back to his office he called to his number two:

'I say, Peters, who's dead, d'you know?'

But Peters knew nothing. The taipan was puzzled. He called one of the native clerks and sent him to the cemetery to ask the coolies. He began to sign his letters. The clerk came back and said the coolies had gone and there was no one to ask. The taipan began to feel vaguely annoyed: he did not like things to happen of which he knew nothing. His own boy would know, his boy always knew everything, and he sent for him; but the boy had heard of no death in the community.

'I knew no one was dead,' said the taipan irritably. 'But what's the grave for?'

He told the boy to go to the overseer of the cemetery and find out what the devil he had dug a grave for when no one was dead.

'Let me have a whisky and soda before you go,' he added, as the boy was leaving the room.

He did not know why the sight of the grave had made him uncomfortable. But he tried to put it out of his mind. He felt better when he had drunk the whisky, and he finished his work. He went upstairs and turned over the pages of *Punch*. In a few minutes he would go to the club and play a rubber or two of bridge before dinner. But it would ease his mind to hear what his boy had to say and he waited for his return. In a little while the boy came back and he brought the overseer with him.

'What are you having a grave dug for?' he asked the overseer point-blank. 'Nobody's dead.'

'I no dig glave,' said the man.

'What the devil do you mean by that? There were two coolies digging a grave this afternoon.'

The two Chinese looked at one another. Then the boy said they had been to the cemetery together. There was no new grave there.

The taipan only just stopped himself from speaking.

'But damn it all, I saw it myself,' were the words on the tip of his tongue.

But he did not say them. He grew very red as he choked them down. The two Chinese looked at him with their steady eyes. For a moment his breath failed him.

'All right. Get out,' he gasped.

But as soon as they were gone he shouted for the boy again, and when he came, maddeningly impassive, he told him to bring some whisky. He rubbed his sweating face with a handkerchief. His hand trembled when he lifted the glass to his lips. They could say what they liked, but he had seen the grave. Why, he could hear still the dull thud as the coolies threw the spadefuls of earth on the ground above them. What did it mean? He could feel his heart beating. He felt strangely ill at ease. But he pulled himself together. It was all nonsense. If there was no grave there it must have been a hallucination. The best thing he could do was to go to the club, and if he ran across the doctor he would ask him to give him a look over.

Everyone in the club looked just the same as ever. He did not know why he should have expected them to look different. It was a comfort. These men, living for many years with one another lives that were methodically regulated, had acquired a number of little idiosyncrasies – one of them hummed incessantly while he played bridge, another insisted on drinking beer through a straw – and these tricks which had so often irritated the taipan now gave him a sense of security. He needed it, for he could not get out of his head that strange sight he had seen; he played bridge very badly; his partner was censorious, and the taipan lost his temper. He thought the men were looking at him oddly. He wondered what they saw in him that was unaccustomed.

Suddenly he felt he could not bear to stay in the club any longer. As he went out he saw the doctor reading *The Times* in the reading-room, but he could not bring himself to speak to him. He wanted to see for himself whether that grave was really there, and stepping into his chair he told his bearers to take him to the cemetery. You couldn't have a hallucination twice, could you? And besides, he would take the overseer in with him and if the grave was not there he wouldn't see it, and if it was he'd give the overseer the soundest thrashing he'd ever had. But the overseer was nowhere to be found. He had gone out and taken the keys with him. When the taipan found he could not get into the cemetery he felt suddenly exhausted. He got back into his chair and told his bearers to take him home. He would lie down for half an hour before dinner. He was tired out. That was it. He had heard that people had hallucinations when they were tired. When his boy came in to put out his clothes for dinner it was only by an effort of will that he got up. He had a strong inclination not to dress that evening, but he resisted it: he made it a rule to dress, he had dressed every evening for twenty years and it would never do to break his rule. But he ordered a bottle of champagne with his dinner and that made him feel more comfortable. Afterwards he told the boy to bring him the best brandy. When he had drunk a couple of glasses of this he felt himself again. Hallucinations be damned! He went to the billiard-room and practised a few difficult shots. There could not be much the matter with him when his eye was so sure. When he went to bed he sank immediately into a sound sleep.

But suddenly he awoke. He had dreamed of that open grave and the coolies digging leisurely. He was sure he had seen them. It was absurd to say it was a hallucination when he had seen them with his own eyes. Then he heard the rattle of the night-watchman going his rounds. It broke upon the stillness of the night so harshly that it made him jump out of his skin. And then terror seized him. He felt a horror of the winding multitudinous streets of the Chinese city, and there was something ghastly and terrible in the convoluted roofs of the temples with their devils grimacing and tortured. He loathed the smells that assaulted his nostrils. And the people. Those myriads of blue-clad coolies, and the beggars in their filthy rags, and the merchants and the magistrates, sleek, smiling, and inscrutable, in their long black gowns. They seemed to press upon him with menace. He hated the country. China. Why had he ever come? He was panic-stricken now. He must get out. He would not stay another year, another month. What did he care about Shanghai?

'Oh, my God,' he cried, 'if I were only safely back in England.'

He wanted to go home. If he had to die he wanted to die in England. He could not bear to be buried among all these yellow men, with their slanting eyes and their grinning faces. He wanted to be buried at home, not in that grave he had seen that day. He could never rest there. Never. What did it matter what people thought? Let them think what they liked. The only thing that mattered was to get away while he had the chance.

He got out of bed and wrote to the head of the firm and said he had discovered he was dangerously ill. He must be replaced. He could not stay longer than was absolutely necessary. He must go home at once.

They found the letter in the morning clenched in the taipan's hand. He had slipped down between the desk and the chair. He was stone dead.

THE CONSUL

MR PETE was in a state of the liveliest exasperation. He had been in the consular service for more than twenty years and he had had to deal with all manner of vexatious people, officials who would not listen to reason, merchants who took the British Government for a debt-collecting agency, missionaries who resented as gross injustice any attempt at fair play; but he never recollected a case which had left him more completely at a loss. He was a mild-mannered man, but for no reason he flew into a passion with his writer and he very nearly sacked the Eurasian clerk because he had wrongly spelt two words in a letter placed before him for his official signature. He was a conscientious man and he could not persuade himself to leave his office before the clock struck four; the moment it did he jumped up and called for his hat and stick. Because his boy did not bring them at once he abused him roundly. They say that the consuls all grow a little odd; and the merchants who can live for thirty-five years in China without learning enough of the language to ask their way in the street say that it is because they have to study Chinese; and there was no doubt that Mr Pete was decidedly odd. He was a bachelor and on that account had been sent to a series of posts which by reason of their isolation were thought unsuited to married men. He had lived so much alone that his natural tendency to eccentricity had developed to an extravagant degree, and he had habits which surprised the stranger. He was very absent-minded. He paid no attention to his house, which was always in great disorder, nor to his food; his boys gave him to eat what they liked and for everything he had made him pay through the nose. He was untiring in his efforts to suppress the opium traffic, but he was the only person in the city who did not know that his servants kept opium in the consulate itself, and a busy traffic in the drug was openly conducted at the back door of the compound. He was an ardent collector and the house provided for him by the government was filled with the various things which he had collected one after the other, pewter, brass, carved wood; these were his more legitimate enterprises; but he also collected stamps, birds' eggs, hotel labels, and post-marks: he boasted that he had a collection of postmarks which was unequalled in the Empire. During his long sojourning in lonely places he had read a great deal, and though he was no sinologue he had a greater knowledge of China, its history, litera-ture, and people, than most of his colleagues; but from his wide reading he had acquired not toleration but vanity. He was a man of a singular appearance. His body was small and frail and when he walked he gave you the idea of a dead leaf dancing before the wind; and then there was something extraordinarily odd in the small Tyrolese hat, with a cock's feather in it, very old and shabby, which he wore perched rakishly on the side of his large head. He was exceedingly bald. You saw that his eyes, blue and pale, were weak behind the spectacles, and a drooping, ragged, dingy moustache did not hide the peevishness of his mouth. And now, turning out of the street in which was the consulate, he made his way on to the city wall, for there only in the multitudinous city was it possible to walk with comfort.

He was a man who took his work hardly, worrying himself to death over every trifle, but as a rule a walk on the wall soothed and rested him. The city stood in the midst of a great plain and often at sundown from the wall you could see in the distance the snow-capped mountains, the mountains of Tibet; but now he walked quickly, looking neither to the right nor to the left, and his fat spaniel frisked about him unobserved. He talked to himself rapidly in a low monotone. The cause of his irritation was a visit that he had that day received from a lady who called herself Mrs Yü and whom he with a consular passion for precision insisted on calling Miss Lambert. This in itself sufficed to deprive their intercourse of amenity. She was an Englishwoman married to a Chinese. She had arrived two years before with her husband from England, where he had been studying at the University of London; he had made her believe that he was a great personage in his own country and she had imagined herself to be coming to a gorgeous palace and a position of consequence. It was a bitter surprise when she found herself brought to a shabby Chinese house crowded with people: there was not even a foreign bed in it, nor a knife and fork: everything seemed to her very dirty and smelly. It was a shock to find that she had to live with her husband's father and mother and he told her that she must do exactly what his mother bade her; but in her complete ignorance of Chinese it was not till she had been two or three days in the house that she realized that she was not her husband's only wife. He had been married as a boy before he left his native city to acquire the knowledge of the barbarians. When she bitterly upbraided him for deceiving her he shrugged his shoulders. There was nothing to prevent a Chinese from having two wives if he wanted them and, he added with some disregard to truth, no Chinese woman looked upon it as a hardship. It was upon making this discovery that she paid her first visit to the consul. He had already heard of her arrival – in China everyone knows everything about everyone – and he received her without surprise. Nor had he much sympathy to show her. That a foreign woman should marry a Chinese at all filled him with indignation, but that she should do so without making proper inquiries vexed him like a personal affront. She was not at all the sort of woman whose appearance led you to imagine that she would be guilty of such a folly. She was a solid, thick-set, young person, short, plain, and matter-of-fact. She was cheaply dressed in a tailor-made suit and she wore a tam-o'-shanter. She had bad teeth and a muddy skin. Her hands were large and red and ill-cared-for. You could tell that she was not unused to hard work. She spoke English with a cockney whine.

'How did you meet Mr Yü?' asked the consul frigidly.

'Well, you see, it's like this,' she answered. 'Dad was in a very good position, and when he died mother said : "Well, it seems a sinful waste to keep all these rooms empty, I'll put a card in the window."'

The consul interrupted her.

'He had lodgings with you?'

'Well, they weren't exactly lodgings,' she said.

'Shall we say apartments then?' replied the consul, with his thin, slightly vain smile.

That was generally the explanation of these marriages. Then because he thought her a very foolish vulgar woman he explained bluntly that according to English law she was not married to Yü and that the best thing she could do was to go back to England at once. She began to cry and his heart softened a little to her. He promised to put her in charge of some missionary ladies who would look after her on the long journey, and indeed, if she liked, he would see if meanwhile she could not live in one of the missions. But while he talked Miss Lambert dried her tears.

'What's the good of going back to England?' she said at last. 'I 'aven't got nowhere to go to.'

'You can go to your mother.'

'She was all against my marrying Mr Yü. I should never hear the last of it if I was to go back now.'

The consul began to argue with her, but the more he argued the more determined she became, and at last he lost his temper.

'If you like to stay here with a man who isn't your husband it's your own look-out, but I wash my hands of all responsibility.'

Her retort had often rankled.

'Then you've got no cause to worry,' she said, and the look on her face returned to him whenever he thought of her.

That was two years ago and he had seen her once or twice since then. It appeared that she got on very badly both with her mother-in-law and with her husband's other wife, and she had come to the consul with preposterous questions about her rights according to Chinese law. He repeated his offer to get her away, but she remained steadfast in her refusal to go, and their interview always ended in the consul's flying into a passion. He was almost inclined to pity the rascally Yü who had to keep the peace between three warring women. According to his English wife's account he was not unkind to her. He tried to act fairly by both his wives. Miss Lambert did not improve. The consul knew that ordinarily she wore Chinese clothes, but when she came to see him she put on European dress. She was become extremely blowsy. Her health suffered from the Chinese food she ate and she was beginning to look wretchedly ill. But really he was shocked when she had been shown into his office that day. She wore no hat and her hair was dishevelled. She was in a highly hysterical state.

'They're trying to poison me,' she screamed and she put before him a bowl of some foul-smelling food. 'It's poisoned,' she said. 'I've been ill for the last ten days, it's only by a miracle I've escaped.'

She gave him a long story, circumstantial and probable enough, enough to convince him: after all, nothing was more likely than that the Chinese women should use familiar methods to get rid of an intruder who was hateful to them.

'Do they know you've come here?'

'Of course they do; I told them I was going to show them up.'

Now at last was the moment for decisive action. The consul looked at her in his most official manner.

'Well, you must never go back there. I refuse to put up with your nonsense any longer. I insist on your leaving this man who isn't your husband.'

But he found himself helpless against the woman's insane obstinacy. He repeated all the arguments he had used so often, but she would not listen, and as usual he lost his temper. It was then, in answer to his final, desperate question, that she had made the remark which had entirely robbed him of his calm.

'But what on earth makes you stay with the man?' he cried.

She hesitated for a moment and a curious look came into her eyes.

'There's something in the way his hair grows on his forehead that I can't help liking,' she answered.

The consul had never heard anything so outrageous. It really was the last straw. And now while he strode along, trying to walk off his anger, though he was not a man who often used bad language he really could not restrain himself, and he said fiercely:

'Women are simply bloody.'

A FRIEND IN NEED

FOR thirty years now I have been studying my fellow-men. I do not know very much about them. I should certainly hesitate to engage a servant on his face, and yet I suppose it is on the face that for the most part we judge the persons we meet. We draw our conclusions from the shape of the jaw, the look in the eyes, the contour of the mouth. I wonder if we are more often right than wrong. Why novels and plays are so often untrue to life is because their authors, perhaps of necessity, make their characters all of a piece. They cannot afford to make them self-contradictory, for then they become incomprehensible, and yet self-contradictory is what most of us are. We are a haphazard bundle of inconsistent qualities. In books on logic they will tell you that it is absurd to say that yellow is tubular or gratitude heavier than air; but in that mixture of incongruities that makes up the self yellow may very well be a horse and cart and gratitude the middle of next week. I shrug my shoulders when people tell me that their first impressions of a person are always right. I think they must have small insight or great vanity. For my own part I find that the longer I know people the more they puzzle me: my oldest friends are just those of whom I can say that I don't know the first thing about them.

These reflections have occurred to me because I read in this morning's paper that Edward Hyde Burton had died at Kobe. He was a merchant and he had been in business in Japan for many years. I knew him very little, but he interested me because once he gave me a great surprise. Unless I had heard the story from his own lips I should never have believed that he was capable of such an action. It was more startling because both in appearance and manner he suggested a very definite type. Here if ever was a man all of a piece. He was a tiny little fellow, not much more than five feet four in height, and very slender, with white hair, a red face much wrinkled, and blue eyes. I suppose he was about sixty when I knew him. He was always neatly and quietly dressed in accordance with his age and station.

Though his offices were in Kobe, Burton often came down to Yokohama. I happened on one occasion to be spending a few days there, waiting for a ship, and I was introduced to him at the British Club. We played bridge together. He played a good game and a generous one. He did not talk very much, either then or later when we were having drinks, but what he said was sensible.

He had a quiet, dry humour. He seemed to be popular at the club and afterwards, when he had gone, they described him as one of the best. It happened that we were both staying at the Grand Hotel and next day he asked me to dine with him. I met his wife, fat, elderly, and smiling, and his two daughters. It was evidently a united and affectionate family. I think the chief thing that struck me about Burton was his kindliness. There was something very pleasing in his mild blue eyes. His voice was gentle; you could not imagine that he could possibly raise it in anger; his smile was benign. Here was a man who attracted you because you felt in him a real love for his fellows. He had charm. But there was nothing mawkish in him: he liked his game of cards and his cocktail, he could tell with point a good and spicy story, and in his youth he had been something of an athlete. He was a rich man and he had made every penny himself. I suppose one thing that made you like him was that he was so small and frail; he aroused your instincts of protection. You felt that he could not bear to hurt a fly.

One afternoon I was sitting in the lounge of the Grand Hotel. This was before the earthquake and they had leather arm-chairs there. From the windows you had a spacious view of the harbour with its crowded traffic. There were great liners on their way to Vancouver and San Francisco or to Europe by way of Shanghai, Hong-Kong, and Singapore; there were tramps of all nations, battered and sea-worn, junks with their high sterns and great coloured sails, and innumerable sampans. It was a busy, exhilarating scene, and yet, I know not why, restful to the spirit. Here was romance and it seemed that you had but to stretch out your hand to touch it.

Burton came into the lounge presently and caught sight of me. He seated himself in the chair next to mine.

'What do you say to a little drink?'

He clapped his hands for a boy and ordered two gin fizzes. As the boy brought them a man passed along the street outside and seeing me waved his hand.

'Do you know Turner?' said Burton as I nodded a greeting.

'I've met him at the club. I'm told he's a remittance man.'

'Yes, I believe he is. We have a good many here.'

'He plays bridge well.'

'They generally do. There was a fellow here last year, oddly enough a namesake of mine, who was the best bridge player I ever met. I suppose you never came across him in London. Lenny Burton he called himself. I believe he'd belonged to some very good clubs.'

'No, I don't believe I remember the name.'

'He was quite a remarkable player. He seemed to have an instinct about the cards. It was uncanny. I used to play with him a lot. He was in Kobe for some time.'

Burton sipped his gin fizz.

'It's rather a funny story,' he said. 'He wasn't a bad chap. I liked him. He was always well-dressed and smart-looking. He was handsome in a way with curly hair and pink-and-white cheeks. Women thought a lot of him. There was no harm in him, you know, he was only wild. Of course he drank too much. Those sort of fellows always do. A bit of money used to come in for him once a quarter and he made a bit more by card-playing. He won a good deal of mine, I know that.'

Burton gave a kindly chuckle. I knew from my own experience that he could lose money at bridge with a good grace. He stroked his shaven chin with his thin hand; the veins stood out on it and it was almost transparent.

'I suppose that is why he came to me when he went broke, that and the fact that he was a namesake of mine. He came to see me in my office one day and asked me for a job. I was rather surprised. He told me that there was no more money coming from home and he wanted to work. I asked him how old he was.

'"Thirty-five," he said.

'"And what have you been doing hitherto?" I asked him.

'"Well, nothing very much," he said.

'I couldn't help laughing.

'"I'm afraid I can't do anything for you just yet," I said. "Come back and see me in another thirty-five years, and I'll see what I can do."

'He didn't move. He went rather pale. He hesitated for a moment and then he told me that he had had bad luck at cards for some time. He hadn't been willing to stick to bridge, he'd been playing poker, and he'd got trimmed. He hadn't a penny. He'd pawned everything he had. He couldn't pay his hotel bill and they wouldn't give him any more credit. He was down and out. If he couldn't get something to do he'd have to commit suicide.

'I looked at him for a bit. I could see now that he was all to pieces. He'd been drinking more than usual and he looked fifty. The girls wouldn't have thought so much of him if they'd seen him then.

'"Well, isn't there anything you can do except play cards?" I asked him.

'"I can swim," he said.

'"Swim!"

'I could hardly believe my ears; it seemed such an insane answer to give.

'"I swam for my university."

'I got some glimmering of what he was driving at. I've known too many men who were little tin gods at their university to be impressed by it.

'"I was a pretty good swimmer myself when I was a young man," I said.

'Suddenly I had an idea.'

Pausing in his story, Burton turned to me.

'Do you know Kobe?' he asked.

'No,' I said, 'I passed through it once, but I only spent a night there.'

'Then you don't know the Shioya Club. When I was a young man I swam from there round the beacon and landed at the creek of Tarumi. It's over three miles and it's rather difficult on account of the currents round the beacon. Well, I told my young name-sake about it and I said to him that if he'd do it I'd give him a job.

'I could see he was rather taken aback.

'"You say you're a swimmer," I said.

'"I'm not in very good condition," he answered.

'I didn't say anything. I shrugged my shoulders. He looked at me for a moment and then he nodded.

'"All right," he said. "When do you want me to do it?"

'I looked at my watch. It was just after ten.

'"The swim shouldn't take you much over an hour and a quarter. I'll drive round to the creek at half past twelve and meet you. I'll take you back to the club to dress and then we'll have lunch together."

'"Done," he said.

'We shook hands. I wished him good luck and he left me. I had a lot of work to do that morning and I only just managed to get to the creek at Tarumi at half past twelve. But I needn't have hurried; he never turned up.'

'Did he funk it at the last moment?' I asked.

'No, he didn't funk it. He started all right. But of course he'd ruined his constitution by drink and dissipation. The currents round the beacon were more than he could manage. We didn't get the body for about three days.'

I didn't say anything for a moment or two. I was a trifle shocked. Then I asked Burton a question.

'When you made him that offer of a job, did you know he'd be drowned?'

He gave a little mild chuckle and he looked at me with those kind and candid blue eyes of his. He rubbed his chin with his hand. 'Well, I hadn't got a vacancy in my office at the moment.'

THE ROUND DOZEN

I LIKE Elsom. It is a seaside resort in the South of England, not very far from Brighton, and it has something of the late Georgian charm of that agreeable town. But it is neither bustling nor garish. Ten years ago, when I used to go there not infrequently, you might still see here and there an old house, solid and pretentious in no unpleasing fashion (like a decayed gentlewoman of good family whose discreet pride in her ancestry amuses rather than offends you), which was built in the reign of the First Gentleman in Europe and where a courtier of fallen fortunes may well have passed his declining years. The main street had a lackadaisical air and the doctor's motor seemed a trifle out of place. The house-wives did their housekeeping in a leisurely manner. They gossiped with the butcher as they watched him cut from his great joint of South Down a piece of the best end of the neck, and they asked amiably after the grocer's wife as he put half a pound of tea and a packet of salt into their string bag. I do not know whether Elsom was ever fashionable: it certainly was not so then; but it was respectable and cheap. Elderly ladies, maiden and widowed, lived there, Indian Civilians and retired soldiers: they looked forward with little shudders of dismay to August and September which would bring holiday-makers; but did not disdain to let them their houses and on the proceeds spend a few worldly weeks in a Swiss pension. I never knew Elsom at that hectic time when the lodging-houses were full and young men in blazers sauntered along the front, when Pierrots performed on the beach and in the billiard-room at the Dolphin you heard the click of balls till eleven at night. I only knew it in winter. Then in every house on the sea-front, stucco houses with bow-windows built a hundred years ago, there was a sign to inform you that apartments were to let; and the guests of the Dolphin were waited on by a single waiter and the boots. At ten o'clock the porter came into the smoking-room and looked at you in so marked a manner that you got up and went to bed. Then Elsom was a restful place and the Dolphin a very comfortable inn. It was pleasing to think that the Prince Regent drove over with Mrs Fitzherbert more than once to drink a dish of tea in its coffee-room. In the hall was a framed letter from Mr Thackeray ordering a sitting-room and two bedrooms overlooking the sea and giving instructions that a fly should be sent to the station to meet him.

One November, two or three years after the war, having had a bad attack of influenza, I went down to Elsom to regain my strength. I arrived in the afternoon and when I had unpacked my things went for a stroll on the front. The sky was overcast and the calm sea grey and cold. A few seagulls flew close to the shore. Sailing-boats, their masts taken down for the winter, were drawn up high on the shingly beach, and the bathing-huts stood side by side in a long, grey, and tattered row. No one was sitting on the benches that the town council had put here and there, but a few people were trudging up and down for exercise. I passed an old colonel with a red nose who stamped along in plus-fours followed by a terrier, two elderly women in short skirts and stout shoes, and a plain girl in a tam-o'-shanter. I had never seen the front so deserted. The lodging-houses looked like bedraggled old maids waiting for lovers who would never return, and even the friendly Dolphin seemed wan and desolate. My heart sank. Life on a sudden seemed very drab. I returned to the hotel, drew the curtains of my sitting-room, poked the fire, and with a book sought to dispel my melancholy. But I was glad enough when it was time to dress for dinner. I went into the coffee-room and found the guests of the hotel already seated. I gave them a casual glance. There was one lady of middle age by herself and there were two elderly gentlemen, golfers probably, with red faces and baldish heads, who ate their food in moody silence. The only other persons in the room were a group of three who sat in the bow-window, and they immediately attracted my surprised attention. The party consisted of an old gentleman and two ladies, one of whom was old and probably his wife, while the other was younger and possibly his daughter. It was the old lady who first excited my interest. She wore a voluminous dress of black silk and a black lace cap; on her wrists were heavy gold bangles and round her neck a substantial gold chain from which hung a large gold locket; at her neck was a large gold brooch. I did not know that anyone still wore jewellery of that sort. Often, passing second-hand jewellers and pawnbrokers, I had lingered for a moment to look at these strangely old-fashioned articles, so solid, costly, and hideous, and thought with a smile in which there was a tinge of sadness, of the women long since dead who had worn them. They suggested the period when the bustle and the flounce were taking the place of the crinoline and the pork-pie hat was ousting the poke-bonnet. The British people liked things solid and good in those days. They went to church on Sunday morning and after church walked in the Park. They gave dinner-parties of twelve courses where the master of the house carved the beef and the chickens, and after dinner the ladies who could play favoured the company with Mendelssohn's *Songs without Words* and the gentleman with the fine baritone voice sang an old English ballad.

The younger woman had her back turned to me and at first I could see only that she had a slim and youthful figure. She had a great deal of brown hair which seemed to be elaborately arranged. She wore a grey dress. The three of them were chatting in low tones and presently she turned her head so that I saw her profile. It was astonishingly beautiful. The nose was straight and delicate, the line of the cheek exquisitely modelled; I saw then that she wore her hair after the manner of Queen Alexandra. The dinner proceeded to its close and the party got up. The old lady sailed out of the room, looking neither to the right nor to the left, and the young one followed her. Then I saw with a shock that she was old. Her frock was simple enough, the skirt was longer than was at that time worn, and there was something slightly old-fashioned in the cut, I dare say the waist was more clearly indicated than was then usual, but it was a girl's frock. She was tall, like a heroine of Tennyson's, slight, with long legs and a graceful carriage. I had seen the nose before, it was the nose of a Greek goddess, her mouth was beautiful, and her eyes were large and blue. Her skin was of course a little tight on the bones and there were wrinkles on her forehead and about her eyes, but in youth it must have been lovely. She reminded you of those Roman ladies with features of an exquisite regularity whom Alma-Tadema used to paint, but who, notwithstanding their antique dress, were so stubbornly English. It was a type of cold perfection that one had not seen for five-and-twenty years. Now it is as dead as the epigram. I was like an archaeologist who finds some long-buried statue and I was thrilled in so unexpected a manner to hit upon this survival of a past era. For no day is so dead as the day before yesterday.

The gentleman rose to his feet when the two ladies left, and then resumed his chair. A waiter brought him a glass of heavy port. He smelt it, sipped it, and rolled it round his tongue. I observed him. He was a little man, much shorter than his imposing wife, well-covered without being stout, with a fine head of curling grey hair. His face was much wrinkled and it bore a faintly humorous expression. His lips were tight and his chin was square. He was, according to our present notions, somewhat extravagantly dressed. He wore a black velvet jacket, a frilled shirt with a low collar and a large black tie, and very wide evening trousers. It gave you vaguely the effect of costume. Having drunk his port with deliberation, he got up and sauntered out of the room.

When I passed through the hall, curious to know who these singular people were, I glanced at the visitors' book. I saw written

in an angular feminine hand, the writing that was taught to young
ladies in modish schools forty years or so ago, the names: Mr and
Mrs Edwin St Clair and Miss Porchester. Their address was given
as 68 Leinster Square, Bayswater, London. These must be the
names and this the address of the persons who had so much interested me. I asked the manageress who Mr St Clair was and she
told me that she believed he was something in the City. I went
into the billiard-room and knocked the balls about for a little
while and then on my way upstairs passed through the lounge.
The two red-faced gentlemen were reading the evening paper and
the elderly lady was dozing over a novel. The party of three sat in
a corner. Mrs St Clair was knitting, Miss Porchester was busy
with embroidery, and Mr St Clair was reading aloud in a discreet
but resonant tone. As I passed I discovered that he was reading
Bleak House.

I read and wrote most of the next day, but in the afternoon I
went for a walk and on my way home I sat down for a little on one
of those convenient benches on the sea-front. It was not quite so
cold as the day before and the air was pleasant. For want of anything better to do I watched a figure advancing towards me from
a distance. It was a man and as he came nearer I saw that it was
rather a shabby little man. He wore a thin black greatcoat and a
somewhat battered bowler. He walked with his hands in his
pockets and looked cold. He gave me a glance as he passed by,
went on a few steps, hesitated, stopped and turned back. When
he came up once more to the bench on which I sat he took a hand
out of his pocket and touched his hat. I noticed that he wore
shabby black gloves, and surmised that he was a widower in strai-
tened circumstances. Or he might have been a mute recovering,
like myself, from influenza.

'Excuse me, sir,' he said, 'but could you oblige me with a
match?'

'Certainly.'

He sat down beside me and while I put my hand in my pocket
for matches he hunted in his for cigarettes. He took out a small
packet of Gold Flake and his face fell.

'Dear, dear, how very annoying! I haven't got a cigarette left.'

'Let me offer you one,' I replied, smiling.

I took out my case and he helped himself.

'Gold?' he asked, giving the case a tap as I closed it. 'Gold?
That's a thing I never could keep. I've had three. All stolen.'

His eyes rested in a melancholy way on his boots, which were
sadly in need of repair. He was a wizened little man with a long
thin nose and pale-blue eyes. His skin was sallow and he was much

lined. I could not tell what his age was; he might have been five-and-thirty or he might have been sixty. There was nothing remarkable about him except his insignificance. But though evidently poor he was neat and clean. He was respectable and he clung to respectability. No, I did not think he was a mute, I thought he was a solicitor's clerk who had lately buried his wife and been sent to Elsom by an indulgent employer to get over the first shock of his grief.

'Are you making a long stay, sir?' he asked me.

'Ten days or a fortnight.'

'Is this your first visit to Elsom, sir?'

'I have been here before.'

'I know it well, sir. I flatter myself there are very few seaside resorts that I have not been to at one time or another. Elsom is hard to beat, sir. You get a very nice class of people here. There's nothing noisy or vulgar about Elsom, if you understand what I mean. Elsom has very pleasant recollections for me, sir. I knew Elsom well in bygone days. I was married in St Martin's Church, sir.'

'Really,' I said feebly.

'It was a very happy marriage, sir.'

'I'm very glad to hear it,' I returned.

'Nine months, that one lasted,' he said reflectively.

Surely the remark was a trifle singular. I had not looked forward with any enthusiasm to the probability which I so clearly foresaw that he would favour me with an account of his matrimonial experiences, but now I waited if not with eagerness at least with curiosity for a further observation. He made none. He sighed a little. At last I broke the silence.

'There don't seem to be very many people about,' I remarked.

'I like it so. I'm not one for crowds. As I was saying just now, I reckon I've spent a good many years at one seaside resort after the other, but I never came in the season. It's the winter I like.'

'Don't you find it a little melancholy?'

He turned towards me and placed his black-gloved hand for an instant on my arm.

'It is melancholy. And because it's melancholy a little ray of sunshine is very welcome.'

The remark seemed to me perfectly idiotic and I did not answer. He withdrew his hand from my arm and got up.

'Well, I mustn't keep you, sir. Pleased to have made your acquaintance.'

He took off his dingy hat very politely and strolled away. It was beginning now to grow chilly and I thought I would return to the Dolphin. As I reached its broad steps a landau drove up, drawn by two scraggy horses, and from it stepped Mr St Clair. He wore a hat that looked like the unhappy result of a union between a bowler and a top-hat. He gave his hand to his wife and then to his niece. The porter carried in after them rugs and cushions. As Mr St Clair paid the driver I heard him tell him to come at the usual time next day and I understood that the St Clairs took a drive every afternoon in a landau. It would not have surprised me to learn that none of them had ever been in a motor-car.

The manageress told me that they kept very much to themselves and sought no acquaintance among the other persons staying at the hotel. I rode my imagination on a loose rein. I watched them eat three meals a day. I watched Mr and Mrs St Clair sit at the top of the hotel steps in the morning. He read *The Times* and she knitted. I suppose Mrs St Clair had never read a paper in her life, for they never took anything but *The Times* and Mr St Clair of course took it with him every day to the City. At about twelve Miss Porchester joined them.

'Have you enjoyed your walk, Eleanor?' asked Mrs St Clair.

'It was very nice, Aunt Gertrude,' answered Miss Porchester.

And I understood that just as Mrs St Clair took 'her drive' every afternoon Miss Porchester took 'her walk' every morning.

'When you have come to the end of your row, my dear,' said Mr St Clair, with a glance at his wife's knitting, 'we might go for a constitutional before luncheon.'

'That will be very nice,' answered Mrs St Clair. She folded up her work and gave it to Miss Porchester. 'If you're going upstairs, Eleanor, will you take my work?'

'Certainly, Aunt Gertrude.'

'I dare say you're a little tired after your walk, my dear.'

'I shall have a little rest before luncheon.'

Miss Porchester went into the hotel and Mr and Mrs St Clair walked slowly along the sea-front, side by side, to a certain point, and then walked slowly back.

When I met one of them on the stairs I bowed and received an unsmiling, polite bow in return, and in the morning I ventured upon a 'good day' but there the matter ended. It looked as though I should never have a chance to speak to any of them. But presently I thought that Mr St Clair gave me now and then a glance, and thinking he had heard my name I imagined, perhaps vainly, that he looked at me with curiosity. And a day or two after that I was sitting in my room when the porter came in with a message.

'Mr St Clair presents his compliments and could you oblige him with the loan of *Whitaker's Almanack*.'

I was astonished.

'Why on earth should he think that I have a *Whitaker's Almanack*?'

'Well, sir, the manageress told him you wrote.'

I could not see the connexion.

'Tell Mr St Clair that I'm very sorry that I haven't got a *Whitaker's Almanack*, but if I had I would very gladly lend it to him.'

Here was my opporunity. I was by now filled with eagerness to know these fantastic persons more closely. Now and then in the heart of Asia I have come upon a lonely tribe living in a little village among an alien population. No one knows how they came there or why they settled in that spot. They live their own lives, speak their own language, and have no communication with their neighbours. No one knows whether they are the descendants of a band that was left behind when their nation swept in a vast horde across the continent or whether they are the dying remnant of some great people that in that country once held empire. They are a mystery. They have no future and no history. This odd little family seemed to me to have something of the same character. They were of an era that is dead and gone. They reminded me of persons in one of those leisurely, old-fashioned novels that one's father read. They belonged to the eighties and they had not moved since then. How extraordinary it was that they could have lived through the last forty years as though the world stood still! They took me back to my childhood and I recollected people who are long since dead. I wonder if it is only distance that gives me the impression that they were more peculiar than anyone is now. When a person was described then as 'quite a character', by heaven, it meant something.

So that evening after dinner I went into the lounge and boldly addressed Mr St Clair.

'I'm sorry I haven't got a *Whitaker's Almanack*,' I said, 'but if I have any other book that can be of service to you I shall be delighted to lend it to you.'

Mr St Clair was obviously startled. The two ladies kept their eyes on their work. There was an embarrassed hush.

'It does not matter at all, but I was given to understand by the manageress that you were a novelist.'

I racked my brain. There was evidently some connexion between my profession and *Whitaker's Almanack* that escaped me.

'In days gone by Mr Trollope used often to dine with us in Leinster Square and I remember him saying that the two most useful books to a novelist were the Bible and *Whitaker's Almanack.'*

'I see that Thackeray once stayed in this hotel,' I remarked, anxious not to let the conversation drop.

'I never very much cared for Mr Thackeray, though he dined more than once with my wife's father, the late Mr Sargeant Saunders. He was too cynical for me. My niece has not read *Vanity Fair* to this day.'

Miss Porchester blushed slightly at this reference to herself. A waiter brought in the coffee and Mrs St Clair turned to her husband.

'Perhaps, my dear, this gentleman would do us the pleasure to have his coffee with us.'

Although not directly addressed I answered promptly:

'Thank you very much.'

I sat down.

'Mr Trollope was always my favourite novelist,' said Mr St Clair. 'He was so essentially a gentleman. I admire Charles Dickens. But Charles Dickens could never draw a gentleman. I am given to understand that young people nowadays find Mr Trollope a little slow. My niece, Miss Porchester, prefers the novels of Mr William Black.'

'I'm afraid I've never read any,' I said.

'Ah, I see that you are like me; you are not up to date. My niece once persuaded me to read a novel by a Miss Rhoda Broughton, but I could not manage more than a hundred pages of it.'

'I did not say I liked it, Uncle Edwin,' said Miss Porchester, defending herself, with another blush, 'I told you it was rather fast, but everybody was talking about it.'

'I'm quite sure it is not the sort of book your Aunt Gertrude would have wished you to read, Eleanor.'

'I remember Miss Broughton telling me once that when she was young people said her books were fast and when she was old they said they were slow, and it was very hard since she had written exactly the same sort of book for forty years.'

'Oh, did you know Miss Broughton?' asked Miss Porchester, addressing me for the first time. 'How very interesting! And did you know Ouida?'

'My dear Eleanor, what will you say next! I'm quite sure you've never read anything by Ouida.'

'Indeed, I have, Uncle Edwin. I've read *Under Two Flags* and I liked it very much.'

'You amaze and shock me. I don't know what girls are coming to nowadays.'

'You always said that when I was thirty you gave me complete liberty to read anything I liked.'

'There is a difference, my dear Eleanor, between liberty and licence,' said Mr St Clair, smiling a little in order not to make his reproof offensive, but with a certain gravity.

I do not know if in recounting this conversation I have managed to convey the impression it gave me of a charming and old-fashioned air. I could have listened all night to them discussing the depravity of an age that was young in the eighteen-eighties. I would have given a good deal for a glimpse of their large and roomy house in Leinster Square. I should have recognized the suite covered in red brocade that stood stiffly about the drawing-room, each piece in its appointed place; and the cabinets filled with Dresden china would have brought me back my childhood. In the dining-room, where they habitually sat, for the drawing-room was used only for parties, was a Turkey carpet and a vast mahogany sideboard 'groaning' with silver. On the walls were the pictures that had excited the admiration of Mrs Humphrey Ward and her uncle Matthew in the Academy of eighteen-eighty.

Next morning, strolling through a pretty lane at the back of Elsom, I met Miss Porchester, who was taking 'her walk'. I should have liked to go a little way with her, but felt certain that it would embarrass this maiden of fifty to saunter alone with a man even of my respectable years. She bowed as I passed her and blushed. Oddly enough, a few yards behind her I came upon the funny shabby little man in black gloves with whom I had spoken for a few minutes on the front. He touched his old bowler hat.

'Excuse me, sir, but could you oblige me with a match?' he said.

'Certainly,' I retorted, 'but I'm afraid I have no cigarettes on me.'

'Allow me to offer you one of mine,' he said, taking out the paper case. It was empty. 'Dear, dear, I haven't got one either. What a curious coincidence!'

He went on and I had a notion that he a little hastened his steps. I was beginning to have my doubts about him. I hoped he was not going to bother Miss Porchester. For a moment I thought of walking back, but I did not. He was a civil little man and I did not believe he would make a nuisance of himself to a single lady.

I saw him again that very afternoon. I was sitting on the front. He walked towards me with little, halting steps. There was something of a wind and he looked like a dried leaf being driven before it. This time he did not hesitate, but sat down beside me.

'We meet again, sir. The world is a small place. If it will not inconvenience you perhaps you will allow me to rest a few minutes. I am a wee bit tired.'

'This is a public bench, and you have just as much right to sit on it as I.'

I did not wait for him to ask me for a match, but at once offered him a cigarette.

'How very kind of you, sir! I have to limit myself to so many cigarettes a day, but I enjoy those I smoke. As one grows older the pleasures of life diminish, but my experience is that one enjoys more those that remain.'

'That is a very consoling thought.'

'Excuse me, sir, but am I right in thinking that you are the well-known author?'

'I am an author,' I replied. 'But what made you think it?'

'I have seen your portrait in the illustrated papers. I suppose you don't recognize me?'

I looked at him again, a weedy little man in neat but shabby black clothes, with a long nose and watery blue eyes.

'I'm afraid I don't.'

'I dare say I've changed,' he sighed. 'There was a time when my photograph was in every paper in the United Kingdom. Of course, those press photographs never do you justice. I give you my word, sir, that if I hadn't seen my name underneath I should never have guessed that some of them were meant for me.'

He was silent for a while. The tide was out and beyond the shingle of the beach was a strip of yellow mud. The breakwaters were half buried in it like the backbones of prehistoric beasts.

'It must be a wonderfully interesting thing to be an author, sir. I've often thought I had quite a turn for writing myself. At one time and another I've done a rare lot of reading. I haven't kept up with it much lately. For one thing my eyes are not so good as they used to be. I believe I could write a book if I tried.'

'They say anybody can write one,' I answered.

'Not a novel, you know. I'm not much of a one for novels; I prefer histories and that-like. But memoirs. If anybody was to make it worth my while I wouldn't mind writing my memoirs.'

'It's very fashionable just now.'

'There are not many people who've had the experiences I've had in one way and another. I did write to one of the Sunday papers about it some little while back, but they never answered my letter.'

He gave me a long, appraising look. He had too respectable an air to be about to ask me for half a crown.

'Of course you don't know who I am, sir, do you?'

'I honestly don't.'

He seemed to ponder for a moment, then he smoothed down his black gloves on his fingers, looked for a moment at a hole in one of them, and then turned to me not without self-consciousness.

'I am the celebrated Mortimer Ellis,' he said.

'Oh?'

I did not know what other ejaculation to make, for to the best of my belief I had never heard the name before. I saw a look of disappointment come over his face, and I was a trifle embarrassed.

'Mortimer Ellis,' he repeated. 'You're not going to tell me you don't know.'

'I'm afraid I must. I'm very often out of England.'

I wondered to what he owed his celebrity. I passed over in my mind various possibilities. He could never have been an athlete, which alone in England gives a man real fame, but he might have been a faith-healer or a champion billiard-player. There is of course no one so obscure as a Cabinet Minister out of office and he might have been the President of the Board of Trade in a defunct administration. But he had none of the look of a politician.

'That's fame for you,' he said bitterly. 'Why, for weeks I was the most talked-about man in England. Look at me. You must have seen my photograph in the papers. Mortimer Ellis.'

'I'm sorry,' I said, shaking my head.

He paused a moment to give his disclosure effectiveness.

'I am the well-known bigamist.'

Now what are you to reply when a person who is practically a stranger to you informs you that he is a well-known bigamist? I will confess that I have sometimes had the vanity to think that I am not as a rule at a loss for a retort, but here I found myself speechless.

'I've had eleven wives, sir,' he went on.

'Most people find one about as much as they can manage.'

'Ah, that's want of practice. When you've had eleven there's very little you don't know about women.'

'But why did you stop at eleven?'

'There now, I knew you'd say that. The moment I set eyes on you I said to myself, he's got a clever face. You know, sir, that's the thing that always grizzles me. Eleven does seem a funny number, doesn't it? There's something unfinished about it. Now

301

three anyone might have, and seven's all right, they say nine's
lucky, and there's nothing wrong with ten. But eleven! That's the
one thing I regret. I shouldn't have minded anything if I could
have brought it up to the Round Dozen.'

He unbuttoned his coat and from an inside pocket produced a
bulging and very greasy pocket-book. From this he took a large
bundle of newspaper cuttings; they were worn and creased and
dirty. But he spread out two or three.

'Now just you look at those photographs. I ask you, are they
like me? It's an outrage. Why, you'd think I was a criminal to
look at them.'

The cuttings were of imposing length. In the opinion of sub-
editors Mortimer Ellis had obviously been a news item of value.
One was headed, A Much Married Man; another, Heartless
Ruffian Brought to Book; a third, Contemptible Scoundrel Meets
his Waterloo.

'Not what you would call a good press,' I murmured.

'I never pay any attention to what the newspapers say,' he
answered, with a shrug of his thin shoulders. 'I've known too
many journalists myself for that. No, it's the judge I blame. He
treated me shocking and it did him no good, mind you; he died
within the year.'

I ran my eyes down the report I held.

'I see he gave you five years.'

'Disgraceful, I call it, and see what it says.' He pointed to a
place with his forefinger. '"Three of his victims pleaded for
mercy to be shown to him." That shows what they thought of me.
And after that he gave me five years. And just look what he called
me, a heartless scoundrel – me, the best-hearted man that ever
lived – a pest of society and a danger to the public. Said he wished
he had the power to give me the cat. I don't so much mind his
giving me five years, though you'll never get me to say it wasn't
excessive, but I ask you, had he the right to talk to me like that?
No, he hadn't, and I'll never forgive him, not if I live to be a
hundred.'

The bigamist's cheeks flushed and his watery eyes were filled
for a moment with fire. It was a sore subject with him.

'May I read them?' I asked him.

'That's what I gave them you for. I want you to read them,
sir. And if you can read them without saying that I'm a much
wronged man, well, you're not the man I took you for.'

As I glanced through one cutting after another I saw why
Mortimer Ellis had so wide an acquaintance with the seaside
resorts of England. They were his hunting-ground. His method

was to go to some place when the season was over and take apartments in one of the empty lodging-houses. Apparently it did not take him long to make acquaintance with some woman or other, widow or spinster, and I noticed that their ages at the time were between thirty-five and fifty. They stated in the witness-box that they had met him first on the sea-front. He generally proposed marriage to them within a fortnight of this and they were married shortly after. He induced them in one way or another to entrust him with their savings and in a few months, on the pretext that he had to go to London on business, he left them never to return. Only one had ever seen him again till, obliged to give evidence, they saw him in the dock. They were women of certain respectability; one was the daughter of a doctor and another of a clergyman; there was a lodging-house keeper, there was the widow of a commercial traveller, and there was a retired dressmaker. For the most part, their fortunes ranged from five hundred to a thousand pounds, but whatever the sum the misguided women were stripped of every penny. Some of them told really pitiful stories of the destitution to which they had been reduced. But they all acknowledged that he had been a good husband to them. Not only had three actually pleaded for mercy to be shown him, but one said in the witness-box that, if he was willing to come, she was ready to take him back. He noticed that I was reading this.

'And she'd have worked for me,' he said, 'there's no doubt about that. But I said, better let bygones be bygones. No one likes a cut off the best end of the neck better than I do, but I'm not much of a one for cold roast mutton, I will confess.'

It was only by an accident that Mortimer Ellis did not marry his twelfth wife and so achieve the Round Dozen which I understand appealed to his love of symmetry. For he was engaged to be married to a Miss Hubbard – 'two thousand pounds she had, if she had a penny, in war-loan,' he confided to me – and the banns had been read, when one of his former wives saw him, made inquiries, and communicated with the police. He was arrested on the very day before his twelfth wedding.

'She was a bad one, she was,' he told me. 'She deceived me something cruel.'

'How did she do that?'

'Well, I met her at Eastbourne, one December it was, on the pier, and she told me in course of conversation that she'd been in the millinery business and had retired. She said she'd made a tidy bit of money. She wouldn't say exactly how much it was, but she gave me to understand it was something like fifteen hundred pounds. And when I married her, would you believe it, she hadn't got three hundred. And that's the one who gave me away. And mind you, I'd never blamed her. Many a man would have cut up rough when he found out he'd been made a fool of. I never showed her that I was disappointed even, I just went away without a word.'

'But not without the three hundred pounds, I take it.'

'Oh come, sir, you must be reasonable,' he returned in an injured tone. 'You can't expect three hundred pounds to last for ever and I'd been married to her four months before she confessed the truth.'

'Forgive my asking,' I said, 'and pray don't think my question suggests a disparaging view of your personal attractions, but – why did they marry you?'

'Because I asked them,' he answered, evidently very much surprised at my inquiry.

'But did you never have any refusals?'

'Very seldom. Not more than four or five in the whole course of my career. Of course I didn't propose till I was pretty sure of my ground and I don't say I didn't draw a blank sometimes. You can't expect to click every time, if you know what I mean, and I've often wasted several weeks making up to a woman before I saw there was nothing doing.'

I surrendered myself for a time to my reflections. But I noticed presently that a broad smile spread over the mobile features of my friend.

'I understand what you mean,' he said. 'It's my appearance that puzzles you. You don't know what it is they see in me. That's what comes of reading novels and going to the pictures. You think what women want is the cowboy type, or the romance of old Spain touch, flashing eyes, an olive skin, and a beautiful dancer. You make me laugh.'

'I'm glad,' I said.

'Are you a married man, sir?'

'I am. But I only have one wife.'

'You can't judge by that. You can't generalize from a single instance, if you know what I mean. Now, I ask you, what would you know about dogs if you'd never had anything but one bull-terrier?'

The question was rhetorical and I felt sure did not require an answer. He paused for an effective moment and went on.

'You're wrong, sir. You're quite wrong. They may take a fancy to a good-looking young fellow, but they don't want to marry him. They don't really care about looks.'

'Douglas Jerrold, who was as ugly as he was witty, used to say that if he was given ten minutes' start with a woman he could cut out the handsomest man in the room.'

'They don't want wit. They don't want a man to be funny; they think he's not serious. They don't want a man who's too handsome; they think he's not serious either. That's what they want, they want a man who's serious. Safety first. And then – attention. I may not be handsome and I may not be amusing, but believe me, I've got what every woman wants. Poise. And the proof is, I've made every one of my wives happy.'

'It certainly is much to your credit that three of them pleaded for mercy to be shown to you and that one was willing to take you back.'

'You don't know what an anxiety that was to me all the time I was in prison. I thought she'd be waiting for me at the gate when I was released and I said to the Governor: "For God's sake, sir, smuggle me out so as no one can see me."'

He smoothed his gloves again over his hands and his eye once more fell upon the hole in the first finger.

'That's what comes of living in lodgings, sir. How's a man to keep himself neat and tidy without a woman to look after him? I've been married too often to be able to get along without a wife. There are men who don't like being married. I can't understand them. The fact is, you can't do a thing really well unless you've got your heart in it, and I like being a married man. It's no difficulty to me to do the little things that women like and that some men can't be bothered with. As I was saying just now, it's attention a woman wants. I never went out of the house without giving my wife a kiss and I never came in without giving her another. And it was very seldom I came in without bringing her some chocolates or a few flowers. I never grudged the expense.'

'After all, it was her money you were spending,' I interposed.

'And what if it was? It's not the money that you've paid for a present that signifies, it's the spirit you give it in. That's what counts with women. No, I'm not one to boast, but I will say this of myself, I am a good husband.'

I looked desultorily at the reports of the trial which I still held.

'I'll tell you what surprises me,' I said. 'All these women were very respectable, of a certain age, quiet, decent persons. And yet they married you without any inquiry after the shortest possible acquaintance.'

He put his hand impressively on my arm.

'Ah, that's what you don't understand, sir. Women have got a craving to be married. It doesn't matter how young they are or how old they are, if they're short or tall, dark or fair, they've all got one thing in common: they want to be married. And mind you, I married them in church. No woman feels really safe unless she's married in church. You say I'm no beauty, well, I never thought I was, but if I had one leg and a hump on my back I could find any number of women who'd jump at the chance of marrying me. It's a mania with them. It's a disease. Why, there's hardly one of them who wouldn't have accepted me the second time I saw her only I like to make sure of my ground before I commit myself. When it all came out there was a rare to-do because I'd married eleven times. Eleven times? Why, it's nothing, it's not even a Round Dozen. I could have married thirty times if I'd wanted to. I give you my word, sir, when I consider my opportunities, I'm astounded at my moderation.'

'You told me you were fond of reading history.'

'Yes, Warren Hastings said that, didn't he? It struck me at the time I read it. It seemed to fit me like a glove.'

'And you never found these constant courtships a trifle monotonous?'

'Well, sir, I think I've got a logical mind, and it always gave me a rare lot of pleasure to see how the same effects followed on the same causes, if you know what I mean. Now, for instance, with a woman who'd never been married before I always passed myself off as a widower. It worked like a charm. You see, a spinster likes a man who knows a thing or two. But with a widow I always said I was a bachelor: a widow's afraid a man who's been married before knows too much.'

I gave him back his cuttings; he folded them up neatly and replaced them in his greasy pocket-book.

'You know, sir, I always think I've been misjudged. Just see what they say about me: a pest of society, unscrupulous villain, contemptible scoundrel. Now just look at me. I ask you, do I look that sort of man? You know me, you're a judge of character, I've told you all about myself; do you think me a bad man?'

'My acquaintance with you is very slight,' I answered with what I thought considerable tact.

'I wonder if the judge, I wonder if the jury, I wonder if the public ever thought about my side of the question. The public booed me when I was taken into the court and the police had to protect me from their violence. Did any of them think what I'd done for these women?'

'You took their money.'

'Of course I took their money. I had to live the same as anybody has to live. But what did I give them in exchange for their money?'

This was another rhetorical question and though he looked at me as though he expected an answer I held my tongue. Indeed I did not know the answer. His voice was raised and he spoke with emphasis. I could see that he was serious.

'I'll tell you what I gave them in exchange for their money. Romance. Look at this place.' He made a wide, circular gesture that embraced the sea and the horizon. 'There are a hundred places in England like this. Look at that sea and that sky; look at these lodging-houses; look at that pier and the front. Doesn't it make your heart sink? It's dead as mutton. It's all very well for you who come down here for a week or two because you're run down. But think of all those women who live here from one year's end to another. They haven't a chance. They hardly know anyone. They've just got enough money to live on and that's all. I wonder if you know how terrible their lives are. Their lives are just like the front, a long, straight, cemented walk that goes on and on from one seaside resort to another. Even in the season there's nothing for them. They're out of it. They might as well be dead. And then I come along. Mind you, I never made advances to a woman who wouldn't have gladly acknowledged to thirty-five. And I give them love. Why, many of them had never known what it was to have a man do them up behind. Many of them had never known what it was to sit on a bench in the dark with a man's arm round their waist. I bring them change and excitement. I give them a new pride in themselves. They were on the shelf and I come along quite quietly and I deliberately take them down. A little ray of sunshine in those drab lives, that's what I was. No wonder they jumped at me, no wonder they wanted me to go back to them. The only one who gave me away was the milliner; she said she was a widow, my private opinion is that she'd never been married at all. You say I did the dirty on them; why, I brought happiness and glamour into eleven lives that never thought they had even a dog's chance of it again. You say I'm a villain and a scoundrel, you're wrong. I'm a philanthropist. Five years, they gave me; they should have given me the medal of the Royal Humane Society.'

He took out his empty packet of Gold Flake and looked at it with a melancholy shake of the head. When I handed him my cigarette case he helped himself without a word. I watched the spectacle of a good man struggling with his emotion.

'And what did I get out of it, I ask you?' he continued presently. 'Board and lodging and enough to buy cigarettes. But I never was able to save, and the proof is that now, when I'm not so young as I was, I haven't got half a crown in my pocket.' He gave me a sidelong glance. 'It's a great come-down for me to find myself in this position. I've always paid my way and I've never asked a friend for a loan in all my life. I was wondering, sir, if you could oblige me with a trifle. It's humiliating to me to have to suggest it, but the fact is, if you could oblige me with a pound it would mean a great deal to me.'

Well, I had certainly had a pound's worth of entertainment out of the bigamist and I dived for my pocket-book.

'I shall be very glad,' I said.

He looked at the notes I took out.

'I suppose you couldn't make it two, sir?'

'I think I could.'

I handed him a couple of pound notes and he gave a little sigh as he took them.

'You don't know what it means to a man who's used to the comforts of home life not to know where to turn for a night's lodging.'

'But there is one thing I should like you to tell me,' I said. 'I shouldn't like you to think me cynical, but I had a notion that women on the whole take the maxim, "It is more blessed to give than to receive," as applicable exclusively to our sex. How did you persuade these respectable, and no doubt thrifty, women to entrust you so confidently with all their savings?'

An amused smile spread over his undistinguished features.

'Well, sir, you know what Shakespeare said about ambition o'erleaping itself. That's the explanation. Tell a woman you'll double her capital in six months if she'll give it you to handle and she won't be able to give you the money quick enough. Greed, that's what it is. Just greed.'

It was a sharp sensation, stimulating to the appetite (like hot sauce with ice cream), to go from this diverting ruffian to the respectability, all lavender bags and crinolines, of the St Clairs and Miss Porchester. I spent every evening with them now. No sooner had the ladies left him than Mr St Clair sent his compliments to my table and asked me to drink a glass of port with him. When we had finished it we went into the lounge and drank coffee. Mr St Clair enjoyed his glass of old brandy. The hour I thus spent with them was so exquisitely boring that it had for me a singular fascination. They were told by the manageress that I had written plays.

'We used often to go to the theatre when Sir Henry Irving was at the Lyceum,' said Mr St Clair. 'I once had the pleasure of meeting him. I was taken to supper at the Garrick Club by Sir

Everard Millais and I was introduced to Mr Irving, as he then was.'

'Tell him what he said to you, Edwin,' said Mrs St Clair.

Mr St Clair struck a dramatic attitude and gave not at all a bad imitation of Henry Irving.

'"You have the actor's face, Mr St Clair," he said to me. "If you ever think of going on the stage, come to me and I will give you a part."' Mr St Clair resumed his natural manner. 'It was enough to turn a young man's head.'

'But it didn't turn yours,' I said.

'I will not deny that if I had been otherwise situated I might have allowed myself to be tempted. But I had my family to think of. It would have broken my father's heart if I had not gone into the business.'

'What is that?' I asked.

'I am a tea merchant, sir. My firm is the oldest in the City of London. I have spent forty years of my life in combating to the best of my ability the desire of my fellow-countrymen to drink Ceylon tea instead of the China tea which was universally drunk in my youth.'

I thought it charmingly characteristic of him to spend a lifetime in persuading the public to buy something they didn't want rather than something they did.

'But in his younger days my husband did a lot of amateur acting and he was thought very clever,' said Mrs St Clair.

'Shakespeare, you know, and sometimes *The School for Scandal*. I would never consent to act trash. But that is a thing of the past. I had a gift, perhaps it was a pity to waste it, but it's too late now. When we have a dinner-party I sometimes let the ladies persuade me to recite the great soliloquies of Hamlet. But that is all I do.'

Oh! Oh! Oh! I thought with shuddering fascination of those dinner-parties and wondered whether I should ever be asked to one of them. Mrs St Clair gave me a little smile, half shocked, half prim.

'My husband was very Bohemian as a young man,' she said.

'I sowed my wild oats. I knew quite a lot of painters and writers, Wilkie Collins, for instance, and even men who wrote for the papers. Watts painted a portrait of my wife, and I bought a picture of Millais. I knew a number of the Pre-Raphaelites.'

'Have you a Rossetti?' I asked.

'No. I admired Rossetti's talent, but I could not approve of his private life. I would never buy a picture by an artist whom I should not care to ask to dinner at my house.'

My brain was reeling when Miss Porchester, looking at her watch, said: 'Are you not going to read to us tonight, Uncle Edwin?'

I withdrew.

It was while I was drinking a glass of port with Mr St Clair one evening that he told me the sad story of Miss Porchester. She was engaged to be married to a nephew of Mrs St Clair, a barrister, when it was discovered that he had had an intrigue with the daughter of his laundress.

'It was a terrible thing,' said Mr St Clair. 'A terrible thing. But of course my niece took the only possible course. She returned him his ring, his letters, and his photograph, and said that she could never marry him. She implored him to marry the young person he had wronged and said she would be a sister to her. It broke her heart. She has never cared for anyone since.'

'And did he marry the young person?'

Mr St Clair shook his head and sighed.

'No, we were greatly mistaken in him. It has been a sore grief to my dear wife to think that a nephew of hers should behave in such a dishonourable manner. Some time later we heard that he was engaged to a young lady in a very good position with ten thousand pounds of her own. I considered it my duty to write to her father and put the facts before him. He answered my letter in a most insolent fashion. He said he would much rather his son-in-law had a mistress before marriage than after.'

'What happened then?'

'They were married and now my wife's nephew is one of His Majesty's Judges of the High Court, and his wife is My Lady. But we've never consented to receive them. When my wife's nephew was knighted Eleanor suggested that we should ask them to dinner, but my wife said that he should never darken our doors and I upheld her.'

'And the laundress's daughter?'

'She married in her own class of life and has a public-house at Canterbury. My niece, who has a little money of her own, did everything for her and is godmother to her eldest child.'

Poor Miss Porchester. She had sacrificed herself on the altar of Victorian morality and I am afraid the consciousness that she had behaved beautifully was the only benefit she had got from it.

'Miss Porchester is a woman of striking appearance,' I said. 'When she was younger she must have been perfectly lovely. I wonder she never married somebody else.'

'Miss Porchester was considered a great beauty. Alma-Tadema admired her so much that he asked her to sit as a model for one

of his pictures, but of course we couldn't very well allow that.'
Mr St Clair's tone conveyed that the suggestion had deeply outraged his sense of decency. 'No, Miss Porchester never cared for
anyone but her cousin. She never speaks of him and it is now
thirty years since they parted, but I am convinced that she loves
him still. She is a true woman, my dear sir, one life, one love,
and though perhaps I regret that she has been deprived of the joys
of marriage and motherhood I am bound to admire her fidelity.'

But the heart of woman is incalculable and rash is the man who
thinks she will remain in one stay. Rash, Uncle Edwin. You have
known Eleanor for many years, for when, her mother having
fallen into a decline and died, you brought the orphan to your comfortable and even luxurious house in Leinster Square, she was but
a child; but what, when it comes down to brass tacks, Uncle
Edwin, do you really know of Eleanor?

It was but two days after Mr St Clair had confided to me the
touching story which explained why Miss Porchester had remained a spinster that, coming back to the hotel in the afternoon
after a round of golf, the manageress came up to me in an agitated manner.

'Mr St Clair's compliments and will you go up to number
twenty-seven the moment you come in.'

'Certainly. But why?'

'Oh, there's a rare upset. They'll tell you.'

I knocked at the door. I heard a 'Come in, come in,' which
reminded me that Mr St Clair had played Shakespearean parts in
probably the most refined amateur dramatic company in London.
I entered and found Mrs St Clair lying on the sofa with a handkerchief soaked in eau-de-Cologne on her brow and a bottle of
smelling-salts in her hand. Mr St Clair was standing in front of
the fire in such a manner as to prevent anyone else in the room
from obtaining any benefit from it.

'I must apologize for asking you to come up in this uncere-
monious fashion, but we are in great distress, and we thought you
might be able to throw some light on what has happened.'

His perturbation was obvious.

'What *has* happened?'

'Our niece, Miss Porchester, has eloped. This morning she sent
in a message to my wife that she had one of her sick headaches.
When she has one of her sick headaches she likes to be left
absolutely alone and it wasn't till this afternoon that my wife
went to see if there was anything she could do for her. The room
was empty. Her trunk was packed. Her dressing-case with silver

311

fittings was gone. And on the pillow was a letter telling us of her rash act.'

'I'm very sorry,' I said. 'I don't know exactly what I can do.'

'We were under the impression that you were the only gentleman at Elsom with whom she had any acquaintance.'

His meaning flashed across me.

'I haven't eloped with her,' I said. 'I happen to be a married man.'

'I see you haven't eloped with her. At the first moment we thought perhaps ... but if it isn't you, who is it?'

'I'm sure I don't know.'

'Show him the letter, Edwin,' said Mrs St Clair from the sofa.

'Don't move, Gertrude. It will bring on your lumbago.'

Miss Porchester had 'her' sick headaches and Mrs St Clair had 'her' lumbago. What had Mr St Clair? I was willing to bet a fiver that Mr St Clair had 'his' gout. He gave me the letter and I read it with an air of decent commiseration.

Dearest Uncle Edwin and Aunt Gertrude –

When you receive this I shall be far away. I am going to be married this morning to a gentleman who is very dear to me. I know I am doing wrong in running away like this, but I was afraid you would endeavour to set obstacles in the way of my marriage and since nothing would induce me to change my mind I thought it would save us all much unhappiness if I did it without telling you anything about it. My fiancé is a very retiring man, owing to his long residence in tropical countries not in the best of health, and he thought it much better that we should be married quite privately. When you know how radiantly happy I am I hope you will forgive me. Please send my box to the luggage office at Victoria Station.

Your loving niece,
Eleanor

'I will never forgive her,' said Mr St Clair as I returned him the letter. 'She shall never darken my doors again. Gertrude, I forbid you ever to mention Eleanor's name in my hearing.'

Mrs St Clair began to sob quietly.

'Aren't you rather hard?' I said. 'Is there any reason why Miss Porchester shouldn't marry?'

'At her age,' he answered angrily. 'It's ridiculous. We shall be the laughing-stock of everyone in Leinster Square. Do you know how old she is? She's fifty-one.'

'Fifty-four,' said Mrs St Clair through her sobs.

'She's been the apple of my eye. She's been like a daughter to us. She's been an old maid for years. I think it's positively improper for her to think of marriage.'

'She was always a girl to us, Edwin,' pleaded Mrs St Clair.

'And who is this man she's married? It's the deception that rankles. She must have been carrying on with him under our very noses. She does not even tell us his name. I fear the very worst.'

Suddenly I had an inspiration. That morning after breakfast I had gone out to buy myself some cigarettes and at the tobacconist's I ran across Mortimer Ellis. I had not seen him for some days.

'You're looking very spruce,' I said.

His boots had been repaired and were neatly blacked, his hat was brushed, he was wearing a clean collar and new gloves. I thought he had laid out my two pounds to advantage.

'I have to go to London this morning on business,' he said.

I nodded and left the shop.

I remembered that a fortnight before, walking in the country, I had met Miss Porchester and, a few yards behind, Mortimer Ellis. Was it possible that they had been walking together and he had fallen back as they caught sight of me? By heaven, I saw it all.

'I think you said that Miss Porchester had money of her own,' I said.

'A trifle. She has three thousand pounds.'

Now I was certain. I looked at them blankly. Suddenly Mrs St Clair, with a cry, sprang to her feet.

'Edwin, Edwin, supposing he doesn't marry her?'

Mr St Clair at this put his hand to his head and in a state of collapse sank into a chair.

'The disgrace would kill me,' he groaned.

'Don't be alarmed,' I said. 'He'll marry her all right. He always does. He'll marry her in church.'

They paid no attention to what I said. I suppose they thought I'd suddenly taken leave of my senses. I was quite sure now. Mortimer Ellis had achieved his ambition after all. Miss Porchester completed the Round Dozen.

THE HUMAN ELEMENT

I SEEM never to find myself in Rome but at the dead season. I pass through in August or September on my way somewhere or other and spend a couple of days revisiting places or pictures that are endeared to me by old associations. It is very hot then and the inhabitants of the city spend their day interminably strolling up and down the Corso. The Caffé Nazionale is crowded with people sitting at little tables for long hours with an empty cup of coffee in front of them and a glass of water. In the Sistine Chapel you see blond and sunburned Germans, in knickerbockers and shirts open at the neck, who have walked down the dusty roads of Italy with knapsacks on their shoulders; and in St Peter's little groups of the pious, tired but eager, who have come on pilgrimage (at an inclusive rate) from some distant country. They are under the charge of a priest and they speak strange tongues. The Hotel Plaza then is cool and restful. The public rooms are dark, silent and spacious. In the lounge at tea-time the only persons are a young, smart officer and a woman with fine eyes, drinking iced lemonade, and they talk intimately, in low tones, with the un-wearying fluency of their race. You go up to your room and read and write letters and come down again two hours later and they are still talking. Before dinner a few people saunter into the bar, but for the rest of the day it is empty and the barman has time to tell you of his mother in Switzerland and his experiences in New York. You discuss life and love and the high cost of liquor.

And on this occasion too I found that I had the hotel almost to myself. When the reception clerk took me to my room he told me that they were pretty full, but when, having bathed and changed, I came down again to the hall, the liftman, an old acquaintance, informed me that there were not more than a dozen people staying there. I was tired after a long and hot journey down Italy and had made up my mind to dine quietly in the hotel and go to bed early. It was late when I went into the dining-room, vast and brightly lit, but not more than three or four tables were occupied. I looked round me with satisfaction. It is very agreeable to find yourself alone in a great city which is yet not quite strange to you and in a large empty hotel. It gives you a delectable sense of freedom. I felt the wings of my spirit give a little flutter of delight. I had paused for ten minutes in the bar and had a dry Martini. I ordered myself a bottle of good red wine. My limbs were weary, but my soul responded wonderfully to food and drink and I began to feel a singular lightness of heart. I ate my soup and my fish and pleasant thoughts filled my mind. Scraps of dialogue occurred to me and my fancy played happily with the persons of a novel I was then at work on. I rolled a phrase on my tongue and it tasted better than the wine. I began to think of the difficulty of describing the looks of people in such a way as to make the reader see them as you see them. To me it has always been one of the most difficult things in fiction. What does the reader really get when you describe a face feature by feature? I should think nothing. And yet the plan some writers adopt of taking a salient characteristic, a crooked smile or shifty eyes, and emphasizing that, though effective, avoids rather than solves the problem. I looked about me and wondered how I would describe the people at the tables round me. There was one man by himself just opposite and for practice I asked myself in what way I should treat him. He was a tall, spare fellow, and what I believe is generally called loose-limbed. He wore a dinner jacket and a boiled shirt. He had a rather long face and pale eyes; his hair was fairish and wavy, but it was growing thin, and the baldness of his temples gave him a certain nobility of brow. His features were undistinguished. His mouth and nose were like everybody else's; he was clean-shaven; his skin was naturally pale, but at the moment sunburned. His appearance suggested an intellectual but slightly commonplace distinction. He looked as though he might have been a lawyer or a don who played a pretty game of golf. I felt that he had good taste and was well-read and would be a very agreeable guest at a luncheon-party in Chelsea. But how the devil one was to describe him so as in a few lines to give a vivid, interesting, and accurate picture I could not imagine. Perhaps it would be better to let all the rest go and dwell only on that rather fatigued distinction which on the whole was the most definite impression he gave. I looked at him reflectively. Suddenly he leaned forwards and gave me a stiff but courtly little bow. I have a ridiculous habit of flushing when I am taken aback and now I felt my cheeks redden. I was startled. I had been staring at him for several minutes as though he were a dummy. He must have thought me extremely rude. I nodded with a good deal of embarrassment and looked away. Fortunately at that moment the waiter was handing me a dish. To the best of my belief I had never seen the fellow before. I asked myself whether his bow was due to my insistent stare, which made him think that he had met me somewhere, or whether I had really run across him and completely forgotten. I have a bad memory for faces and I had in this case the excuse that he looked exactly like a great many other people. You saw a dozen of him at every golf course round London on a fine Sunday.

He finished his dinner before me. He got up, but on his way out stopped at my table. He stretched out his hand.

'How d'you do?' he said. 'I didn't recognize you when you first came in. I wasn't meaning to cut you.'

He spoke in a pleasant voice with the tones cultivated at Oxford and copied by many who have never been there. It was evident that he knew me and evident too that he had no notion that I did not also know him. I had risen and since he was a good deal taller than I he looked down on me. He held himself with a sort of languor. He stooped a little, which added to the impression he gave me of having about him an air that was vaguely apologetic. His manner was a trifle condescending and at the same time a trifle shy.

'Won't you come and have your coffee with me?' he said. 'I'm quite alone.'

'Yes, I shall be glad to.'

He left me and I still had no notion who he was or where I had met him. I had noticed one curious thing about him. Not once during the few sentences we exchanged, when we shook hands, or when with a nod he left me, did even the suspicion of a smile cross his face. Seeing him more closely I observed that he was in his way good-looking; his features were regular, his grey eyes were handsome, he had a slim figure; but it was a way that I found uninteresting. A silly woman would say he looked romantic. He reminded you of one of the knights of Burne-Jones though he was on a larger scale and there was no suggestion that he suffered from the chronic colitis that afflicted those unfortunate creatures. He was the sort of man whom you expected to look wonderful in fancy dress till you saw him in it and then you found that he looked absurd.

Presently I finished my dinner and went into the lounge. He was sitting in a large arm-chair and when he saw me he called a waiter. I sat down. The waiter came up and he ordered coffee and liqueurs. He spoke Italian very well. I was wondering by what means I could find out who he was without offending him. People are always a little disconcerted when you do not recognize them, they are so important to themselves, it is a shock to discover of what small importance they are to others. The excellence of his Italian recalled him to me. I remembered who he was and remembered at the same time that I did not like him. His name was Humphrey Carruthers. He was in the Foreign Office and he had a position of some importance. He was in charge of I know not what department. He had been attached to various embassies and

I supposed that a sojourn in Rome accounted for his idiomatic Italian. It was stupid of me not to have seen at once that he was connected with the diplomatic service. He had all the marks of the profession. He had the supercilious courtesy that is so well calculated to put up the backs of the general public and the aloofness due to the consciousness the diplomat has that he is not as other men are, joined with the shyness occasioned by his uneasy feeling that other men do not quite realize it. I had known Carruthers for a good many years, but had met him infrequently, at luncheon-parties where I said no more than how do you do to him and at the opera where he gave me a cool nod. He was generally thought intelligent; he was certainly cultured. He could talk of all the right things. It was inexcusable of me not to have remembered him, for he had lately acquired a very considerable reputation as a writer of short stories. They had appeared first in one or other of those magazines that are founded now and then by well-disposed persons to give the intelligent reader something worthy of his attention and that die when their proprietors have lost as much money as they want to; and in their discreet and handsomely printed pages had excited as much attention as an exiguous circulation permitted. Then they were published in book form. They created a sensation. I have seldom read such unanimous praise in the weekly papers. Most of them gave the book a column and the Literary Supplement of *The Times* reviewed it not among the common ruck of novels but in a place by itself cheek by jowl with the memoirs of a distinguished statesman. The critics welcomed Humphrey Carruthers as a new star in the firmament. They praised his distinction, his subtlety, his delicate irony, and his insight. They praised his style, his sense of beauty, and his atmosphere. Here at last was a writer who had raised the short story from the depths into which in English-speaking countries it had fallen and here was work to which an Englishman could point with pride; it bore comparison with the best compositions in this manner of Finland, Russia, and Czecho-Slovakia.

Three years later Humphrey Carruthers brought out his second book and the critics commented on the interval with satisfaction. Here was no hack prostituting his talent for money! The praise it received was perhaps a little cooler than that which welcomed his first volume, the critics had had time to collect themselves, but it was enthusiastic enough to have delighted any common writer who earns his living by his pen and there was no doubt that his position in the world of letters was secure and honourable. The story that attracted most commendation was called *The Shaving Mop* and all the best critics pointed out with what beauty the author in three or four pages had laid bare the tragic soul of a barber's assistant.

But his best-known story, which was also his longest, was called *Week End*. It gave its title to his first book. It narrated the adventures of a number of people who left Paddington Station on Saturday afternoon to stay with friends at Taplow and on Monday morning returned to London. It was so delicate that it was a little difficult to know exactly what happened. A young man, parliamentary secretary to a Cabinet Minister, very nearly proposed to a baronet's daughter, but didn't. Two or three others went on the river in a punt. They all talked a great deal in an allusive way, but none of them ever finished a sentence and what they meant was very subtly indicated by dots and dashes. There were a good many descriptions of flowers in the garden and a sensitive picture of the Thames under the rain. It was all seen through the eyes of the German governess and everyone agreed that Carruthers had conveyed her outlook on the situation with quite delicious humour.

I read both Humphrey Carruthers's books. I think it part of the writer's business to make himself aware of what is being written by his contemporaries. I am very willing to learn and I thought I might discover in them something that would be useful to me. I was disappointed. I like a story to have a beginning, a middle, and an end. I have a weakness for a point. I think atmosphere is all very well, but atmosphere without anything else is like a frame without a picture; it has not much significance. But it may be that I could not see the merit of Humphrey Carruthers on account of defects in myself, and if I have described his two most successful stories without enthusiasm the cause perhaps lies in my own wounded vanity. For I was perfectly conscious that Humphrey Carruthers looked upon me as a writer of no account. I am convinced that he had never read a word I had written. The popularity I enjoyed was sufficient to persuade him that there was no occasion for him to give me any of his attention. For a moment, such was the stir he created, it looked as though he might himself be faced with that ignominy, but it soon appeared that his exquisite work was above the heads of the public. One can never tell how large the intelligentsia is, but one can tell fairly well how many of its members are prepared to pay money to patronize the arts they cherish. The plays that are of too fine a quality to attract the patrons of the commercial theatre can count on an audience of ten thousand, and the books that demand from their readers more comprehension than can be expected from the common herd sell twelve hundred copies. For the intelligentsia, notwithstanding their sensitiveness to beauty, prefer to go to the theatre on the nod and to get a book from the library.

I am sure this did not distress Carruthers. He was an artist. He was also a clerk in the Foreign Office. His reputation as a writer was distinguished; he was not interested in the vulgar, and to sell well would possibly have damaged his career. I could not surmise what had induced him to invite me to have coffee with him. It is true he was alone, but I should have supposed he found his thoughts excellent company, and I could not believe he imagined that I had anything to say that would interest him. Nevertheless I could not but see that he was doing his dreary best to be affable. He reminded me of where we had last met and we talked for a moment of common friends in London. He asked me how I came to be in Rome at this season and I told him. He volunteered the information that he had arrived that morning from Brindisi. Our conversation did not go easily and I made up my mind that as soon as I civilly could I would get up and leave him. But presently I had an odd sensation, I hardly know what caused it, that he was conscious of this and was desperately anxious not to give me the opportunity. I was surprised. I gathered my wits about me. I noticed that whenever I paused he broke in with a new topic. He was trying to find something to interest me so that I should stay. He was straining every nerve to be agreeable. Surely he could not be lonely; with his diplomatic connexions he must know plenty of people with whom he could have spent the evening. I wondered indeed that he was not dining at the Embassy; even though it was summer there must be someone there he knew. I noticed also that he never smiled. He talked with a sort of harsh eagerness as though he were afraid of a moment's silence and the sound of his voice shut out of his mind something that tortured him. It was very strange. Though I did not like him, though he meant nothing to me and to be with him irked me somewhat, I was against my will a trifle interested. I gave him a searching glance. I wondered if it was my fancy that I saw in those pale eyes of his the cowed look of a hunted dog and, notwithstanding his neat features and his expression so civilly controlled, in his aspect something that suggested the grimace of a soul in pain. I could not understand. A dozen absurd notions flashed through my mind. I was not particularly sympathetic: like an old war horse scenting the fray I roused myself. I had been feeling very tired, but now I grew alert. My sensibilities put out tentacles. I was suddenly alive to every expression of his face and every gesture. I put aside the thought that had come to me that he had written a play and wanted my advice. These exquisite persons succumb strangely to

the glamour of the footlights and they are not averse from getting
a few tips from the craftsman whose competence they super-
ciliously despise. No, it was not that. A single man in Rome, of
aesthetic leanings, is liable to get into trouble, and I asked myself
whether Carruthers had got into some difficulty to extricate himself from which the Embassy was the last place he could go to.
The idealist, I have noticed, is apt at times to be imprudent in the
affairs of the flesh. He sometimes finds love in places which the
police inconveniently visit. I tittered in my heart. Even the gods
laugh when a prig is caught in an equivocal situation.

Suddenly Carruthers said something that staggered me.

'I'm so desperately unhappy,' he muttered.

He said it without warning. He obviously meant it. There was
in his tone a sort of gasp. It might very well have been a sob. I
cannot describe what a shock it was to me to hear him say those
words. I felt as you do when you turn a corner of the street and on
a sudden a great blast of wind meets you, takes your breath away,
and nearly blows you off your feet. It was so unexpected. After all
I hardly knew the fellow. We were not friends. I did not like him;
he did not like me. I have never looked on him as quite human. It
was amazing that a man so self-controlled, so urbane, accustomed
to the usages of polite society, should break in upon a stranger
with such a confession. I am naturally reticent. I should be
ashamed, whatever I was suffering, to disclose my pain to another.
I shivered. His weakness outraged me. For a moment I was filled
with a passion of anger. How dared he thrust the anguish of his
soul on me? I very nearly cried:

'What the hell do I care?'

But I didn't. He was sitting huddled up in the big arm-chair.
The solemn nobility of his features, which reminded one of the
marble statue of a Victorian statesman, had strangely crumpled
and his face sagged. He looked almost as though he were going to
cry. I hesitated. I faltered. I had flushed when he spoke and now I
felt my face go white. He was a pitiable object.

'I'm awfully sorry,' I said.

'Do you mind if I tell you about it?'

'No.'

It was not the moment for many words. I suppose Carruthers
was in the early forties. He was a well-made man, athletic in his
way, and with a confident bearing. Now he looked twenty years
older and strangely shrivelled. He reminded me of the dead soldiers I had seen during the war and how oddly small death had
made them. I was embarrassed and looked away, but I felt his
eyes claiming mine and I looked back.

'Do you know Betty Welldon-Burns?' he asked me.

'I used to meet her sometimes in London years ago. I've not seen her lately.'

'She lives in Rhodes now, you know. I've just come from there. I've been staying with her.'

'Oh?'

He hesitated.

'I'm afraid you'll think it awfully strange of me to talk to you like this. I'm at the end of my tether. If I don't talk to somebody I shall go off my head.'

He had ordered double brandies with the coffee and now calling the waiter he ordered himself another. We were alone in the lounge. There was a little shaded lamp on the table between us. Because it was a public room he spoke in a low voice. The place gave one oddly enough a sense of intimacy. I cannot repeat all that Carruthers said to me in the words he said it; it would be impossible for me to remember them; it is more convenient for me to put it in my own fashion. Sometimes he could not bring himself to say a thing right out and I had to guess at what he meant. Sometimes he had not understood, and it seemed to me that in certain ways I saw the truth more clearly than he. Betty Welldon-Burns had a very keen sense of humour and he had none. I perceived a good deal that had escaped him.

I had met her a good many times, but I knew her chiefly from hearsay. In her day she had made a great stir in the little world of London and I had heard of her often before I met her. This was at a dance in Portland Place soon after the war. She was then already at the height of her celebrity. You could not open an illustrated paper without seeing in it a portrait of her, and her mad pranks were a staple of conversation. She was twenty-four. Her mother was dead, her father, the Duke of St Erth, old and none too rich, spent most of the year in his Cornish castle and she lived in London with a widowed aunt. At the outbreak of the war she went to France. She was just eighteen. She was a nurse in a hospital at the Base and then drove a car. She acted in a theatrical tour designed to amuse the troops; she posed in *tableaux* at home for charitable purposes, held auctions for this object and that, and sold flags in Piccadilly. Every one of her activities was widely advertised and in every new role she was profusely photographed. I suppose that she managed to have a very good time. But now that the war was over she was having her fling with a vengeance. Just then everybody a little lost his head. The young, relieved of the burden that for five years had oppressed them, indulged in one wild escapade after another. Betty took part in them all. Sometimes, for one reason or another, an account of them found its way into the newspapers and her name was always in the headlines. At that time night clubs were in the first flush of their success and she was to be seen at them every night. She lived a life of hectic gaiety. It can only be described in a hackneyed phrase, because it was a hackneyed thing. The British public in its odd way took her to its heart and Lady Betty was a sufficient description of her throughout the British islands. Women mobbed her when she went to a wedding and the gallery applauded her at first nights as though she were a popular actress. Girls copied the way she did her hair and manufacturers of soap and face cream paid her money to use her photograph to advertise their wares.

Of course dull, stodgy people, the people who remembered and regretted the old order, disapproved of her. They sneered at her constant appearance in the limelight. They said she had an insane passion for self-advertisement. They said she was fast. They said she drank too much. They said she smoked too much. I will admit that nothing I had heard of her had predisposed me to think very well of her. I held cheap the women who seemed to look upon the war as an occasion to enjoy themselves and be talked about. I am bored by the papers in which you see photographs of persons in society walking in Cannes or playing golf at St Andrew's. I have always found the Bright Young People extremely tedious. The gay life seems dull and stupid to the onlooker, but the moralist is unwise to judge it harshly. It is as absurd to be angry with the young things who lead it as with a litter of puppies scampering aimlessly around, rolling one another over and chasing their tails. It is well to bear it with fortitude if they cause havoc in the flower beds or break a piece of china. Some of them will be drowned because their points are not up to the mark and the rest will grow up into well-behaved dogs. Their unruliness is due only to the vitality of youth.

And it was vitality that was Betty's most shining characteristic. The urge of life flowed through her with a radiance that dazzled you. I do not think I shall ever forget the impression she made on me at the party at which I first saw her. She was like a maenad. She danced with an abandon that made you laugh, so obvious was her intense enjoyment of the music and the movement of her young limbs. Her hair was brown, slightly disordered by the vigour of her gestures, but her eyes were deep blue, and her skin was milk and roses. She was a great beauty, but she had none of the coldness of great beauty. She laughed constantly and when she was not laughing she smiled and her eyes danced with the joy of living. She was like a milkmaid on the farmstead of the gods. She had the strength and health of the people; and yet the independence of her bearing, a sort of noble frankness of carriage, suggested the great lady. I do not quite know how to put the feeling she gave me, that though so simple and unaffected she was not unconscious of her station. I fancied that if occasion arose she could get on her dignity and be very grand indeed. She was charming to everybody because, probably without being quite aware of it, in the depths of her heart she felt that the rest of the world was perfectly insignificant. I understood why the factory girls in the East End adored her and why half a million people who had never seen her except in a photograph looked upon her with the intimacy of personal friendship. I was introduced to her and she spent a few minutes talking to me. It was extraordinarily flattering to see the interest she showed in you; you knew she could not really be so pleased to meet you as she seemed or so delighted with what you said, but it was very attractive. She had the gift of being able to jump over the first difficult phases of acquaintance and you had not known her for five minutes before you felt you had known her all her life. She was snatched away from me by someone who wanted to dance with her and she surrendered herself to her partner's arms with just the same eager happiness as she had shown when she sank into a chair by my side. I was surprised when I met her at luncheon a fortnight later to find that she remembered exactly what we had talked about during those noisy ten minutes at the dance. A young woman with all the social graces.

I mentioned the incident to Carruthers.

'She was no fool,' he said. 'Very few people knew how intelligent she was She wrote some very good poetry. Because she was so gay, because she was so reckless and never cared a damn for anybody, people thought she was scatter-brained. Far from it. She was as clever as a monkey. You would never have thought she'd had the time to read all the things she had. I don't suppose anyone knew that side of her as well as I did. We used to take walks together, in the country at week-ends, and in London we'd drive out to Richmond Park and walk there, and talk. She loved flowers and trees and grass. She was interested in everything. She had a lot of information and a lot of sense. There was nothing she couldn't talk about. Sometimes when we'd been for a walk in the afternoon and we met at a night club and she'd had a couple of glasses of champagne, that was enough to make her completely buffy, you know, and she was the life and soul of the party, I couldn't help thinking how amazed the rest of them would be if they knew how seriously we'd been talking only a few hours before. It was an extraordinary contrast. There seemed to be two entirely different women in her.'

Carruthers said all this without a smile. He spoke with the melancholy he might have used if he had been speaking of some person snatched from the pleasant company of the living by untimely death. He gave a deep sigh.

'I was madly in love with her. I proposed to her half a dozen times. Of course I knew I hadn't a chance, I was only a very junior clerk at the F.O., but I couldn't help myself. She refused me, but she was always frightfully nice about it. It never made any difference to our friendship. You see, she really liked me. I gave her something that other people didn't. I always thought that she was really fonder of me than of anybody. I was crazy about her.'

'I don't suppose you were the only one,' I said, having to say something.

'Far from it. She used to get dozens of love letters from men she'd never seen or heard of, farmers in Africa, miners, and policemen in Canada. All sorts of people proposed to her. She could have married anyone she liked.'

'Even royalty, one heard.'

'Yes, she said she couldn't stand the life. And then she married Jimmie Welldon-Burns.'

'People were rather surprised, weren't they?'

'Did you ever know him?'

'No, I don't think so. I may have met him, but he left no impression on me.'

'He wouldn't. He was the most insignificant fellow that ever breathed. His father was a big manufacturer up in the North. He'd made a lot of money during the war and bought a baronetcy. I believe he hadn't an aitch to his name. Jimmy was at Eton with me, they'd tried hard to make a gentleman of him, and in London after the war he was about a good deal. He was always willing to throw a party. No one ever paid any attention to him. He just paid the bill. He was the most crashing bore. You know, rather prim, terribly polite; he made you rather uncomfortable because he was so anxious not to do the wrong thing. He always wore his clothes as though he'd just put them on for the first time and they were a little too tight for him.'

When Carruthers innocently opened his *Times* one morning and casting his eyes down the fashionable intelligence of the day saw that a marriage had been arranged between Elizabeth, only daughter of the Duke of St Erth, and James, eldest son of Sir

John Welldon-Burns, Bart, he was dumbfounded. He rang Betty up and asked if it was true.

'Of course,' she said.

He was so shocked that for the moment he found nothing to say. She went on speaking.

'He's bringing his family to luncheon today to meet father. I dare say it'll be a bit grim. You might stand me a cocktail at Claridge's to fortify me, will you?'

'At what time?' he asked.

'One.'

'All right. I'll meet you there.'

He was waiting for her when she came in. She walked with a sort of spring as though her eager feet itched to break into a dance. She was smiling. Her eyes shone with the joy that suffused her because she was alive and the world was such a pleasant place to live in. People recognizing her whispered to one another as she came in. Carruthers really felt that she brought sunshine and the scent of flowers into the sober but rather overwhelming splendour of Claridge's lounge. He did not wait to say how do you do to her.

'Betty, you can't do it,' he said. 'It's simply out of the question.'

'Why?'

'He's awful.'

'I don't think he is. I think he's rather nice.'

A waiter came up and took their order. Betty looked at Carruthers with those beautiful blue eyes of hers that managed to be at the same time so gay and so tender.

'He's such a frightful bounder, Betty.'

'Oh, don't be so silly, Humphrey. He's just as good as anybody else. I think you're rather a snob.'

'He's so dull.'

'No, he's rather quiet. I don't know that I want a husband who's too brilliant. I think he'll make a very good background. He's quite good-looking and he has nice manners.'

'My God, Betty.'

'Oh, don't be idiotic, Humphrey.'

'Are you going to pretend you're in love with him?'

'I think it would be tactful, don't you?'

'Why are you going to marry him?'

She looked at him coolly.

'He's got pots of money. I'm nearly twenty-six.'

There was nothing much more to be said. He drove her back to her aunt's house. She had a very grand marriage, with dense crowds lining the approach to St Margaret's, Westminster, presents from practically all the royal family, and the honeymoon was passed on the yacht her father-in-law had lent them. Carruthers applied for a post abroad and was sent to Rome (I was right in guessing that he had thus acquired his admirable Italian) and later to Stockholm. Here he was counsellor and here he wrote the first of his stories.

Perhaps Betty's marriage had disappointed the British public who expected much greater things of her, perhaps only that as a young married woman she no longer appealed to the popular sense of romance; the fact was plain that she soon lost her place in the public eye. You ceased to hear very much about her. Not long after the marriage it was rumoured that she was going to have a baby and a little later that she had had a miscarriage. She did not drop out of society, I suppose she continued to see her friends, but her activities were no longer spectacular. She was certainly but seldom seen any more in those raffish assemblies where the members of a tarnished aristocracy hob-nob with the hangers-on of the arts and flatter themselves that they are being at once smart and cultured. People said she was settling down. They wondered how she was getting on with her husband and no sooner did they do this than they concluded that she was not getting on very well. Presently gossip said that Jimmie was drinking too much and then, a year or two later, one heard that he had contracted tuberculosis. The Welldon-Burnses spent a couple of winters in Switzerland. Then the news spread that they had separated and Betty had gone to live in Rhodes. An odd place to choose.

'It must be deadly,' her friends said.

A few of them went to stay with her now and then and came back with reports of the beauty of the island and the leisurely charm of the life. But of course it was very lonely. It seemed strange that Betty, with her brilliance and her energy, should be content to settle there. She had bought a house. She knew no one but a few Italian officials, there was indeed no one to know; but she seemed perfectly happy. Her visitors could not make it out. But the life of London is busy and memories are short. People ceased to concern themselves with her. She was forgotten. Then, a few weeks before I met Humphrey Carruthers in Rome, *The Times* announced the death of Sir James Welldon-Burns, second baronet. His younger brother succeeded him in the title. Betty had never had a child.

Carruthers continued to see her after the marriage. Whenever he came to London they lunched together. She had the ability to take up a friendship after a long separation as though no passage of time had intervened, so that there was never any strangeness in their meetings. Sometimes she asked him when he was going to marry.

'You're getting on, you know, Humphrey. If you don't marry soon you'll get rather old-maidish.'

'D'you recommend marriage?'

It was not a very kindly thing to say, because like everyone else he had heard that she was not getting on too well with her husband, but her remark piqued him.

'On the whole. I think probably an unsatisfactory marriage is better than no marriage at all.'

'You know quite well that nothing would induce me to marry and you know why.'

'Oh, my dear, you're not going to pretend that you're still in love with me?'

'I am.'

'You are a damned fool.'

'I don't care.'

She smiled at him. Her eyes always had that look, partly bantering, partly tender, that gave him such a happy pain in his heart. Funny, he could almost localize it.

'You're rather sweet, Humphrey. You know I'm devoted to you, but I wouldn't marry you even if I were free.'

When she left her husband and went to live in Rhodes Carruthers ceased to see her. She never came to England. They maintained an active correspondence.

'Her letters were wonderful,' he said. 'You seemed to hear her talking. They were just like her. Clever and witty, inconsequent and yet so shrewd.'

He suggested coming to Rhodes for a few days, but she thought he had better not. He understood why. Everyone knew he had been madly in love with her. Everyone knew he was still. He did not know in what circumstances exactly the Welldon-Burnses had separated. It might be that there had been a good deal of bad feeling. Betty might think that his presence on the island would compromise her.

'She wrote a charming letter to me when my first book came out. You know I dedicated it to her. She was surprised that I had done anything so good. Everyone was very nice about it, and she was delighted with that. I think her pleasure was the chief thing that pleased me. After all I'm not a professional writer, you know: I don't attach much importance to literary success.'

Fool, I thought, and liar. Did he think I had not noticed the self-satisfaction that consumed him on account of the favourable reception of his books? I did not blame him for feeling that, nothing could be more pardonable, but why be at such pains to deny it. But it was doubtless true that it was mostly for Betty's sake that he relished the notoriety they had brought him. He had a positive achievement to offer her. He could lay at her feet now not only his love, but a distinguished reputation. Betty was not very young any more, she was thirty-six; her marriage, her sojourn abroad, had changed things; she was no longer surrounded by suitors; she had lost the halo with which the public admiration had surrounded her. The distance between them was no longer insuperable. He alone had remained faithful through the years. It was absurd that she should continue to bury her beauty, her wit, her social grace in an island in the corner of the Mediterranean. He knew she was fond of him. She could hardly fail to be touched by his long devotion. And the life he had to offer her now was one that he knew would appeal to her. He made up his mind to ask her once more to marry him. He was able to get away towards the end of July. He wrote and said that he was going to spend his leave in the Greek islands and if she would be glad to see him he would stop off at Rhodes for a day or two where he had heard the Italians had opened a very good hotel. He put his suggestion in this casual way out of delicacy. His training at the Foreign Office had taught him to eschew abruptness. He never willingly put himself in a position from which he could not if necessary withdraw with tact. Betty sent him a telegram in reply. She said it was too marvellous that he was coming to Rhodes and of course he must come and stay with her, for at least a fortnight, and he was to wire what boat he was coming by.

He was in a state of wild excitement when at last the ship he had taken at Brindisi steamed, soon after sunrise, into the neat and pretty harbour of Rhodes. He had hardly slept a wink all night and getting up early had watched the island loom grandly out of the dawn and the sun rise over the summer sea. Boats came out as the ship dropped her anchor. The gangway was lowered. Humphrey, leaning over the rail, watched the doctor and the port officials and the hotel couriers swarm up it. He was the only Englishman on board. His nationality was obvious. A man came on deck and immediately walked up to him.

'Are you Mr Carruthers?'

'Yes.'

He was about to smile and put out his hand, but he perceived in the twinkling of an eye that the person who addressed him, an Englishman like himself, was not a gentleman. Instinctively his manner, remaining exceedingly polite, became a trifle stiff. Of course Carruthers did not tell me this, but I see the scene so clearly that I have no hesitation in describing it.

'Her ladyship hopes you don't mind her not coming to meet you, but the boat got in so early and it's more than an hour's drive to where we live.'

'Oh, of course. Her ladyship well?'

'Yes, thank you. Got your luggage ready?'

'Yes.'

'If you'll show me where it is I'll tell one of these fellows to put it in a boat. You won't have any difficulty at the Customs. I've fixed that up all right, and then we'll get off. Have you had breakfast?'

'Yes, thank you.'

The man was not quite sure of his aitches. Carruthers wondered who he was. You could not say he was uncivil, but he was certainly a little offhand. Carruthers knew that Betty had rather a large estate; perhaps he was her agent. He seemed very competent. He gave the porters instructions in fluent Greek and when they got in the boat and the boatmen asked for more money than he gave them, he said something that made them laugh and they shrugged their shoulders satisfied. The luggage was passed through the Customs without examination, Humphrey's guide shaking hands with the officials, and they went into a sunny place where a large yellow car was standing.

'Are you going to drive me?' asked Carruthers.

'I'm her ladyship's chauffeur.'

'Oh, I see. I didn't know.'

He was not dressed like a chauffeur. He wore white duck trousers and espadrilles on his bare feet, a white tennis shirt, with no tie and open at the neck, and a straw hat. Carruthers frowned. Betty oughtn't to let her chauffeur drive the car like that. It was true that he had had to get up before daybreak and it looked like being a hot drive up to the villa. Perhaps under ordinary conditions he wore uniform. Though not so tall as Carruthers, who was six feet one in his socks, he was not short; but he was broad-shouldered and squarely built, so that he looked stocky. He was not fat, but plump rather; he looked as though he had a hearty appetite and ate well. Young still, thirty perhaps or thirty-one, he had already a massive look and one day would be very beefy. Now he was a hefty fellow. He had a broad face deeply sunburned, a short thickish nose, and a somewhat sullen look. He wore a short fair moustache. Oddly enough Carruthers had a vague feeling that he had seen him before.

'Have you been with her ladyship long?' he asked.

'Well, I have, in a manner of speaking.'

Carruthers became a trifle stiffer. He did not quite like the manner in which the chauffeur spoke. He wondered why he did not say 'sir' to him. He was afraid Betty had let him get a little above himself. It was like her to be a bit careless about such things. But it was a mistake. He'd give her a hint when he got a chance. Their eyes met for an instant and he could have sworn that there was a twinkle of amusement in the chauffeur's. Carruthers could not imagine why. He was not aware that there was anything amusing in him.

'That, I suppose, is the old city of the Knights,' he said distantly, pointing to the battlemented walls.

'Yes. Her ladyship'll take you over. We get a rare lot of tourists here in the season.'

Carruthers wished to be affable. He thought it would be nicer of him to offer to sit by the chauffeur rather than behind by himself and was just going to suggest it when the matter was taken out of his hands. The chauffeur told the porters to put Carruther's bags at the back, and settling himself at the wheel said:

'Now if you'll hop in we'll get along.'

Carruthers sat down beside him and they set off along a white road that ran by the sea. In a few minutes they were in the open country. They drove in silence. Carruthers was a little on his dignity. He felt that the chauffeur was inclined to be familiar and he did not wish to give him occasion to be so. He flattered himself that he had a manner with him that puts his inferiors in their place. He thought with sardonic grimness that it would not be long before the chauffeur would be calling him 'sir'. But the morning was lovely; the white road ran between olive groves and the farmhouses they passed now and then, with their white walls and flat roofs, had an Oriental look that took the fancy. And Betty was waiting for him. The love in his heart disposed him to kindliness towards all men and lighting himself a cigarette he thought it would be a generous act to offer the chauffeur one too. After all, Rhodes was very far away from England and the age was democratic. The chauffeur accepted the gift and stopped the car to light up.

'Have you got the baccy?' he asked suddenly.

'Have I got what?'

The chauffeur's face fell.

'Her ladyship wired to you to bring two pounds of Player's

Navy Cut. That's why I fixed it up with the Customs people not to open your luggage.'

'I never got the wire.'

'Damn!'

'What on earth does her ladyship want with two pounds of Player's Navy Cut?'

He spoke with hauteur. He did not like the chauffeur's exclamation. The fellow gave him a sidelong glance in which Carruthers read a certain insolence.

'We can't get it here,' he said briefly.

He threw away with what looked very like exasperation the Egyptian cigarette Carruthers had given him and started off again. He looked sulky. He said nothing more. Carruthers felt that his efforts at sociability had been a mistake. For the rest of the journey he ignored the chauffeur. He adopted the frigid manner that he had used so successfully as secretary at the Embassy when a member of the British public came to him for assistance. For some time they had been running up hill and now they came to a long low wall and then to an open gate. The chauffeur turned in.

'Have we arrived?' cried Carruthers.

'Sixty-five kilometres in fifty-seven minutes,' said the chauffeur, a smile suddenly showing his fine white teeth. 'Not so bad considering the road.'

He sounded his klaxon shrilly. Carruthers was breathless with excitement. They drove up a narrow road through an olive grove, and came to a low, white, rambling house. Betty was standing at the door. He jumped out of the car and kissed her on both cheeks. For a moment he could not speak. But subconsciously he noticed that at the door stood an elderly butler in white ducks and a couple of footmen in the fustanellas of their country. They were smart and picturesque. Whatever Betty permitted her chauffeur it was evident that the house was run in the civilized style suited to her station. She led him through the hall, a large apartment with whitewashed walls in which he was vaguely conscious of handsome furniture, into the drawing-room. This also was large and low, with the same whitewashed walls, and he had immediately an impression of comfort and luxury.

'The first thing you must do is to come and look at my view,' she said.

'The first thing I must do is to look at you.'

She was dressed in white. Her arms, her face, her neck, were deeply burned by the sun; her eyes were bluer than he had ever seen them and the whiteness of her teeth was startling. She looked extremely well. She was very trim and neat. Her hair was waved, her nails were manicured; he had had a moment's anxiety that in the easy life she led on this romantic isle she had let herself go.

'Upon my word you look eighteen, Betty. How do you manage it?'

'Happiness,' she smiled.

It gave him a momentary pang to hear her say this. He did not want her to be too happy. He wanted to give her happiness. But now she insisted on taking him out on the terrace. The drawing-room had five long windows that led out to it and from the terrace the olive-clad hill tumbled steeply to the sea. There was a tiny bay below in which a white boat, mirrored on the calm water, lay at anchor. On a further hill, round the corner, you saw the white houses of a Greek village and beyond it a huge grey crag surmounted by the battlements of a medieval castle.

'It was one of the strongholds of the Knights,' she said. 'I'll take you up there this evening.'

The scene was quite lovely. It took your breath away. It was peaceful and yet it had a strange air of life. It moved you not to contemplation, but stirred you to activity.

'You've got the tobacco all right, I suppose.'

He started.

'I'm afraid I haven't. I never got your wire.'

'But I wired to the Embassy and I wired to the Excelsior.'

'I stayed at the Plaza.'

'What a bore! Albert'll be furious.'

'Who is Albert?'

'He drove you out. Player's is the only tobacco he likes and he can't get it here.'

'Oh, the chauffeur.' He pointed to the boat that lay gleaming beneath them. 'Is that the yacht I've heard about?'

'Yes.'

It was a large caïque that Betty had bought, fitted with a motor auxiliary and smartened up. In it she wandered about the Greek islands. She had been as far north as Athens and as far south as Alexandria.

'We'll take you for a trip if you can spare the time,' she said. 'You ought to see Cos while you're here.'

'Who runs it for you?'

'Of course I have a crew, but Albert chiefly. He's very clever with motors and all that.'

He did not know why it gave him a vague discomfort to hear her speak of the chauffeur again. Carruthers wondered if she did not leave too much in his hands. It was a mistake to give a servant too much leeway.

'You know, I couldn't help thinking I'd seen Albert before somewhere. But I can't place him.'

She smiled brightly, her eyes shining, with that sudden gaiety of hers that gave her face its delightful frankness.

'You ought to remember him. He was the second footman at Aunt Louise's. He must have opened the door to you hundreds of times.'

Aunt Louise was the aunt with whom Betty had lived before her marriage.

'Oh, is that who he is? I suppose I must have seen him there without noticing him. How does he happen to be here?'

'He comes from our place at home. When I married he wanted to come with me, so I took him. He was Jimmie's valet for some time and then I sent him to some motor works, he was mad about cars, and eventually I took him on as my chauffeur. I don't know what I should do without him now.'

'Don't you think it's rather a mistake to get too dependent on a servant?'

'I don't know. It never occurred to me.'

Betty showed him the rooms that had been got ready for him, and when he had changed they strolled down to the beach. A dinghy was waiting for them and they rowed out to the caïque and bathed from there. The water was warm and they sunned themselves on the deck. The caïque was roomy, comfortable, and luxurious. Betty showed him over and they came upon Albert tinkering with the engines. He was in filthy overalls, his hands were black and his face was smeared with grease.

'What's the matter, Albert?' said Betty.

He raised himself and faced her respectfully.

'Nothing, m'lady. I was just 'aving a look round.'

'There are only two things Albert loves in the world. One is the car and the other's the yacht. Isn't that true, Albert?'

She gave him a gay smile and Albert's rather stolid face lit up. He showed his beautiful white teeth.

'That's true, m'lady.'

'He sleeps on board, you know. We rigged up a very nice cabin for him aft.'

Carruthers fell into the life very easily. Betty had bought the estate from a Turkish pasha exiled to Rhodes by Abdul Hamid and she had added a wing to the picturesque house. She had made a wild garden of the olive grove that surrounded it. It was planted with rosemary and lavender and asphodel, broom that she had had sent from England and the roses for which the island was famous. In the spring, she told him, the ground was carpeted with anemones. But when she showed him her property, telling him her plans and what alterations she had in mind, Carruthers could not help feeling a little uneasy.

'You talk as though you were going to live here all your life,' he said.

'Perhaps I am,' she smiled.

'What nonsense! At your age.'

'I'm getting on for forty, old boy,' she answered lightly.

He discovered with satisfaction that Betty had an excellent cook and it gratified his sense of propriety to dine with her in the splendid dining-room, with its Italian furniture, and be waited on by the dignified Greek butler and the two handsome footmen in their flamboyant uniforms. The house was furnished with taste; the rooms contained nothing that was not essential, but every piece was good. Betty lived in considerable state. When, the day after his arrival, the Governor with several members of his staff came over to dinner she displayed all the resources of the household. The Governor entering the house passed between a double row of flunkeys magnificent in their starched petticoats, embroidered jackets, and velvet caps. It was almost a bodyguard. Carruthers liked the grand style. The dinner-party was very gay. Betty's Italian was fluent and Carruthers spoke it perfectly. The young officers in the Governor's suite were uncommonly smart in their uniforms. They were very attentive to Betty and she treated them with easy cordiality. She chaffed them. After dinner the gramophone was turned on and they danced with her one after the other.

When they were gone Carruthers asked her:

'Aren't they all madly in love with you?'

'I don't know about that. They hint occasionally at alliances permanent or otherwise, but they take it very good-naturedly when I decline with thanks.'

They were not serious. The young ones were callow and the not so young were fat and bald. Whatever they might feel about her Carruthers could not for a moment believe that Betty would make a fool of herself with a middle-class Italian. But a day or two later a curious thing happened. He was in his rooms dressing for dinner; he heard a man's voice outside in the passage, he could not hear what was said or what language was spoken, and then ringing out suddenly Betty's laughter. It was a charming laugh, rippling and gay, like a young girl's, and it had a joyous

abandon that was infectious. But whom could she be laughing
with? It was not the way you would laugh with a servant. It had a
curious intimacy. It may seem strange that Carruthers read all
this into a peal of laughter, but it must be remembered that
Carruthers was very subtle. His stories were remarkable for such
touches.

When they met presently on the terrace and he was shaking a
cocktail he sought to gratify his curiosity.

'What were you laughing your head off over just now? Has
anyone been here?'

'No.'

She looked at him with genuine surprise.

'I thought one of your Italian officers had come to pass the time
of day.'

'No.'

Of course the passage of years had had its effect on Betty. She
was beautiful, but her beauty was mature. She had always had
assurance, but now she had repose; her serenity was a feature,
like her blue eyes and her candid brow, that was part of her
beauty. She seemed to be at peace with all the world; it rested you
to be with her as it rested you to lie among the olives within sight
of the wine-coloured sea. Though she was as gay and witty as
ever, the seriousness which once he had been alone to know was
now patent. No one could accuse her any longer of being scatter-
brained; it was impossible not to perceive the fineness of her
character. It had even nobility. That was not a trait it was usual
to find in the modern woman and Carruthers said to himself that
she was a throw-back; she reminded him of the great ladies of the
eighteenth century. She had always had a feeling for literature,
the poems she wrote as a girl were graceful and melodious, and he
was more interested than surprised when she told him that she
had undertaken a solid historical work. She was getting materials
together for an account of the Knights of St John in Rhodes.
It was a story of romantic incidents. She took Carruthers to the
city and showed him the noble battlements and together they
wandered through austere and stately buildings. They strolled up
the silent Street of the Knights with the lovely stone façades and
the great coats of arms that recalled a dead chivalry. She had a
surprise for him here. She had bought one of the old houses and
with affectionate care had restored it to its old state. When you
entered the little courtyard, with its carved stone stairway,
you were taken back into the middle ages. It had a tiny walled
garden in which a fig-tree grew and roses. It was small and
secret and silent. The old knights had been in contact with the

East long enough to have acquired Oriental ideas of privacy.

'When I'm tired of the villa I come here for two or three days and picnic. It's a relief sometimes not to be surrounded by people.'

'But you're not alone here?'

'Practically.'

There was a little parlour austerely furnished.

'What is this?' said Carruthers pointing with a smile to a copy of the *Sporting Times* that lay on a table.

'Oh, that's Albert's. I suppose he left it here when he came to meet you. He has the *Sporting Times* and the *News of the World* sent him every week. That is how he keeps abreast of the great world.'

She smiled tolerantly. Next to the parlour was a bedroom with nothing much in it but a large bed.

'The house belonged to an Englishman. That's partly why I bought it. He was a Sir Giles Quern, and one of my ancestors married a Mary Quern who was a cousin of his. They were Cornish people.'

Finding that she could not get on with her history without such a knowledge of Latin as would enable her to read the medieval documents with ease, Betty had set about learning the classical language. She troubled to acquire only the elements of grammar and then started, with a translation by her side, to read the authors that interested her. It is a very good method of learning a language and I have often wondered that it is not used in schools. It saves all the endless turning over of dictionaries and the fumbling search for meaning. After nine months Betty could read Latin as fluently as most of us can read French. It seemed a trifle ridiculous to Carruthers that this lovely, brilliant creature should take her work so seriously and yet he was moved; he would have liked to snatch her in his arms and kiss her, not at that moment as a woman, but as a precocious child whose cleverness suddenly enchants you. But later he reflected upon what she had told him. He was of course a very clever man, otherwise he could not have attained the position he held in the Foreign Office, and it would be silly to claim that those two books of his could have made so much stir without some merit; if I have made him look a bit of a fool it is only because I did not happen to like him, and if I have derided his stories it is merely because stories of that sort seem to me rather silly. He had tact and insight. He had a conviction that there was but one way to win her. She was in a groove and happy in it, her plans were definite; but her life at Rhodes was so well-ordered, so complete and satisfying, that for that very reason its hold over her could be combated. His chance was to arouse in her the restlessness that lies deep in the heart of the English. So he talked to Betty of England and London, their common friends and the painters, writers, and musicians with whom his literary success had brought him acquaintance. He talked of the Bohemian parties in Chelsea, and of the opera, of trips to Paris *en bande* for a fancy-dress ball, or to Berlin to see the new plays. He recalled to her imagination a life rich and easy, varied, cultured, intelligent, and highly civilized. He tried to make her feel that she was stagnating in a backwater. The world was hurrying on, from one new and interesting phase to another, and she was standing still. They were living in a thrilling age and she was missing it. Of course he did not tell her this; he left her to infer it. He was amusing and spirited, he had an excellent memory for a good story, he was whimsical and gay. I know I have not made Humphrey Carruthers witty any more than I have shown Lady Betty brilliant. The reader must take my word for it that they were. Carruthers was generally reckoned an entertaining companion, and that is half the battle; people were willing to find him amusing and they vowed the things he said were marvellous. Of course his wit was social. It needed a particular company, who understood his allusions and shared his exclusive sense of humour. There are a score of journalists in Fleet Street who could knock spots off the most famous of the society wits; it is their business to be witty and brilliance is in their day's work. There are a few of the society beauties whose photographs appear in the papers who could get a job at three pounds a week in the chorus of a song-and-dance show. Amateurs must be judged with tolerance. Carruthers knew that Betty enjoyed his society. They laughed a great deal together. The days passed in a flash.

'I shall miss you terribly when you go,' she said in her frank way. 'It's been a treat having you here. You are a sweet, Humphrey.'

'Have you only just discovered it?'

He patted himself on the back. His tactics had been right. It was interesting to see how well his simple plan had worked. Like a charm. The vulgar might laugh at the Foreign Office, but there was no doubt it taught you how to deal with difficult people. Now he had but to choose his opportunity. He felt that Betty had never been more attached to him. He would wait till the end of his visit. Betty was emotional. She would be sorry that he was going. Rhodes would seem very dull without him. Whom would she have to talk to when he was gone? After dinner they usually sat on the terrace looking at the starry sea; the air was warm and balmy and vaguely scented: it was then he would ask her to marry him, on the eve of his departure. He felt it in his bones that she would accept him.

One morning when he had been in Rhodes a little over a week, he happened to be coming upstairs as Betty was walking along the passage.

'You've never shown me your room, Betty,' he said.

'Haven't I? Come in and have a look now. It's rather nice.'

She turned back and he followed her in. It was over the drawing-room and nearly as large. It was furnished in the Italian style, and as is the present way more like a sitting-room than a bedroom. There were fine Paninis on the walls and one or two handsome cabinets. The bed was Venetian and beautifully painted.

'That's a couch of rather imposing dimensions for a widow lady,' he said facetiously.

'It is enormous, isn't it? But it was so lovely, I had to buy it. It cost a fortune.'

His eye took in the bed-table by the side. There were two or three books on it, a box of cigarettes, and on an ash-tray a briar pipe. Funny! What on earth had Betty got a pipe by her bed for?

'Do look at this *cassone*. Isn't the painting marvellous? I almost cried when I found it.'

'I suppose that cost a fortune too.'

'I daren't tell you what I paid.'

When they were leaving the room he cast another glance at the bed-table. The pipe had vanished.

It was odd that Betty should have a pipe in her bedroom, she certainly didn't smoke one herself, and if she had would have made no secret of it, but of course there were a dozen reasonable explanations. It might be a present she was making to somebody, one of the Italians or even Albert, he had not been able to see if it was new or old, or it might be a pattern that she was going to ask him to take home to have others of the same sort sent out to her. After the moment's perplexity, not altogether unmingled with amusement, he put the matter out of his mind. They were going for a picnic that day, taking their luncheon with them, and Betty was driving him herself. They had arranged to go for a cruise of a couple of days before he left so that he should see Patmos and Cos, and Albert was busy with the engines of the caïque. They had a wonderful day. They visited a ruined castle and climbed a mountain on which grew asphodel, hyacinth, and narcissus, and returned dead beat. They separated not long after dinner and Carruthers went to bed. He read for a little and then turned out his light. But he could not sleep. It was hot under his mosquito-net. He turned and tossed. Presently he thought he would go down to the little beach at the foot of the hill and bathe. It was not more than three minutes' walk. He put on his espa-drilles and took a towel. The moon was full and he saw it shining on the sea through the olive-trees. But he was not alone to have thought that this radiant night would be lovely to bathe in, for just before he came out on to the beach sounds reached his ears. He muttered a little damn of vexation, some of Betty's servants were bathing, and he could not very well disturb them. The olive-trees came almost to the water's edge and undecided he stood in their shelter. He heard a voice that gave him a sudden start.

'Where's my towel?'

English. A woman waded out of the water and stood for a moment at its edge. From the darkness a man came forward with nothing but a towel round his loins. The woman was Betty. She was stark naked. The man wrapped a bath-robe round her and began drying her vigorously. She leaned on him while she put on first one shoe and then the other and to support her he placed his arm round her shoulders. The man was Albert.

Carruthers turned and fled up the hill. He stumbled blindly. Once he nearly fell. He was gasping like a wounded beast. When he got into his room he flung himself on the bed and clenched his fists and the dry, painful sobs that tore his chest broke into tears. He evidently had a violent attack of hysterics. It was all clear to him, clear with the ghastly vividness with which on a stormy night a flash of lightning can disclose a ravaged landscape, clear, horribly clear. The way the man had dried her and the way she leaned against him pointed not to passion, but to a long-con-tinued intimacy, and the pipe by the bedside, the pipe had a hideously conjugal air. It suggested the pipe a man might smoke while he was reading in bed before going to sleep. The *Sporting Times!* That was why she had that little house in the Street of the Knights, so that they could spend two or three days together in domestic familiarity. They were like an old married couple. Hum-phrey asked himself how long the hateful thing had lasted and suddenly he knew the answer; for years. Ten, twelve, four-teen; it had started when the young footman first came to London, he was a boy then and it was obvious enough that it was not he who had made the advances; all through those years when she was the idol of the British public, when everyone adored her and she could have married anyone she liked, she was living with the second footman at her aunt's house. She took him with her when she married. Why had she made that surprising marriage?

And the still-born child that came before its time. Of course that was why she had married Jimmie Welldon-Burns, because she was going to have a child by Albert. Oh, shameless, shameless! And then, when Jimmie's health broke down she had made him take Albert as his valet. And what had Jimmie known and what had he suspected? He drank, that was what had started his tuberculosis; but why had he started drinking? Perhaps it was to still a suspicion that was so ugly that he could not face it. And it was to live with Albert that she had left Jimmie and it was to live with Albert that she had settled in Rhodes. Albert, his hands with their broken nails stained by his work on the motors, coarse of aspect and stocky, rather like a butcher with his high colour and clumsy strength, Albert not even very young any more and running to fat, uneducated and vulgar, with his common way of speaking. Albert, Albert, how could she?

Carruthers got up and drank some water. He threw himself into a chair. He could not bear his bed. He smoked cigarette after cigarette. He was a wreck in the morning. He had not slept at all. They brought him in his breakfast; he drank the coffee but could eat nothing. Presently there was a brisk knock on his door.

'Coming down to bathe, Humphrey?'

That cheerful voice sent the blood singing through his head. He braced himself and opened the door.

'I don't think I will today. I don't feel very well.'

She gave him a look.

'Oh, my dear, you look all in. What's the matter with you?'

'I don't know. I think I must have got a touch of the sun.'

His voice was dead and his eyes were tragic. She looked at him more closely. She did not say anything for a moment. He thought she went pale. He *knew*. Then a faintly mocking smile crossed her eyes; she thought the situation comic.

'Poor old boy, go and lie down, I'll send you in some aspirin. Perhaps you'll feel better at luncheon.'

He lay in his darkened room. He would have given anything to get away then so that he need not set eyes on her again, but there was no means of that, the ship that was to take him back to Brindisi did not touch at Rhodes till the end of the week. He was a prisoner. And the next day they were to go to the islands. There was no escape from her there; in the caïque they would be in one another's pockets all day long. He couldn't face that. He was so ashamed. But she wasn't ashamed. At that moment when it had been plain to her that nothing was hidden from him any longer she had smiled. She was capable of telling him all about it. He could not bear that. That was too much. After all she couldn't be certain that he knew, at best she could only suspect; if he behaved as if nothing had happened, if at luncheon and during the days that remained he was as gay and jolly as usual she would think she had been mistaken. It was enough to know what he knew, he would not suffer the crowning humiliation of hearing from her own lips the disgraceful story. But at luncheon the first thing she said was:

'Isn't it a bore. Albert says something's gone wrong with the motor, we shan't be able to go on our trip after all. I daren't trust to sail at this time of the year. We might be becalmed for a week.'

She spoke lightly and he answered in the same casual fashion.

'Oh, I'm sorry, but still I don't really care. It's so lovely here, I really didn't much want to go.'

He told her that the aspirin had done him good and he felt much better; to the Greek butler and the two footmen in fustanellas it must have seemed that they talked as vivaciously as usual. That night the British consul came to dinner and the night after some Italian officers. Carruthers counted the days, he counted the hours. Oh, if the moment would only come when he could step on the ship and be free from the horror that every moment of the day obsessed him! He was growing so tired. But Betty's manner was so self-possessed that sometimes he asked himself if she really knew that he was aware of her secret. Was it the truth that she had told about the caïque and not, as had at once struck him, an excuse; and was it an accident that a succession of visitors prevented them from ever being alone together? The worst of having so much tact was that you never quite knew whether other people were acting naturally or being tactful too. When he looked at her, so easy and calm, so obviously happy, he could not believe the odious truth. And yet he had seen with his own eyes. And the future. What would her future be? It was horrible to think of. Sooner or later the truth must become notorious. And to think of Betty a mock and an outcast, in the power of a coarse and common man, growing older, losing her beauty; and the man was five years younger than she. One day he would take a mistress, one of her own maids, perhaps, with whom he would feel at home as he had never felt with the great lady, and what could she do then? What humiliation then must she be prepared to put up with! He might be cruel to her. He might beat her. Betty. Betty.

Carruthers wrung his hands. And on a sudden an idea came to him that filled him with a painful exaltation; he put it away from him, but it returned; it would not let him be. He must save her, he had loved her too much and too long to let her sink, sink as she was sinking; a passion of self-sacrifice welled up in him. Notwithstanding everything, though his love now was dead and he felt for her an almost physical repulsion, he would marry her. He laughed mirthlessly. What would his life be? He couldn't help that. He didn't matter. It was the only thing to do. He felt wonderfully uplifted, and yet very humble, for he was awed at the thought of the heights which the divine spirit of man could reach.

His ship was to sail on Saturday and on Thursday when the guests who had been dining left them, he said:

'I hope we're going to be alone tomorrow.'

'As a matter of fact I've asked some Egyptians who spend the summer here. She's a sister of the ex-Khedive and very intelligent. I'm sure you'll like her.'

'Well, it's my last evening. Couldn't we spend it alone?'

She gave him a glance. There was a faint amusement in her eyes, but his were grave.

'If you like. I can put them off.'

'Then do.'

He was to start early in the morning and his luggage was packed. Betty had told him not to dress, but he had answered that he preferred to. For the last time they sat down to dinner facing one another. The dining-room, with its shaded lights, was bare and formal, but the summer night flooding in through the great open windows gave it a sober richness. It had the effect of the private refectory in a convent to which a royal lady had retired in order to devote the remainder of her life to a piety not too austere. They had their coffee on the terrace. Carruthers drank a couple of liqueurs. He was feeling very nervous.

'Betty, my dear, I've got something I want to say to you,' he began.

'Have you? I wouldn't say it if I were you.'

She answered gently. She remained perfectly calm, watching him shrewdly, but with the glimmer of a smile in her blue eyes.

'I must.'

She shrugged her shoulders and was silent. He was conscious that his voice trembled a little and he was angry with himself.

'You know I've been madly in love with you for many years. I don't know how many times I've asked you to marry me. But, after all, things change and people change too, don't they? We're neither of us so young as we were. Won't you marry me now, Betty?'

She gave him the smile that had always been such an attractive thing in her; it was so kindly, so frank, and still, still so wonderfully innocent.

'You're very sweet, Humphrey. It's awfully nice of you to ask me again. I can't tell you how touched I am. But you know, I'm a creature of habit, I've got in the habit of saying no to you now, and I can't change it.'

'Why not?'

There was something aggressive in his tone, something almost ominous, that made her give him a quick look. Her face blanched with sudden anger, but she immediately controlled herself.

'Because I don't want to,' she smiled.

'Are you going to marry anyone else?'

'I? No. Of course not.'

For a moment she seemed to draw herself up as though a wave of ancestral pride swept through her and then she began to laugh. But whether she laughed at the thought that had passed through her mind or because something in Humphrey's proposal had amused her none but she could have told.

'Betty. I implore you to marry me.'

'Never.'

'You can't go on living this life.'

He put into his voice all the anguish of his heart and his face was drawn and tortured. She smiled affectionately.

'Why not? Don't be such a donkey. You know I adore you, Humphrey, but you are rather an old woman.'

'Betty. Betty.'

Did she not see that it was for her sake that he wanted it? It was not love that made him speak, but human pity and shame. She got up.

'Don't be tiresome, Humphrey. You'd better go to bed, you know you have to be up with the lark. I shan't see you in the morning. Good-bye and God bless you. It's been wonderful having you here.'

She kissed him on both cheeks.

Next morning, early, for he had to be on board at eight, when Carruthers stepped out of the front door he found Albert waiting for him in the car. He wore a singlet, duck trousers, and a beret basque. Carruthers' luggage was in the back. He turned to the butler.

'Put my bags beside the chauffeur,' he said. 'I'll sit behind.'

Albert made no remark. Carruthers got in and they drove off. When they arrived at the harbour, porters ran up. Albert got out of the car. Carruthers looked down at him from his greater height.

'You need not see me on board. I can manage perfectly well by myself. Here's a tip for you.'

He gave him a five-pound note. Albert flushed. He was taken aback, he would have liked to refuse it, but did not know how to, and the servility of years asserted itself. Perhaps he did not know what he said.

'Thank you, sir.'

Carruthers gave him a curt nod and walked away. He had forced Betty's lover to call him 'sir'. It was as though he had struck her a blow across that smiling mouth of hers and flung in her face an opprobrious word. It filled him with a bitter satisfaction.

He shrugged his shoulders and I could see that even this small triumph now seemed vain. For a little while we were silent. There was nothing for me to say. Then he began again.

'I dare say you think it's very strange that I should tell you all this. I don't care. You know, I feel as if nothing mattered any more. I feel as if decency no longer existed in the world. Heaven knows, I'm not jealous. You can't be jealous unless you love and my love is dead. It was killed in a flash. After all those years. I can't think of her now without horror. What destroys me, what makes me so frightfully unhappy is to think of her unspeakable degradation.'

So it has been said that it was not jealousy that caused Othello to kill Desdemona, but an agony that the creature that he believed angelic should be proved impure and worthless. What broke his noble heart was that virtue should so fall.

'I thought there was no one like her. I admired her so much. I admired her courage and her frankness, her intelligence and her love of beauty. She's just a sham and she's never been anything else.'

'I wonder if that's true. Do you think any of us are all of a piece? Do you know what strikes me? I should have said that Albert was only the instrument, her toll to the solid earth, so to speak; that left her soul at liberty to range the empyrean. Perhaps the mere fact that he was so far below her gave her a sense of freedom in her relations with him that she would have lacked with a man of her own class. The spirit is very strange, it never soars so high as when the body has wallowed for a period in the gutter.'

'Oh, don't talk such rot,' he answered angrily.

'I don't think it is rot. I don't put it very well, but the idea's sound.'

'Much good it does me. I'm broken and done for. I'm finished.'

'Oh, nonsense. Why don't you write a story about it?'

'I?'

'You know, that's the great pull a writer has over other people. When something has made him terribly unhappy, and he's tortured and miserable, he can put it all into a story and it's astonishing what a comfort and relief it is.'

'It would be monstrous. Betty was everything in the world to me. I couldn't do anything so caddish.'

He paused for a little and I saw him reflect. I saw that notwithstanding the horror that my suggestion caused him he did for one minute look at the situation from the standpoint of the writer. He shook his head.

'Not for her sake, for mine. After all I have some self-respect. Besides, there's no story there.'

JANE

I REMEMBER very well the occasion on which I first saw Jane Fowler. It is indeed only because the details of the glimpse I had of her then are so clear that I trust my recollection at all, for, looking back, I must confess that I find it hard to believe that it has not played me a fantastic trick. I had lately returned to London from China and was drinking a dish of tea with Mrs Tower. Mrs Tower had been seized with the prevailing passion for decoration; and with the ruthlessness of her sex had sacrificed chairs in which she had comfortably sat for years, tables, cabinets, ornaments on which her eyes had dwelt in peace since she was married, pictures that had been familiar to her for a generation; and delivered herself into the hands of an expert. Nothing remained in her drawing-room with which she had any association, or to which any sentiment was attached; and she had invited me that day to see the fashionable glory in which she now lived. Everything that could be pickled was pickled and what couldn't be pickled was painted. Nothing matched, but everything harmonized.

'Do you remember that ridiculous drawing-room suite that I used to have?' asked Mrs Tower.

The curtains were sumptuous yet severe; the sofa was covered with Italian brocade; the chair on which I sat was in *petit point*. The room was beautiful, opulent without garishness, and original without affectation; yet to me it lacked something; and while I praised with my lips I asked myself why I so much preferred the rather shabby chintz of the despised suite, the Victorian watercolours that I had known so long, and the ridiculous Dresden china that had adorned the chimney-piece. I wondered what it was that I missed in all these rooms that the decorators were turning out with a profitable industry. Was it heart? But Mrs Tower looked about her happily.

'Don't you like my alabaster lamps?' she said. 'They give such a soft light.'

'Personally I have a weakness for a light that you can see by,' I smiled.

'It's so difficult to combine that with a light that you can't be too much seen by,' laughed Mrs Tower.

I had no notion what her age was. When I was quite a young man she was a married woman a good deal older than I, but now she treated me as her contemporary. She constantly said that she made no secret of her age, which was forty, and then added with a smile that all women took five years off. She never sought to conceal the fact that she dyed her hair (it was a very pretty brown with reddish tints), and she said she did this because hair was hideous while it was going grey; as soon as hers was white she would cease to dye it.

'Then they'll say what a young face I have.'

Meanwhile it was painted, though with discretion, and her eyes owed not a little of their vivacity to art. She was a handsome woman, exquisitely gowned, and in the sombre glow of the alabaster lamps did not look a day more than the forty she gave herself.

'It is only at my dressing-table that I can suffer the naked brightness of a thirty-two-candle electric bulb,' she added with smiling cynicism. 'There I need it to tell me first the hideous truth and then to enable me to take the necessary steps to correct it.'

We gossiped pleasantly about our common friends and Mrs Tower brought me up to date in the scandal of the day. After roughing it here and there it was very agreeable to sit in a comfortable chair, the fire burning brightly on the hearth, charming tea-things set out on a charming table, and talk with this amusing, attractive woman. She treated me as a prodigal returned from his husks and was disposed to make much of me. She prided herself on her dinner-parties; she took no less trouble to have her guests suitably assorted than to give them excellent food; and there were few persons who did not look upon it as a treat to be bidden to one of them. Now she fixed a date and asked me whom I would like to meet.

'There's only one thing I must tell you. If Jane Fowler is still here I shall have to put it off.'

'Who is Jane Fowler?' I asked.

Mrs Tower gave a rueful smile.

'Jane Fowler is my cross.'

'Oh!'

'Do you remember a photograph that I used to have on the piano before I had my room done, of a woman in a tight dress with tight sleeves and a gold locket, with her hair drawn back from a broad forehead and her ears showing and spectacles on a rather blunt nose? Well, that was Jane Fowler.'

'You had so many photographs about the room in your unregenerate days,' I said, vaguely.

'It makes me shudder to think of them. I've made them into a huge brown-paper parcel and hidden them in an attic.'

'Well, who is Jane Fowler?' I asked again, smiling.

'She's my sister-in-law. She was my husband's sister and she married a manufacturer in the North. She's been a widow for many years, and she's very well-to-do.'

'And why is she your cross?'

'She's worthy, she's dowdy, she's provincial. She looks twenty years older than I do and she's quite capable of telling anyone she meets that we were at school together. She has an overwhelming sense of family affection and because I am her only living connexion she's devoted to me. When she comes to London it never occurs to her that she should stay anywhere but here – she thinks it would hurt my feelings – and she'll pay me visits of three or four weeks. We sit here and she knits and reads. And sometimes she insists on taking me to dine at Claridge's and she looks like a funny old charwoman and everyone I particularly don't want to be seen by is sitting at the next table. When we are driving home she says she loves giving me a little treat. With her own hands she makes me tea-cosies that I am forced to use when she is here and doilies and centrepieces for the dining-room table.'

Mrs Tower paused to take breath.

'I should have thought a woman of your tact would find a way to deal with a situation like that.'

'Ah, but don't you see, I haven't a chance. She's so immeasurably kind. She has a heart of gold. She bores me to death, but I wouldn't for anything let her suspect it.'

'And when does she arrive?'

'Tomorrow.'

But the answer was hardly out of Mrs Tower's mouth when the bell rang. There were sounds in the hall of a slight commotion and in a minute or two the butler ushered in an elderly lady.

'Mrs Fowler,' he announced.

'Jane,' cried Mrs Tower, springing to her feet. 'I wasn't expecting you today.'

'So your butler has just told me. I certainly said today in my letter.'

Mrs Tower recovered her wits.

'Well, it doesn't matter. I'm very glad to see you whenever you come. Fortunately I'm doing nothing this evening.'

'You mustn't let me give you any trouble. If I can have a boiled egg for my dinner, that's all I shall want.'

A faint grimace for a moment distorted Mrs Tower's handsome features. A boiled egg!

'Oh, I think we can do a little better than that.'

I chuckled inwardly when I recollected that the two ladies were

JANE

contemporaries. Mrs Fowler looked a good fifty-five. She was a rather big woman; she wore a black straw hat with a wide brim and from it a black lace veil hung over her shoulders, a cloak that oddly combined severity with fussiness, a long black dress, voluminous as though she wore several petticoats under it, and stout boots. She was evidently short-sighted, for she looked at you through large gold-rimmed spectacles.

'Won't you have a cup of tea?' asked Mrs Tower.

'If it wouldn't be too much trouble. I'll take off my mantle.'

She began by stripping her hands of the black gloves she wore, and then took off her cloak. Round her neck was a solid gold chain from which hung a large gold locket in which I felt certain was a photograph of her deceased husband. Then she took off her hat and placed it neatly with her gloves and cloak on the sofa corner. Mrs Tower pursed her lips. Certainly those garments did not go very well with the austere but sumptuous beauty of Mrs Tower's redecorated drawing-room. I wondered where on earth Mrs Fowler had found the extraordinary clothes she wore. They were not old and the materials were expensive. It was astounding to think that dressmakers still made things that had not been worn for a quarter of a century. Mrs Fowler's grey hair was very plainly done, showing all her forehead and her ears, with a parting in the middle. It had evidently never known the tongs of Monsieur Marcel. Now her eyes fell on the tea-table with its teapot of Georgian silver and its cups in old Worcester.

'What have you done with the tea-cosy I gave you last time I came up, Marion?' she asked. 'Don't you use it?'

'Yes, I used it every day, Jane,' answered Mrs Tower glibly. 'Unfortunately we had an accident with it a little while ago. It got burnt.'

'But the last one I gave you got burnt.'

'I'm afraid you'll think us very careless.'

'It doesn't really matter,' smiled Mrs Fowler. 'I shall enjoy making you another. I'll go to Liberty's tomorrow and buy some silks.'

Mrs Tower kept her face bravely.

'I don't deserve it, you know. Doesn't your vicar's wife need one?'

'Oh, I've just made her one,' said Mrs Fowler brightly.

I noticed that when she smiled she showed white, small, and regular teeth. They were a real beauty. Her smile was certainly very sweet.

But I felt it high time for me to leave the two ladies to themselves, so I took my leave.

Early next morning Mrs Tower rang me up and I heard at once from her voice that she was in high spirits.

'I've got the most wonderful news for you,' she said. 'Jane is going to be married.'

'Nonsense.'

'Her fiancé is coming to dine here tonight to be introduced to me and I want you to come too.'

'Oh, but I shall be in the way.'

'No, you won't. Jane suggested herself that I should ask you. Do come.'

She was bubbling over with laughter.

'Who is he?'

'I don't know. She tells me he's an architect. Can you imagine the sort of man Jane would marry?'

I had nothing to do and I could trust Mrs Tower to give me a good dinner.

When I arrived Mrs Tower, very splendid in a tea-gown a little too young for her, was alone.

'Jane is putting the finishing touches to her appearance. I'm longing for you to see her. She's all in a flutter. She says he adores her. His name is Gilbert and when she speaks of him her voice gets all funny and tremulous. It makes me want to laugh.'

'I wonder what he's like.'

'Oh, I'm sure I know. Very big and massive, with a bald head and an immense gold chain across an immense tummy. A large, fat, clean-shaven, red face and a booming voice.'

Mrs Fowler came in. She wore a very stiff black silk dress with a wide skirt and a train. At the neck it was cut into a timid V and the sleeves came down to the elbows. She wore a necklace of diamonds set in silver. She carried in her hands a long pair of black gloves and a fan of black ostrich feathers. She managed (as so few people do) to look exactly what she was. You could never have thought her anything in the world but the respectable relict of a North-country manufacturer of ample means.

'You've really got quite a pretty neck, Jane,' said Mrs Tower with a kindly smile.

It was indeed astonishingly young when you compared it with her weather-beaten face. It was smooth and unlined and the skin was white. And I noticed then that her head was very well placed on her shoulders.

'Has Marion told you my news?' she said, turning to me with that really charming smile of hers as if we were already old friends.

'I must congratulate you,' I said.

'Wait to do that till you've seen my young man.'

'I think it's too sweet to hear you talk of your young man,' smiled Mrs Tower.

Mrs Fowler's eyes certainly twinkled behind her preposterous spectacles.

'Don't expect anyone too old. You wouldn't like me to marry a decrepit old gentleman with one foot in the grave, would you?'

This was the only warning she gave us. Indeed there was no time for any further discussion, for the butler flung open the door and in a loud voice announced:

'Mr Gilbert Napier.'

There entered a youth in a very well-cut dinner jacket. He was slight, not very tall, with fair hair in which there was a hint of a natural wave, clean-shaven, and blue-eyed. He was not particularly good-looking, but he had a pleasant, amiable face. In ten years he would probably be wizened and sallow; but now, in extreme youth, he was fresh and clean and blooming. For he was certainly not more than twenty-four. My first thought was that this was the son of Jane Fowler's fiancé (I had not known he was a widower) come to say that his father was prevented from dining by a sudden attack of gout. But his eyes fell immediately on Mrs Fowler, his face lit up, and he went towards her with both hands outstretched. Mrs Fowler gave him hers, a demure smile on her lips, and turned to her sister-in-law.

'This is my young man, Marion,' she said.

He held out his hand.

'I hope you'll like me, Mrs Tower,' he said. 'Jane tells me you're the only relation she has in the world.'

Mrs Tower's face was wonderful to behold. I saw then to admiration how bravely good breeding and social usage could combat the instincts of the natural woman. For the astonishment and then the dismay that for an instant she could not conceal were quickly driven away, and her face assumed an expression of affable welcome. But she was evidently at a loss for words. It was not unnatural if Gilbert felt a certain embarrassment and I was too busy preventing myself from laughing to think of anything to say. Mrs Fowler alone kept perfectly calm.

'I know you'll like him, Marion. There's no one enjoys good food more than he does.' She turned to the young man. 'Marion's dinners are famous.'

'I know,' he beamed.

Mrs Tower made some quick rejoinder and we went down stairs. I shall not soon forget the exquisite comedy of that meal. Mrs Tower could not make up her mind whether the pair of them were playing a practical joke on her or whether Jane by wilfully concealing her fiancé's age had hoped to make her look foolish. But then Jane never jested and she was incapable of doing a malicious thing. Mrs Tower was amazed, exasperated, and perplexed. But she had recovered her self-control, and for nothing would she have forgotten that she was a perfect hostess whose duty it was to make her party go. She talked vivaciously; but I wondered if Gilbert Napier saw how hard and vindictive was the expression of her eyes behind the mask of friendliness that she turned to him. She was measuring him. She was seeking to delve into the secret of his soul. I could see that she was in a passion, for under her rouge her cheeks glowed with an angry red.

'You've got a very high colour, Marion,' said Jane, looking at her amiably through her great round spectacles.

'I dressed in a hurry. I dare say I put on too much rouge.'

'Oh, is it rouge? I thought it was natural. Otherwise I shouldn't have mentioned it.' She gave Gilbert a shy little smile. 'You know, Marion and I were at school together. You would never think it to look at us now, would you? But of course I've lived a very quiet life.'

I do not know what she meant by these remarks; it was almost incredible that she made them in complete simplicity; but anyhow they goaded Mrs Tower to such a fury that she flung her own vanity to the winds. She smiled brightly.

'We shall neither of us see fifty again, Jane,' she said.

If the observation was meant to discomfit the widow it failed.

'Gilbert says I mustn't acknowledge to more than forty-nine for his sake,' she answered blandly.

Mrs Tower's hands trembled slightly, but she found a retort.

'There is of course a certain disparity of age between you,' she smiled.

'Twenty-seven years,' said Jane. 'Do you think it's too much? Gilbert says I'm very young for my age. I told you I shouldn't like to marry a man with one foot in the grave.'

I was really obliged to laugh and Gilbert laughed too. His laughter was frank and boyish. It looked as though he were amused at everything Jane said. But Mrs Tower was almost at the end of her tether and I was afraid that unless relief came she would for once forget that she was a woman of the world. I came to the rescue as best I could.

'I suppose you're very busy buying your trousseau,' I said.

'No. I wanted to get my things from the dressmaker in Liverpool I've been to ever since I was first married. But Gilbert won't let me. He's very masterful, and of course he has wonderful taste.'

She looked at him with a little affectionate smile, demurely, as though she were a girl of seventeen.

Mrs Tower went quite pale under her make-up.

'We're going to Italy for our honeymoon. Gilbert has never had a chance of studying Renaissance architecture and of course it's important for an architect to see things for himself. And we shall stop in Paris on the way and get my clothes there.'

'Do you expect to be away long?'

'Gilbert has arranged with his office to stay away for six months. It will be such a treat for him, won't it? You see, he's never had more than a fortnight's holiday before.'

'Why not?' asked Mrs Tower in a tone that no effort of will could prevent from being icy.

'He's never been able to afford it, poor dear.'

'Ah!' said Mrs Tower, and into the exclamation put volumes.

Coffee was served and the ladies went upstairs. Gilbert and I began to talk in the desultory way in which men talk who have nothing whatever to say to one another; but in two minutes a note was brought in to me by the butler. It was from Mrs Tower and ran as follows:

'Come upstairs quickly and then go as soon as you can. Take him with you. Unless I have it out with Jane at once I shall have a fit.

I told a facile lie.

'Mrs Tower has a headache and wants to go to bed. I think if you don't mind we'd better clear out.'

'Certainly,' he answered.

We went upstairs and five minutes later were on the doorstep. I called a taxi and offered the young man a lift.

'No, thanks,' he answered. 'I'll just walk to the corner and jump on a bus.'

Mrs Tower sprang to the fray as soon as she heard the front-door close behind us.

'Are you crazy, Jane?' she cried.

'Not more than most people who don't habitually live in a lunatic asylum, I trust,' Jane answered blandly.

'May I ask why you're going to marry this young man?' asked Mrs Tower with formidable politeness.

'Partly because he won't take no for an answer. He's asked me five times. I grew positively tired of refusing him.'

'And why do you think he's so anxious to marry you?'

'I amuse him.'

Mrs Tower gave an exclamation of annoyance.

'He's an unscrupulous rascal. I very nearly told him so to his face.'

'You would have been wrong, and it wouldn't have been very polite.'

'He's penniless and you're rich. You can't be such a besotted fool as not to see that he's marrying you for your money.'

Jane remained perfectly composed. She observed her sister-in-law's agitation with detachment.

'I don't think he is, you know,' she replied. 'I think he's very fond of me.'

'You're an old woman, Jane.'

'I'm the same age as you are, Marion,' she smiled.

'I've never let myself go. I'm very young for my age. No one would think I was more than forty. But even I wouldn't dream of marrying a boy twenty years younger than myself.'

'Twenty-seven,' correct Jane.

'Do you mean to tell me that you can bring yourself to believe that it's possible for a young man to care for a woman old enough to be his mother?'

'I've lived very much in the country for many years. I dare say there's a great deal about human nature that I don't know. They tell me there's a man called Freud, an Austrian, I believe . . . '

But Mrs Tower interrupted her without any politeness at all.

'Don't be ridiculous, Jane. It's so undignified. It's so ungraceful. I always thought you were a sensible woman. Really you're the last person I should ever have thought likely to fall in love with a boy.'

'But I'm not in love with him. I've told him that. Of course I like him very much or I wouldn't think of marrying him. I thought it only fair to tell him quite plainly what my feelings were towards him.'

Mrs Tower gasped. The blood rushed to her head and her breathing oppressed her. She had no fan, but she seized the evening paper and vigorously fanned herself with it.

'If you're not in love with him why do you want to marry him?'

'I've been a widow a very long time and I've led a very quiet life. I thought I'd like a change.'

'If you want to marry just to be married why don't you marry a man of your own age?'

'No man of my own age has asked me five times. In fact no man of my own age has asked me at all.'

Jane chuckled as she answered. It drove Mrs Tower to the final pitch of frenzy.

'Don't laugh, Jane. I won't have it. I don't think you can be right in your mind. It's dreadful.'

It was altogether too much for her and she burst into tears. She knew that at her age it was fatal to cry, her eyes would be swollen for twenty-four hours and she would look a sight. But there was no help for it. She wept. Jane remained perfectly calm. She looked at Marion through her large spectacles and reflectively smoothed the lap of her black silk dress.

'You're going to be so dreadfully unhappy,' Mrs Tower sobbed, dabbing her eyes cautiously in the hope that the black on her lashes would not smudge.

'I don't think so, you know,' Jane answered in those equable, mild tones of hers, as if there were a little smile behind the words. 'We've talked it over very thoroughly. I always think I'm a very easy person to live with. I think I shall make Gilbert very happy and comfortable. He's never had anyone to look after him properly. We're only marrying after mature consideration. And we've decided that if either of us wants his liberty the other will place no obstacles in the way of his getting it.'

Mrs Tower had by now recovered herself sufficiently to make a cutting remark.

'How much has he persuaded you to settle on him?'

'I wanted to settle a thousand a year on him, but he wouldn't hear of it. He was quite upset when I made the suggestion. He says he can earn quite enough for his own needs.'

'He's more cunning than I thought,' said Mrs Tower acidly.

Jane paused a little and looked at her sister-in-law with kindly but resolute eyes.

'You see, my dear, it's different for you,' she said. 'You've never been so very much a widow, have you?'

Mrs Tower looked at her. She blushed a little. She even felt slightly uncomfortable. But of course Jane was much too simple to intend an innuendo. Mrs Tower gathered herself together with dignity.

'I'm so upset that I really must go to bed ' she said. 'We'll resume the conversation tomorrow morning.'

'I'm afraid that won't be very convenient, dear. Gilbert and I are going to get the licence tomorrow morning.'

Mrs Tower threw up her hands in a gesture of dismay, but she found nothing more to say.

The marriage took place at a registrar's office. Mrs Tower and I were the witnesses. Gilbert in a smart blue suit looked absurdly young and he was obviously nervous. It is a trying moment for any man. But Jane kept her admirable composure. She might have been in the habit of marrying as frequently as a woman of fashion. Only a slight colour on her cheeks suggested that beneath her calm was some faint excitement. It is a thrilling moment for any woman. She wore a very full dress of silvery grey velvet in the cut of which I recognized the hand of the dressmaker in Liverpool (evidently a widow of unimpeachable character) who had made her gowns for so many years; but she had so far succumbed to the frivolity of the occasion as to wear a large picture hat covered with blue ostrich feathers. Her gold-rimmed spectacles made it extraordinarily grotesque. When the ceremony was over the registrar (somewhat taken aback, I thought, by the difference of age between the pair he was marrying) shook hands with her, tendering his strictly official congratulations; and the bridegroom, blushing slightly, kissed her. Mrs Tower, resigned but implacable, kissed her; and then the bride looked at me expectantly. It was evidently fitting that I should kiss her too. I did. I confess that I felt a little shy as we walked out of the registrar's office past loungers who waited cynically to see the bridal pairs, and it was with relief that I stepped into Mrs Tower's car. We drove to Victoria Station, for the happy couple were to go over to Paris by the two o'clock train, and Jane had insisted that the wedding-breakfast should be eaten at the station restaurant. She said it always made her nervous not to be on the platform in good time. Mrs Tower, present only from a strong sense of family duty, was able to do little to make the party go off well; she ate nothing (for which I could not blame her, since the food was execrable, and anyway I hate champagne at luncheon) and talked in a strained voice. But Jane went through the menu conscientiously.

'I always think one should make a hearty meal before starting out on a journey,' she said.

We saw them off, and I drove Mrs Tower back to her house.

'How long do you give it?' she said. 'Six months?'

'Let's hope for the best,' I smiled.

'Don't be so absurd. There can be no "best". You don't think he's marrying her for anything but her money, do you? Of course it can't last. My only hope is that she won't have to go through as much suffering as she deserves.'

I laughed. The charitable words were spoken in such a tone as to leave me in small doubt of Mrs Tower's meaning.

'Well, if it doesn't last you'll have the consolation of saying: "I told you so",' I said.

'I promise you I'll never do that.'

'Then you'll have the satisfaction of congratulating yourself on your self-control in not saying: "I told you so".'

'She's old and dowdy and dull.'

'Are you sure she's dull?' I said. 'It's true she doesn't say very much, but when she says anything it's very much to the point.'

'I've never heard her make a joke in my life.'

I was once more in the Far East when Gilbert and Jane returned from their honeymoon and this time I remained away for nearly two years. Mrs Tower was a bad correspondent and though I sent her an occasional picture-postcard I received no news from her. But I met her within a week of my return to London; I was dining out and found that I was seated next to her. It was an immense party, I think we were four-and-twenty, like the blackbirds in the pie, and, arriving somewhat late, I was too confused by the crowd in which I found myself to notice who was there. But when we sat down, looking round the long table I saw that a good many of my fellow-guests were well known to the public from their photographs in the illustrated papers. Our hostess had a weakness for the persons technically known as celebrities and this was an unusually brilliant gathering. When Mrs Tower and I had exchanged the conventional remarks that two people make when they have not seen one another for a couple of years I asked about Jane.

'She's very well,' said Mrs Tower with a certain dryness.

'How has the marriage turned out?'

Mrs Tower paused a little and took a salted almond from the dish in front of her.

'It appears to be quite a success.'

'You were wrong then?'

'I said it wouldn't last and I still say it won't last. It's contrary to human nature.'

'Is she happy?'

'They're both happy.'

'I suppose you don't see very much of them.'

'At first I saw quite a lot of them. But now...' Mrs Tower pursed her lips a little. 'Jane is becoming very grand.'

'What *do* you mean?' I laughed.

'I think I should tell you that she's here tonight.'

'Here?'

I was startled. I looked round the table again. Our hostess was a delightful and an entertaining woman, but I could not imagine that she would be likely to invite to a dinner such as this the elderly and dowdy wife of an obscure architect. Mrs Tower saw my perplexity and was shrewd enough to see what was in my mind. She smiled thinly.

'Look on the left of our host.'

I looked. Oddly enough the woman who sat there had by her fantastic appearance attracted my attention the moment I was ushered into the crowded drawing-room. I thought I noticed a gleam of recognition in her eye, but to the best of my belief I had never seen her before. She was not a young woman, for her hair was iron-grey; it was cut very short and clustered thickly round her well-shaped head in tight curls. She made no attempt at youth, for she was conspicuous in that gathering by using neither lipstick, rouge, nor powder. Her face, not a particularly handsome one, was red and weather-beaten; but because it owed nothing to artifice had a naturalness that was very pleasing. It contrasted oddly with the whiteness of her shoulders. They were really magnificent. A woman of thirty might have been proud of them. But her dress was extraordinary. I had not often seen anything more audacious. It was cut very low, with short skirts, which were then the fashion, in black and yellow; it had almost the effect of fancy-dress and yet so became her that though on anyone else it would have been outrageous, on her it had the inevitable simplicity of nature. And to complete the impression of an eccentricity in which there was no pose and of an extravagance in which there was no ostentation she wore, attached by a broad black ribbon, a single eyeglass.

'You're not going to tell me *that* is your sister-in-law,' I gasped.

'That is Jane Napier,' said Mrs Tower icily.

At that moment she was speaking. Her host was turned towards her with an anticipatory smile. A baldish white-haired man, with a sharp, intelligent face, who sat on her left, was leaning forward eagerly, and the couple who sat opposite, ceasing to talk with one another, listened intently. She said her say and they all, with a sudden movement, threw themselves back in their chairs and burst into vociferous laughter. From the other side of the table a man addressed Mrs Tower: I recognized a famous statesman.

'Your sister-in-law has made another joke, Mrs Tower,' he said.

Mrs Tower smiled.

'She's priceless, isn't she?'

'Let me have a long drink of champagne and then for heaven's sake tell me all about it,' I said.

Well, this is how I gathered it had all happened. At the beginning of their honeymoon Gilbert took Jane to various dress-makers in Paris and he made no objection to her choosing a number of 'gowns' after her own heart; but he persuaded her to have a 'frock' or two made according to his own design. It appeared that he had a knack for that kind of work. He engaged a smart French maid. Jane had never had such a thing before. She did her own mending and when she wanted 'doing up' was in the habit of ringing for the housemaid. The dresses Gilbert had devised were very different from anything she had worn before; but he had been careful not to go too far too quickly, and because it pleased him she persuaded herself, though not without mis-givings, to wear them in preference to those she had chosen her-self. Of course she could not wear them with the voluminous petticoats she had been in the habit of using, and these, though it cost her an anxious moment, she discarded.

'Now if you please,' said Mrs Tower, with something very like a sniff of disapproval, 'she wears nothing but thin silk tights. It's a wonder to me she doesn't catch her death of cold at her age.'

Gilbert and the French maid taught her how to wear her clothes, and, unexpectedly enough, she was very quick at learning. The French maid was in raptures over Madame's arms and shoulders. It was a scandal not to show anything so fine.

'Wait a little, Alphonsine,' said Gilbert. 'The next lot of clothes I design for Madame we'll make the most of her.'

The spectacles of course were dreadful. No one could look really well in gold-rimmed spectacles. Gilbert tried some with tortoiseshell rims. He shook his head.

'They'd look all right on a girl,' he said. 'You're too old to wear spectacles, Jane.' Suddenly he had an inspiration. 'By George, I've got it. You must wear an eyeglass.'

'Oh, Gilbert, I couldn't.'

She looked at him and his excitement, the excitement of the artist, made her smile. He was so sweet to her she wanted to do what she could to please him.

'I'll try,' she said.

When they went to an optician and, suited with the right size, she placed an eyeglass jauntily in her eye Gilbert clapped his hands. There and then, before the astonished shopman, he kissed her on both cheeks.

'You look wonderful,' he cried.

So they went down to Italy and spent happy months studying Renaissance and Baroque architecture. Jane not only grew accustomed to her changed appearance, but found she liked it.

At first she was a little shy when she went into the dining-room of an hotel and people turned round to stare at her, no one had ever raised an eyelid to look at her before, but presently she found that the sensation was not disagreeable. Ladies came up to her and asked her where she got her dress.

'Do you like it?' she answered demurely. 'My husband designed it for me.'

'I should like to copy it if you don't mind.'

Jane had certainly for many years lived a very quiet life, but she was by no means lacking in the normal instincts of her sex. She had her answer ready.

'I'm so sorry, but my husband's very particular and he won't hear of anyone copying my frocks. He wants me to be unique.'

She had an idea that people would laugh when she said this, but they didn't; they merely answered:

'Oh, of course I quite understand. You *are* unique.'

But she saw them making mental notes of what she wore, and for some reason this quite 'put her about'. For once in her life that she wasn't wearing what everybody else did, she reflected, she didn't see why everybody else should want to wear what she did.

'Gilbert,' said she, quite sharply for her, 'next time you're designing dresses for me I wish you'd design things that people *can't* copy.'

'The only way to do that is to design things that only you can wear.'

'Can't you do that?'

'Yes, if you'll do something for me.'

'What is it?'

'Cut off your hair.'

I think this was the first time that Jane jibbed. Her hair was long and thick and as a girl she had been quite vain of it; to cut it off was a very drastic proceeding. This really was burning her boats behind her. In her case it was not the first step that cost so much, it was the last; but she took it ('I know Marion will think me a perfect fool, and I shall *never* be able to go to Liverpool again,' she said), and when they passed through Paris on their way home Gilbert led her (she felt quite sick, her heart was beating so fast) to the best hairdresser in the world. She came out of his shop with a jaunty, saucy, impudent head of crisp grey curls. Pygmalion had finished his fantastic masterpiece: Galatea was come to life.

'Yes,' I said, 'but that isn't enough to explain why Jane is here tonight amid this crowd of duchesses, Cabinet Ministers, and suchlike; nor why she is sitting on one side of her host with an Admiral of the Fleet on the other.'

'Jane is a humorist,' said Mrs Tower. 'Didn't you see them all laughing at what she said?'

There was no doubt now of the bitterness in Mrs Tower's heart.

'When Jane wrote and told me they were back from their honeymoon I thought I must ask them both to dinner. I didn't much like the idea, but I felt it had to be done. I knew the party would be deadly and I wasn't going to sacrifice any of the people who really mattered. On the other hand I didn't want Jane to think I hadn't any nice friends. You know I never have more than eight, but on this occasion I thought it would make things go better if I had twelve. I'd been too busy to see Jane until the evening of the party. She kept us all waiting a little – that was Gilbert's cleverness – and at last she sailed in. You could have knocked me down with a feather. She made the rest of the women look dowdy and provincial. She made me feel like a painted old trollop.'

Mrs Tower drank a little champagne.

'I wish I could describe the frock to you. It would have been quite impossible on anyone else; on her it was perfect. And the eyeglass! I'd known her for thirty-five years and I'd never seen her without spectacles.'

'But you knew she had a good figure.'

'How should I? I'd never seen her except in the clothes you first saw her in. Did *you* think she had a good figure? She seemed not to be unconscious of the sensation she made but to take it as a matter of course. I thought of my dinner and I heaved a sigh of relief. Even if she was a little heavy in hand, with that appearance it didn't so very much matter. She was sitting at the other end of the table and I heard a good deal of laughter. I was glad to think that the other people were playing up well; but after dinner I was a good deal taken aback when no less than three men came up to me and told me that my sister-in-law was priceless, and did I think she would allow them to call on her? I didn't quite know whether I was standing on my head or my heels. Twenty-four hours later our hostess of tonight rang me up and said she had heard my sister-in-law was in London and she was priceless and would I ask her to luncheon to meet her? She has an infallible instinct, that woman: in a month everyone was talking about Jane. I am here tonight, not because I've known our hostess for twenty years and have asked her to dinner a hundred times, but because I'm Jane's sister-in-law.'

Poor Mrs Tower. The position was galling, and though I could not help being amused, for the tables were turned on her with a vengeance, I felt that she deserved my sympathy.

'People never can resist those who make them laugh,' I said, trying to console her.

'She never makes *me* laugh.'

Once more from the top of the table I heard a guffaw and guessed that Jane had said another amusing thing.

'Do you mean to say that you are the only person who doesn't think her funny?' I asked, smiling.

'Had it struck *you* that she was a humorist?'

'I'm bound to say it hadn't.'

'She says just the same things as she's said for the last thirty-five years. I laugh when I see everyone else does because I don't want to seem a perfect fool, but I am not amused.'

'Like Queen Victoria,' I said.

It was a foolish jest and Mrs Tower was quite right sharply to tell me so. I tried another tack.

'Is Gilbert here?' I asked, looking down the table.

'Gilbert was asked because she won't go out without him, but tonight he's at a dinner of the Architects' Institute or whatever it's called.'

'I'm dying to renew my acquaintance with her.'

'Go and talk to her after dinner. She'll ask you to her Tuesdays.'

'Her Tuesdays?'

'She's at home every Tuesday evening. You'll meet there everyone you ever heard of. They're the best parties in London. She's done in one year what I've failed to do in twenty.'

'But what you tell me is really miraculous. How has it been done?'

Mrs Tower shrugged her handsome but adipose shoulders.

'I shall be glad if you'll tell me,' she replied.

After dinner I tried to make my way to the sofa on which Jane was sitting, but I was intercepted and it was not till a little later that my hostess came up to me and said:

'I must introduce you to the star of my party. Do you know Jane Napier? She's priceless. She's much more amusing than your comedies.'

I was taken up to the sofa. The admiral who had been sitting beside her at dinner was with her still. He showed no sign of moving and Jane, shaking hands with me, introduced me to him.

'Do you know Sir Reginald Frobisher?'

We began to chat. It was the same Jane as I had known before, perfectly simple, homely and unaffected, but her fantastic appearance certainly gave a peculiar savour to what she said. Suddenly I found myself shaking with laughter. She had made a remark, sensible and to the point, but not in the least witty, which her manner of saying and the bland look she gave me through her eyeglass made perfectly irresistible. I felt light-hearted and buoyant. When I left her she said to me:

'If you've got nothing better to do, come and see us on Tuesday evening. Gilbert will be so glad to see you.'

'When he's been a month in London he'll know that he *can* have nothing better to do,' said the admiral.

So, on Tuesday but rather late, I went to Jane's. I confess I was a little surprised at the company. It was a quite a remarkable collection of writers, painters and politicians, actors, great ladies and great beauties: Mrs Tower was right, it was a grand party; I had seen nothing like it in London since Stafford House was sold. No particular entertainment was provided. The refreshments were adequate without being luxurious. Jane in her quiet way seemed to be enjoying herself; I could not see that she took a great deal of trouble with her guests, but they seemed to like being there and the gay, pleasant party did not break up till two in the morning. After that I saw much of her. I not only went often to her house, but seldom went out to luncheon or to dinner without meeting her. I am an amateur of humour and I sought to discover in what lay her peculiar gift. It was impossible to repeat anything she said, for the fun, like certain wines, would not travel. She had no gift for epigram. She never made a brilliant repartee. There was no malice in her remarks nor sting in her rejoinders. There are those who think that impropriety, rather than brevity, is the soul of wit; but she never said a thing that could have brought a blush to a Victorian cheek. I think her humour was unconscious and I am sure it was unpremeditated. It flew like a butterfly from flower to flower, obedient only to its own caprice and pursuivant of neither method nor intention. It depended on the way she spoke and on the way she looked. Its subtlety gained by the flaunting and extravagant appearance that Gilbert had achieved for her; but her appearance was only an element in it. Now of course she was the fashion and people laughed if she but opened her mouth. They no longer wondered that Gilbert had married a wife so much older than himself. They saw that Jane was a woman with whom age did not count. They thought him a devilish lucky young fellow. The admiral quoted Shakespeare to me: 'Age cannot wither her, nor custom stale her infinite variety.' Gilbert was delighted with her success. As I came to know him better I grew to like him. It was quite evident that he was neither a rascal nor a fortune-hunter. He was not only immensely proud of Jane but genuinely devoted to her. His kindness to her was touching. He was a very unselfish and sweet-tempered young man.

'Well, what do you think of Jane now?' he said to me once, with boyish triumph.

'I don't know which of you is more wonderful,' I said. 'You or she.'

'Oh, I'm nothing.'

'Nonsense. You don't think I'm such a fool as not to see that it's you, and you only, who've made Jane what she is.'

'My only merit is that I saw what was there when it wasn't obvious to the naked eye,' he answered.

'I can understand your seeing that she had in her the possibility of that remarkable appearance, but how in the world have you made her into a humorist?'

'But I always thought the things she said a perfect scream. She was always a humorist.'

'You're the only person who ever thought so.'

Mrs Tower, not without magnanimity, acknowledged that she had been mistaken in Gilbert. She grew quite attached to him. But notwithstanding appearances she never faltered in her opinion that the marriage could not last. I was obliged to laugh at her.

'Why, I've never seen such a devoted couple,' I said.

'Gilbert is twenty-seven now. It's just the time for a pretty girl to come along. Did you notice the other evening at Jane's that pretty little neice of Sir Reginald's? I thought Jane was looking at them both with a good deal of attention, and I wondered to myself.'

'I don't believe Jane fears the rivalry of any girl under the sun.'

'Wait and see,' said Mrs Tower.

'You gave it six months.'

'Well, now I give it three years.'

When anyone is very positive in an opinion it is only human nature to wish him proved wrong. Mrs Tower was really too cocksure. But such a satisfaction was not mine, for the end that she had always and confidently predicted to the ill-assorted match did in point of fact come. Still, the fates seldom give us what we want in the way we want it, and though Mrs Tower could flatter herself that she had been right, I think after all she would sooner have been wrong. For things did not happen at all in the way she expected.

One day I received an urgent message from her and fortunately went to see her at once. When I was shown into the room Mrs Tower rose from her chair and came towards me with the stealthy swiftness of a leopard stalking his prey. I saw that she was excited.

'Jane and Gilbert have separated,' she said.

'Not really? Well, you were right after all.'

Mrs Tower looked at me with an expression I could not understand.

'Poor Jane,' I muttered.

'Poor Jane!' she repeated, but in tones of such derision that I was dumbfounded.

She found some difficulty in telling me exactly what had occurred.

Gilbert had left her a moment before she leaped to the telephone to summon me. When he entered the room, pale and distraught, she saw at once that something terrible had happened. She knew what he was going to say before he said it.

'Marion, Jane has left me.'

She gave him a little smile and took his hand.

'I knew you'd behave like a gentleman. It would have been dreadful for her for people to think that *you* had left her.'

'I've come to you because I knew I could count on your sympathy.'

'Oh, I don't blame you, Gilbert,' said Mrs Tower, very kindly. 'It was bound to happen.'

He sighed.

'I suppose so. I couldn't hope to keep her always. She was too wonderful and I'm a perfectly commonplace fellow.'

Mrs Tower patted his hand. He was really behaving beautifully.

'And what's going to happen now?'

'Well, she's going to divorce me.'

'Jane always said she'd put no obstacle in your way if ever you wanted to marry a girl.'

'You don't think it's likely I should ever be willing to marry anyone else after being Jane's husband,' he answered.

Mrs Tower was puzzled.

'Of course you mean that *you*'ve left Jane.'

'I? That's the last thing I should ever do.'

'Then why is she divorcing you?'

'She's going to marry Sir Reginald Frobisher as soon as the decree is made absolute.'

Mrs Tower positively screamed. Then she felt so faint that she had to get her smelling salts.

'After all you've done for her?'

'I've done nothing for her.'

'Do you mean to say you're going to allow yourself to be made use of like that?'

'We arranged before we married that if either of us wanted his liberty the other should put no hindrance in the way.'

'But that was done on your account. Because you were twenty-seven years younger than she was.'

'Well, it's come in very useful for her,' he answered bitterly.

Mrs Tower expostulated, argued, and reasoned; but Gilbert insisted that no rules applied to Jane, and he must do exactly what she wanted. He left Mrs Tower prostrate. It relieved her a good deal to give me a full account of this interview. It pleased her to see that I was as surprised as herself and if I was not so indignant with Jane as she was she ascribed that to the criminal lack of morality incident to my sex. She was still in a state of extreme agitation when the door was opened and the butler showed in – Jane herself. She was dressed in black and white as no doubt befitted her slightly ambiguous position, but in a dress so original and fantastic, in a hat so striking, that I positively gasped at the sight of her. But she was as ever bland and collected. She came forward to kiss Mrs Tower, but Mrs Tower withdrew herself with icy dignity.

'Gilbert has been here,' she said.

'Yes, I know,' smiled Jane. 'I told him to come and see you. I'm going to Paris tonight and I want you to be very kind to him while I'm away. I'm afraid just at first he'll be rather lonely and I shall feel more comfortable if I can count on your keeping an eye on him.'

Mrs Tower clasped her hands.

'Gilbert has just told me something that I can hardly bring myself to believe. He tells me that you're going to divorce him to marry Reginald Frobisher.'

'Don't you remember, before I married Gilbert you advised me to marry a man of my own age? The admiral is fifty-three.'

'But, Jane, you owe everything to Gilbert,' said Mrs Tower indignantly. 'You wouldn't exist without him. Without him to design your clothes, you'll be nothing.'

'Oh, he's promised to go on designing my clothes,' Jane answered blandly.

'No woman could want a better husband. He's always been kindness itself to you.'

'Oh, I know he's been sweet.'

'How *can* you be so heartless?'

'But I was never in love with Gilbert,' said Jane. 'I always told him that. I'm beginning to feel the need of the companionship of a man of my own age. I think I've probably been married to Gilbert long enough. The young have no conversation.' She paused a little and gave us both a charming smile. 'Of course I shan't lose sight of Gilbert. I've arranged that with Reginald. The admiral has a niece that would just suit him. As soon as we're married we'll ask them to stay with us at Malta – you know that the admiral is to have the Mediterranean Command – and I shouldn't be at all surprised if they fell in love with one another.'

Mrs Tower gave a little sniff.

'And have you arranged with the admiral that if you want your liberty neither should put any hindrance in the way of the other?'

'I suggested it,' Jane answered with composure. 'But the admiral says he knows a good thing when he sees it and he won't want to marry anyone else, and if anyone wants to marry me – he has eight twelve-inch guns on his flagship and he'll discuss the matter at short range.' She gave us a look through her eyeglass which even the fear of Mrs Tower's wrath could not prevent me from laughing at. 'I think the admiral's a very passionate man.'

Mrs Tower gave me an angry frown.

'I never thought you funny, Jane,' she said. 'I never understood why people laughed at the things you said.'

'I never thought I was funny myself, Marion,' smiled Jane, showing her bright, regular teeth. 'I am glad to leave London before too many people come round to our opinion.'

'I wish you'd tell me the secret of your astonishing success,' I said.

She turned to me with that bland, homely look I knew so well.

'You know, when I married Gilbert and settled in London and people began to laugh at what I said no one was more surprised than I was. I'd said the same things for thirty years and no one ever saw anything to laugh at. I thought it must be my clothes or my bobbed hair or my eyeglass. Then I discovered it was because I spoke the truth. It was so unusual that people thought it humorous. One of these days someone else will discover the secret and when people habitually tell the truth of course there'll be nothing funny in it.'

'And why am I the only person not to think it funny?' asked Mrs Tower.

Jane hesitated a little as though she were honestly searching for a satisfactory explanation.

'Perhaps you don't know the truth when you see it, Marion dear,' she answered in her mild good-natured way.

It certainly gave her the last word. I felt that Jane would always have the last word. She *was* priceless.

FOOTPRINTS IN THE JUNGLE

THERE is no place in Malaya that has more charm than Tanah Merah. It lies on the sea, and the sandy shore is fringed with casuarinas. The government offices are still in the old Raad Huis that the Dutch built when they owned the land, and on the hill stand the grey ruins of the fort by aid of which the Portuguese maintained their hold over the unruly natives. Tanah Merah has a history and in the vast labyrinthine houses of the Chinese merchants, backing on the sea so that in the cool of the evening they may sit in their loggias and enjoy the salt breeze, families dwell that have been settled in the country for three centuries. Many have forgotten their native language and hold intercourse with one another in Malay and pidgin English. The imagination lingers here gratefully, for in the Federated Malay States the only past is within the memory for the most part of the fathers of living men.

Tanah Merah was for long the busiest mart of the Middle East and its harbour was crowded with shipping when the clipper and the junk still sailed the China seas. But now it is dead. It has the sad and romantic air of all places that have once been of importance and live now on the recollection of a vanished grandeur. It is a sleepy little town and strangers that come to it, losing their native energy, insensibly drop into its easy and lethargic ways. Successive rubber booms bring it no prosperity and the ensuing slumps hasten its decay.

The European quarter is very silent. It is trim and neat and clean. The houses of the white men – government servants and agents of companies – stand round an immense padang, agreeable and roomy bungalows shaded by great cassias, and the padang is vast and green and well cared for, like the lawn of a cathedral close, and indeed there is in the aspect of this corner of Tanah Merah something quiet and delicately secluded that reminds you of the precincts of Canterbury.

The club faces the sea; it is a spacious but shabby building; it has an air of neglect and when you enter you feel that you intrude. It gives you the impression that it is closed really, for alterations and repairs, and that you have taken indiscreet advantage of an open door to go where you are not wanted. In the morning you may find there a couple of planters who have come in from their estates on business and are drinking a gin-sling before starting back again; and latish in the afternoon a lady or two may perhaps be seen looking with a furtive air through old numbers of the *Illustrated London News*. At nightfall a few men saunter in and sit about the billiard-room watching the play and drinking sukas. But on Wednesdays there is a little more animation. On that day the gramophone is set going in the large room upstairs and people come in from the surrounding country to dance. There are sometimes no less than a dozen couples and it is even possible to make up two tables of bridge.

It was on one of these occasions that I met the Cartwrights. I was staying with a man called Gaze who was head of the police and he came into the billiard-room, where I was sitting, and asked me if I would make up a four. The Cartwrights were planters and they came in to Tanah Merah on Wednesdays because it gave their girl a chance of a little fun. They were very nice people, said Gaze, quiet and unobtrusive, and played a very pleasant game of bridge. I followed Gaze into the card-room and was introduced to them. They were already seated at a table and Mrs Cartwright was shuffling the cards. It inspired me with confidence to see the competent way in which she did it. She took half the pack in each hand, and her hands were large and strong, deftly inserted the corners of one half under the corners of the other, and with a click and a neat bold gesture cascaded the cards together.

It had all the effect of a conjuring trick. The card-player knows that it can be done perfectly only after incessant practice. He can be fairly sure that anyone who can so shuffle a pack of cards loves cards for their own sake.

'Do you mind if my husband and I play together?' asked Mrs Cartwright. 'It's no fun for us to win one another's money.'

'Of course not.'

We cut for deal and Gaze and I sat down.

Mrs Cartwright drew an ace and while she dealt, quickly and neatly, chatted with Gaze of local affairs. But I was aware that she took stock of me. She looked shrewd, but good-natured.

She was a woman somewhere in the fifties (though in the East, where people age quickly, it is difficult to tell their ages), with white hair very untidily arranged, and a constant gesture with her was an impatient movement of the hand to push back a long wisp of hair that kept falling over her forehead. You wondered why she did not, by the use of a hairpin or two, save herself so much trouble. Her blue eyes were large, but pale and a little tired; her face was lined and sallow; I think it was her mouth that gave it the expression which I felt was characteristic of caustic but tolerant irony. You saw that here was a woman who knew her mind and was never afraid to speak it. She was a chatty player (which some people object to strongly, but which does not disconcert me, for I do not see why you should behave at the card-table as though you were at a memorial service) and it was soon apparent that she had an effective knack of badinage. It was pleasantly acid, but it was amusing enough to be offensive only to a fool. If now and then she uttered a remark so sarcastic that you wanted all your sense of humour to see the fun in it, you could not but quickly see that she was willing to take as much as she gave. Her large, thin mouth broke into a dry smile and her eyes shone brightly when by a lucky chance you brought off a repartee that turned the laugh against her.

I thought her a very agreeable person. I liked her frankness. I liked her quick wit. I liked her plain face. I never met a woman who obviously cared so little how she looked. It was not only her head that was untidy, everything about her was slovenly; she wore a high-necked silk blouse, but for coolness had unbuttoned the top buttons and showed a gaunt and withered neck; the blouse was crumpled and none too clean, for she smoked innumerable cigarettes and covered herself with ash. When she got up for a moment to speak to somebody I saw that her blue skirt was rather ragged at the hem and badly needed a brush, and she wore heavy, low-heeled boots. But none of this mattered. Everything she wore was perfectly in character.

And it was a pleasure to play bridge with her. She played very quickly, without hesitation, and she had not only knowledge but flair. Of course she knew Gaze's game, but I was a stranger and she soon took my measure. The team-work between her husband and herself was admirable; he was sound and cautious, but knowing him, she was able to be bold with assurance and brilliant with safety. Gaze was a player who founded a foolish optimism on the hope that his opponents would not have the sense to take advantage of his errors, and the pair of us were no match for the Cartwrights. We lost one rubber after another, and there was nothing to do but smile and look as if we liked it.

'I don't know what's the matter with the cards,' said Gaze at last, plaintively. 'Even when we have every card in the pack we go down.'

'It can't be anything to do with your play,' answered Mrs Cartwright, looking him full in the face with those pale blue eyes of hers, 'it must be bad luck pure and simple. Now if you hadn't had your hearts mixed up with your diamonds in that last hand you'd have saved the game.'

Gaze began to explain at length how the misfortune, which had cost us dear, occurred, but Mrs Cartwright, with a deft flick of the hand, spread out the cards in a great circle so that we should cut for deal. Cartwright looked at the time.

'This will have to be the last, my dear,' he said.

'Oh, will it?' She glanced at her watch and then called to a young man who was passing through the room. 'Oh, Mr Bullen, if you're going upstairs tell Olive that we shall be going in a few minutes.' She turned to me. 'It takes us the best part of an hour to get back to the estate and poor Theo has to be up at the crack of dawn.'

'Oh, well, we only come in once a week' said Cartwright, 'and it's the one chance Olive gets of being gay and abandoned.'

I thought Cartwright looked tired and old. He was a man of middle height, with a bald, shiny head, a stubbly grey moustache, and gold-rimmed spectacles. He wore white ducks and a black-and-white tie. He was rather neat and you could see he took much more pains with his clothes than his untidy wife. He talked little, but it was plain that he enjoyed his wife's caustic humour and sometimes he made quite a neat retort. They were evidently very good friends. It was pleasing to see so solid and tolerant an affection between two people who were almost elderly and must have lived together for so many years.

It took but two hands to finish the rubber and we had just ordered a final gin and bitters when Olive came down.

'Do you really want to go already, Mumsey?' she asked.

Mrs Cartwright looked at her daughter with fond eyes.

'Yes, darling. It's nearly half past eight. It'll be ten before we get our dinner.'

'Damn our dinner,' said Olive gaily.

'Let her have one more dance before we go,' suggested Cartwright.

'Not one. You must have a good night's rest.'

Cartwright looked at Olive with a smile.

'If your mother has made up her mind, my dear, we may just as well give in without any fuss.'

'She's a determined woman,' said Olive, lovingly stroking her mother's wrinkled cheek.

Mrs Cartwright patted her daughter's hand, and kissed it.

Olive was not very pretty, but she looked extremely nice. She was nineteen or twenty, I suppose, and she had still the plumpness of her age; she would be more attractive when she had fined down a little. She had none of the determination that gave her mother's face so much character, but resembled her father; she had his dark eyes and slightly aquiline nose, and his look of rather weak good nature. It was plain that she was strong and healthy. Her cheeks were red and her eyes bright. She had a vitality that he had long since lost. She seemed to be the perfectly normal English girl, with high spirits, a great desire to enjoy herself, and an excellent temper.

When we separated, Gaze and I set out to walk to his house.

'What did you think of the Cartwrights?' he asked me.

'I liked them. They must be a great asset in a place like this.'

'I wish they came oftener. They live a very quiet life.'

'It must be dull for the girl. The father and mother seem very well satisfied with one another's company.'

'Yes, it's been a great success.'

'Olive is the image of her father, isn't she?'

Gaze gave me a sidelong glance.

'Cartwright isn't her father. Mrs Cartwright was a widow when he married her. Olive was born four months after her father's death.'

'Oh!'

I drew out the sound in order to put in it all I could of surprise, interest, and curiosity. But Gaze said nothing and we walked the rest of the way in silence. The boy was waiting at the door as we entered the house and after a last gin pahit we sat down to dinner.

At first Gaze was inclined to be talkative. Owing to the restriction of the output of rubber there had sprung up a considerable activity among the smugglers and it was part of his duty to circumvent their knavishness. Two junks had been captured that day and he was rubbing his hands over his success. The go-downs were full of confiscated rubber and in a little while it was going to be solemnly burnt. But presently he fell into silence and we finished without a word. The boys brought in coffee and brandy and we lit our cheroots. Gaze leaned back in his chair. He looked at me reflectively and then looked at his brandy. The boys had left the room and we were alone.

'I've known Mrs Cartwright for over twenty years,' he said slowly. 'She wasn't a bad-looking woman in those days. Always untidy, but when she was young it didn't seem to matter so much. It was rather attractive. She was married to a man called Bronson. Reggie Bronson. He was a planter. He was manager of an estate up in Selantan and I was stationed at Alor Lipis. It was a much smaller place than it is now; I don't suppose there were more than twenty people in the whole community, but they had a jolly little club, and we used to have a very good time. I remember the first time I met Mrs Bronson as though it was yesterday. There were no cars in those days and she and Bronson had ridden in on their bicycles. Of course then she didn't look so determined as she looks now. She was much thinner, she had a nice colour, and her eyes were very pretty – blue, you know – and she had a lot of dark hair. If she'd only taken more trouble with herself she'd have been rather stunning. As it was she was the best-looking woman there.'

I tried to construct in my mind a picture of what Mrs Cartwright – Mrs Bronson as she was then – looked like from what she was now and from Gaze's not very graphic description. In the solid woman, with her well-covered bones, who sat rather heavily at the bridge-table, I tried to see a slight young thing with buoyant movements and graceful, easy gestures. Her chin now was square and her nose decided, but the roundness of youth must have masked this: she must have been charming with a pink-and-white skin and her hair, carelessly dressed, brown and abundant. At that period she wore a long skirt, a tight waist, and a picture hat. Or did women in Malaya still wear the topees that you see in old numbers of the illustrated papers?

'I hadn't seen her for – oh, nearly twenty years,' Gaze went on. 'I knew she was living somewhere in the F.M.S., but it was a surprise when I took this job and came here to run across her in the club just as I had up in Selantan so many years before. Of course she's an elderly woman now and she's changed out of all recognition. It was rather a shock to see her with a grown-up daughter, it made me realize how the time had passed; I was a young fellow when I met her last and now, by Jingo, I'm due to retire on the age limit in two or three years. Bit thick, isn't it?'

Gaze, a rueful grin on his ugly face, looked at me with faint indignation, as though I could help the hurrying march of the years as they trod upon one another's heels.

'I'm no chicken myself,' I replied.

'You haven't lived out East all your life. It ages one before one's time. One's an elderly man at fifty and at fifty-five one's good for nothing but the scrap-heap.'

But I did not want Gaze to wander off into a disquisition on old age.

'Did you recognize Mrs Cartwright when you saw her again?' I asked.

'Well, I did and I didn't. At the first glance I thought I knew her, but couldn't quite place her. I thought perhaps she was someone I'd met on board ship when I was going on leave and had known only by sight. But the moment she spoke I remembered at once. I remembered the dry twinkle in her eyes and the crisp sound of her voice. There was something in her voice that seemed to mean: You're a bit of a damned fool, my lad, but you're not a bad sort and upon my soul I rather like you.'

'That's a good deal to read into the sound of a voice,' I smiled.

'She came up to me in the club and shook hands with me. "How do you do, Major Gaze? Do you remember me?" she said.

'"Of course I do."

'"A lot of water has passed under the bridge since we met last. We're none of us as young as we were. Have you seen Theo?"

'For a moment I couldn't think whom she meant. I suppose I looked rather stupid, because she gave a little smile, that chaffing smile that I knew so well, and explained.

'"I married Theo, you know. It seemed the best thing to do. I was lonely and he wanted it."

'"I heard you married him," I said. "I hope you've been very happy."

'"Oh, very. Theo's a perfect duck. He'll be here in a minute. He'll be so glad to see you."

'I wondered. I should have thought I was the last man Theo would wish to see. I shouldn't have thought she would wish it very much either. But women are funny.'

'Why shouldn't she wish him to see you?' I asked.

'I'm coming to that later,' said Gaze. 'Then Theo turned up. I don't know why I call him Theo; I never called him anything but Cartwright, I never thought of him as anything but Cartwright. Theo was a shock. You know what he looks like now; I remembered him as a curly-headed youngster, very fresh and clean-looking. He was always neat and dapper, he had a good figure, and he held himself well, like a man who's used to taking a lot of exercise. Now I come to think of it he wasn't bad-looking, not in a big, massive way, but graceful, you know, and lithe. When I saw this bowed, cadaverous, bald-headed old buffer with spectacles I could hardly believe my eyes. I shouldn't have known him from Adam. He seemed pleased to see me, at least, interested; he wasn't effusive, but he'd always been on the quiet side and I didn't expect him to be.

'"Are you surprised to find us here?" he asked me.

'"Well, I hadn't the faintest notion where you were."

'"We've kept track of your movements more or less. We've seen your name in the paper every now and then. You must come out one day and have a look at our place. We've been settled there a good many years, and I suppose we shall stay there till we go home for good. Have you ever been back to Alor Lipis?"

'"No, I haven't," I said.

'"It was a nice little place. I'm told it's grown. I've never been back."

'"It hasn't got the pleasantest recollections for us," said Mrs Cartwright.

'I asked them if they'd have a drink and we called the boy. I dare say you noticed that Mrs Cartwright likes her liquor; I don't mean that she gets tight or anything like that, but she drinks her stengah like a man. I couldn't help looking at them with a certain amount of curiosity. They seemed perfectly happy; I gathered that they hadn't done at all badly, and I found out later that they were quite well off. They had a very nice car, and when they went on leave they denied themselves nothing. They were on the best of terms with one another. You know how jolly it is to see two people who've been married a great many years obviously better pleased with their own company than anyone else's. Their marriage had evidently been a great success. And they were both of them devoted to Olive and very proud of her, Theo especially.'

'Although she was only his step-daughter?' I said.

'Although she was only his step-daughter,' answered Gaze. 'You'd think that she would have taken his name. But she hadn't. She called him Daddy, of course, he was the only father she'd ever known, but she signed her letters, Olive Bronson.'

'What was Bronson like, by the way?'

'Bronson? He was a great big fellow, very hearty, with a loud voice and a bellowing laugh, beefy, you know, and a fine athlete. There was not very much to him, but he was as straight as a die. He had a red face and red hair. Now I come to think of it I remember that I never saw a man sweat as much as he did. Water just poured off him, and when he played tennis he always used to bring a towel on the court with him.'

'It doesn't sound very attractive.'

'He was a handsome chap. He was always fit. He was keen on that. He hadn't much to talk about but rubber and games, tennis, you know, and golf and shooting; and I don't suppose he read a book from year's end to year's end. He was the typical public-school boy. He was about thirty-five when I first knew him, but he had the mind of a boy of eighteen. You know how many fellows when they come out East seem to stop growing.'

I did indeed. One of the most disconcerting things to the traveller is to see stout, middle-aged gentlemen, with bald heads, speaking and acting like schoolboys. You might almost think that no idea has entered their heads since they first passed through the Suez Canal. Though married and the fathers of children, and perhaps in control of a large business, they continue to look upon life from the standpoint of the sixth form.

'But he was no fool,' Gaze went on. 'He knew his work from A to Z. His estate was one of the best managed in the country and he knew how to handle his labour. He was a damned good sort, and if he did get on your nerves a little you couldn't help liking him. He was generous with his money, and always ready to do anybody a good turn. That's how Cartwright happened to turn up in the first instance.'

'Did the Bronsons get on well together?'

'Oh, yes, I think so. I'm sure they did. He was good-natured and she was very jolly and gay. She was very outspoken, you know. She can be damned amusing when she likes even now, but there's generally a sting lurking in the joke; when she was a young woman and married to Bronson it was just pure fun. She had high spirits and liked having a good time. She never cared a hang what she said, but it went with her type, if you understand what I mean; there was something so open and frank and careless about her that you didn't care what she said to you. They seemed very happy.

'Their estate was about five miles from Alor Lipis. They had a trap and they used to drive in most evenings about five. Of course it was a very small community and men were in the majority. There were only about six women. The Bronsons were a god-send. They bucked things up the moment they arrived. We used to have very jolly times in that little club. I've often thought of them since and I don't know that on the whole I've ever enjoyed myself more than I did when I was stationed there. Between six and eight-thirty the club at Alor Lipis twenty years ago was about as lively a place as you could find between Aden and Yokohama.

'One day Mrs Bronson told us that they were expecting a friend to stay with them and a few days later they brought Cartwright along. It appeared that he was an old friend of Bronson's, they'd been at school together, Marlborough, or some place like that, and they'd first come out East on the same ship. Rubber had taken a toss and a lot of fellows had lost their jobs. Cartwright was one of them. He'd been out of work for the greater part of a year and he hadn't anything to fall back on. In those days planters were even worse paid than they are now and a man had to be very lucky to put by something for a rainy day. Cartwright had gone to Singapore. They all go there when there's a slump, you know. It's awful then, I've seen it; I've known of planters sleeping in the street because they hadn't the price of a night's lodging. I've known them stop strangers outside the Europe and ask for a dollar to get a meal, and I think Cartwright had had a pretty rotten time.

'At last he wrote to Bronson and asked him if he couldn't do something for him. Bronson asked him to come and stay till things got better, at least it would be free board and lodging, and Cartwright jumped at the chance, but Bronson had to send him the money to pay his railway fare. When Cartwright arrived at Alor Lipis he hadn't ten cents in his pocket. Bronson had a little money of his own, two or three hundred a year, I think, and though his salary had been cut, he'd kept his job, so that he was better off than most planters. When Cartwright came Mrs Bronson told him that he was to look upon the place as his home and stay as long as he liked.'

'It was very nice of her, wasn't it?' I remarked.

'Very.'

Gaze lit himself another cheroot and filled his glass. It was very still and but for the occasional croak of the chik-chak the silence was intense. We seemed to be alone in the tropical night and heaven only knows how far from the habitations of men. Gaze did not speak for so long that at last I was forced to say something.

'What sort of a man was Cartwright at that time?' I asked. 'Younger, of course, and you told me rather nice-looking; but in himself?'

'Well, to tell you the truth, I never paid much attention to him. He was pleasant and unassuming. He's very quiet now, as I dare say you noticed; well, he wasn't exactly lively then. But he was perfectly inoffensive. He was fond of reading and he played the piano rather nicely. You never minded having him about, he was never in the way, but you never bothered very much about him. He danced well and the women rather liked that, but he also played billiards quite decently and he wasn't bad at tennis. He fell into our little groove very naturally. I wouldn't say that he ever became wildly popular, but everyone liked him. Of course we were sorry for him, as one is for a man who's down and out, but there was nothing we could do, and, well, we just accepted him and then forgot that he hadn't always been there. He used to come in with the Bronsons every evening and pay for his drinks like everyone else, I suppose Bronson had lent him a bit of money for current expenses, and he was always very civil. I'm rather vague about him, because really he didn't make any particular impression on me; in the East one meets such a lot of people, and he seemed very much like anybody else. He did everything he could to get something to do, but he had no luck; the fact is, there were no jobs going, and sometimes he seemed rather depressed about it. He was with the Bronsons for over a year. I remember his saying to me once:

'"After all I can't live with them for ever. They've been most awfully good to me, but there are limits."

'"I should think the Bronsons would be very glad to have you," I said. "It's not particularly gay on a rubber estate, and as far as your food and drink go, it must make precious little difference if you're there or not."'

Gaze stopped once more and looked at me with a sort of hesitation.

'What's the matter?' I asked.

'I'm afraid I'm telling you this story very badly,' he said. 'I seem to be just rambling on. I'm not a damned novelist, I'm a policeman, and I'm just telling you the facts as I saw them at the time; and from my point of view all the circumstances are important; it's important, I mean, to realize what sort of people they were.'

'Of course. Fire away.'

'I remember someone, a woman, I think it was, the doctor's wife, asking Mrs Bronson if she didn't get tired sometimes of having a stranger in the house. You know, in places like Alor Lipis there isn't very much to talk about, and if you didn't talk about your neighbours there'd be nothing to talk about at all.

'"Oh, no," she said, "Theo's no trouble." She turned to her husband, who was sitting there mopping his face. "We like having him, don't we?"

'"He's all right," said Bronson.

'"What does he do with himself all day long?"

'"Oh, I don't know," said Mrs Bronson. "He walks round the estate with Reggie sometimes, and he shoots a bit. He talks to me."

'"He's always glad to make himself useful," said Bronson. "The other day when I had a go of fever, he took over my work and I just lay in bed and had a good time."'

'Hadn't the Bronsons any children?' I asked.

'No,' Gaze answered. 'I don't know why, they could well have afforded it.'

Gaze leant back in his chair. He took off his glasses and wiped them. They were very strong and hideously distorted his eyes. Without them he wasn't so homely. The chik-chak on the ceiling gave its strangely human cry. It was like the cackle of an idiot child.

'Bronson was killed,' said Gaze suddenly.

'Killed?'

'Yes, murdered. I shall never forget that night. We'd been playing tennis, Mrs Bronson and the doctor's wife, Theo Cartwright and I; and then we played bridge. Cartwright had been off his game and when we sat down at the bridge-table Mrs Bronson said to him: "Well, Theo, if you play bridge as rottenly as you played tennis we shall lose our shirts."

'We'd just had a drink, but she called the boy and ordered another round.

'"Put that down your throat," she said to him, "and don't call without top honours and an outside trick."

'Bronson hadn't turned up, he'd cycled in to Kabulong to get the money to pay his coolies their wages and was to come along to the club when he got back. The Bronsons' estate was nearer Alor Lipis than it was to Kabulong, but Kabulong was a more important place commercially, and Bronson banked there.

'"Reggie can cut in when he turns up," said Mrs Bronson.

'"He's late, isn't he?" said the doctor's wife.

'"Very. He said he wouldn't get back in time for tennis, but would be here for a rubber. I have a suspicion that he went to the club at Kabulong instead of coming straight home and is having drinks, the ruffian."

'"Oh, well, he can put away a good many without their having much effect on him," I laughed.

'"He's getting fat, you know. He'll have to be careful."

'We sat by ourselves in the card-room and we could hear the crowd in the billiard-room talking and laughing. They were all on the merry side. It was getting on to Christmas Day and we were all letting ourselves go a little. There was going to be a dance on Christmas Eve.

'I remembered afterwards that when we sat down the doctor's wife asked Mrs Bronson if she wasn't tired.

'"Not a bit," she said. "Why should I be?"

'I didn't know why she flushed.

'"I was afraid the tennis might have been too much for you," said the doctor's wife.

'"Oh, no," answered Mrs Bronson, a trifle abruptly, I thought, as though she didn't want to discuss the matter.

'I didn't know what they meant, and indeed it wasn't till later that I remembered the incident.

'We played three or four rubbers and still Bronson didn't turn up.

'"I wonder what's happened to him," said his wife. "I can't think why he should be so late."

'Cartwright was always silent, but this evening he had hardly opened his mouth. I thought he was tired and asked him what he'd been doing.

'"Nothing very much," he said. "I went out after tiffin to shoot pigeon."

'"Did you have any luck?" I asked.

'"Oh, I got half a dozen. They were very shy."

'But now he said: "If Reggie got back late, I dare say he thought it wasn't worth while to come here. I expect he's had a bath and when we get in we shall find him asleep in his chair."

'"It's a good long ride from Kabulong," said the doctor's wife.

'"He doesn't take the road, you know," Mrs Bronson explained. "He takes the short cut through the jungle."

'"Can he get along on his bicycle?" I asked.

'"Oh, yes, it's a very good track. It saves about a couple of miles."

'We had just started another rubber when the bar-boy came in and said there was a police-sergeant outside who wanted to speak to me.

'"What does he want?" I asked.

'The boy said he didn't know, but he had two coolies with him.

'"Curse him," I said. "I'll give him hell if I find he's disturbed me for nothing."

'I told the boy I'd come and I finished playing the hand. Then I got up.

'"I won't be a minute," I said. "Deal for me, will you?" I added to Cartwright.

'I went out and found the sergeant with two Malays waiting for me on the steps. I asked him what the devil he wanted. You can imagine my consternation when he told me that the Malays had come to the police-station and said there was a white man lying dead on the path that led through the jungle to Kabulong. I immediately thought of Bronson.

'"Dead?" I cried.

'"Yes, shot. Shot through the head. A white man with red hair."

'Then I knew it was Reggie Bronson, and indeed, one of them naming his estate said he'd recognized him as the man. It was an awful shock. And there was Mrs Bronson in the card-room waiting impatiently for me to sort my cards and make a bid. For a moment I really didn't know what to do. I was frightfully upset. It was dreadful to give her such a terrible and unexpected blow without a word of preparation, but I found myself quite unable to think of any way to soften it. I told the sergeant and the coolies to wait and went back into the club. I tried to pull myself together. As I entered the card-room Mrs Bronson said: "You've been an awful long time." Then she caught sight of my face. "Is anything the matter?" I saw her clench her fists and go white. You'd have thought she had a presentiment of evil.

'"Something dreadful has happened," I said, and my throat was all closed up so that my voice sounded even to myself hoarse and uncanny. "There's been an accident. Your husband's been wounded."

'She gave a long gasp, it was not exactly a scream, it reminded me oddly of a piece of silk torn in two.

'"Wounded?"

'She leapt to her feet and with her eyes starting from her head stared at Cartwright. The effect on him was ghastly, he fell back in his chair and went as white as death.

'"Very, very badly, I'm afraid," I added.

'I knew that I must tell her the truth, and tell it then, but I couldn't bring myself to tell it all at once.

'"Is he," her lips trembled so that she could hardly form the words, "is he – conscious?"

'I looked at her for a moment without answering. I'd have given a thousand pounds not to have to.

'"No, I'm afraid he isn't."

'Mrs Bronson stared at me as though she were trying to see right into my brain.

'"Is he dead?"

'I thought the only thing was to get it out and have done with it.

'"Yes, he was dead when they found him."

'Mrs Bronson collapsed into her chair and burst into tears.

'"Oh, my God," she muttered. "Oh, my God."

'The doctor's wife went to her and put her arms round her. Mrs Bronson with her face in her hands swayed to and fro weeping hysterically. Cartwright, with that livid face, sat quite still, his mouth open, and stared at her. You might have thought he was turned to stone.

'"Oh, my dear, my dear," said the doctor's wife, "you must try and pull yourself together." Then, turning to me, "Get her a glass of water and fetch Harry."

'Harry was her husband and he was playing billiards. I went in and told him what had happened.

'"A glass of water be damned," he said. "What she wants is a good long peg of brandy."

'We took it in to her and forced her to drink it and gradually

382

the violence of her emotion exhausted itself. In a few minutes the doctor's wife was able to take her into the ladies' lavatory to wash her face. I'd made up my mind now what had better be done. I could see that Cartwright wasn't good for much; he was all to pieces. I could understand that it was a fearful shock to him, for after all Bronson was his greatest friend and had done everything in the world for him.

'"You look as though you'd be all the better for a drop of brandy yourself, old man," I said to him.

'He made an effort.

'"It's shaken me, you know," he said. "I ... I didn't ..." He stopped as though his mind was wandering; he was still fearfully pale; he took out a packet of cigarettes and struck a match, but his hand was shaking so that he could hardly manage it.

'"Yes, I'll have a brandy."

'"Boy," I shouted, and then to Cartwright: "Now, are you fit to take Mrs Bronson home?"

'"Oh, yes," he answered.

'"That's good. The doctor and I will go along with the coolies and some police to where the body is."

'"Will you bring him back to the bungalow?" asked Cartwright.

'"I think he'd better be taken straight to the mortuary," said the doctor before I could answer. "I shall have to do a P.M."

'When Mrs Bronson, now so much calmer that I was amazed, came back, I told her what I suggested. The doctor's wife, kind woman, offered to go with her and spend the night at the bungalow, but Mrs Bronson wouldn't hear of it. She said she would be perfectly all right, and when the doctor's wife insisted – you know how bent some people are on forcing their kindness on those in trouble – she turned on her almost fiercely.

'"No, no, I must be alone," she said. "I really must. And Theo will be there."

'They got into the trap. Theo took the reins and they drove off. We started after them, the doctor and I, while the sergeant and the coolies followed. I had sent my seis to the police-station with instructions to send two men to the place where the body was lying. We soon passed Mrs Bronson and Cartwright.

'"All right?" I called.

'"Yes," he answered.

'For some time the doctor and I drove without saying a word; we were both of us deeply shocked. I was worried as well. Somehow or other I'd got to find the murderers and I foresaw that it would be no easy matter.

'"Do you suppose it was gang robbery?" said the doctor at last.

'He might have been reading my thoughts.

'"I don't think there's a doubt of it," I answered. "They knew he'd gone into Kabulong to get the wages and lay in wait for him on the way back. Of course he should never have come alone through the jungle when everyone knew he had a packet of money with him."

'"He'd done it for years," said the doctor. "And he's not the only one."

'"I know. The question is, how we're going to get hold of the fellows that did it."

'"You don't think the two coolies who say they found him could have had anything to do with it?"

'"No. They wouldn't have the nerve. I think a pair of Chinks might think out a trick like that, but I don't believe Malays would. They'd be much too frightened. Of course we'll keep an eye on them. We shall soon see if they seem to have any money to fling about."

'"It's awful for Mrs Bronson," said the doctor. "It would have been bad enough at any time, but now she's going to have a baby . . ."

'"I didn't know that," I said, interrupting him.

'"No, for some reason she wanted to keep it dark. She was rather funny about it, I thought."

'I recollected then that little passage between Mrs Bronson and the doctor's wife. I understood why that good woman had been so anxious that Mrs Bronson should not overtire herself.

'"It's strange her having a baby after being married so many years."

'"It happens, you know. But it was a surprise to her. When first she came to see me and I told her what was the matter she fainted, and then she began to cry. I should have thought she'd be as pleased as Punch. She told me that Bronson didn't like children and he'd be awfully bored at the idea, and she made me promise to say nothing about it till she had had a chance of breaking it to him gradually."

'I reflected for a moment.

'"He was the kind of breezy, hearty cove whom you'd expect to be as keen as mustard on having kids."

'"You never can tell. Some people are very selfish and just don't want the bother."

'"Well, how did he take it when she did tell him? Wasn't he rather bucked?"

'"I don't know that she ever told him. Though she couldn't have waited much longer; unless I'm very much mistaken she ought to be confined in about five months."

'"Poor devil," I said. "You know, I've got a notion that he'd have been most awfully pleased to know."

'We drove in silence for the rest of the way and at last came to the point at which the short cut to Kabulong branched off from the road. Here we stopped and in a minute or two my trap, in which were the police-sergeant and the two Malays, came up. We took the head-lamps to light us on our way. I left the doctor's seis to look after the ponies and told him that when the policemen came they were to follow the path till they found us. The two coolies, carrying the lamps, walked ahead, and we followed them. It was a fairly broad track, wide enough for a small cart to pass, and before the road was built it had been the highway between Kabulong and Alor Lipis. It was firm to the foot and good walking. The surface here and there was sandy and in places you could see quite plainly the mark of a bicycle wheel. It was the track Bronson had left on his way to Kabulong.

'We walked twenty minutes, I should think, in single file, and on a sudden the coolies, with a cry, stopped sharply. The sight had come upon them so abruptly that notwithstanding they were expecting it they were startled. There, in the middle of the pathway lit dimly by the lamps the coolies carried, lay Bronson; he'd fallen over his bicycle and lay across it in an ungainly heap. I was too shocked to speak, and I think the doctor was, too. But in our silence the din of the jungle was deafening; those damned cicadas and the bull-frogs were making enough row to wake the dead. Even under ordinary circumstances the noise of the jungle at night is uncanny; because you feel that at that hour there should be utter silence it has an odd effect on you, that ceaseless and invisible uproar that beats upon your nerves. It surrounds you and hems you in. But just then, believe me, it was terrifying. That poor fellow lay dead and all round him the restless life of the jungle pursued its indifferent and ferocious course.

'He was lying face downwards. The sergeant and the coolies looked at me as though awaiting an order. I was a young fellow then and I'm afraid I felt a little frightened. Though I couldn't see the face I had no doubt that it was Bronson, but I felt that I ought to turn the body over to make sure. I suppose we all have our little squeamishnesses; you know, I've always had a horrible distaste for touching dead bodies. I've had to do it fairly often now, but it still makes me feel slightly sick.

'"It's Bronson, all right," I said.

'The doctor – by George, it was lucky for me he was there – the doctor bent down and turned the head. The sergeant directed the lamp on the dead face.

'"My God, half his head's been shot away," I cried.

'"Yes."

'The doctor stood up straight and wiped his hands on the leaves of a tree that grew beside the path.

'"Is he quite dead?" I asked.

'"Oh, yes. Death must have been instantaneous. Whoever shot him must have fired at pretty close range."

'"How long has he been dead, d'you think?"

'"Oh, I don't know, several hours."

'"He would have passed here about five o'clock, I suppose, if he was expecting to get to the club for a rubber at six."

'"There's no sign of any struggle," said the doctor.

'"No, there wouldn't be. He was shot as he was riding along."

'I looked at the body for a little while. I couldn't help thinking how short a time ago it was since Bronson, noisy and loud-voiced, had been so full of hearty life.

'"You haven't forgotten that he had the coolies' wages on him," said the doctor.

'"No, we'd better search him."

'"Shall we turn him over?"

'"Wait a minute. Let us just have a look at the ground first."

'I took the lamp and as carefully as I could looked all about me. Just where he had fallen the sandy pathway was trodden and confused; there were our footprints and the footprints of the coolies who had found him. I walked two or three paces and then saw quite clearly the mark of his bicycle wheels; he had been riding straight and steadily. I followed it to the spot where he had fallen, to just before that, rather, and there saw very distinctly the prints on each side of the wheels of his heavy boots. He had evidently stopped there and put his feet to the ground, then he'd started off again, there was a great wobble of the wheel, and he'd crashed.

'"Now let's search him," I said.

'The doctor and the sergeant turned the body over and one of the coolies dragged the bicycle away. They laid Bronson on his back. I supposed he would have had the money partly in notes and partly in silver. The silver would have been in a bag attached to the bicycle and a glance told me that it was not there. The notes he would have put in a wallet. It would have been a good thick bundle. I felt him all over, but there was nothing; then I turned out the pockets, they were all empty except the right trouser pocket, in which there was a little small change.

'"Didn't he always wear a watch?" asked the doctor.

'"Yes, of course he did."

'I remembered that he wore the chain through the buttonhole in the lapel of his coat and the watch and some seals and things in his handkerchief pocket. But watch and chain were gone.

'"Well, there's not much doubt now, is there?" I said.

'It was clear that he had been attacked by gang robbers who knew he had money on him. After killing him they had stripped him of everything. I suddenly remembered the footprints that proved that for a moment he had stood still. I saw exactly how it had been done. One of them had stopped him on some pretext and then, just as he started off again, another, slipping out of the jungle behind him, had emptied the two barrels of a gun into his head.

'"Well," I said to the doctor, "it's up to me to catch them, and I'll tell you what, it'll be a real pleasure to me to see them hanged."

'Of course there was an inquest. Mrs Bronson gave evidence, but she had nothing to say that we didn't know already. Bronson had left the bungalow about eleven, he was to have tiffin at Kabulong and was to be back between five and six. He asked her not to wait for him, he said he would just put the money in the safe and come straight to the club. Cartwright confirmed this. He had lunched alone with Mrs Bronson and after a smoke had gone out with a gun to shoot pigeon. He had got in about five, a little before perhaps, had a bath and changed to play tennis. He was shooting not far from the place where Bronson was killed, but never heard a shot. That, of course, meant nothing; what with the cicadas and the frogs and the other sounds of the jungle, he would have had to be very near to hear anything; and besides, Cartwright was probably back in the bungalow before Bronson was killed. We traced Bronson's movements. He had lunched at the club, he had got money at the bank just before it closed, had gone back to the club and had one more drink, and then started off on his bicycle. He had crossed the river by the ferry; the ferryman remembered distinctly seeing him, but was positive that no one else with a bicycle had crossed. That looked as though the murderers were not following, but lying in wait for him. He rode along the main road for a couple of miles and then took the path which was a short cut to his bungalow.

'It looked as though he had been killed by men who knew his habits, and suspicion, of course, fell immediately on the coolies of his estate. We examined them all – pretty carefully – but there was not a scrap of evidence to connect any of them with the crime. In fact, most of them were able satisfactorily to account for their actions and those who couldn't seemed to me for one reason and another out of the running. There were a few bad characters among the Chinese at Alor Lipis and I had them looked up. But somehow I didn't think it was the work of the Chinese; I had a feeling that Chinese would have used revolvers and not a shot-gun. Anyhow, I could find out nothing there. So then we offered a reward of a thousand dollars to anyone who could put us in the way of discovering the murderers. I thought there were a good many people to whom it would appeal to do a public service and at the same time earn a tidy sum. But I knew that an informer would take no risks, he wouldn't want to tell what he knew till he knew he could tell it safely, and I armed myself with patience. The reward had brightened the interest of my police and I knew they would use every means they had to bring the criminals to trial. In a case like this they could do more than I.

'But it was strange, nothing happened; the reward seemed to tempt no one. I cast my net a little wider. There were two or three kampongs along the road and I wondered if the murderers were there; I saw the headmen, but got no help from them. It was not that they would tell me nothing, I was sure they had nothing to tell. I talked to the bad hats, but there was absolutely nothing to connect them with the murder. There was not the shadow of a clue.

'"Very well, my lads," I said to myself, as I drove back to Alor Lipis, "there's no hurry; the rope won't spoil by keeping."

'The scoundrels had got away with a considerable sum, but money is no good unless you spend it. I felt I knew the native temperament enough to be sure that the possession of it was a constant temptation. The Malays are an extravagant race, and a race of gamblers, and the Chinese are gamblers, too; sooner or later someone would start flinging his money about, and then I should want to know where it came from. With a few well-directed questions I thought I could put the fear of God into the fellow and then, if I knew my business, it shouldn't be hard to get a full confession.

'The only thing now was to sit down and wait till the hue and cry had died down and the murderers thought the affair was forgotten. The itch to spend those ill-gotten dollars would grow more and more intolerable till at last it could be resisted no longer. I would go about my business, but I meant never to relax my watch, and one day, sooner or later, my time must come.

'Cartwright took Mrs Bronson down to Singapore. The

company Bronson had worked for asked him if he would care to take Bronson's place, but he said, very naturally, that he didn't like the idea of it; so they put another man in and told Cartwright that he could have the job that Bronson's successor had vacated. It was the management of the estate that Cartwright lives on now. He moved in at once. Four months after this Olive was born at Singapore, and a few months later, when Bronson had been dead just over a year, Cartwright and Mrs Bronson were married. I was surprised; but on thinking it over I couldn't help confessing that it was very natural. After the trouble Mrs Bronson had leant much on Cartwright and he had arranged everything for her; she must have been lonely, and rather lost, and I dare say she was grateful for his kindness, he did behave like a brick; and so far as he was concerned I imagined he was sorry for her, it was a dreadful position for a woman, she had nowhere to go, and all they'd gone through must have been a tie between them. There was every reason for them to marry and it was probably the best thing for them both.

'It looked as though Bronson's murderers would never be caught, for that plan of mine didn't work; there was no one in the district who spent more money than he could account for, and if anyone had that hoard buried away under his floor he was showing a self-control that was superhuman. A year had passed and to all intents and purposes the thing was forgotten. Could anyone be so prudent as after so long not to let a little money dribble out? It was incredible. I began to think that Bronson had been killed by a couple of wandering Chinese who had got away, to Singapore perhaps, where there would be small chance of catching them. At last I gave it up. If you come to think of it, as a rule, it's just those crimes, crimes of robbery, in which there is least chance of getting the culprit; for there's nothing to attach suspicion to him, and if he's caught it can only be by his own carelessness. It's different with crimes of passion or vengeance, then you can find out who had a motive to put the victim out of the way.

'It's no use grizzling over one's failures, and bringing my common sense to bear I did my best to put the matter out of my mind. No one likes to be beaten, but beaten I was and I had to put as good a face on it as I could. And then a Chinaman was caught trying to pawn poor Bronson's watch.

'I told you that Bronson's watch and chain had been taken, and of course Mrs Bronson was able to give us a fairly accurate description of it. It was a half-hunter, by Benson, there was a gold chain, three or four seals, and a sovereign purse. The pawnbroker was a smart fellow and when the Chinaman brought the watch he recognized it at once. On some pretext he kept the man waiting and sent for a policeman. The man was arrested and immediately brought to me. I greeted him like a long-lost brother. I was never so pleased to see anyone in my life. I have no feeling about criminals, you know; I'm rather sorry for them, because they're playing a game in which their opponents hold all the aces and kings; but when I catch one it gives me a little thrill of satisfaction, like bringing off a neat finesse at bridge. At last the mystery was going to be cleared up, for if the Chinaman hadn't done the thing himself we were pretty sure through him to trace the murderers. I beamed on him.

'I asked him to account for his possession of the watch. He said he had bought it from a man he didn't know. That was very thin. I explained the circumstances briefly and told him he would be charged with murder. I meant to frighten him and I did. He said then that he'd found the watch.

'"Found it?" I said. "Fancy that. Where?"

'His answer staggered me; he said he'd found it in the jungle. I laughed at him; I asked him if he thought watches were likely to be left lying about in the jungle; then he said he'd been coming along the pathway that led from Kabulong to Alor Lipis, and had gone into the jungle and caught sight of something gleaming and there was the watch. That was odd. Why should he have said he found the watch just there? It was either true or excessively astute. I asked him where the chain and the seals were, and he produced them immediately. I'd got him scared, and he was pale and shaking; he was a knock-kneed little fellow and I should have been a fool not to see that I hadn't got hold of the murderer there. But his terror suggested that he knew something.

'I asked him when he'd found the watch.

'"Yesterday," he said.

'I asked him what he was doing on the short-cut from Kabulong to Alor Lipis. He said he'd been working in Singapore and had gone to Kabulong because his father was ill, and that he himself had come to Alor Lipis to work. A friend of his father, a carpenter by trade, had given him a job. He gave me the name of the man with whom he had worked in Singapore and the name of the man who had engaged him at Alor Lipis. All he said seemed plausible and could so easily be verified that it was hardly likely to be false. Of course it occurred to me that if he had found the watch as he said, it must have been lying in the jungle for more than a year. It could hardly be in very good condition; I tried to open it, but couldn't. The pawnbroker had come to the police-station and was waiting in the next room. Luckily he was also something of a watch-maker. I sent for him and asked him to look at the watch; when he opened it he gave a little whistle, the works were thick with rust.

'"This watch no good," he said, shaking his head. "Him never go now."

'I asked him what had put it in such a state, and without a word from me he said that it had been long exposed to wet. For the moral effect I had the prisoner put in a cell and I sent for his employer. I sent a wire to Kabulong and another to Singapore. While I waited I did my best to put two and two together. I was inclined to believe the man's story true; his fear might be ascribed to no more guilt than consisted in his having found something and tried to sell it. Even quite innocent persons are apt to be nervous when they're in the hands of the police; I don't know what there is about a policeman, people are never very much at their ease in his company. But if he really had found the watch where he said, someone had thrown it there. Now that was funny. Even if the murderers had thought the watch a dangerous thing to possess, one would have expected them to melt down the gold case; that would be a very simple thing for any native to do; and the chain was of so ordinary a pattern they could hardly have thought it possible to trace that. There were chains like it in every jeweller's shop in the country. Of course there was the possibility that they had plunged into the jungle and having dropped the watch in their hurry had been afraid to go back and look for it. I didn't think that very likely: the Malays are used to keeping things tucked away in their sarongs, and the Chinese have pockets in their coats. Besides, the moment they got into the jungle they knew there was no hurry; they probably waited and divided the swag then and there.

'In a few minutes the man I had sent for came to the police-station and confirmed what the prisoner had said, and in an hour I got an answer from Kabulong. The police had seen his father, who told them that the boy had gone to Alor Lipis to get a job with a carpenter. So far everything he had said seemed true. I had him brought in again, and told him I was going to take him to the place where he said he had found the watch and he must show me the exact spot. I handcuffed him to a policeman, though it was hardly necessary, for the poor devil was shaking with fright, and took a couple of men besides. We drove out to where the track joined the road and walked along it; within five yards of the place where Bronson was killed the Chinaman stopped.

'"Here," he said.

'He pointed to the jungle and we followed him in. We went

in about ten yards and he pointed to a chink between two large boulders and said that he found the watch there. It could only have been by the merest chance that he noticed it, and if he really had found it there it looked very much as though someone had put it there to hide it.'

Gaze stopped and gave me a reflective look.

'What would you have thought then?' he asked.

'I don't know,' I answered.

'Well, I'll tell you what I thought. I thought that if the watch was there the money might be there, too. It seemed worth while having a look. Of course, to look for something in the jungle makes looking for a needle in a bundle of hay a drawing-room pastime. I couldn't help that. I released the Chinaman, I wanted all the help I could get, and set him to work. I set my three men to work, and I started in myself. We made a line – there were five of us – and we searched from the road; for fifty yards on each side of the place at which Bronson was murdered and for a hundred yards in we went over the ground foot by foot. We routed among dead leaves and peered in bushes, we looked under boulders and in the hollows of trees. I knew it was a foolish thing to do, for the chances against us were a thousand to one; my only hope was that anyone who had just committed a murder would be rattled and if he wanted to hide anything would hide it quickly; he would choose the first obvious hiding-place that offered itself. That is what he had done when he hid the watch. My only reason for looking in so circumscribed an area was that as the watch had been found so near the road, the person who wanted to get rid of the things must have wanted to get rid of them quickly.

'We worked on. I began to grow tired and cross. We were sweating like pigs. I had a maddening thirst and nothing in the world to drink. At last I came to the conclusion that we must give it up as a bad job, for that day at least, when suddenly the Chinaman – he must have had sharp eyes, that young man – uttered a guttural cry. He stooped down and from under the winding root of a tree drew out a messy, mouldering, stinking thing. It was a pocket-book that had been out in the rain for a year, that had been eaten by ants and beetles and God knows what, that was sodden and foul, but it was a pocket-book all right, Bronson's, and inside were the shapeless, mushed-up, fetid remains of the Singapore notes he had got from the bank at Kabulong. There was still the silver and I was convinced that it was hidden somewhere about, but I wasn't going to bother about that. I had found out something very important; whoever had murdered Bronson had made no money out of it.

'Do you remember my telling you that I'd noticed the print of Bronson's feet on each side of the broad line of the pneumatic tyre, where he had stopped, and presumably spoken to someone? He was a heavy man and the prints were well marked. He hadn't just put his feet on the soft sand and taken them off, but must have stopped at least for a minute or two. My explanation was that he had stopped to chat with a Malay or a Chinaman, but the more I thought of it the less I liked it. Why the devil should he? Bronson wanted to get home, and though a jovial chap, he certainly was not hail-fellow-well-met with the natives. His relations towards them were those of master and servants. Those footprints had always puzzled me. And now the truth flashed across me. Whoever had murdered Bronson hadn't murdered him to rob and if he'd stopped to talk with someone it could only be with a friend. I knew at last who the murderer was.'

I have always thought the detective story a most diverting and ingenious variety of fiction, and have regretted that I never had the skill to write one, but I have read a good many, and I flatter myself it is rarely that I have not solved the mystery before it was disclosed to me; and now for some time I had foreseen what Gaze was going to say, but when at last he said it I confess that it gave me, notwithstanding, somewhat of a shock.

'The man he met was Cartwright. Cartwright was pigeon-shooting. He stopped and asked him what sport he had had, and as he rode on Cartwright raised his gun and discharged both barrels into his head. Cartwright took the money and the watch in order to make it look like the work of gang robbers and hurriedly hid them in the jungle, then made his way along the edge till he got to the road, went back to the bungalow, changed into his tennis things, and drove with Mrs Bronson to the club.

'I remembered how badly he'd played tennis, and how he'd collapsed when, in order to break the news more gently to Mrs Bronson, I said Bronson was wounded and not dead. If he was only wounded he might have been able to speak. By George, I bet that was a bad moment. The child was Cartwright's. Look at Olive: why, you saw the likeness yourself. The doctor had said that Mrs Bronson was upset when he told her she was going to have a baby and made him promise not to tell Bronson. Why? Because Bronson knew that he couldn't be the father of the child.'

'Do you think that Mrs Bronson knew what Cartwright had done?' I asked.

'I'm sure of it. When I look back on her behaviour that evening at the club I am convinced of it. She was upset, but not because Bronson was killed; she was upset because I said he was wounded; on my telling her that he was dead when they found him she burst out crying, but from relief. I know that woman. Look at that square chin of hers and tell me that she hasn't got the courage of the devil. She has a will of iron. She made Cartwright do it. She planned every detail and every move. He was completely under her influence; he is now.'

'But do you mean to tell me that neither you nor anyone else ever suspected that there was anything between them?'

'Never. Never.'

'If they were in love with one another and knew that she was going to have a baby, why didn't they just bolt?'

'How could they? It was Bronson who had the money; she hadn't a bean and neither had Cartwright. He was out of a job. Do you think he would have got another with that story round his neck? Bronson had taken him in when he was starving and he'd stolen his wife from him. They wouldn't have had a dog's chance. They couldn't afford to let the truth come out, their only chance was to get Bronson out of the way, and they got him out of the way.'

'They might have thrown themselves on his mercy.'

'Yes, but I think they were ashamed. He'd been so good to them, he was such a decent chap, I don't think they had the heart to tell him the truth. They preferred to kill him.'

There was a moment's silence while I reflected over what Gaze said.

'Well, what did you do about it?' I asked.

'Nothing. What was there to do? What was the evidence? That the watch and notes had been found? They might easily have been hidden by someone who was afterwards afraid to come and get them. The murderer might have been quite content to get away with the silver. The footprints? Bronson might have stopped to light a cigarette or there might have been a tree-trunk across the path and he waited while the coolies he met there by chance moved it away. Who could prove that the child that a perfectly decent, respectable woman had had four months after her husband's death was not his child? No jury would have convicted Cartwright. I held my tongue and the Bronson murder was forgotten.'

'I don't suppose the Cartwrights have forgotten,' I suggested.

'I shouldn't be surprised. Human memory is astonishingly short and if you want my professional opinion I don't mind telling you that I don't believe remorse for a crime ever sits very heavily on a man when he's absolutely sure he'll never be found out.'

I thought once more of the pair I had met that afternoon, the thin, elderly, bald man with gold-rimmed spectacles, and that white-haired untidy woman with her frank speech and kindly, caustic smile. It was almost impossible to imagine that in the distant past they had been swayed by so turbulent a passion, for that alone made their behaviour explicable, that it had brought them in the end to such a pass that they could see no other issue than a cruel and cold-blooded murder.

'Doesn't it make you feel a little uncomfortable to be with them?' I asked Gaze. 'For, without wishing to be censorious, I'm bound to say that I don't think they can be very nice people.'

'That's where you're wrong. They are very nice people; they're about the pleasantest people here. Mrs Cartwright is a thoroughly good sort and a very amusing woman. It's my business to prevent crime and to catch the culprit when crime is committed, but I've known far too many criminals to think that on the whole they're worse than anybody else. A perfectly decent fellow may be driven by circumstances to commit a crime and if he's found out he's punished; but he may very well remain a perfectly decent fellow. Of course society punishes him if he breaks its laws, and it's quite right, but it's not always his actions that indicate the essential man. If you'd been a policeman as long as I have, you'd know it's not what people do that really matters, it's what they are. Luckily a policeman has nothing to do with their thoughts, only with their deeds; if he had, it would be a very different, a much more difficult matter.'

Gaze flicked the ash from his cheroot and gave me his wry, sardonic, but agreeable smile.

'I'll tell you what, there's one job I *shouldn't* like,' he said.

'What is that?' I asked.

'God's, at the Judgement Day,' said Gaze. 'No, sir.'

THE DOOR OF OPPORTUNITY

THEY got a first-class carriage to themselves. It was lucky, because they were taking a good deal in with them, Alban's suit-case and a hold-all, Anne's dressing-case and her hat-box. They had two trunks in the van, containing what they wanted immediately, but all the rest of their luggage Alban had put in the care of an agent who was to take it up to London and store it till they had made up their minds what to do. They had a lot, pictures and books, curios that Alban had collected in the East, his guns and saddles. They had left Sondurah for ever. Alban, as was his way, tipped the porter generously and then went to the bookstall and bought papers. He bought the *New Statesman* and the *Nation*, and the *Tatler* and the *Sketch*, and the last number of the *London Mercury*. He came back to the carriage and threw them on the seat.

'It's only an hour's journey,' said Anne.

'I know, but I wanted to buy them. I've been starved so long. Isn't it grand to think that tomorrow morning we shall have tomorrow's *Times*, and the *Express* and the *Mail*?'

She did not answer and he turned away, for he saw coming towards them two persons, a man and his wife, who had been fellow-passengers from Singapore.

'Get through the Customs all right?' he cried to them cheerily.

The man seemed not to hear, for he walked straight on, but the woman answered.

'Yes, they never found the cigarettes.'

She saw Anne, gave her a friendly little smile, and passed on. Anne flushed.

'I was afraid they'd want to come in here,' said Alban. 'Let's have the carriage to ourselves if we can.'

She looked at him curiously.

'I don't think you need worry,' she answered. 'I don't think anyone will come in.'

He lit a cigarette and lingered at the carriage door. On his face was a happy smile. When they had passed through the Red Sea and found a sharp wind in the Canal, Anne had been surprised to see how much the men who had looked presentable enough in the white ducks in which she had been accustomed to see them, were changed when they left them off for warmer clothes. They looked like nothing on earth then. Their ties were awful and their shirts all wrong. They wore grubby flannel trousers and shabby old

396

golf-coats that had too obviously been bought off the nail, or blue serge suits that betrayed the provincial tailor. Most of the passengers had got off at Marseilles, but a dozen or so, either because after a long period in the East they thought the trip through the Bay would do them good, or, like themselves, for economy's sake, had gone all the way to Tilbury, and now several of them walked along the platform. They wore solar topees or double-brimmed terais, and heavy greatcoats, or else shapeless soft hats or bowlers, not too well brushed, that looked too small for them. It was a shock to see them. They looked suburban and a trifle second-rate. But Alban had already a London look. There was not a speck of dust on his smart greatcoat, and his black Homburg hat looked brand-new. You would never have guessed that he had not been home for three years. His collar fitted closely round his neck and his foulard tie was neatly tied. As Anne looked at him she could not but think how good-looking he was. He was just under six feet tall, and slim, and he wore his clothes well, and his clothes were well cut. He had fair hair, still thick, and blue eyes and the faintly yellow skin common to men of that complexion after they have lost the pink-and-white freshness of early youth. There was no colour in his cheeks. It was a fine head, well-set on rather a long neck, with a somewhat prominent Adam's apple; but you were more impressed with the distinction than with the beauty of his face. It was because his features were so regular, his nose so straight, his brow so broad that he photographed so well. Indeed, from his photographs you would have thought him extremely handsome. He was not that, perhaps because his eyebrows and his eyelashes were pale, and his lips thin, but he looked very intellectual. There was refinement in his face and a spirituality that was oddly moving. That was how you thought a poet should look; and when Anne became engaged to him she told her girl friends who asked her about him that he looked like Shelley. He turned to her now with a little smile in his blue eyes. His smile was very attractive.

'What a perfect day to land in England!'

It was October. They had steamed up the Channel on a grey sea under a grey sky. There was not a breath of wind. The fishing boats seemed to rest on the placid water as though the elements had for ever forgotten their old hostility. The coast was incredibly green, but with a bright cosy greenness quite unlike the luxuriant, vehement verdure of Eastern jungles. The red towns they passed here and there were comfortable and homelike. They seemed to welcome the exiles with a smiling friendliness. And when they drew into the estuary of the Thames they saw the rich levels of

Essex and in a little while Chalk Church on the Kentish shore, lonely in the midst of weather-beaten trees, and beyond it the woods of Cobham. The sun, red in a faint mist, set on the marshes, and night fell. In the station the arc-lamps shed a light that spotted the darkness with cold hard patches. It was good to see the porters lumbering about in their grubby uniforms and the station-master fat and important in his bowler hat. The stationmaster blew a whistle and waved his arm. Alban stepped into the carriage and seated himself in the corner opposite to Anne. The train started.

'We're due in London at six-ten,' said Alban. 'We ought to get to Jermyn Street by seven. That'll give us an hour to bath and change and we can get to the Savoy for dinner by eight-thirty. A bottle of pop tonight, my pet, and a slap-up dinner.' He gave a chuckle. 'I heard the Strouds and the Maundys arranging to meet at the Trocadero Grill-Room.'

He took up the papers and asked if she wanted any of them. Anne shook her head.

'Tired?' he smiled.

'No.'

'Excited?'

In order not to answer she gave a little laugh. He began to look at the papers, starting with the publishers' advertisements, and she was conscious of the intense satisfaction it was to him to feel himself through them once more in the middle of things. They had taken in those same papers in Sondurah, but they arrived six weeks old, and though they kept them abreast of what was going on in the world that interested them both, they emphasized their exile. But these were fresh from the press. They smelt different. They had a crispness that was almost voluptuous. He wanted to read them all at once. Anne looked out of the window. The country was dark, and she could see little but the lights of their carriage reflected on the glass, but very soon the town encroached upon it, and then she saw little sordid houses, mile upon mile of them, with a light in a window here and there, and the chimneys made a dreary pattern against the sky. They passed through Barking and East Ham and Bromley – it was silly that the name on the platform as they went through the station should give her such a tremor – and then Stepney. Alban put down his papers.

'We shall be there in five minutes now.'

He put on his hat and took down from the racks the things the porter had put in them. He looked at her with shining eyes and his lips twitched. She saw that he was only just able to control his emotion. He looked out of the window, too, and they passed over brightly lighted thoroughfares, close packed with tram-cars, buses, and motor-vans, and they saw the streets thick with people. What a mob! The shops were all lit up. They saw the hawkers with their barrows at the kerb.

'London,' he said.

He took her hand and gently pressed it. His smile was so sweet that she had to say something. She tried to be facetious.

'Does it make you feel all funny inside?'

'I don't know if I want to cry or if I want to be sick.'

Fenchurch Street. He lowered the window and waved his arm for a porter. With a grinding of brakes the train came to a standstill. A porter opened the door and Alban handed him out one package after another. Then in his polite way, having jumped out, he gave his hand to Anne to help her down to the platform. The porter went to fetch a barrow and they stood by the pile of their luggage. Alban waved to two passengers from the ship who passed them. The man nodded stiffly.

'What a comfort it is that we shall never have to be civil to those awful people any more,' said Alban lightly.

Anne gave him a quick glance. He was really incomprehensible. The porter came back with his barrow, the luggage was put on, and they followed him to collect their trunks. Alban took his wife's arm and pressed it.

'The smell of London. By God, it's grand.'

He rejoiced in the noise and the bustle, and the crowd of people who jostled them; the radiance of the arc-lamps and the black shadows they cast, sharp but full-toned, gave him a sense of elation. They got out into the street and the porter went off to get them a taxi. Alban's eyes glittered as he looked at the buses and the policemen trying to direct the confusion. His distinguished face bore a look of something like inspiration. The taxi came. Their luggage was stowed away and piled up beside the driver, Alban gave the porter half-a-crown, and they drove off. They turned down Gracechurch Street and in Cannon Street were held up by a block in the traffic. Alban laughed out loud.

'What's the matter?' said Anne.

'I'm so excited.'

They went along the Embankment. It was relatively quiet there. Taxis and cars passed them. The bells of the trams were music in his ears. At Westminster Bridge they cut across Parliament Square and drove through the green silence of St James's Park. They had engaged a room at a hotel just off Jermyn Street. The reception clerk took them upstairs and a porter brought up their luggage. It was a room with twin beds and a bathroom.

'This looks all right,' said Alban. 'It'll do us till we can find a flat or something.'

He looked at his watch.

'Look here, darling, we shall only fall over one another if we try to unpack together. We've got oodles of time and it'll take you longer to get straight and dress than me. I'll clear out. I want to go to the club and see if there's any mail for me. I've got my dinner jacket in my suit-case and it'll only take me twenty minutes to have a bath and dress. Does that suit you?'

'Yes. That's all right.'

'I'll be back in an hour.'

'Very well.'

He took out of his pocket the little comb he always carried and passed it through his long fair hair. Then he put on his hat. He gave himself a glance in the mirror.

'Shall I turn on the bath for you?'

'No, don't bother.'

'All right. So long.'

He went out.

When he was gone Anne took her dressing-case and her hat-box and put them on the top of her trunk. Then she rang the bell. She did not take off her hat. She sat down and lit a cigarette. When a servant answered the bell she asked for the porter. He came. She pointed to the luggage.

'Will you take those things and leave them in the hall for the present. I'll tell you what to do with them presently.'

'Very good, ma'am.'

She gave him a florin. He took the trunk out and the other packages and closed the door behind him. A few tears slid down Anne's cheeks, but she shook herself; she dried her eyes and powdered her face. She needed all her calm. She was glad that Alban had conceived the idea of going to his club. It made things easier and gave her a little time to think them out.

Now that the moment had come to do what she had for weeks determined, now that she must say the terrible things she had to say, she quailed. Her heart sank. She knew exactly what she meant to say to Alban, she had made up her mind about that long ago, and had said the very words to herself a hundred times, three or four times a day every day of the long journey from Singapore, but she was afraid that she would grow confused. She dreaded an argument. The thought of a scene made her feel slightly sick. It was something at all events to have an hour in which to collect herself. He would say she was heartless and cruel and unreasonable. She could not help it.

'No, no, no,' she cried aloud.

She shuddered with horror. And all at once she saw herself again in the bungalow, sitting as she had been sitting when the whole thing started. It was getting on towards tiffin time and in a few minutes Alban would be back from the office. It gave her pleasure to reflect that it was an attractive room for him to come back to, the large veranda which was their parlour, and she knew that though they had been there eighteen months he was still alive to the success she had made of it. The jalousies were drawn now against the midday sun, and the mellowed light filtering through them gave an impression of cool silence. Anne was house-proud, and though they were moved from district to district according to the exigencies of the Service and seldom stayed anywhere very long, at each new post she started with new enthusiasm to make their house cosy and charming. She was very modern. Visitors were surprised because there were no knick-knacks. They were taken aback by the bold colour of her curtains and could not at all make out the tinted reproductions of pictures by Marie Laurencin and Gauguin in silvered frames which were placed on the walls with such cunning skill. She was conscious that few of them quite approved, and the good ladies of Port Wallace and Pemberton thought such arrangements odd, affected, and out of place; but this left her calm. They would learn. It did them good to get a bit of a jolt. And now she looked round the long, spacious veranda with the complacent sigh of the artist satisfied with his work. It was gay. It was bare. It was restful. It refreshed the spirit and gently excited the fancy. Three immense bowls of yellow cannas completed the colour scheme. Her eyes lingered for a moment on the book-shelves filled with books; that was another thing that disconcerted the colony, all the books they had, and strange books too, heavy they thought them for the most part; and she gave them a little affectionate look as though they were living things. Then she gave the piano a glance. A piece of music was still open on the rack, it was something of Debussy, and Alban had been playing it before he went to the office.

Her friends in the colony had condoled with her when Alban was appointed D.O. at Daktar, for it was the most isolated district in Sondurah. It was connected with the town which was the headquarters of the Government neither by telegraph nor telephone. But she liked it. They had been there for some time and she hoped they would remain till Alban went home on leave in another twelve months. It was as large as an English county, with a long coast-line, and the sea was dotted with little islands. A broad, winding river ran through it, and on each side of this stretched hills densely covered with virgin forest. The station, a good way up the river, consisted of a row of Chinese shops and a native village nestling amid coconut trees, the District Office, the D.O.'s bungalow, the clerk's quarters, and the barracks. Their only neighbours were the manager of a rubber estate a few miles up the river, and the manager and his assistant, Dutchmen both, of a timber camp on one of the river's tributaries. The rubber estate's launch went up and down twice a month and was their only means of regular communication with the outside world. But though they were lonely they were not dull. Their days were full. Their ponies waited for them at dawn and they rode while the day was still fresh and in the bridle-paths through the jungle lingered the mystery of the tropical night. They came back, bathed, changed, and had breakfast, and Alban went to the office. Anne spent the morning writing letters and working. She had fallen in love with the country from the first day she arrived in it and had taken pains to master the common language spoken. Her imagination was inflamed by the stories she heard of love and jealousy and death. She was told romantic tales of a time that was only just past. She sought to steep herself in the lore of those strange people. Both she and Alban read a great deal. They had for the country a considerable library and new books came from London by nearly every mail. Little that was noteworthy escaped them. Alban was fond of playing the piano. For an amateur he played very well. He had studied rather seriously, and he had an agreeable touch and a good ear; he could read music with ease, and it was always a pleasure to Anne to sit by him and follow the score when he tried something new. But their great delight was to tour the district. Sometimes they would be away for a fortnight at a time. They would go down the river in a prahu and then sail from one little island to another, bathe in the sea, and fish, or else row upstream till it grew shallow and the trees on either bank were so close to one another that you only saw a slim strip of sky between. Here the boatmen had to pole and they would spend the night in a native house. They bathed in a river pool so clear that you could see the sand shining silver at the bottom; and the spot was so lovely, so peaceful and remote, that you felt you could stay there for ever. Sometimes, on the other hand, they would tramp for days along the jungle paths, sleeping under canvas, and notwithstanding the mosquitoes that tormented them and the leeches that sucked their blood, enjoy every moment. Whoever slept so well as on a camp bed? And then there was the gladness of getting back, the delight in the comfort of the well-ordered establishment, the mail that had arrived with letters from home and all the papers, and the piano.

Alban would sit down to it then, his fingers itching to feel the keys, and in what he played, Stravinsky, Ravel, Darius Milhaud, she seemed to feel that he put in something of his own, the sounds of the jungle at night, dawn over the estuary, the starry nights, and the crystal clearness of the forest pools.

Sometimes the rain fell in sheets for days at a time. Then Alban worked at Chinese. He was learning it so that he could communicate with the Chinese of the country in their own language, and Anne did the thousand-and-one things for which she had not had time before. Those days brought them even more closely together; they always had plenty to talk about, and when they were occupied with their separate affairs they were pleased to feel in their bones that they were near to one another. They were wonderfully united. The rainy days that shut them up within the walls of the bungalow made them feel as if they were one body in face of the world.

On occasion they went to Port Wallace. It was a change, but Anne was always glad to get home. She was never quite at her ease there. She was conscious that none of the people they met liked Alban. They were very ordinary people, middle-class and suburban and dull, without any of the intellectual interests that made life so full and varied to Alban and her, and many of them were narrow-minded and ill-natured; but since they had to pass the better part of their lives in contact with them, it was tiresome that they should feel so unkindly towards Alban. They said he was conceited. He was always very pleasant with them, but she was aware that they resented his cordiality. When he tried to be jovial they said he was putting on airs, and when he chaffed them they thought he was being funny at their expense.

Once they stayed at Government House, and Mrs Hannay, the Governor's wife, who liked her, talked to her about it. Perhaps the Governor had suggested that she should give Anne a hint.

'You know, my dear, it's a pity your husband doesn't try to be more come-hither with people. He's very intelligent; don't you think it would be better if he didn't let others see he knows it quite so clearly? My husband said to me only yesterday: Of course I know Alban Torel is the cleverest young man in the Service, but he does manage to put my back up more than anyone I know. I am the Governor, but when he talks to me he always gives me the impression that he looks upon me as a damned fool.'

The worst of it was that Anne knew how low an opinion Alban had of the Governor's parts.

'He doesn't mean to be superior,' Anne answered, smiling. 'And he really isn't in the least conceited. I think it's only because he has a straight nose and high cheek-bones.'

'You know, they don't like him at the club. They call him Powder-Puff Percy.'

Anne flushed. She had heard that before and it made her very angry. Her eyes filled with tears.

'I think it's frightfully unfair.'

Mrs Hannay took her hand and gave it an affectionate little squeeze.

'My dear, you know I don't want to hurt your feelings. Your husband can't help rising very high in the Service. He'd make things so much easier for himself if he were a little more human. Why doesn't he play football?'

'It's not his game. He's always only too glad to play tennis.'

'He doesn't give that impression He gives the impression that there's no one here who's worth his while to play with.'

'Well, there isn't,' said Anne, stung.

Alban happened to be an extremely good tennis-player. He had played a lot of tournaments in England and Anne knew that it gave him a grim satisfaction to knock those beefy, hearty men all over the court. He could make the best of them look foolish. He could be maddening on the tennis court and Anne was aware that sometimes he could not resist the temptation.

'He does play to the gallery, doesn't he?' said Mrs Hannay.

'I don't think so. Believe me, Alban has no idea he isn't popular. As far as I can see he's always pleasant and friendly with everybody.'

'It's then he's most offensive,' said Mrs Hannay dryly.

'I know people don't like us very much,' said Anne, smiling a little. 'I'm very sorry, but really I don't know what we can do about it.'

'Not you, my dear,' cried Mrs Hannay. 'Everybody adores you. That's why they put up with your husband. My dear, who could help liking you?'

'I don't know why they should adore me,' said Anne.

But she did not say it quite sincerely. She was deliberately playing the part of the dear little woman and within her she bubbled with amusement. They disliked Alban because he had such an air of distinction, and because he was interested in art and literature; they did not understand these things and so thought them unmanly; and they disliked him because his capacity was greater than theirs. They disliked him because he was better bred than they. They thought him superior; well, he was superior, but not in the sense they meant. They forgave her because she was an ugly little thing. That was what she called herself, but she wasn't that, or if she was it was with an ugliness that was most attractive. She was like a little monkey, but a very sweet little monkey and very human. She had a neat figure. That was her best point. That and her eyes. They were very large, of a deep brown, liquid and shining; they were full of fun, but they could be tender on occasion with a charming sympathy. She was dark, her frizzy hair was almost black, and her skin was swarthy; she had a small fleshy nose, with large nostrils, and much too big a mouth. But she was alert and vivacious. She could talk with a show of real interest to the ladies of the colony about their husbands and their servants and their children in England, and she could listen appreciatively to the men who told her stories that she had often heard before. They thought her a jolly good sort. They did not know what clever fun she made of them in private. It never occurred to them that she thought them narrow, gross, and pretentious. They found no glamour in the East because they looked at it vulgarly with material eyes. Romance lingered at their threshold and they drove it away like an importunate beggar. She was aloof. She repeated to herself Landor's line:

'*Nature I loved, and next to nature, art.*'

She reflected on her conversation with Mrs Hannay, but on the whole it left her unconcerned. She wondered whether she should say anything about it to Alban; it had always seemed a little odd to her that he should be so little aware of his unpopularity; but she was afraid that if she told him of it he would become self-conscious. He never noticed the coldness of the men at the club. He made them feel shy and therefore uncomfortable. His appearance then caused a sort of awkwardness, but he, happily insensible, was breezily cordial to all and sundry. The fact was that he was strangely unconscious of other people. She was in a class by herself, she and a little group of friends they had in London, but he could never quite realize that the people of the colony, the government officials and the planters and their wives, were human beings. They were to him like pawns in a game. He laughed with them, chaffed them, and was amiably tolerant of them; with a chuckle Anne told herself that he was rather like the master of a preparatory school taking little boys out on a picnic and anxious to give them a good time.

She was afraid it wasn't much good telling Alban. He was incapable of the dissimulation which, she happily realized, came so easily to her. What was one to do with these people? The men had come out to the colony as lads from second-rate schools, and life had taught them nothing. At fifty they had the outlook of hobbledehoys. Most of them drank a great deal too much. They read nothing worth reading. Their ambition was to be like everybody else. Their highest praise was to say that a man was a damned good sort. If you were interested in the things of the spirit you were a prig. They were eaten up with envy of one another and devoured by petty jealousies. And the women, poor things, were obsessed by petty rivalries. They made a circle that was more provincial than any in the smallest town in England. They were prudish and spiteful. What did it matter if they did not like Alban? They would have to put up with him because his ability was so great. He was clever and energetic. They could not say that he did not do his work well. He had been successful in every post he had occupied. With his sensitiveness and his imagination he understood the native mind and he was able to get the natives to do things that no one in his position could. He had a gift for languages, and he spoke all the local dialects. He not only knew the common tongue that most of the government officials spoke, but was acquainted with the niceties of the language and on occasion could make use of a ceremonial speech that flattered and impressed the chiefs. He had a gift for organization. He was not afraid of responsibility. In due course he was bound to be made a Resident. Alban had some interest in England; his father was a brigadier-general killed in the war, and though he had no private means he had influential friends. He spoke of them with pleasant irony.

'The great advantage of democratic government,' he said, 'is that merit, with influence to back it, can be pretty sure of receiving its due reward.'

Alban was so obviously the ablest man in the Service that there seemed no reason why he should not eventually be made Governor. Then, thought Anne, his air of superiority, of which they complained, would be in place. They would accept him as their master and he would know how to make himself respected and obeyed. The position she foresaw did not dazzle her. She accepted it as a right. It would be fun for Alban to be Governor and for her to be the Governor's wife. And what an opportunity! They were sheep, the government servants and the planters; when Government House was the seat of culture they would soon fall into line. When the best way to the Governor's favour was to be intelligent, intelligence would become the fashion. She and Alban would cherish the native arts and collect carefully the memorials of a vanished past. The country would make an advance it had never dreamed of. They would develop it, but along lines of order and beauty. They would instil into their subordinates a passion for that beautiful land and a loving interest in these romantic races. They would make them realize what music meant. They would cultivate literature. They would create beauty. It would be the golden age.

Suddenly she heard Alban's footstep. Anne awoke from her day-dream. All that was far away in the future. Alban was only a District Officer yet and what was important was the life they were living now. She heard Alban go into the bath-house and splash water over himself. In a minute he came in. He had changed into a shirt and shorts. His fair hair was still wet.

'Tiffin ready?' he asked.

'Yes.'

He sat down at the piano and played the piece that he had played in the morning. The silvery notes cascaded coolly down the sultry air. You had an impression of a formal garden with great trees and elegant pieces of artificial water and of leisurely walks bordered with pseudo-classical statues. Alban played with a peculiar delicacy. Lunch was announced by the head boy. He rose from the piano. They walked into the dining-room hand in hand. A punkah lazily fanned the air. Anne gave the table a glance. With its bright-coloured tablecloth and the amusing plates it looked very gay.

'Anything exciting at the office this morning?' she asked.

'No, nothing much. A buffalo case. Oh, and Prynne has sent along to ask me to go up to the estate. Some coolies have been damaging the trees and he wants me to come along and look into it.'

Prynne was manager of the rubber estate up the river and now and then they spent a night with him. Sometimes when he wanted a change he came down to dinner and slept at the D.O.'s bungalow. They both liked him. He was a man of five-and-thirty, with a red face, with deep furrows in it, and very black hair. He was quite uneducated, but cheerful and easy, and being the only Englishman within two days' journey they could not but be friendly with him. He had been a little shy of them at first. News spreads quickly in the East and long before they arrived in the district he heard that they were highbrows. He did not know what he would make of them. He probably did not know that he had charm, which makes up for many more commendable qualities, and Alban with his almost feminine sensibilities was peculiarly susceptible to this. He found Alban much more human than he expected, and of course Anne was stunning. Alban played ragtime for him, which he would not have done for the Governor, and played dominoes with him. When Alban was making his first tour of the district with Anne, and suggested that they would like to spend a couple of nights on the estate, he had thought it as well to warn him that he lived with a native woman and had two children by her. He would do his best to keep them out of Anne's sight, but he could not send them away, there was nowhere to send them. Alban laughed.

'Anne isn't that sort of woman at all. Don't dream of hiding them. She loves children.'

Anne quickly made friends with the shy, pretty little native woman and soon was playing happily with the children. She and the girl had long confidential chats. The children took a fancy to her. She brought them lovely toys from Port Wallace. Prynne, comparing her smiling tolerance with the disapproving acidity of the other white women of the colony, described himself as knocked all of a heap. He could not do enough to show his delight and gratitude.

'If all highbrows are like you,' he said, 'give me highbrows every time.'

He hated to think that in another year they would leave the district for good and the chances were that, if the next D.O. was married, his wife would think it dreadful that, rather than live alone, he had a native woman to live with him and, what was more, was much attached to her.

But there had been a good deal of discontent on the estate of late. The coolies were Chinese and infected with communist ideas. They were disorderly. Alban had been obliged to sentence several of them for various crimes to terms of imprisonment.

'Prynne tells me that as soon as their term is up he's going to send them all back to China and get Javanese instead,' said Alban. 'I'm sure he's right. They're much more amenable.'

'You don't think there's going to be any serious trouble?'

'Oh, no. Prynne knows his job and he's a pretty determined fellow. He wouldn't put up with any nonsense and with me and our policemen to back him up I don't imagine they'll try any monkey tricks.' He smiled. 'The iron hand in the velvet glove.'

The words were barely out of his mouth when a sudden shouting arose. There was a commotion and the sound of steps. Loud voices and cries.

'Tuan, Tuan.'

'What the devil's the matter?'

Alban sprang from his chair and went swiftly on to the veranda. Anne followed him. At the bottom of the steps was a group of natives. There was the sergeant, and three or four policemen, boatmen, and several men from the kampong.

'What is it?' called Alban.

Two or three shouted back in answer. The sergeant pushed others aside and Alban saw lying on the ground a man in a shirt and khaki shorts. He ran down the steps. He recognized the man as the assistant manager of Prynne's estate. He was a half-caste. His shorts were covered with blood and there was clotted blood all over one side of his face and head. He was unconscious.

'Bring him up here,' called Anne.

Alban gave an order. The man was lifted up and carried on to the veranda. They laid him on the floor and Anne put a pillow under his head. She sent for water and for the medicine-chest in which they kept things for emergency.

'Is he dead?' asked Alban.

'No.'

'Better try to give him some brandy.'

The boatmen brought ghastly news. The Chinese coolies had risen suddenly and attacked the manager's office. Prynne was killed, and the assistant manager, Oakley by name, had escaped only by the skin of his teeth. He had come upon the rioters when they were looting the office, he had seen Prynne's body thrown out of the window, and had taken to his heels. Some of the Chinese saw him and gave chase. He ran for the river and was wounded as he jumped into the launch. The launch managed to put off before the Chinese could get on board and they had come down-stream for help as fast as they could go. As they went they saw flames rising from the office buildings. There was no doubt that the coolies had burned down everything that would burn.

Oakley gave a groan and opened his eyes. He was a little, dark-skinned man, with flattened features and thick coarse hair. His great native eyes were filled with terror.

'You're all right,' said Anne. 'You're quite safe.'

He gave a sigh and smiled. Anne washed his face and swabbed it with antiseptics. The wound on his head was not serious.

'Can you speak yet?' said Alban.

'Wait a bit,' she said. 'We must look at his leg.'

Alban ordered the sergeant to get the crowd out of the veranda. Anne ripped up one leg of the shorts. The material was clinging to the coagulated wound.

'I've been bleeding like a pig,' said Oakley.

It was only a flesh wound. Alban was clever with his fingers, and though the blood began to flow again they staunched it. Alban put on a dressing and a bandage. The sergeant and a policeman lifted

Oakley on to a long chair. Alban gave him a brandy and soda, and soon he felt strong enough to speak. He knew no more than the boatmen had already told. Prynne was dead and the estate was in flames.

'And the girl and the children?' asked Anne.

'I don't know.'

'Oh, Alban.'

'I must turn out the police. Are you sure Prynne is dead?'

'Yes, sir. I saw him.'

'Have the rioters got fire-arms?'

'I don't know, sir.'

'How d'you mean, you don't know?' Alban cried irritably. 'Prynne had a gun, hadn't he?'

'Yes, sir.'

'There must have been more on the estate. You had one, didn't you? The head overseer had one.'

The half-caste was silent. Alban looked at him sternly.

'How many of those damned Chinese are there?'

'A hundred and fifty.'

Anne wondered that he asked so many questions. It seemed waste of time. The important thing was to collect coolies for the transport up-river, prepare the boats, and issue ammunition to the police.

'How many policemen have you got, sir?' asked Oakley.

'Eight and the sergeant.'

'Could I come too? That would make ten of us. I'm sure I shall be all right now I'm bandaged.'

'I'm not going,' said Alban.

'Alban, you must,' cried Anne. She could not believe her ears.

'Nonsense. It would be madness. Oakley's obviously useless. He's sure to have a temperature in a few hours. He'd only be in the way. That leaves nine guns. There are a hundred and fifty Chinese and they've got fire-arms and all the ammunition in the world.'

'How d'you know?'

'It stands to reason they wouldn't have started a show like this unless they had. It would be idiotic to go.'

Anne stared at him with open mouth. Oakley's eyes were puzzled.

'What are you going to do?'

'Well, fortunately we've got the launch. I'll send it to Port Wallace with a request for reinforcements.'

'But they won't be here for two days at least.'

'Well, what of it? Prynne's dead and the estate burned to the

410

ground. We couldn't do any good by going up now. I shall send a native to reconnoitre so that we can find out exactly what the rioters are doing.' He gave Anne his charming smile. 'Believe me, my pet, the rascals won't lose anything by waiting a day or two for what's coming to them.'

Oakley opened his mouth to speak, but perhaps he hadn't the nerve. He was a half-caste assistant manager and Alban, the D.O., represented the power of the Government. But the man's eyes sought Anne's and she thought she read in them an earnest and personal appeal.

'But in two days they're capable of committing the most frightful atrocities,' she cried. 'It's quite unspeakable what they may do.'

'Whatever damage they do they'll pay for. I promise you that.'

'Oh, Alban, you can't sit still and do nothing. I beseech you to go yourself at once.'

'Don't be so silly. I can't quell a riot with eight policemen and a sergeant. I haven't got the right to take a risk of that sort. We'd have to go in boats. You don't think we could get up unobserved. The lalang along the banks is perfect cover and they could just take pot shots at us as we came along. We shouldn't have a chance.'

'I'm afraid they'll only think it weakness if nothing is done for two days, sir,' said Oakley.

'When I want your opinion I'll ask for it,' said Alban acidly. 'So far as I can see when there was danger the only thing you did was to cut and run. I can't persuade myself that your assistance in a crisis would be very valuable.'

The half-caste reddened. He said nothing more. He looked straight in front of him with troubled eyes.

'I'm going down to the office,' said Alban. 'I'll just write a short report and send it down the river by launch at once.'

He gave an order to the sergeant, who had been standing all this time stiffly at the top of the steps. He saluted and ran off. Alban went into a little hall they had to get his topee. Anne swiftly followed him.

'Alban, for God's sake listen to me a minute,' she whispered.

'I don't want to be rude to you, darling, but I am pressed for time. I think you'd much better mind your own business.'

'You can't do nothing, Alban. You must go. Whatever the risk.'

'Don't be such a fool,' he said angrily.

He had never been angry with her before. She seized his hand to hold him back.

'I tell you I can do no good by going.'

411

'You don't know. There's the woman and Prynne's children. We must do something to save them. Let me come with you. They'll kill them.'

'They've probably killed them already.'

'Oh, how can you be so callous! If there's a chance of saving them it's your duty to try.'

'It's my duty to act like a reasonable human being. I'm not going to risk my life and my policemen's for the sake of a native woman and her half-caste brats. What sort of a damned fool do you take me for?'

'They'll say you were afraid.'

'Who?'

'Everyone in the colony.'

He smiled disdainfully.

'If you only knew what a complete contempt I have for the opinion of everyone in the colony.'

She gave him a long searching look. She had been married to him for eight years and she knew every expression of his face and every thought in his mind. She stared into his blue eyes as if they were open windows. She suddenly went quite pale. She dropped his hand and turned away. Without another word she went back on to the veranda. Her ugly little monkey face was a mask of horror.

Alban went to his office, wrote a brief account of the facts, and in a few minutes the motor launch was pounding down the river.

The next two days were endless. Escaped natives brought them news of happenings on the estate. But from their excited and terrified stories it was impossible to get an exact impression of the truth. There had been a good deal of bloodshed. The head overseer had been killed. They brought wild tales of cruelty and outrage. Anne could hear nothing of Prynne's woman and the two children. She shuddered when she thought of what might have been their fate. Alban collected as many natives as he could. They were armed with spears and swords. He commandeered boats. The situation was serious, but he kept his head. He felt that he had done all that was possible and nothing remained but for him to carry on normally. He did his official work. He played the piano a great deal. He rode with Anne in the early morning. He appeared to have forgotten that they had had the first serious difference of opinion in the whole of their married life. He took it that Anne had accepted the wisdom of his decision. He was as amusing, cordial, and gay with her as he had always been. When he spoke of the rioters it was with grim irony: when the time came to settle matters a good many of them would wish they had never been born.

'What'll happen to them?' asked Anne.

'Oh, they'll hang.' He gave a shrug of distaste. 'I hate having to be present at executions. It always makes me feel rather sick.'

He was very sympathetic to Oakley, whom they had put to bed and whom Anne was nursing. Perhaps he was sorry that in the exasperation of the moment he had spoken to him offensively, and he went out of his way to be nice to him.

Then on the afternoon of the third day, when they were drinking their coffee after luncheon, Alban's quick ears caught the sound of a motor boat approaching. At the same moment a policeman ran up to say that the government launch was sighted.

'At last,' cried Alban.

He bolted out of the house. Anne raised one of the jalousies and looked out at the river. Now the sound was quite loud and in a moment she saw the boat come round the bend. She saw Alban on the landing-stage. He got into a prahu and as the launch dropped her anchor he went on board. She told Oakley that the reinforcements had come.

'Will the D.O. go up with them when they attack?' he asked her.

'Naturally,' said Anne coldly.

'I wondered.'

Anne felt a strange feeling in her heart. For the last two days she had had to exercise all her self-control not to cry. She did not answer. She went out of the room.

A quarter of an hour later Alban returned to the bungalow with the captain of constabulary who had been sent with twenty Sikhs to deal with the rioters. Captain Stratton was a little red-faced man with a red moustache and bow legs, very hearty and dashing, whom she had met often at Port Wallace.

'Well, Mrs Torel, this is a pretty kettle of fish,' he cried, as he shook hands with her, in a loud jolly voice. 'Here I am, with my army all full of pep and ready for a scrap. Up, boys, and at 'em. Have you go anything to drink in this benighted place?'

'Boy,' she cried, smiling.

'Something long and cool and faintly alcoholic, and then I'm ready to discuss the plan of campaign.'

His breeziness was very comforting. It blew away the sullen apprehension that had seemed ever since the disaster to brood over the lost peace of the bungalow. The boy came in with a tray and Stratton mixed himself a stengah. Alban put him in possession of the facts. He told them clearly, briefly, and with precision.

'I must say I admire you,' said Stratton. 'In your place I should

413

never have been able to resist the temptation to take my eight cops and have a whack at the blighters myself.'

'I thought it was a perfectly unjustifiable risk to take.'

'Safety first, old boy, eh, what?' said Stratton jovially. 'I'm jolly glad you didn't. It's not often we get the chance of a scrap. It would have been a dirty trick to keep the whole show to yourself.'

Captain Stratton was all for steaming straight up the river and attacking at once, but Alban pointed out to him the inadvisability of such a course. The sound of the approaching launch would warn the rioters. The long grass at the river's edge offered them cover and they had enough guns to make a landing difficult. It seemed useless to expose the attacking force to their fire. It was silly to forget that they had to face a hundred and fifty desperate men and it would be easy to fall into an ambush. Alban expounded his own plan. Stratton listened to it. He nodded now and then. The plan was evidently a good one. It would enable them to take the rioters in the rear, surprise them, and in all probability finish the job without a single casualty. He would have been a fool not to accept it.

'But why didn't you do that yourself?' asked Stratton.

'With eight men and a sergeant?'

Stratton did not answer.

'Anyhow it's not a bad idea and we'll settle on it. It gives us plenty of time, so with your permission, Mrs Torel, I'll have a bath.'

They set out at sunset, Captain Stratton and his twenty Sikhs, Alban with his policemen and the natives he had collected. The night was dark and moonless. Trailing behind them were the dugouts that Alban had gathered together and into which after a certain distance they proposed to transfer their force. It was important that no sound should give warning of their approach. After they had gone for about three hours by launch they took to the dug-outs and in them silently paddled up-stream. They reached the border of the vast estate and landed. Guides led them along a path so narrow that they had to march in single file. It had been long unused and the going was heavy. They had twice to ford a stream. The path led them circuitously to the rear of the coolie lines, but they did not wish to reach them till nearly dawn and presently Stratton gave the order to halt. It was a long cold wait. At last the night seemed to be less dark; you did not see the trunks of the trees, but were vaguely sensible of them against its darkness. Stratton had been sitting with his back to a tree. He gave a whispered order to a sergeant and in a few minutes the column was once more on the march. Suddenly they found themselves on a road. They formed fours. The dawn broke and in the ghostly light the surrounding objects were wanly visible. The column stopped on a whispered order. They had come in sight of the coolie lines. Silence reigned in them. The column crept on again and again halted. Stratton, his eyes shining, gave Alban a smile.

'We've caught the blighters asleep.'

He lined up his men. They inserted cartridges in their guns. He stepped forward and raised his hand. The carbines were pointed at the coolie lines.

'Fire.'

There was a rattle as the volley of shots rang out. Then suddenly there was a tremendous din and the Chinese poured out, shouting and waving their arms, but in front of them, to Alban's utter bewilderment, bellowing at the top of his voice and shaking his fists at them, was a white man.

'Who the hell's that?' cried Stratton.

A very big, very fat man, in khaki trousers and a singlet, was running towards them as fast as his fat legs would carry him and as he ran shaking both fists at them and yelling:

'*Smerige flikkers! Vervloekte ploerten!*'

'My God, it's Van Hasseldt,' said Alban.

This was the Dutch manager of the timber camp which was situated on a considerable tributary of the river about twenty miles away.

'What the hell do you think you're doing?' he puffed as he came up to them.

'How the hell did you get here?' asked Stratton in turn.

He saw that the Chinese were scattering in all directions and gave his men instructions to round them up. Then he turned again to Van Hasseldt.

'What's it mean?'

'Mean? Mean?' shouted the Dutchman furiously. 'That's what I want to know. You and your damned policemen. What do you mean by coming here at this hour in the morning and firing a damned volley. Target practice? You might have killed me. Idiots!'

'Have a cigarette,' said Stratton.

'How did you get here, Van Hasseldt?' asked Alban again, very much at sea. 'This is the force they've sent from Port Wallace to quell the riot.'

'How did I get here? I walked. How did you think I got here? Riot be damned. I quelled the riot. If that's what you came for you can take your damned policemen home again. A bullet came within a foot of my head.'

'I don't understand,' said Alban.

'There's nothing to understand,' spluttered Van Hasseldt, still fuming. 'Some coolies came to my estate and said the Chinks had killed Prynne and burned the bally place down, so I took my assistant and my head overseer and a Dutch friend I had staying with me and came over to see what the trouble was.'

Captain Stratton opened his eyes wide.

'Did you just stroll in as if it was a picnic?' he asked.

'Well, you don't think after all the years I've been in this country I'm going to let a couple of hundred Chinks put the fear of God into me? I found them all scared out of their lives. One of them had the nerve to pull a gun on me and I blew his bloody brains out. And the rest surrendered. I've got the leaders tied up. I was going to send a boat down to you this morning to come up and get them.'

Stratton stared at him for a minute and then burst into a shout of laughter. He laughed till the tears ran down his face. The Dutchman looked at him angrily, then began to laugh too; he laughed with the big belly laugh of a very fat man and his coils of fat heaved and shook. Alban watched them sullenly. He was very angry.

'What about Prynne's girl and the kids?' he asked.

'Oh, they got away all right.'

It just showed how wise he had been not to let himself be influenced by Anne's hysteria. Of course the children had come to no harm. He never thought they would.

Van Hasseldt and his little party started back for the timber camp, and as soon after as possible Stratton embarked his twenty Sikhs and leaving Alban with his sergeant and his policemen to deal with the situation departed for Port Wallace. Alban gave him a brief report for the Governor. There was much for him to do. It looked as though he would have to stay for a considerable time; but since every house on the estate had been burned to the ground and he was obliged to install himself in the coolie lines he thought it better that Anne should not join him. He sent her a note to that effect. He was glad to be able to reassure her of the safety of poor Prynne's girl. He set to work at once to make his preliminary inquiry. He examined a host of witnesses. But a week later he received an order to go to Port Wallace at once. The launch that brought it was to take him and he was able to see Anne on the way down for no more than an hour. Alban was a trifle vexed.

'I don't know why the Governor can't leave me to get things straight without dragging me off like this. It's extremely inconvenient.'

'Oh, well, the Government never bothers very much about the convenience of its subordinates, does it?' smiled Anne.

'It's just red-tape. I would offer to take you along, darling, only I shan't stay a minute longer than I need. I want to get my evidence together for the Sessions Court as soon as possible. I think in a country like this it's very important that justice should be prompt.'

When the launch came in to Port Wallace one of the harbour police told him that the harbour-master had a chit for him. It was from the Governor's secretary and informed him that His Excellency desired to see him as soon as convenient after his arrival. It was ten in the morning. Alban went to the club, had a bath and shaved, and then in clean ducks, his hair neatly brushed, he called a rickshaw and told the boy to take him to the Governor's office. He was at once shown in to the secretary's room. The secretary shook hands with him.

'I'll tell H.E. you're here,' he said. 'Won't you sit down?'

The secretary left the room and in a little while came back.

'H.E. will see you in a minute. Do you mind if I get on with my letters?'

Alban smiled. The secretary was not exactly come-hither. He waited, smoking a cigarette, and amused himself with his own thoughts. He was making a good job of the preliminary inquiry. It interested him. Then an orderly came in and told Alban that the Governor was ready for him. He rose from his seat and followed him into the Governor's room.

'Good morning, Torel.'

'Good morning, sir.'

The Governor was sitting at a large desk. He nodded to Alban and motioned to him to take a seat. The Governor was all grey. His hair was grey, his face, his eyes; he looked as though the tropical suns had washed the colour out of him; he had been in the country for thirty years and had risen one by one through all the ranks of the Service; he looked tired and depressed. Even his voice was grey. Alban liked him because he was quiet; he did not think him clever, but he had an unrivalled knowledge of the country, and his great experience was a very good substitute for intelligence. He looked at Alban for a full moment without speaking and the odd idea came to Alban that he was embarrassed. He very nearly gave him a lead.

'I saw Van Hasseldt yesterday,' said the Governor suddenly.

'Yes, sir?'

'Will you give me your account of the occurrences at the Alud Estate and of the steps you took to deal with them.'

Alban had an orderly mind. He was self-possessed. He marshalled his facts well and was able to state them with precision. He chose his words with care and spoke them fluently.

'You had a sergeant and eight policemen. Why did you not immediately go to the scene of the disturbance?'

'I thought the risk was unjustifiable.'

A thin smile was outlined on the Governor's grey face.

'If the officers of this Government had hesitated to take unjustifiable risks it would never have become a province of the British Empire.'

Alban was silent. It was difficult to talk to a man who spoke obvious nonsense.

'I am anxious to hear your reasons for the decision you took.'

Alban gave them coolly. He was quite convinced of the rightness of his action. He repeated, but more fully, what he had said in the first place to Anne. The Governor listened attentively.

'Van Hasseldt, with his manager, a Dutch friend of his, and a native overseer, seems to have coped with the situation very efficiently,' said the Governor.

'He had a lucky break. That doesn't prevent him from being a damned fool. It was madness to do what he did.'

'Do you realize that by leaving a Dutch planter to do what you should have done yourself, you have covered the Government with ridicule?'

'No, sir.'

'You've made yourself a laughing-stock in the whole colony.'

Alban smiled.

'My back is broad enough to bear the ridicule of persons to whose opinion I am entirely indifferent.'

'The utility of a government official depends very largely on his prestige, and I'm afraid his prestige is likely to be inconsiderable when he lies under the stigma of cowardice.'

Alban flushed a little.

'I don't quite know what you mean by that, sir.'

'I've gone into the matter very carefully. I've seen Captain Stratton, and Oakley, poor Prynne's assistant, and I've seen Van Hasseldt. I've listened to your defence.'

'I didn't know that I was defending myself, sir.'

'Be so good as not to interrupt me. I think you committed a grave error of judgement. As it turns out, the risk was very small, but whatever it was, I think you should have taken it. In such matters promptness and firmness are essential. It is not for me to conjecture what motive led you to send for a force of constabulary and do nothing till they came. I am afraid, however, that I consider that your usefulness in the Service is no longer very great.'

Alban looked at him with astonishment.

'But would you have gone under the circumstances?' he asked him.

'I should.'

Alban shrugged his shoulders.

'Don't you believe me?' rapped out the Governor.

'Of course I believe you, sir. But perhaps you will allow me to say that if you had been killed the colony would have suffered an irreparable loss.'

The Governor drummed on the table with his fingers. He looked out of the window and then looked again at Alban. When he spoke it was not unkindly.

'I think you are unfitted by temperament for this rather rough-and-tumble life, Torel. If you'll take my advice you'll go home. With your abilities I feel sure that you'll soon find an occupation much better suited to you.'

'I'm afraid I don't understand what you mean, sir.'

'Oh, come, Torel, you're not stupid. I'm trying to make things easy for you. For your wife's sake as well as for your own I do not wish you to leave the colony with the stigma of being dismissed from the Service for cowardice. I'm giving you the opportunity of resigning.'

'Thank you very much, sir. I'm not prepared to avail myself of the opportunity. If I resign I admit that I committed an error and that the charge you make against me is justified. I don't admit it.'

'You can please yourself. I have considered the matter very carefully and I have no doubt about it in my mind. I am forced to discharge you from the Service. The necessary papers will reach you in due course. Meanwhile you will return to your post and hand over to the officer appointed to succeed you on his arrival.'

'Very good, sir,' replied Alban, a twinkle of amusement in his eyes. 'When do you desire me to return to my post?'

'At once.'

'Have you any objection to my going to the club and having tiffin before I go?'

The Governor looked at him with surprise. His exasperation was mingled with an unwilling admiration.

'Not at all. I'm sorry, Torel, that this unhappy incident should have deprived the Government of a servant whose zeal has always been so apparent and whose tact, intelligence, and industry seemed to point him out in the future for very high office.'

'Your Excellency does not read Schiller, I suppose. You are

probably not acquainted with his celebrated line: *mit der Dummheit kämpfen die Götter selbst vergebens.*'

'What does it mean?'

'Roughly: Against stupidity the gods themselves battle in vain.'

'Good morning.'

With his head in the air, a smile on his lips, Alban left the Governor's office. The Governor was human, and he had the curiosity to ask his secretary later in the day if Alban Torel had really gone to the club.

'Yes, sir. He had tiffin there.'

'It must have wanted some nerve.'

Alban entered the club jauntily and joined the group of men standing at the bar. He talked to them in the breezy, cordial tone he always used with them. It was designed to put them at their ease. They had been discussing him ever since Stratton had come back to Port Wallace with his story, sneering at him and laughing at him, and all who had resented his superciliousness, and they were the majority, were triumphant because his pride had had a fall. But they were so taken aback at seeing him now, so confused to find him as confident as ever, that it was they who were embarrassed.

One man, though he knew perfectly, asked him what he was doing in Port Wallace.

'Oh, I came about the riot on the Alud Estate. H.E. wanted to see me. He does not see eye to eye with me about it. The silly old ass has fired me. I'm going home as soon as he appoints a D.O. to take over.'

There was a moment of awkwardness. One, more kindly disposed than the others, said:

'I'm awfully sorry.'

Alban shrugged his shoulders.

'My dear fellow, what can you do with a perfect damned fool? The only thing is to let him stew in his own juice.'

When the Governor's secretary had told his chief as much of this as he thought discreet, the Governor smiled.

'Courage is a queer thing. I would rather have shot myself than go to the club just then and face all those fellows.'

A fortnight later, having sold to the incoming D.O. all the decorations that Anne had taken so much trouble about, with the rest of their things in packing-cases and trunks, they arrived at Port Wallace to await the local steamer that was to take them to Singapore. The padre's wife invited them to stay with her, but Anne refused; she insisted that they should go to the hotel. An hour after their arrival she received a very kind little letter from

the Governor's wife asking her to go and have tea with her. She
went. She found Mrs Hannay alone, but in a minute the Governor
joined them. He expressed his regret that she was leaving and told
her how sorry he was for the cause.

'It's very kind of you to say that,' said Anne, smiling gaily,
'but you mustn't think I take it to heart. I'm entirely on Alban's
side. I think what he did was absolutely right and if you
don't mind my saying so I think you've treated him most
unjustly.'

'Believe me, I hated having to take the step I took.'

'Don't let's talk about it,' said Anne.

'What are your plans when you get home?' asked Mrs Hannay.

Anne began to chat brightly. You would have thought she had
not a care in the world. She seemed in great spirits at going home.
She was jolly and amusing and made little jokes. When she took
leave of the Governor and his wife she thanked them for all their
kindness. The Governor escorted her to the door.

The next day but one, after dinner, they went on board the
clean and comfortable little ship. The padre and his wife saw
them off. When they went into their cabin they found a large
parcel on Anne's bunk. It was addressed to Alban. He opened it
and saw that it was an immense powder-puff.

'Hullo, I wonder who sent us this,' he said, with a laugh. 'It
must be for you, darling.'

Anne gave him a quick look. She went pale. The brutes! How
could they be so cruel? She forced herself to smile.

'It's enormous, isn't it? I've never seen such a large powder-
puff in my life.'

But when he had left the cabin and they were out at sea, she
threw it passionately overboard.

And now, now that they were back in London and Sondurah
was nine thousand miles away, she clenched her hands as she
thought of it. Somehow, it seemed the worst thing of all. It was
so wantonly unkind to send that absurd object to Alban, Powder-
Puff Percy; it showed such a petty spite. Was that their idea of
humour? Nothing had hurt her more and even now she felt that
it was only by holding on to herself that she could prevent herself
from crying. Suddenly she started, for the door opened and Alban
came in. She was still sitting in the chair in which he had left
her.

'Hullo, why haven't you dressed?' He looked about the room.
'You haven't unpacked.'

'No.'

'Why on earth not?'

'I'm not going to unpack. I'm not going to stay here. I'm leaving you.'

'What are you talking about?'

'I've stuck it out till now. I made up my mind I would till we got home. I set my teeth, I've borne more than I thought it possible to bear, but now it's finished. I've done all that could be expected of me. We're back in London now and I can go.'

He looked at her in utter bewilderment.

'Are you mad, Anne?'

'Oh, my God, what I've endured! The journey to Singapore, with all the officers knowing, and even the Chinese stewards. And at Singapore, the way people looked at us at the hotel, and the sympathy I had to put up with, the bricks they dropped and their embarrassment when they realized what they'd done. My God, I could have killed them. That interminable journey home. There wasn't a single passenger on the ship who didn't know. The contempt they had for you and the kindness they went out of their way to show me. And you so self-complacent and so pleased with yourself, seeing nothing, feeling nothing. You must have the hide of a rhinoceros. The misery of seeing you so chatty and agreeable. Pariahs, that's what we were. You seemed to ask them to snub you. How can anyone be so shameless?'

She was flaming with passion. Now that at last she need not wear the mask of indifference and pride that she had forced herself to assume she cast aside all reserve and all self-control. The words poured from her trembling lips in a virulent stream.

'My dear, how can you be so absurd?' he said good-naturedly, smiling. 'You must be very nervous and high-strung to have got such ideas in your head. Why didn't you tell me? You're like a country bumpkin who comes to London and thinks everyone is staring at him. Nobody bothered about us, and if they did what on earth did it matter? You ought to have more sense than to bother about what a lot of fools say. And what do you imagine they were saying?'

'They were saying you'd been fired.'

'Well, that was true,' he laughed.

'They said you were a coward.'

'What of it?'

'Well, you see, that was true too.'

He looked at her for a moment reflectively. His lips tightened a little.

'And what makes you think so?' he asked acidly.

'I saw it in your eyes, that day the news came, when you refused to go to the estate and I followed you into the hall when you went to fetch your topee. I begged you to go, I felt that whatever the danger you must take it, and suddenly I saw the fear in your eyes. I nearly fainted with the horror.'

'I should have been a fool to risk my life to no purpose. Why should I? Nothing that concerned me was at stake. Courage is the obvious virtue of the stupid. I don't attach any particular importance to it.'

'How do you mean that nothing that concerned you was at stake? If that's true then your whole life is a sham. You've given away everything you stood for, everything we both stand for. You've let all of us down. We did set ourselves up on a pinnacle, we did think ourselves better than the rest of them because we loved literature and art and music, we weren't content to live a life of ignoble jealousies and vulgar tittle-tattle, we did cherish the things of the spirit, and we loved beauty. It was our food and drink. They laughed at us and sneered at us. That was inevitable. The ignorant and the common naturally hate and fear those who are interested in things they don't understand. We didn't care. We called them Philistines. We despised them and we had a right to despise them. Our justification was that we were better and nobler and wiser and braver than they were. And you weren't better, you weren't nobler, you weren't braver. When the crisis came you slunk away like a whipped cur with his tail between his legs. You of all people hadn't the right to be a coward. They despise *us* now and they have the right to despise us. Us and all we stood for. Now they can say that art and beauty are all rot; when it comes to a pinch people like us always let you down. They never stopped looking for a chance to turn and rend us and you gave it to them. They can say that they always expected it. It's a triumph for them. I used to be furious because they called you Powder-Puff Percy. Did you know they did?'

'Of course. I thought it very vulgar, but it left me entirely indifferent.'

'It's funny that their instinct should have been so right.'

'Do you mean to say you've been harbouring this against me all these weeks? I should never have thought you capable of it.'

'I couldn't let you down when everyone was against you. I was too proud for that. Whatever happened I swore to myself that I'd stick to you till we got home. It's been torture.'

'Don't you love me any more?'

'Love you? I loathe the very sight of you.'

'Anne!'

'God knows I loved you. For eight years I worshipped the

423

ground you trod on. You were everything to me. I believed in you as some people believe in God. When I saw the fear in your eyes that day, when you told me that you weren't going to risk your life for a kept woman and her half-caste brats, I was shattered. It was as though someone had wrenched my heart out of my body and trampled on it. You killed my love there and then, Alban. You killed it stone-dead. Since then when you've kissed me I've had to clench my hands so as not to turn my face away. The mere thought of anything else makes me feel physically sick. I loathe your complacence and your frightful insensitiveness. Perhaps I could have forgiven it if it had been just a moment's weakness and if afterwards you'd been ashamed. I should have been miserable, but I think my love was so great that I should only have felt pity for you. But you're incapable of shame. And now I believe in nothing. You're only a silly, pretentious, vulgar poseur. I would rather be the wife of a second-rate planter so long as he had the common human virtues of a man than the wife of a fake like you.'

He did not answer. Gradually his face began to discompose. Those handsome, regular features of his horribly distorted and suddenly he broke out into loud sobs. She gave a little cry.

'Don't, Alban, don't.'

'Oh, darling, how can you be so cruel to me? I adore you. I'd give my whole life to please you. I can't live without you.'

She put out her arms as though to ward off a blow.

'No, no, Alban, don't try to move me. I can't. I must go. I can't live with you any more. It would be frightful. I can never forget. I must tell you the truth, I have only contempt for you and repulsion.'

He sank down at her feet and tried to cling to her knees. With a gasp she sprang up and he buried his head in the empty chair. He cried painfully with sobs that tore his chest. The sound was horrible. The tears streamed from Anne's eyes and, putting her hands to her ears to shut out that dreadful, hysterical sobbing, blindly stumbling she rushed to the door and ran out.

FOR THE BEST IN PAPERBACKS, LOOK FOR THE

In every corner of the world, on every subject under the sun, Penguin represents quality and variety—the very best in publishing today.

For complete information about books available from Penguin—including Puffins, Penguin Classics, and Arkana—and how to order them, write to us at the appropriate address below. Please note that for copyright reasons the selection of books varies from country to country.

In the United Kingdom: Please write to *Dept. JC, Penguin Books Ltd, FREEPOST, West Drayton, Middlesex UB7 0BR.*

If you have any difficulty in obtaining a title, please send your order with the correct money, plus ten percent for postage and packaging, to *P.O. Box No. 11, West Drayton, Middlesex UB7 0BR*

In the United States: Please write to *Consumer Sales, Penguin USA, P.O. Box 999, Dept. 17109, Bergenfield, New Jersey 07621-0120.* VISA and MasterCard holders call 1-800-253-6476 to order all Penguin titles

In Canada: Please write to *Penguin Books Canada Ltd, 10 Alcorn Avenue, Suite 300, Toronto, Ontario M4V 3B2*

In Australia: Please write to *Penguin Books Australia Ltd, P.O. Box 257, Ringwood, Victoria 3134*

In New Zealand: Please write to *Penguin Books (NZ) Ltd, Private Bag 102902, North Shore Mail Centre, Auckland 10*

In India: Please write to *Penguin Books India Pvt Ltd, 706 Eros Apartments, 56 Nehru Place, New Delhi 110 019*

In the Netherlands: Please write to *Penguin Books Netherlands bv, Postbus 3507, NL-1001 AH Amsterdam*

In Germany: Please write to *Penguin Books Deutschland GmbH, Metzlerstrasse 26, 60594 Frankfurt am Main*

In Spain: Please write to *Penguin Books S. A., Bravo Murillo 19, 1° B, 28015 Madrid*

In Italy: Please write to *Penguin Italia s.r.l., Via Felice Casati 20, I-20124 Milano*

In France: Please write to *Penguin France S. A., 17 rue Lejeune, F–31000 Toulouse*

In Japan: Please write to *Penguin Books Japan, Ishikiribashi Building, 2–5–4, Suido, Bunkyo-ku, Tokyo 112*

In Greece: Please write to *Penguin Hellas Ltd, Dimocritou 3, GR–106 71 Athens*

In South Africa: Please write to *Longman Penguin Southern Africa (Pty) Ltd, Private Bag X08, Bertsham 2013*

BY THE SAME AUTHOR

Cakes and Ale

Of all W. Somerset Maugham's novels, *Cakes and Ale* is the gayest. The entrancing character of Rosie, a barmaid with a history and a heart of gold, places the book, as creative literature, on a level with *Of Human Bondage*.

Liza of Lambeth

Into London's East End of the 1890s came a young medical student; from this experience of life that was hard, unpredictable, and sordid emerged one of the greatest novelists of this century. This is his first novel: the story of strong-willed Liza, who overstepped the conventions of her world.

The Merry-Go-Round

The Merry-Go-Round is a round of misalliances orchestrated by a droll, original heroine – an elderly spinster who takes a cool view of emotional entanglements – an acute observation of the manners and preoccupations of the Edwardians.

The Moon and Sixpence

A disturbing study of single-minded genius, *The Moon and Sixpence* confirmed Maugham's reputation as a novelist and is probably his best-known book.

The Razor's Edge

The Razor's Edge is the most serious and the most ambitious of W. Somerset Maugham's novels. Published when he was seventy, it prompted Cyril Connolly to speak of 'a great writer determined to tell the truth in a form which releases all the possibilities of his art'. Largely set in France, *The Razor's Edge* tells the story of the spiritual odyssey of a young American in search of God and the infinite.

The Summing Up

The Summing Up might aptly be described as the *Religio Medici* of a great modern writer (who, as it happens, ascribes much of his literary success to his medical training). Maugham had already completed the bulk of his best work when, in 1938, he published this personal statement. Here is Maugham's impartial judgement on Maugham, a considered comment on life and on his own life's work, a careful weighing of religion, philosophy, and the arts. On every page the reader is charmed by the directness, the lucidity, and the sincerity of the author's tone.

Up At The Villa

Up at the Villa so shocked the New York editor who commissioned it that it never appeared as the magazine serial it was intended to be, but, in the end, it proved to be one of the most popular books Maugham ever wrote. A short novel, *Up at the Villa* tells the story of a beautiful woman who, though she could have chosen at will from the highly eligible men who courted her, gives herself to a comparative stranger – and tragedy follows . . .

Mrs Craddock

'Extremely daring' was the publisher's verdict in 1900. Today's readers, though they are unlikely to share that opinion, will certainly find W. Somerset Maugham's story of a woman who 'marries beneath her' still has the power to move and surprise.

The Narrow Corner

The Narrow Corner recalls the best of Maugham's short stories in its location in the Far East, its subtlety, and its wry penetration of human nature. Money talked the shifty Captain Nichols into whisking a young Australian over the horizon for a discreet period, but it was love that lured the luckless Fred Blake into disaster. Ultimately it is money that ironically winds up this partnership of gamblers in a book that utters a tart comment on the futility of idealism.

Of Human Bondage

Of Human Bondage is generally considered to be Maugham's masterpiece in a long, versatile, and extremely distinguished literary career. First published in 1915, the book was described by Maugham as an autobiographical novel in which fact and fiction are inextricably mixed. Philip Carey, a handicapped orphan, is brought up by a self-indulgent Victorian clergyman. Shedding his religious faith as a young man, he begins to study art in Paris but finally returns to London to become a doctor.

The Painted Veil

The Painted Veil is probably the only novel that Maugham based on a story rather than a character. Nevertheless, on publication in 1925 it was twice threatened with libel actions. Maugham gives a modern setting to the curious plot, which was suggested by a few lines of Dante. Detected in an affair with the Assistant Colonial Secretary of Hong Kong, Kitty Fane is forced by her husband, a bacteriologist, to accompany him to the heart of a cholera epidemic. In the course of this harsh penance she learns the true meaning of love, but her discovery comes too late.

BY THE SAME AUTHOR

Collected Short Stories

W. Somerset Maugham's short stories are masterpieces of the art. No more need be said, except that in their precision of form and beauty of expression, they are jewels of their kind.

Volume 1

Of the thirty stories in this volume some take place on Pacific islands, and some in England, Spain, and France. They include 'Rain', the sardonic tragedy of Mr Davidson, the prudish missionary, and Sadie Thompson, the prostitute.

Volume 3

This volume contains the famous Ashenden series of stories. These are stories of espionage in the First World War, told by Ashenden, a secret-service agent, who, Maugham has stated, can be taken as a flattering self-portrait of himself.

Volume 4

Most of the thirty stories in this final volume are set in Malaya and Southeast Asia, always favourite Maugham territory. The author brings home the charged atmosphere of remote colonial stations. 'The Out-station' immortalizes in Warburton a significant type of colonial administrator.